LUCKY BUNNY

LUCKY BUNNY

JILL DAWSON

ISIS
LARGE PRINT
Oxford

First published in Great Britain 2011
by
Sceptre
An imprint of Hodder & Stoughton

Published in Large Print 2012 by ISIS Publishing Ltd.,
7 Centremead, Osney Mead, Oxford OX2 0ES
by arrangement with
Hodder & Stoughton
An Hachette UK Company

British Library Cataloguing in Publication Data
Dawson, Jill.
    Lucky bunny.
    1. Female offenders - - Fiction.
    2. London (England) - - Social life and customs - -
    20th century - - Fiction.
    3. Large type books.
    I. Title
    823.9'2–dc23

ISBN 978–0–7531–9018–0 (hb)
ISBN 978–0–7531–9019–7 (pb)

Printed and bound in Great Britain by
T. J. International Ltd., Padstow, Cornwall

For the Dawson girls:
Maud, Debra, Beth, Lotte and Rose.

And for Meredith, with love, as ever.

Stolen sweets are always sweeter;
Stolen kisses much completer;
Stolen looks are nice in chapels;
Stolen, stolen be your apples.

James Leigh Hunt, "Fairies' Song", 1830

Part One

Queenie's not my real name, of course. The name I was given at birth is plain enough, well known, and easily looked-up. Queenie's the name I took, chose for myself. Only the best for me, I remember thinking, at the time: the Queen of everything. A cracking name. I wanted it, I took it, I made it mine. As there might be some proper consequences attached to my real name, it wouldn't be right to set my given name down. I shouldn't even call that one my *real* name because, now I think of it, isn't that the point? Queenie's real, to me. For the purposes of this account, then, best you think of me as Queenie throughout: the name I've gone by for most of my life.

My best friend Stella knows my given name, but never calls me it. Yesterday she drove me up here, to my new home by the river, and as we picked up the keys from the estate agent's office and I signed "Queenie Dove" on the contract, she was giggling and shoving me in the ribs and trying to hide her excitement, whispering in my ear, "Can you believe your luck sometimes? Go on — can you?"

When I'd turned the key to my own front door, Stella went on: "Don't you ever ask yourself, 'Blimey, how did I end up here in one piece, and *get away with it all?*' "

You might find this strange but, honestly, I never *have* asked myself that. And it struck me hard, Stella saying it. As if, now that she's mentioned it, I'll have to pinch myself. My luck might fly off. I don't think I've breathed out yet. Am I safe? This old cottage has a back door and a garden that can't be seen from the front, and a garden wall with a door in it that leads to the river: an escape route. I noticed it right away. And it's nothing flash, either, doesn't draw attention to itself. I'm not swanking — it's nothing like what I could actually afford. Bricks and mortar and my own garden shed, a wad of money all cosy in the silk lining of my red leather handbag, a child sleeping outside in the car: those things are real — those are things, not ideas. But luck, and getting away with it? How did I get here, after all?

So, after Stella's gone back to London, and it's late, midnight, and I'm lying for the first time in the brand-new, stiffly squeaking bed, snuggling in the fresh shop-scented linen, and geese are honking outside by the water, and there's the rest of the money, fat and solid, all piled up high in the otherwise empty white cupboard, I can't sleep for thinking about it, for wanting to answer Stella's question.

I'm so wide awake I have to get out of bed and wander into the front room, bumping into a crate. I put the light on and blink hard. My eyes fall on the open door to the kitchen, on the wooden table, to the cherries, bought from a roadside stall, that Stella's

4

dumped in a blue china bowl — her contribution to the unpacking. Crumpled newspaper springs around the bowl, the purple-red cherries pretty against the blue china. I pop one in my mouth. I spread the newspaper out, glance at the headlines. Even now, years later, I expect to read about more arrests, see names I know, wonder if one day something will be said that could lead to me. But so far, so good. Stella's right then, surely? This is luck. I'm here, in one piece. Because don't we all believe that bad behaviour will be punished, that those who stick to the rules will get their reward eventually? If not in heaven, then in a beautiful cottage by the river, with a healthy child and a table with fresh cherries in a bowl.

Not me, though. I don't think I ever believed in fairness. Where would I have learned to expect that? No moaning and groaning and tearing at my clothes either. You won't catch me repenting. Puzzling, yes, but not repenting . . .

Mum once showed me a picture. Of her as a really young girl, with my dad, standing in Docklands at the edge of the water, men loading in the background and those huge cranes towering over her, like weird insects, and I remember saying, "Where am I in that photo, then?" and her answer: "Oh, you wasn't even a twinkle in your dad's eye then." A shiver ran through me. Like I could see my own ghost there. How could that be? How could I be looking at a picture of a time when I didn't exist? But we can, can't we? It's what school-teachers praise us for, and then tell us we have too much of: it's called having an imagination. I'm

5

good at that, I've learned. Making things up. Not telling tales, though; I'm not a tell-tale. I don't want to drop certain people in it, so I might change some names and the odd fact here and there, but not the relevant things, not the gist of it. I don't think I'm a confessional person. Bit of a story-teller, that's all.

Take what I say with a pinch of salt, if you like: luck always beggars belief. The more someone insists something's true, the more you've got to doubt it, wouldn't you say? It's important to me that you don't know the name my mother chose for me. I hope I've left that other-named little girl behind; I've worked bloody hard at it.

This magistrate, a woman, once said to me, "I am rather tired of hearing time and again from those breaking the law that they had a terribly troubled childhood. Everyone who passes through this court claims to have had an appalling childhood. Surely some people can transcend their childhood, once in a while. Could we at least stop using it as an excuse for everything?"

She had this glossy black hair, like the oiled hair of a Doberman Pinscher, and she flashed a smile round the court as she said it — you know, like a dog baring its teeth. What did I think, listening to her, back then? I thought she had a point. I was all for not making excuses. But she annoyed me, too, I'll admit. I didn't examine things too much in those days, but dimly I might have wondered, does anyone "transcend" their childhood? I mean, did she? Did she rise above it, to be someone different from the shape cut out for her? Did her family expect a tearaway, a hoister, a criminal or a madam, for instance, and instead they got her — a homework-producing head girl?

I wasn't allowed to answer back, of course. I knew she didn't want an answer. She was bright and hard, skin stretched tight over that smile. It was probably a throwaway remark; she was just fed up, hearing the same sob stories time and again. It's funny how that comment from years ago — *ten* years ago — sailed back just now.

My Early Years

I was born in Poplar, East London, in 1933. In school we used to sing, "God made the Earth, and God made me." And all this other stuff that God made. "The flowers and the rivers and the bumblebee." And me! I loved that song. Did God make me? Or was it Moll and "Lucky Boy Tommy" one night in Tunnel Gardens, down on East India Dock Wall Road, the tree-lined bit between Blackwall Tunnel and the docks, when he'd plied her with gin and persuaded her to roll up that pink, surgical-looking girdle she wore. A girdle she would never have needed to wear, Moll, because she was only seventeen and weighed about seven stone, but it was the fashion back then, that kind of underwear. She thought she should and it would look sophisticated. And sexy. Which, to Tommy, it probably did. It turned him on, no doubt: he *was* Thomas bloody Dove. He would have been insistent, he wouldn't have taken no for an answer — is it possible to think this, to think about the point when your own father's juices start flowing, the first moment you're being brought into production, down some tube . . . the first little throb? The idea of me, the dot. Well, yes. Just about possible.

But we'll skip that, because I never did ask them, and I'm only . . . speculating. We'll go straight to my birth.

I wonder how I knew, one day, that it was my time to arrive (doctors still don't agree on that, do they? A mystery, how labour is triggered.) I like to think it was me who decided, that in some tiny, seed-like part of my consciousness, I heard the rag-and-bone man in the street — my granddad! — shouting, "Raaaaagaboooagh," and decided, yep, sounds good, time's up, here I come.

He had a horse and cart. Granddad, I mean. But he died the year I was born so I only got to ride in it once. There's a photo of me, and whenever I look at it, I'm there: the smell of the horse-shit steaming on the street, the bumpiness of that cracked leather seat, the feeling of being Lady of the Manor in my knitted lace baby bonnet and my tie-at-the-neck bouncing pom-poms sodden with dribble, propped up on a bunch of cushions, gazing down from a grand height, jolting round the Isle of Dogs. You might think this couldn't possibly be a real memory, I was too young. It must be something the photograph calls up. What's the difference? It feels real enough to me.

We lived then in a flat in the tenements built to house dock workers. My mum, Molly, who was seventeen, like I said, and Irish, was a slattern. That's my word for it. Nicer than slut, don't you think? She'd arrived in London with her big sister Brodie just a few years before and met my dad, Thomas, at a dance. Dad was twenty-five and all dark and hairy, with the most spectacular temper. He had — she told me — a good job down the docks when she first met him. Those jobs were well paid and really sought after in the Depression, and my uncle Charlie was the gang-leader so he made sure Dad would always get chosen for work, but everyone knew Dad wouldn't last long, because the job was full of "temptations".

One thing about Dad that was true his whole life was that he couldn't work for anybody but himself. He always fell out with a boss, as soon as the poor sod tried to tell him what to do. Dad couldn't abide being told. And in that moment, when his temper went off, when he yelled all the joined-up obscenities that come to mind or put his face awful close to someone's and pressed his nose against theirs, he loved the *freedom* of really saying what he felt, of losing it completely. You could feel the joy crackle around him, like a sparkler flaring into life, and nothing else mattered.

Our tenements were densely packed buildings with external stone steps, about six storeys high, set between Blackwall Tunnel and Blackwall Stairs. All the flats were light-starved, facing inwards towards a courtyard, heaped with strings of sopping washing where the women would stand, where my nan would be, most days, peg in her mouth, basket at her feet, chatting, laughing, surrounded by bins that were always overflowing.

Moll had wanted to give birth at home, I know, because she was too lazy to get herself to the hospital, but home was a tip, I mean *filthy*. It always stank to high heaven: of urine, my dad's sweaty baked-bean armpit smell, cigarettes, spilled beer, unwashed clothes, paraffin for the heater. Those were the smells that would have greeted me after that clean pure smell of blood and adrenalin and the whoosh of arrival. Shit. I should have been warned. But I was an optimist, from day one, and in that respect maybe I was more like my nan, not my mum. Or more like myself, perhaps. Surely there's a bit of me that's just me. It can't only be genetics and environment, can it? Otherwise, well, wouldn't we be repeating everything, walking round like clones? I was never one of those kids who shouted, "I never asked to be born," because it wasn't true. I *longed* to be born — I was even two weeks early. I jumped out, I really did. I couldn't wait.

I remember Nan telling me that the midwife was just a slip of twenty-two. Her name was something like Jennifer, or perhaps Rosie — let's call her Rosie — and she was still in training with the nuns who delivered babies in our part of London; she would have had a uniform on, and worn a handkerchief over her nose and chin. This girl had managed, with Nan's help, to get the flat into some sort of state to greet me. I can imagine her young high voice squeaking while I was starting my descent, saying things to my mum like "The heartbeat's 126, that's very good," and "Oh — oh, Mrs Dove, why didn't you say the baby was breech?" and Nan, clacking her dentures, saying things like "Well, for God's sake, she didn't know!" And then to herself: "I'll find someone to tell that good-for-nothing son of mine that he's been and got another one on the way," and her knees snapping and creaking, like twigs on a fire, as she knelt by the bed. She could never be sure where Lucky Boy Tommy was, although even at the cell-dividing

LUCKY BUNNY

stage I could have told her: the betting shop was always
worth a try.

I was pushed about, then, or whatever it is that a
baby feels, pulled and pummelled, in a corkscrew
fashion, and all around me the seething walls sort of
pumping me and squeezing me. Nan says I poked one
little foot out and it was dramatic: it caused such a
shriek — "What's that? My God — what's that?" —
that I tried again.

I was still in the sac, all nicely sealed up and wet, and
you know mine had to be an original entrance — not a
slimy red head like the cliché, no, not for me, but a foot
inside a bulging bubble; like the eye of some fantastical
insect or a sea monster, something like that. Nan said
they couldn't believe it when they first saw me: they
thought I'd come from the moon! She said the midwife,
young Rosie, actually *screamed* with astonishment:
"Oh, my word, a footling breech!"

In a rush of liquid, all at once, there I was, then, one
foot after the other, and no time really for Moll to
push, that's what Nan said: when a baby's in that
position there's no stopping her. They were shouting
and fussing, the midwife, Nan, Mum . . . and I was
making my first great escape, feet first, leaping, heading
for the open, for the light!

That, then, was the fanfare and kerfuffle when I
arrived, in such an unusual way, and a few hours later,
when he was found (yes, at the betting shop, and in a
grand mood, Nan told me, because he'd won two
pounds and brought home a crate of beer) would have
been the first time I met my gorgeous dad.

12

It must have been late by then. The midwife would have been long gone, and Nan would have been snoozing by the fire, her knitting pattern sliding off her knee; churning a giant bullseye against her dentures, one foot in a pink slipper on the cradle she'd popped me in to rock me now and then. Mum was probably lying on a bed in the same room, her long auburn hair spread out on the pillow like a mess of hay. I guess Mum was sometimes a looker — I think I learned that over the years, the reactions she got when she pranced down the park with us all bound up in her tightest skirt and her clickiest heels, her hair washed and piled on top of her head in curls. But that was rare. She mostly lay in bed in those early years, with her face to the wall, and allowed Nan to do any taking care of us that happened. If she did get herself tarted up, she did it with a giddy smile and we knew things were going to end badly.

So now Dad came in, and he had his wild black hair slicked down, and such a big, big grin on his face and such pale icy blue eyes. He scooped me up from the cradle — and if I close my eyes now I can imagine the massive beating of his heart beside me and the metal buttons on his jacket digging into me and the tickly hair rising up from inside his collar and the powerful smell of him, beer, tobacco, the leather strap from his watch, which was too big for him and he'd been piercing with a knife; a strong, animal smell, sort of bitter and warm all at once. "Look what I've been and got for my little rosebud," he's saying, producing from inside his jacket a bunny rabbit, white and sprawling-legged, and dangling it in front of me.

Did he really? Did he bring me that bunny the night I was born? I have a vivid memory of it. It travelled through my childhood with me, turning grey eventually, like all of us, one ear flopping hopelessly over its eye, but then it would have been new, made of felted wool, with soft white ears carrying little flecks of crumbed leather from Dad's watch strap and smelling of him. It had a glamorous pink bow around its neck, so I knew the bunny was a girl. Why do I think he must have given me it then and there, the first time we met? Because the shape of my life had begun and I feel certain it was Dad who began it. Things. That was what he gave me from the start in place of anything else, and it was what I ended up craving. Gifts and glamour and novelty, and if it came with a whiff of naughtiness so much the better.

Nan told me I opened just one newborn baby eye because the other was crusted with gunk and the eyelid wouldn't budge and my dad laughed, saying to my mum, "That baby is winking at me! The gel's on my side, Molly, and don't you forget it," and he tucked the rabbit into the blanket I was wrapped in and snuggled me back into the cradle. That was it, in fact. He was gone three weeks and didn't so much as *ask* after his new daughter — or her mother — in that time, but why would I care about that? I had the bunny. "Came in here like bleedin' King Kong . . . upsetting the baby," Nan said, describing him later, unimpressed. *King*

14

Kong was showing at the new Troxy cinema on Commercial Road: everyone was talking about it.

My brother Bobby came along barely ten months later and looked like a scrappy black-haired doll. I do remember staring into the drawer they'd pulled out and laid him in, like he was a pet guinea pig or something, and pushing the empty teat of a bottle towards his mouth and watching his tiny eyes stare at me over the top of it, grateful, I suppose, or desperate.

There was one tap for cold running water and one lavatory shed down in the courtyard for a whole row of families to use. But even when I was old enough to reach it I wouldn't dare to venture there if it was dark and raining, when the corridor and stairs would gleam slick as the skin of a black slug, preferring to use the chipped china pot in the corner of the bedroom. It seems to me a little easier to forgive Mum for being so disgusting in her personal habits when I remember that. That was the first five years of my life.

Nan lived one flight down. She was Dad's *muvver*. She'd had a great band of boys, no girls, and all of them "bad as socks" and sure to be "the death of her". Like lots of women at that time, she'd had all her teeth removed for no good reason except that she couldn't afford dentist's bills, and if she'd had any beauty, I think it went that day with the teeth.

The boys had long since left, all except Charlie and her eldest and wildest, my dad, Lucky Boy Tommy, who she doted on, for all he'd been such a "bleedin' handful", for all he got the needle so often and with such dramatic results. She was horrified by his choice of wife. Skinny, hopeless Irish Moll, who had no "good Irish" left in her. Moll's mum had died when she was a girl so, in Nan's view, Moll had "no idea on God's bleedin' green earth" how to be a mother. Mum'd been raised by her older sisters and only one of them had come to London with her. Those sisters had been useless, as far as Nan was concerned: "They didn't half bugger up the raising of Moll," by imparting no practical skills and indulging Moll's laziness and helplessness. Nan had been teetotal all her life, despite the many times when Dad and his brother Charlie had tried to hoodwink her with a slug of Haig in her tea. Molly, now eighteen, and a mother of two, already drank like a fish.

My nan used to say to me when I was little, "Who did she get you off of, eh? Where'd she find you?" It worried me, though I think she meant it kindly. I thought that if it wasn't the moon, it must have been somewhere far away, like Canada. Somewhere icy and clean. I worked out years later that all Nan meant was, how did I get to be so clever? And that was before they tested me, before they knew *how* clever. Nan couldn't quite believe I was one of the Dove family. But when she said it then, shaking her head and pursing her mouth, I thought she meant to disown me, or suggest I was the milk-man's daughter, like people did with Beryl Davis.

Mum was depressed, yes, but she was jealous too. She liked to be the baby herself, the centre of attention, and when she clicked first with me and then with Bobby, she loved the fuss. But once the babies came

16

that all changed. It was just crying and pooping and work, work, work. She'd once said to my dad, "Why don't *you* do all the bleedin' nappy-changing and nappy-washing if you love kids so much?" and he'd said (apparently), "You never ought to have had any, you — and all right, then, I *will* do the nappies and I'll do it a hell of a lot better'n you do." So she started this campaign, where she'd never change Bobby until Dad got home so that she could hand him over. I needn't tell you that in those days men did not change nappies.

Bobby would be sore and red and his little bum kind of scalded-looking, but even if Dad didn't turn up for days on end, Mum still wouldn't change him. She'd just leave his nappy off and let him piddle and poop anywhere in the flat, like a little rabbit. She was on a protest. I don't know how she dared because she must have known it would make Dad mad, mad in a way that always meant fireworks. When he finally did show up, she'd be ready for him. She'd stand in her dressing-gown, the house stinking, drawing on her cigarette as she propped up an old cupboard, smoking and pretending to be calm. Her heartbeat, the sense that she was ticking, like a bomb ready to go off . . . I could feel it, the moment I heard his key in the door. I'd tug on Bobby's hand and hide somewhere, under the beds in our bedroom, where we could put our hands over our ears.

Once I crept out, saw them in the hall. Watched from behind a door-crack as he took off his shoe and threw it at her. It hit her on the shoulder and thudded off the wall, leaving a black smudge, but she just brushed at her shoulder and carried on walking into the kitchen. "Huh! You think that fucking hurt?" she tossed back, over her shoulder.

So he took off the other one . . . I ran into bed then, back under the pillow, Bunny next to me and only the sound of my own sputtering heart for company. *The gel's on my side, Molly.* I'm not like her, I thought. I had no sympathy at all for her. No one's ever going to throw a shoe at me.

But Moll was stubborn too, and defiant in her way, so perhaps my stubbornness was as much from her as Dad. When Nan visited at first she was horrified by the state of our place and would spend her whole time on her hands and knees with a dustpan and brush, while Bobby would stand playing by the mouse-hole next to the fire, poking a pencil into it to see if he could make the mouse come out. Nan would be scooping up dry filth and crying, "What's got into you, Moll? What on earth are you thinking? I'm telling you, these kids will get sick if you carry on like this . . . it's the worst pen . . ."

Pen and ink. Stink.

Nan decided, finally, that she was the only one who could improve things in her daughter-in-law's home, so she took it on herself to bathe us, hauling buckets of water up the stairs from the tap in the courtyard and setting up a chipped china basin in front of the fire. Bobby would always scream and get a mere dunk: he'd soon be rolled in a thin blanket — there were never any towels — and left in front of the fire, where he'd wriggle out right away: he could never be still for long.

Moll and Bobby hated water, but I loved it. I loved that trickling feeling as Nan splashed it over me. I loved sitting up in my cramped bowl, once I could, and gazing at Nan — how she always seemed to me, right from the very beginning, just like a tortoise, with her neck stretching out, all folded and criss-crossed, so many hundreds of times ... I loved the tinkle of the drips between her fingers, as she lifted up the old grey flannel and squeezed it; and the way the droplets looked like gold beads when a little flame from the kitchen fire was reflected in them. I loved water ... baths, pools, the sea ... That was another way that I was different from my mum, who had a suspicion of any place green or wet, or not made of bricks.

We didn't get to go to any place green, though, until war broke out and Bobby and I were evacuated. We'd moved from Canada Buildings by then to a house at the Well Street end of Lauriston Road in South Hackney, near the church; I'd started at Lauriston School and Bobby was in the nursery class. That was the most extraordinary change. I mean, Lucky Boy Tommy bought us that house, and he bought a car too, a Chrysler — we were the only family in the neighbourhood who had one. Looking back now, I realise I did have some dim understanding of how unusual it was, but on the other hand, like any child, I just accepted it as an enchanting change in my life, like the Tizer and coconut ice he suddenly treated us to, and the little shilling knife he bought Bobby, with the bone handle and the leather sheath. The car was a buttery yellow, with a top that peeled back and these

19

little canvas flaps in the windows that you could coil up around the window rails when the roof was off, and big sweeping curves over the wheels, and it was so delicious I used to think it was like one giant ice-cream cone when Dad rolled up outside our house.

It was money that had made this magic, I knew that much. Dad would produce a silver sixpence from behind my ear and pop it on my tongue, or fold a ten-bob note and poke it in the top pocket of my pinafore dress, patting it and telling me to go and buy myself something nice. Silver coins tasted bitter and pennies tasted like blood, but the inky tang of folded notes when I slipped out my tongue and tried it was the best taste on earth. *Rule Britannia, two tanners make a bob* . . . Dad used to sing. He'd throw me up in the air when I was still small enough and there would be breath-holding seconds before he caught me again, when my heart would sail through the air with me, but he always did, and then he'd laugh, and snuggle my face with his, brushing me with his prickly chin.

Those early days in Lauriston Road, I'd stand at the corner shop with Bobby, mouth watering over the coconut ice and liquorice sticks, and know that we could choose them and take them home, where there'd be coal in the fire and faggots and gravy and Sally Lunns from Smulevitch's bakery in Well Street and our lives would be full of calm. I knew that money did this: turned us into children in books — safe and good, with kind parents. I even saw myself differently during this time: I was a girl with auburn ringlets, reading a book in a broderie-anglaise dress under a cherry tree in a garden full of light.

But, being magic, it went up in a puff soon enough. After the thrill of the move and Mum's joy in riding round the streets in the Chrysler, with her conker-coloured hair pinned tightly into a pale pink scarf patterned with rosebuds and wearing a white dress with thin straps and a sweetheart neck-line — well, after that there was a dreadful ugly night, when we had a spin. The police, the cozzers, came round, opening drawers and cupboards and tugging at things, until our spanking new place looked just like a hamster's hutch with all its stuffing pulled out.

Dad sat through it all, glowering on his brand-new red sofa, wearing a vest where hair snaked out from his armpits, smoking and refusing to say anything. Mum was crying, Bobby was crouching behind the sofa, and I was right next to him. Bobby and me stared right into each other's eyes, but said nothing. Bobby had the sweetest little face, with cropped black hair and round, sticking-out ears: his nickname was "Monkey" — also because he was cheeky and a scamp and always dangling from some tree or rung of a ladder or something. His favourite game was to go over to Vicky Park with his shilling knife with the bone handle — all the boys had knives in those days — and practise throwing it at trees, while the crows tottered on the grass, like fat vicars, and the Jewish boys chased each other around Vicky Fountain, throwing their black caps in the air.

Bobby sat now, with his knees up and long arms dangling. I could smell him: sweaty-socks-and-shoes, and the smell of those hard sweets he loved, hard black liquorice pips that Nan would give him from a tin and sometimes stuck to his teeth so that he could pretend to be a toothless pirate. I had the strongest feeling that to say anything, I mean a *word*, not just the wrong word, could make the worst thing ever happen. Could make my dad disappear. So when this policeman's face loomed over the sofa and said, "Hello there, and who have we got here?" I wouldn't answer him. I squinted at Bobby, who squinted right back, snapping his mouth tight shut. There was another baby by then: Vera, a big fat jowly kind of baby, who looked just like a Baby Grumpy doll, and who was lying in her fancy white crib, a little distance from the sofa, staring up at the coloured balls of string, which, on one of her rare visits, Nan had pegged to hang over her head.

The policeman soon gave up, straightening and taking his notebook out of his top pocket, and we watched as he and another man tried to manhandle our dad out of the room. They told him to get a shirt. We held our breath, wondering what Dad would do. No one spoke to him like that! Even Mum stopped sobbing for a minute to peep from behind her hands.

When he wouldn't move, the policeman made a noise with his tongue and went wandering round our house. We listened in hot silence as he thudded up the stairs and came down with a white shirt from the airing cupboard. The room crackled with the smell of Dad's anger, with the feeling I always had when I knew Dad was angry. But to my surprise — to everyone's surprise — Dad just put the shirt on, grinning all the while, fiddling at his cuffs to do them up really, really carefully, taking the longest time to do up every button, right up to the collar, and then gave a short laugh. He had this weird laugh. It wasn't when he found things funny. That laugh frightened me, in fact, because he'd put his face too close to you when he did it, and sort of barked at you, right at you, until you could feel the spray. He did this now, and the room felt very silent and small, like a cupboard.

Dad had turned rigid, stood with his legs apart, pretending not to notice what they were doing as the two men got his arms behind him, clamped these clinky cuffs on him and locked Dad to one of the cozzers.

I covered my face with my hands.

But I had to look, I had to glance, as I saw the two policemen move behind him, give him a poke in the back. The one he was locked to had to sort of stumble behind him, like this toy I had once, a little walking toy with a rod between the two wooden characters. Dad looked proud, then, with his ice-blue eyes staring straight ahead, his sweet-scented hair, his strange smile not wobbling at all. They kept on pushing him, shoving him in the back, and they got him to move in the end.

Just as he was leaving he wheeled around and ducked his head over the top of the sofa to say to me (and only me), "That's right, my gel. Don't you ever go and be a grass. Worst thing in the world. Rather die than be a grass, eh?" I thought he might be about to smack me, he looked so furious, but instead he gave me this whopper of a kiss, a big hard kiss landing like a fist on my head, and that was it: in a whirl of smoke and the sound of Vera wailing, he was gone.

That night I took Bunny to bed with me and sniffed her, trying to breathe some enchantment, something of Dad — the feelings he always brought, the sense that something good might happen to us at last. That rabbit was magic. Dad had produced it, a magician conjuring it from a hat. Dad could snatch at your nose and pretend to pinch it, and then — puff! — it would reappear between his fingers. So maybe Dad would reappear, if I longed for him enough. I slept with Bunny's pink silky ribbon under my cheek and in the morning there was a red strip there. I ran my finger along it, the strange ridge on my skin, thinking, if only it would never fade.

I knew we were going to be hungry then. Where would the money for food come from, if Dad wasn't around? Moll could survive on cigarettes, on "air-pie and a walk around", as Nan used to say. We often felt hungry, we were used to it, but it started up that night, a more desperate clawing feeling than I'd had before, and I knew it was there to stay, for a long, long time.

Dad got nine months. The prison was in the country and we never went to visit him. We didn't know what he'd done; no one mentioned it to us. I somehow got the impression that the house would be taken from us, that what he'd done was connected to that, but it never was. Mum told us we should look sad if anyone asked and say Daddy was a soldier in Burma — this was before the war had started — and how much we missed him.

"Let me see you say it," she said to me, and I put my head on one side and slumped my shoulders and said, "My poor daddy is a soldier over-overcease and we're all on our own."

"No!" she said. "Don't ham it up, gel," and I had to try again, especially with the "overseas" word, until I got it just right, and she sat back on her heels and laughed and said, "Well, would you look at that! The gel's a proper bleedin' *actress*. Ain't she good at lying?"

I beamed at that: the first — maybe only — compliment she ever paid me.

So then the leafleting started. It must have been the summer of '39 and Mum picked one up one day standing waiting in the butcher's on Well Street market, where she couldn't afford anything and was just chatting to Sly Roger, the butcher, who was a friend of my dad's — in fact he was a friend of quite a few men who were inside at that time, and Sly Roger made it his business to look out for them, women whose husbands were "away", to help them out occasionally. He wasn't actually called Sly, of course, that was Nan's name for him. She would say, "Roger the Dodger the Dirty Old Lodger," and some other rhymes, so that's how I thought of him. Mum picked a leaflet up from the dusty window ledge of Sly Roger's shop, with flakes of sawdust on it and that blood-and-sawdust butcher's smell, and read it out to me and Bobby as we were leaving, pushing Vera, with the bouncing pom-poms on her hat, in her pram up Well Street.

"MOTHERS SEND THEM OUT OF LONDON," she read.

Moll stood there with a cigarette in one hand, a leaflet in the other and fanned her face with it, and she suddenly seemed all whipped up in a hot, angry feeling and she was saying, "Shall I, then? Shall I send ya?"

At home, once her mood was quiet again and she had her feet up and her nose in *My Weekly*, I read the leaflet myself. It had a little crown at the top and an arc, a bit like a rainbow, and the words: "EVACUA-TION — Why and How? *Public Information Leaflet No 3. Read this and keep it carefully. You may need it.*" The words were easy for me, the best reader in my class — in fact, Miss Clarkson said, the best little reader she'd ever come across. But even so. It made no sense. Why did we need to evacuate? I decided to ask Nan when next I saw her, on a visit from Poplar to give me and Vera a bath (she'd given up on Bobby — who stank to high heaven, though if she could manage it she'd try to bring him a *Knockout* comic that was a few weeks old: she found them in a bin outside the shops on Well Street).

I'd learned from Nan where Mum's mood swings came from. If Mum had been to the shops and come back with a bottle in brown paper I knew she'd be merry for a while, squeezing our bottoms as she suddenly clutched us in a fierce squishy cuddle. Then she'd slump out, snoring, skirt all rucked up and her knickers on show, on the replacement sofa, a green thing with exploded insides, which we'd rescued from a skip and smelt of dogs.

Nan had said on her last visit that Dad was lucky to be inside because no one outside had a job anyway and, knowing him, he'd have only gone and fought the Blackshirts and got himself into more trouble. She saw him as "lucky", no matter what. She had a blind spot about Dad, for all her goodness, but she didn't know the half about the way we were living, about how hungry we were and how it was for Vera, and I never thought to tell her. What could she have done? She had no money, I knew that much. Only Dad could make a silver coin appear from nowhere.

We were so poor by then. We were still living in that big house but every twig of furniture had been pawned and Moll had no idea, without Dad, how to do anything at all. There was nothing in for breakfast. There was no coal in the fire. The baby cried all night long, and Mum would sleep heavily through it, helped by a visit to Sly Roger and whatever gift he'd given her. Bobby and me took turns to walk Vera, to lift her from her crib and put her against our shoulders, the weight of her bouncing against us, to — when we felt really desperate — sneak our hand under Mum's pillow, brave the stink of her breath and dab at her gin with our fingers, so that we could let Vera suck on them to quieten her.

That was when I did it. The first time. It was a stroke of brilliance, if I say it myself. A talent I didn't know I had was born.

It's like this: me and Bobby are running along Lauriston Road towards school. The spire of St John of

27

Jerusalem church points up towards God in heaven. Bobby is nipping about in his monkey-boy style, sometimes jumping up from the pavement and scampering along a wall instead. We've had no breakfast, and we left Vera at home crying, snuggled up in bed with Mum, and something about this worries me, even though it's the same every day. On this day I don't feel good at all. We love to go to school, though Mum is always trying to keep us home with her. Today she's not fierce: she's in one of her heavy moods. She's slow and — well, I just don't have a good feeling about her. Maybe she'll roll over on Vera and crush her. I'm thinking of this and not really listening to Bobby, but then I do hear him, his little tuppence-ha'penny voice as he leaps down from a wall, saying, "I'm star-ving," and "My stomach's aching." As he says this, school is there, with its big arch and the word "BOYS" calling to Bobby, who is in the first year, the youngest class; but for some reason, I think it might be that I get a sniff of bread from the baker's boy in his van, or just for mischief, I don't know, I suddenly grab Bobby's hand and snatch him away from that arch, and go back the way we've come, running. Bobby laughs and follows me.

We run back past the churchyard and the double arched doorway of St John of Jerusalem, with its funny Jesus with his hand missing and the message saying. *Be not afraid*, and I think, Right, I'm not, ta very much, I'm not afraid! And we run as far as Cassland Road, past privet hedges and grave-stones and droopy bluebells in people's gardens, and dustbins and tweety morning birds and propped-up bicycles, and past the stinky beer smell of the Albion pub and past a sweep carrying all his brushes, and now there are no children going to school, and we're on our own and the light is sticky, warm, and making you feel like you're a wasp in a jar of honey.

The milk van has already been up the street, the horse with its nose stuck in its nosebag. And on one of the steps of one of the fancier houses, in this little neat bit called Cassland Crescent, a maid or a housewife or someone has left it there on the step: a pint of milk in a bottle with the top all curling and pecked by the birds. The street seems suddenly quiet. I look up and down it and don't see a soul. I can't even hear a dog barking, or the clop of the horse from the milk van, which must be long gone, away to Hackney Wick.

Birds hold their breath, watching me. I'm listening to my own heartbeat. Bobby is bouncing on one leg, and then snivelling, and the white milk bottle smiles at me, glowing, handsome. Take me. I'm yours. Come on, gel. You can do it. Come on.

I watch the long, tall houses, staring down their noses at me, from the high-falutin' street. I walk over towards the gate, and quietly undo the latch. The door is painted a colour Nan always calls royal blue. It has one of those huge brass knockers, a lion's head, but he's just peering towards the front step like he's lost his body down there. Bobby is a stride away, one finger in his mouth. My heart is thumping: loud, now. Steady, though.

So then I dart forward. I snatch at it, at the bottle, and it's cold, the glass slippery. I hold it tight, clutch it to my chest, and half run, half walk back towards the gate. I'm not sure if I imagine it, but there seems to be someone at the window of the house, or was there a voice, did someone shout, "Oi! You, gel"? I grab Bobby, almost spinning him round, and shove him towards Cassland Road, and in a kind of running walk, carefully so as not to drop the milk, I follow him.

We stop then, in the doorway of a house on Gascoyne Road, and start laughing and shrieking, and Bobby is saying, "Give it, then, give us a drink!" and I'm scared I might drop it because it's slippery and I've hugged it to me like a doll, or like my beloved white Bunny.

We've found ourselves now far away from school and near to the Cawley Gate bit of Vicky Park. So we hop over the low fence, run towards the Vicky Fountain and sit down behind it on the stone, right beneath the fat cherub riding an elephant. At least, I think it's an elephant — it could be a dolphin with teeth like a shark. But that would be silly.

I pass the milk to Bobby, and let him take a sip.

"Wonder if Flash Gordon has got himself to Mars?" Bobby says happily, after glugging a huge amount. He wipes his mouth with his sleeve.

"Give it me, then . . ." I take a sip myself.

All the time we rushed away from that house, my heart was jabbering, sort of shouting at me. Something inside me rushing, rushing. Is my blood flowing faster? Something else too. Something like the thing I described when Dad loses his temper. A feeling like shredding things, tearing things up, making them flutter in the wind. It's such a blowy day, I notice suddenly. I glance around, at a stand of big trees near Victoria Park Road, staring down at me like a row of teachers. A paper bag bowls along between them. It doesn't matter. They'll never stop me. I can do it — do what I like. It's mine, not theirs, this world, and I want it, I do — I do!

It's brilliant to watch Bobby put his mouth to the lip of the bottle and glug glug glug the milk down. His eyes wide and his ears waggling as he drinks, and his little nose all milky. He's not a bit worried about what I've just done: he's too busy thinking about Flash Gordon. But I am, and not because I think I'll get caught. I can sit under this sign here, above the fat cherub, saying something like *For the love of God and the Gooded* or does it even say, *For the love of God and Good Food*? Perfect! The words are a bit scratched out, being old.

I let Bobby take his time, and slurp the rest when he's ready. The reason I'm worried is because it was so easy and I know that this won't be the last time. The world is full of milk on doorsteps. And bread left by bakers' vans, and coal from the coalman. As long as I don't pick the same doorstep, as long as no one spies me, I can do it every morning, can't I? I can drink it then and there, the way the birds do sometimes, perching on rims to dip their heads into the skin of milk.

Only yesterday we were sitting in St John of Jerusalem, moss under our fingernails where we'd been picking it from the tops of walls, green smells under our noses, and the church organ plonking away and the vicar booming about Proverbs and saying, "Open thy mouth, judge righteously, and plead the cause of the poor and needy."

Cheers! The poor and needy. Ta very much. I be not afraid. I can take some home for Vera and say I found it, somebody left it behind. Finders keepers. It's not as if Mum will ask. I don't think I've eaten anything since the pie and mash Nan brought us last Friday.

So I'm thinking this on my way home, a little later that morning, as the clouds roll over the rooftops and everything, leaves, paper, is caught up and flapping, wheeling along as fast as a child's hoop . . . I'm happily picturing Vera holding out her chubby little arms for a bottle of milk. I'm a bit surprised to see the knitted figure of Nan at the front door of our house and, from the way she's standing, that she's been there a while. I turn to go back, but she's already spotted me and Bobby, who's bouncing from one foot to the other behind me.

She clacks her dentures at us as we get up close, moves the gob-stopper to the side of her mouth so that it bulges scarily as she speaks, stretching her tortoise neck out. "And where you bin, my gel?"

"School, course."

"School my arse. School's the other way. It's nearly ten o'clock. And where's your mum? I can't get no answer at this door. Is she in?"

That scares me. As she says it I realise something: I've had this feeling, a cold stone-in-the-stomach kind of feeling, all morning, and I suddenly know that the reason I didn't want to go to school with Bobby was to get away from it. And I *did* for a bit, stronger feelings blotted it out, but now they're gone and the stone in my stomach is back, all cold-stone heavy again. I don't understand why, or what it was that I was dreading. I only know that now it's happening. Something bad. Happening to Mum, or Vera.

Nan gets her umbrella then and starts bashing the door. She peeks in at the window but the curtains are closed and all she can see is the back-side of green velvet.

"Might be asleep," I say. "She was asleep when we left. She had Vera in bed with her."

Nan stops bashing the door and stares at me. She looks into my face for a minute. The gob-stopper balloons in her cheek like a giant boil. "Had your mum . . . What kind of state was she in, when you two went out this morning?"

I know what she's asking but I can't say it. Cat's got my tongue.

So now Nan seems really worried, and goes next door, and starts knocking on that door instead.

Mr Barry appears in his shirt-sleeves. This is a posh street, not used to the likes of us. Mr Barry is a night-watchman and he sleeps in the day, so we've just woken him too. He gives Nan a bad look.

"Molly. My daughter-in-law. I think she's had an . . . accident," Nan says, and I notice her voice changes a little, and she's trying to speak "proper". My stomach twists: I feel embarrassed for her. "You couldn't . . . Could you help us get inside?"

Mr Barry goes back inside his house without a word, and then he comes out again and says to Bobby and me, in a very important voice, "Stand Back, Children." He has this big crowbar and he's going to bash the door down.

As he lifts it, swinging it behind him, Nan suddenly says, "I thought Moll might have given you a spare key."

At this, his missus, Glenda, appears, and after a chat it seems clear that Mum *did* give Glenda a spare key and the door is opened without the need to smash it up, and Mr Barry puts his crow-bar down and his handkerchief over his mouth and says, "What the . . ." and me and Bobby hang back and I know again, with the same stone-heavy feeling, that this is going to be as bad as Dad going away, maybe even worse. That something too bad to say has happened.

And it has, because now Nan is in the front room and screaming, a sound I've never heard before, and Glenda is crying jesus christ almighty and they're pushing us back outside into the front garden, and trying to block our eyes and not let Bobby squeeze under their legs and run back into the front room. I think that it's Mum — Mum must be dead — and I start screaming too, until Nan stops and her skin is the colour of ash from the fire and she says ssh ssssh and I do at last push past Nan's knobbly knitted shape into the front room and I see then Mr Barry is helping Mum up from the bed on the floor and she's not dead, and I rush to her, and try to cuddle her. I bury my face in her legs in her shiny stockings, but she smells bad, really bad, like petrol or beer or something, but the crying is now from Nan, and Nan is holding my baby sister Vera, wrapped mostly in a sopping wet blanket, and the baby is all wrong, I can see that, with her head over to one side like a chicken when its neck is broken. Nan takes the baby and sits on the stairs, and now Mr Barry is helping Mum over to their house, but I hear Glenda asking if we have a telephone, does anyone have a telephone (we don't) in the street? And I know she's going to ring the Old Bill, that she's going to tell them, to "grass", which can only be a Terrible Thing.

That night we spend at Nan's, back in Poplar. Mum is in hospital, and the cozzers are waiting to talk to her.

Vera is in heaven. No one tells us why or what happened. Whenever I think of it, of what they were all trying to hide from us — we kept getting shooed back outside, on to the street — I remember the kettle, and the fire in the grate, and then I have a funny surprise: Mum lit a fire? Mum got some coal from somewhere? Then I picture the kettle on its side, lying on the floor with no whistle in it, and remember there was water everywhere, as if it had been dropped from high up. Mum's mattress was on the floor in the front room where she always slept in the day and I could see that the bed was wet. Did she drop boiling water on Vera? Would that be enough to kill a baby? Vera did look terrible, her head a blackened red colour.

But no one explains. That night we sleep high up in Nan's big bed, in her bedroom; the bed with a black snaky spring bursting through one little hole in the mattress at the bottom sometimes to poke at your foot.

I usually loved Nan's candle-wick spread with the patterns to pluck at, and the tickly tassels that Bobby likes hiding under and chewing. But I hardly sleep at all, because every time I close my eyes Vera rolls up, and she's crying, and scolding me, and won't stop.

The next morning Nan says the welfare lady is coming to talk to us because Mum is going to be in a special hospital for a while and that we should be glad because it could be worse. We wonder how it could be worse.

"Your dad'll have to be told . . . and there'll have to be a bleedin' funeral for poor little Vera . . . and that ain't no place for you nippers," Nan says, eyes wet. The old tortoise seems older than ever — she hasn't even done her hair, which bounces out from her ears like tufts of cotton wool now that it isn't caught in a net, and I stare into her old blue eyes thinking, how many times has her face folded up that way, like a nice clean handkerchief, crumpled and crumpled in your hand?

The welfare lady wants to send us to Elephant and Castle to be with a foster family, Nan says, but she — Nan — has a better idea and will do her "bleedin' best" for us. Nan's legs are gnarly with veins and don't work so well, and the dirt at our house is too much, these days, even for her, she says, and she'd love to keep us, but she knows they'd never let her. If she makes a fuss they might send us to a home. I can't believe those legs can hold her up at all, let alone take her up the flights of stairs she has to climb to get to her flat: they look so spindly, like twigs, so I know she's telling the truth.

36

Nan has been listening to the wireless, and since May the government has been warning parents about something, about the "biggest sacrifice of all": sending their children to the country. Sounds quite nice to me. She smiles a bit, ducking her head to look really closely at me and Bobby. There's a huge creaky noise as she bends down to whisper in my ear, and a whiff of her, the perfume smell of Parma violet sweets, "And I'm telling you, at least you'll get a bleedin' wash there, and fed too, and you can't do any worse than Moll now, can you?" It sounds like a holiday, a trip to the country, Bobby says. He can't wait.

That night in Nan's Parma-violet-scented bed I have another horrible dream. Little Vera is an angel in heaven but she's unhappy. She's crying and waving her red arms — really in pain. In my hand I'm clutching a bottle of milk and I'm holding it out towards Bobby, and Vera is howling. Give me the milk! I'm the baby! What about me? *Look what you've done.*

It's my fault, I think. I'm the cleverest: I can see things differently from Bobby and Mum and Nan. I'm more like Dad. I'm the one who *does* things. I'm the only one who can make things happen like he can — like he made a car appear from nowhere, and that's my job too.

Waking up I remember something. "Like taking sweets from a baby." I don't know where I first heard that, but I picture the milk on the doorstep. How easy it was to nick it. And then more from that boring vicar, Proverbs again: *The wicked flee when no man pursueth: but the righteous are bold as a lion.* Yes. Bold

37

as a lion — that's me. Lying in the bed with Nan snoring beside me, a hot lump like a meat pie cooking, and Bobby's elbow sticking in me on the other side. I think, I must take care of Bobby. And next time, when Mum is there, I'll bring the milk home. If only I'd done it this time, I would have saved Vera. *Give me not poverty, lest I steal.* Another funny sentence, heard somewhere, all mixing up. I want my mum, I'm thinking. I remember trying to hug her, at the house, trying to wrap my arms around her legs while they were taking her, and how she was being led by Mr Barry, and how she stumbled against me and didn't seem to see me and trod on my foot, and it hurt. "I want Mum," I'm saying, into my pillow. Where is she? I don't understand. "Bad as Nan says you are, Mum, *I want you* . . ."

A Trip to the Country

So then it's Saturday early in September, and Bobby and me are in the playground of Lauriston School, with the other children, all wearing our gas masks on strings round our necks, and a great big label with our names in black ink. (I've written Bobby's label for him. All the children asked me to write their names for them, and to tie their shoelaces. I don't understand why they can't do this themselves. They say how come a six-year-old like me can remember all the identity-card numbers? I only have to glance at them once, that's it, and the number has gone in and stuck there, and even Mr

38

Hitler himself would never un-wedge it.) We're finally going to the country.

We've already had a go at trying on the gas masks, fiddling with the straps at the back so they're tied snug under the chin. I put Bobby's on him and the eye-piece steams up straight away so that he looks funny. Like a weird bug. He pushes it off.

"It's stinky!"

"It's just the rubber, silly . . ."

But then he finds that if you blow hard, this nose-bit, the duck's beak, flaps around and makes farting noises. He looks for his friend Archie Markham to show him and they make the noise together. That cheers him up.

It made me feel panicky too, the first time I put it on, like I couldn't breathe. And the smell was rubber and chemicals, bleach. I threw it down, and Nan was there, watching me. She'd been sewing something. Now she got up. "Look what I made your little rabbit, gel. See what I been and made Bunny. Because we all got to wear one, even her, you know . . ."

Nan showed me what she'd made: a black material gas mask, a tiny one, with ribbon at the back, to tie on my rabbit. I tied it on her; Nan winked at me. She hadn't made anything like that for Bobby, even though he's the youngest. It's our secret, something just for me. Bunny is safely in my bag now. Miss Clarkson's watching us, and we're in line with all the other children and she's checking that we're standing straight and not poking the person in front.

> "*These are the actions I must do:*
> *salute to the King and bow to the Queen,*
> *and turn around to the boys in green . . .*"

Peggy Burchwell sings, under her breath.

I wonder if Peggy remembered her skipping-rope. I haven't got one. I use Nan's washing-line.

"Rub some soap on your finger, and run it along the mask. That'll stop it misting up," Miss Clarkson says to Archie, who is putting his mask away.

"I ain't got no soap, Miss . . ." Archie says, but she's already way down the line, clicking and snapping at Peggy Burchwell.

> "*Mabel, Mabel, set the table.*
> *Do it as fast as you are able . . .*"
> *Peggy sings. Peggy is the best skipper.*
> "*Salt, mustard, vinegar, pepper . . .*"

"Has Mum got a mask?" Bobby asks, now. "What if she gets gassed, in hospital?"

"Yeah . . . oh, I don't blinkin' know . . ."

Does Mum have one? What about Nan? We were given ours a week ago, but I don't know where Mum is, and I haven't seen her since the day Vera went to heaven. All I know is what Nan said to me this morning: "You look after Bobby, now, gel. You're the smartest — you know he's a few currants short of a teacake. And he's only little. Stick together and don't let anyone split you two up — ever, you hear?"

Last night was the first night of the black-out. Nan did it: she drew her curtains and taped up the brown paper, in case the glass all shattered. But later that evening we went outside, me and Bobby, and the streetlights were on, so we could play Knock Down Ginger. Then everything went black. I stood still and looked around me. I put my hand out. There was a sooty blackness and I didn't dare to step into it. I heard Bobby — he'd been running, and now his footsteps skittered up beside me. If only I'd been quick I could have pinched something. I didn't know what, but we were hungry again and Nan had only given us bread and dripping for tea. There would have been milk bottles, but I was like a blind man. (I'd have got better at it, though.) We stumbled towards Nan's flat. The darkness was a different kind of dark, and Bobby was scared of it.

He told me he thought he saw Vera's little head, floating in the stairwell like a pumpkin. We both ran up the stairs howling.

Nan didn't sleep well last night — I felt her huff and puff in the bed beside me, and at one point she climbed out, and I heard her pick herself a paregoric sweet from a packet she has hidden in the bottom of her drawers, among her bloomers, all so big they can keep the sun out of her eyes, she says, and then laughs, and I know it makes no sense but it's funny.

I heard her climb back into bed, putting her dentures — kept in a glass by the bed — back in her mouth, so that she could rattle the cough sweet against them. I smelt its vinegary nurse-and-hospital kind of smell.

41

Nan lay there for a long time, her nose in the darkness pointing towards the ceiling.

Before we leave she kisses us both, and pulls up Bobby's socks, tucking a grey handkerchief into them. I rub my cheek, thinking of the crinkly feel of Nan's papery skin. She gives us our bags with all our things in them, and tells us that the country is a good place, and we're to take care of one another and not get separated. And then she repeats the thing that seems to have been worrying her most, which is about this list the teachers gave us, of things to bring with us. "Mackintosh! Petticoat! Two pairs of bleedin' stockings! Who the bejabas am I meant to get them off of?" She puts us on the bus that drops us at the school playground, she doesn't come to school with us. She says it's hard enough, without that.

Now that we're all in the coach leaving the school, I look again for her, or for Mum, but there's only one person running along Lauriston Road beside the coach. It's Martin Jacobs's mum, carrying a toddler — a baby about the same age as Vera — and his mum is pretty and young and she's got a perky little red hat and a navy coat and she's smiling and lifting the baby's arm and waggling it, as if the baby's a doll.

Miss Clarkson tuts as the bus stops at the roundabout and the woman's face is at the window for a second. "Mrs Jacobs. We nearly left without you."

Martin Jacobs is embarrassed. He's the only one whose mum and sister are coming too. It's because his sister is a baby. Vera would have come, if we'd still needed to keep her safe. The coach is all hubbub, chatter. There's a paper packet going around. We're each grabbing it and then screaming. It's sweets so we don't feel sick. Bobby's on the seat beside me, sucking the barley sugar, waggling his big ears. He's never had barley sugar before. His eyes are wide. You can see from the shape his mouth is making that the crispy golden stick is splintering in there, spreading sweetness all over his tongue.

I press my face to the glass. Where's Mum? Does she even know we're going away, going to the country, like Dad? Perhaps we'll be nearer to him . . . maybe we'll even see him there. Is this how Dad felt, being taken away from everyone? And not knowing where he was going, like us? (It's a secret; it would help Mr Hitler if we all knew where we were being sent so we're not to know and Nan hasn't been told either.)

I remember Dad then, that day in our house, his hands behind his back, being handcuffed. I remember the way he stood, his legs apart, his head up. His chin was trembling, but it was lifted, hoisted high. Chin up. His eyes moved to the window. He didn't turn his head but he saw them driving away his lovely ice-cream Chrysler, slamming the door, using his own key that they'd made him give them. But Dad even grinned, a cheeky grin for the copper doing the handcuffing.

That's how I'm going to be. Like Dad, not Mum. Look after my little brother like Nan told me to. Chin up, and proud.

The station . . . I've never been to a station. I've never seen the bookstalls with their rainbow stacks of magazines and the little shops with all that mouth-watering fruit and the porters with their peaked caps rushing by, with their trolleys of mail-bags and luggage, smiling and elbowing each other, nodding at Miss Clarkson, who sniffs and looks away. Best of all: penny bars of Nestlés from a machine. Of course we don't have a penny. Bobby kicks the machine when Miss isn't looking.

We're told again to form lines and wait. Then we're told to "March!" and we rush on to the train making a noise like bees. We fling our bags and gas masks on the racks above our seats and fight for the best places.

"Bobby, you can have the rest of my barley sugar, if you let me sit next to the window," I shout.

He nods, and I take the tiny pointed stick — it looks like a glass tooth — from my mouth and pop it into Bobby's. Archie leans over the seat and bats Bobby on the head with his gas mask. Bobby sucks hard on the sweet.

I press my face to the scratched window pane. As the train pulls out there are women on the station who wave their hankies at us, and blow us kisses, and shout, "Good luck, me darlings!" and "Be good now!" and we don't even know them.

Peggy and Patricia rush to the window, holding their bald, stupid-looking dolls, taking their hats off their heads to wave back. I cross my arms over my chest. I don't have a doll and Bunny is packed away in my canvas bag, on the rack. Anyhow, I don't want to lose my seat by getting up. I mean, lots of the others have to sit in the corridors and we might be on this train for hours . . .

One of the porters on the station, an old man with whiskers on his chin, rubs his eyes and waves.

I've never seen a man crying. A grown-up man as old as Dad. And we're not even his children.

We all jump up again, crowding round the window and doors: the train is stopping. Is this where we're staying? We've already had a False Alarm, Miss Clarkson called it, when we stopped at a station a while back (with its sign blacked out so no one could know where it was) and there were ladies in flowered aprons giving us sandwiches and half-pint bottles of milk, and patting our heads and some of them crying. Funny how the grown-ups keep crying.

Bobby keeps going on about these lavatories they make us use. All the children are lined up beside these canvas curtains, with flaps in them, and behind them there's a tin bucket, and as Bobby pees, laughing, you can hear him trying to hit the side of the bucket and make that louder noise, the tinny, sloshing sound . . . and his friend Archie's competing with him in the bucket beside his and the pair of them giggling away.

Then it's back on the train again, but this time it's slower. We see water, boats, a bridge, a thin line of geese flying together making shapes like the letters M and V. I stare at them for ages. They look like they're writing something in the sky — the geese I mean — and I wonder for a moment if they are, but maybe it's in a different language out here in the country, one that girls from Lauriston Road can't read. The train is slowing down and in the distance there's a big, big church, dark and high-up and frightening, with two sticking-up towers, one big and one smaller, which make me think of a snail and its hump, or a castle.

"Look, Miss! A castle!" Pat Beveridge says.

"It's Ely Cathedral," Miss Clarkson says, then quickly presses a hand to her mouth to push the words back in. We're not meant to know where we're going. This station sign has paper pasted over it.

"My dad made that," Bobby says, looking at the cathedral.

I know what he means but Martin Jacobs thumps him and says, "He did not!"

"Did too. We got one in our front room. Ship of the Fens. He made it out of matchsticks."

Miss Clarkson gathers all the children from Lauriston School, claps her hands and blows a whistle to tell us to get off the train and on to the platform. Guards open doors for us. They put their arms out to help the girls and hold the hands of the littlest ones. Some people in uniforms are watching us and they step forward and talk to Miss Clarkson and they're all looking at us and we hear for the first time these new words "billet" and "billeting officer" and then we're told to form another line, and we have to set off, across the road and up a hill, with our bags and gas masks strapped on again, towards the giant church snail-building.

There are children pouring out of other carriages, from other schools. Jewish children, dark-haired girls, tall, in their posh coats and shiny shoes. They stand away from us, with their smart teacher, who is patting their heads and crying. I look round for Miss Clarkson.

She's powdering her cheeks from a little compact, and snapping it shut, into her bag, and she's patting one of the younger children on the head, but not looking at him or any of us. Now she's saying something to the guard, and turning away from us. Her navy coat and clicky shoes disappear down a tunnel towards another platform. She doesn't look back, and she doesn't say goodbye or good luck. Her hat bounces with every step. She looks like she's in a hurry.

I hold Bobby's hand and tear off my paper name label, which keeps getting caught in the string of my gas mask. Then I step on it, and the heel of my shoe makes a giant black print on it. That's my old name. Here I'm somebody else and I'm going to have a new one.

"Queenie, Queenie, who's got the ball?
Is she short or is she tall?
Is she hairy or is she bald?
You don't know cos you ain't got the ball!"

That's what we play in the playground. I'm brilliant at it. I'm always Queenie, and I always do know who's got the ball. I can read their faces, their shifting about, their shuffling. Queenie. That's me. A lovely name, I like it much better than mine. Why shouldn't I have it? Marching in a long crocodile towards the biggest blinkin' building I've ever seen, that Ship of the Fens,

47

built for a queen too, Miss said. Queen Etheldreda: Ely Cathedral.

OK, that might be a fabrication. That's how I remember it, changing my name, but you know — there'll be plenty who knew me, knew me later I mean, as an adult and, reading this, might say, "That's not right, you didn't change your name till later, when you had good reason to," but this is my story and that's the way I remember it. In any case, that's just the detail — was there a pint of milk on the step, was it jugs of milk back then? The facts are just as I told you. First thing I ever nicked was milk. My dad was banged up for God knows what and my mum was depressed, a drinker who, through neglect or an accident or whatever, things I never really knew about properly and were never explained to me, caused the death of her own child. Oh, and Dad must have been inside before, come to think of it. That's why those matchstick models — his Ship of the Fens — produced a loud sigh from Nan whenever she looked at them. We lived in the East End and our fortunes changed constantly and we were sent away during the war. Don't listen to those who tell you that billeting officers didn't marshal any evacuated kids in Ely Cathedral. Stick with the facts, as outlined above. It's all true.

What strikes me now in any case, is not all of that but this: Bobby's immediate acceptance of my new name. You'll see. He opened his mouth once to protest, and closed it again. After that, he never slipped up. He never called me anything but Queenie. That tells you a lot about my little brother, that detail. How loving he was. How he let me be who I wanted to be and never mocked it. He understood somehow. That's a rare thing: to love someone not for how you think of them but for how they think of themselves.

Me and Bobby are among the last to be picked. The crowd of children is now down to a straggle. We're sitting with our knees up to our chests, on the floor of this enormous cold church, bigger than any stone dungeon, our bags and boxes at our feet, our bums aching because the tiles are icy, tiles that look like patterns on a draughts board. The place smells of nurse-and-hospital and sweaty feet because some of the boys have taken their shoes off. When we first got here we sounded just like a big hive of bees, or like we were at the swimming baths; it was deafening. But now it's just us and the noise is down to a trickle.

There are some tiny candles lit and they splutter as new people come in, go to the billeting lady and look over at us. Right now I'm staring up at the ceiling, at the coloured glass above us with the nudie figures, showing Bobby, trying to stop him being bored, stop him whispering about Nan — where's Nan, when are we going back to Nan? Wondering, what is it about us? Why are we among the last to be picked?

Bobby's playing with some conkers he picked up on the way over here, jiggling them in his pockets and rolling them in his palm like shiny wooden marbles, then suddenly leaping on Archie and wrestling him to the floor, accusing him of nicking one.

49

We haven't eaten since the sandwiches on the station and, as ever, we're hungry and tired, and a little picture of Nan pops into my head, back home taping up that brown paper for a black-out curtain like yesterday, sighing and showing her nylon slip as she stretches up to peg it to the top of the curtain rail. She would at least have brought us some tea, and the kettle would be whistling and she'd be getting out the *Review* and settling down with a cuppa, having made me and Bobby a half-cup each with lots of sugar.

I screw up my eyes tight because I don't like the leaky feeling in them when I think of Nan, and imagine sleeping in bed beside her with her rustling hairnet that she wears at night, with little wisps of white hair poking out, like the grandmother in *Red Riding Hood* (only our grandmother smells of paregoric lozenges and Parma violets, not apples). Nan's mouth closes down into this strange gummy line, and sometimes when she's asleep and I'm not, I stare at it, and want to open it, and look inside at the place where all the teeth used to be.

A lady's voice suddenly: "But he looks puny. What d'you think, Bert? The one with the ears. What's your name, boy?"

A man and a woman. The man silent, like a tree, and with so much black hair and big red hands. They stand in front of us, staring at us.

"Bit of a rum lot left, isn't it?" says the man. I get a sniff of pipe tobacco as he steps over to us; he's slipping the pipe into the pocket of his jacket but it still peeps out, like a snake's head.

"At least they're not Jews! I wouldn't know what to do with a Jew," the lady says. Then to me, "What's your name?" She's wearing a thick coat, which Nan would call a "camel coat" for the colour and the way it looks like an animal's skin, and men's shoes, and her skin has a rough coating on each cheek, like the skin of some apples. I'm wondering what she might be like underneath, if you peeled her with a knife, like an apple.

"Queenie," I answer.

Bobby stares at me. He opens his mouth a little, like a big fish.

"I don't think there's any Queenie left . . . only Beryl, Mary, Robert, Archibald . . ." says the billeting lady, coming over to us. She has a clipboard, a pen parked above her ear, the way Dad does with a cigarette.

"It's my nickname. Everyone calls me Queenie." I point to the place on her list where my real name is. Bobby closes his mouth tight. "And we have to stay together," I add. "My nan said."

"It's the start of the Campaign," the man says to Bobby. "You're little . . . skin and bone. Can you work hard?" This man's hair is long for a grown-up's. It sticks up from his head like a brush you use to sweep the hearth. His cheeks have these puffs of hair sprouting from them. I suppose it's a beard but it looks more like the stuff you get growing on potatoes when you leave them for too long.

"Yes," I pipe up. "We're grand. We're good in all — campaigns." We don't know what they mean, and

Bobby's mouth is now firm shut, like a letter-box stuck with glue.

The lady in the camel coat laughs. I think she knows I don't know what the man means, but she likes my cheek. The man and the lady — she's quite fat, bundled up to the neck in the coat, her apple-skinned face not very smiley — turn to go, as if that decides it, nodding to the billeting officer, and then the man jerks his head towards Bobby to follow them towards the great big dark doors of the cathedral. I scramble up.

And that's it. The billeting lady crosses our names off the list and nods at the man and the lady, and they lead us out towards the huge doors, with the iron patterns on them, and we hear them clank behind us, like the doors of a castle.

Bobby holds my hand. I wrap my fingers around his fist, feeling through his fingers that he's still tightly holding his conkers. Somehow we both know that if the brush-haired man and the camel-coat woman see them, we'll have to give them up.

"It's ten shillings and eightpence for the first one. How much do we get if we have the girl, too?" the lady asks.

The man says something we don't hear, and again looks back at us, nodding towards a great big black horse with a sort of cart behind it, parked across from the cathedral on a very posh bit of grass. Surely they don't mean us to get in that. Don't they know my dad had a *Chrysler*? The horse is eating the grass near the cathedral and the gardens look so bright and neat that, somehow, I think this must be naughty.

"Just the dregs left," says the lady, as we scramble up on to the high seat behind them. Bobby holds his bag to his chest and bites his bottom lip.

"Call me Auntie Elsie," the lady turns over her shoulder to talk to us, "and this is — Uncle Bert."

The horse clops across the marketplace and down a hill that I read is called "Fore Hill". There's a cottage at the bottom near the river, and as I go past it I turn my head, because I have a very strange feeling about it. As if somebody is inside it, someone I know. I turn back, and think for a minute about saying something to Bobby — did he see anyone at the window, did he have the same funny feeling? — but when I look at his face I see his eyes are like saucers and I know that if I say anything he'll cry. A big cloud of geese bursts from somewhere, making this horrible honking, a really frightening noise, something I've never heard before: it makes me think of children, unfriendly children, shouting and cackling at you. Bobby and I watch the geese go over us, over the high towers of the cathedral. But the man and the woman don't see them.

"Come on, you little old boy . . ." the man says, jerking at the horse's reins. The horse makes a loud, sharp snort and I jump in my seat. Then I start whistling, in case anyone thought I was scared.

After the road to the river, we turn on to a rough, bumpy lane, and it's quiet, a sort of quiet I've never heard. It makes me feel quiet too. I hold Bobby's hand and want to whisper to him, but I don't. Where are the shops and the cars and the smoke and the cinemas and the schools? It's just flat, as if we're rolling along on a big flat blanket of green. No cranes or chimneys or buildings at all, just empty. Bobby's hand is hot and sweaty, so I sing a skipping song and lean closer to him so that he can hear it: *Bluebell, cockleshell, Evie, ivy, over* . . .

Beside us the fields stretch away in black squares, with the soil all folded in lines and oily-looking where it's rained. Bobby whispers that they look like chocolate — do you think we could eat some? His voice is very small. Then he says, "Do you think this is what it's like where Vera is? Are we in heaven?"

The way he says it, heaven doesn't sound nice, it sounds empty and scary. I tell him to shush, not wanting the lady and man to hear.

The road we're on is straight and strict as a ruler. Beside us there's a high bank of green but I somehow know there's water behind it, some kind of river. My bottom keeps jolting on my seat, bouncing me up and down really hard, and bumping me into Bobby. Suddenly, from behind the bank, a big bird appears, like a monster — a bird bigger than anything we've ever seen, with hunched wings in the shape of a giant pair of eyebrows and a beak like a knife. Bobby screams and flings himself at me. The lady — Elsie — turns around and laughs. "Oh, that's just a heron. Never seen a heron before? He won't hurt you . . . After a fish, he is, not a skinny little boy . . ."

Bobby straightens up to try and look like he's not scared, and watches the bird fly off, its wings making a noise like a man flapping his arms in a wet raincoat.

Now it's quiet again, the rattle of the wheels and the heron's wings and then . . . nothing. I'm listening hard. There must be other noises in the country, other things? Where are the *people*?

The journey goes on for ever. Bert is smoking his pipe and the only good thing about it is the smell I keep getting of his tobacco, which smells like my uncle Charlie. We don't pass a single car or cart or person. The sky turns a peachy pink, but in long, flat stripes, like lines in a school exercise book. Bobby's head bounces against me with every step of the horse's hoofs.

I think of Bunny, in my bag on the floor at my feet, and a song that Nan used to sing:

> "*My bunny lies over the ocean,*
> *My bunny lies over the sea.*
> *My bunny lies over the ocean,*
> *Oh, let's have a nice cup of tea.*"

I listen and listen, trying hard to hear the country. It's not what I thought at all. I had no idea anywhere in the world could ever be this quiet. Just the rattle of the cart, the clop, clop of the horse. Just Bobby's breathing.

"Not scared of horses, are we?" Elsie asks suddenly, over her shoulder.

"No," I say. Then a little more loudly: "Me and him have got a horse at home. We've got one in our . . . stables. A white one. She's called Betty — I mean *Betsy*."

Elsie doesn't turn round to look at me. Her neck stiffens. Bobby continues to rest his head against my shoulder; I know from the way he's holding it that he's not resting at all, but listening.

"That can be your job then," Elsie says, after a snort, a glance at Bert and a long pause. "To feed the horse. His name is Highflyer. Highflyer was a famous horse, buried near the pub. Pub's named after him. And *our* horse is named after the pub."

"Or the other horse," I mutter.

Elsie's a bit stupid, surely. Feed a horse? (I know that Bobby wants to whisper to me, to laugh and giggle and tease me, but I pretend not to see; I don't want him to break the spell.) I can feed a horse named after a pub. My granddad had a horse like that. Easy-peasy. And I have a beautiful white horse. Her soft mane feels like the tassels on Nan's bedspread. I imagine her soft munching mouth on my hand as I feed her apples in the stables we own behind our house . . . Oh, and a pink silk ribbon round her neck. A little wash of sadness, as the details come to me. I *miss* her so much, I say to myself. I try her name on my tongue. *Betsy*.

I sit back in my seat, feeling for Bunny in my bag. Nan will be drawing the curtains at home, putting the kettle on. Don't they have black-out out here in this flat open moon country? How do they cover up that sky colour, now red as the inside of a mouth? Hitler would see *that* right away. See that big cathedral behind us, black against it.

I turn my head back for one last look at it. It doesn't seem to matter how far you go in the country, you can always see the cathedral. It's higher than everywhere else — it's like it's sitting on a cloud. It *does* look like the models Dad makes. Men in prison make them, boats, cathedrals, all out of matches, thousands and thousands of them, every last bit, every little window and port-hole (you have to soften and bend them for those, really carefully, so they don't snap) so that Nan always says, "Gawd, Tommy, you had *time* all right," and sighs when she sees them. Why did they send us away? Are we really so safe here? I feel like we've gone back to the olden days before houses and buildings. I feel like we've gone to the moon, and I've changed for ever. I'm different here: my name is Queenie and I'm not scared of horses or giant birds or dogs. I've got a white horse, all of my own, back home in the stables we own. A really, *really* pretty horse, and her name is Betsy.

Weeks go by and it doesn't feel so strange. There are noises at last. I hear owls hooting at night and guns going off in the morning, and the clang of a milk pail. There's thunder sometimes and the horse whinnying at night, and the rattle of the honey-spinner in the kitchen, and the *thump thump thump* of Bert chopping wood, and the dog barking, tied up outside the house, and the swish of Elsie sweeping. We get a bit used to it, I suppose. Bobby more than me. Bert teaches Bobby to shoot rabbits. At night Bobby teases me, lying on his side in the dark to sing: "Run, rabbit, run, rabbit, run, run, run . . ."

But what about Bunny? "Poor rabbits," I say to Bobby. "I ain't never going to eat them. You're just mean."

They wake Bobby up when the air's all crackly and dark to work on the Campaign. We work out what the Campaign is: they just mean help in the fields picking up the sugar-beets, walking behind the horse with this long, sharp thing, poking it at the sugar-beets, then chucking the smelly things into the back of the trailer, but I refuse to do it, scream and shout when Bert tries to wake me, flap my arms and then go all stiff so he can't get me out of bed and has to give up.

Later that morning I put my coat on over my nightie and go out into the fields — Bert calls it the Fen — to see what they're doing: Bert is sitting on another kind of cart that the horse is dragging and Bobby is lifting and picking and throwing into the trailer. Bobby's cheeks are pink, and the tips of his ears too, and his eyes shine. He wants me to laugh at the beets with him, see how rude they look, dirty and pointy, like a giant pile of big rude willies. But I turn around and stamp back indoors. I don't want to see Bert and Bobby take them to the river to heap them on the boats. I'm going back to bed.

Elsie has been calling me so I put my head under the pillow. She shouts that my breakfast has been on the table for hours and it's stone cold now and she'll throw it in the bin if I don't come soon. I'm hungry, I'm *so* hungry, but I can't seem to make myself get up. I think I fall asleep again: I'm sure Elsie must have thrown it in the bin by now. Somewhere, between falling asleep and hearing her call, I think she said she'd wallop the hide off me.

Next time I wake up, it feels like it could be dinner time. The sky is bright in the window, and I stand and stare out until a spider falls on to my shoulder and startles me. I brush it off and it plops to the floor like a tangle of brown cotton and suddenly I feel a bit more awake, so I put a jumper on, hoping that Elsie might have gone out. I tiptoe down the stairs but I can hear her pounding something in a bowl, and I want to go right back upstairs again, but she's heard me and now she's out in the hall and shouting again.

"If you're not going to help Bert come and help me in here — you can't spend all day in bed."

"I want to go to school. Ain't there no school in the country? I like school," I tell her, from halfway down the stairs. Not too close to the open kitchen door. I can hear the wireless but it doesn't sound cosy.

Elsie comes into the hall to look at me, still holding the bowl and spoon. "School? School's six miles away. No one goes to school when the Campaign's on. You're needed *here*."

She gives me a brush and a bucket, and pushes me out towards the back yard. I spy my breakfast on the table, a plate of stuck-on bacon and eggs, but she's already flicking it into the pig bucket, with nasty scraping noises. I won't show her that I mind.

One tea-time, weeks later — well, I think it's weeks, but who knows? We don't have calendars or newspapers and we've no idea, really, how long we've been here; it feels like for ever and it's getting dark at five o'clock and the blackberries we find are small and screwed up, like old men's faces — anyhow, one time, Elsie makes us a pie and it has plums in it, so sour I can hardly eat them. I take the stones out and put them on the side of the plate, counting them up. *What shall I be? Lady, baby, gipsy, queen. What shall I wear? Silk, satin, cotton, rags*.

Elsie hears me and says, "Eat up your pie."

"It's nasty," I say, without meaning to.

"Nasty?" Elsie whirls around, and snatches the plate from under my nose. "So grand, aren't we?" she says.

I'm still counting stones. *How shall I get my wedding clothes? Given, borrowed, bought, stolen?*

"We have bread and jam for breakfast," I say. It's just me and Elsie, the others aren't here, but she acts like I haven't spoken. "My dad's got this proper shop called Cooke's Eel, Pie and Mash Shop. In Dalston. My dad's the boss of it. My nan says it's the Buckingham Palace of pie shops. When you go in you can see the eels in this wooden drawer at the back, all alive and wiggling. You can catch them with a little net and eat as many as you like. Well, I can. Or we can, me and Bobby. Because our dad's the boss."

"I thought your family owned a stables. Pie and mash shop now, is it?"

Elsie stands with her back to me, so that I'm staring at the tied string of her red-checked pinny and her grey-skinned elbow. I wait for a minute, chewing my lip, and then say, "Both." When she says nothing to this, I add, "And I can go in any time I want. And I can eat how many I want, with parsley sauce," and that's it, that does it, at last.

Elsie spins around and says, in a strange voice, "You're funny."

This is the first time she's really looked at me. She crouches on the kitchen floor in front of me with her knees creaking, wiping her hands on her pinny, and looks hard into my face. I feel scared, but I don't blink or move away. I feel glad too. I wanted to know how bad Elsie could be, and now she's going to show me.

"I heard your baby sister died. I heard your mum's a drunk and can't look after you, and your dad's — well, the less said about where *he* is, the better, eh, *Queenie*?"

I kick her then. Not a hard kick. I run at her and just stab at what I can reach. I'm short, and my leg flings out, and I'm not even wearing shoes so it's just my foot bumping up against her fat woolly stockings. Still, it does the trick. She limps off out of the open kitchen door and into the yard to where Bert and Bobby are now fiddling with some farm machinery, fixing something. The black dog chained up outside barks and strains, his mouth dribbling. His eyes are red and he's a Fen Dog, Bert says. You should Watch Him.

I hear Elsie's voice, out in the yard. She's had enough of the little townie bastards. Bert will have to get himself into Ely and talk to that old mawther, the billeting lady. They've tried human charity. They've tried home cooking. Out of the goodness of their hearts, they've let those East End slum kids into their home. But, I ask you. Enough is enough.

I run inside and grab my case from under the bed. My heart is pumping. I'm sure Bobby will be cross with me because, in some funny way, he seems to like Bert. Or like doing things with Bert, who says so little and lets you be around him, as long as you're working. And Bert is in the same mood every day: calm. Pipe-smoking and slow-talking.

With a wild feeling, a funny feeling, strong and strange like the way I felt towards that house at the bottom of Fore Hill when we first arrived, like a memory when it couldn't really be a memory yet, I suddenly picture something I saw in Elsie's bathroom. She didn't let us go in there, but I'd sneaked in one day. I hated the lavatory outside with the squares of newspaper hanging on a nail and all the spiders . . . I wanted to see Elsie's proper lavatory, and her best china jug and bowl with the blue flowers on, for washing in. So I sneaked in and there, on a little dish, was a bar of pure white soap, just sitting there like a princess on a throne. When I put my face up close to it, it smelt even better than it looked. It smelt of all my favourite things: lemons and roses and cleanness and specialness, of Betsy my perfect white pony (yes, pony, surely that was the word I wanted before), of Bunny and her silky ribbon, and Nan's Parma-violet cheeks, and money.

I'm chucking my gas mask into its box, into my case, and that makes me remember Miss Clarkson saying you need soap to stop the lens misting up. And if we're going to see Nan again she'll need some soap, won't she, for her gas mask? The bar in my hand is cool, smooth. I think it must be brand new. There are no suds on it, or black veins in it, like the soap I've seen before.

That phrase. East End slum kids. Hearing it made my skin prickle. Then I felt something else. Not *shamed*, as Bobby always called it. No, not me.

She hates us. She can tell we're poor and she hates us. I don't know how she knows because I didn't tell her but somebody must have done. I picture Elsie's skin, its scaled redness. Outdoor skin, hard and nasty. Elsie doesn't need soap, does she? Nothing will make *her* beautiful. But lovely Nan, with her soft, crumpled face. Nan, at home right now, knitting and clacking her gob-stoppers. I close my eyes and I can see her so clearly, lifting up the soap and sniffing it and smiling. Yes. This lovely, perfect thing is surely hers.

So we arrive back at the billeting lady's house, and because there are so many unhappy children, and unhappy people looking after them, it seems quite a few of us are going home. She can't think what else to do with Bobby and me, she says, if a decent home like the Salmons' at Drove Farm isn't good enough for us. (We've never heard Elsie and Bert's name before. "Salmon's a fish!" Bobby says. That explains it, then. She was a cold fish, with scaly red skin, not an apple, after all.)

"Didn't you even like the horses?" the billeting lady asks, fetching her whistle and getting us to line up outside her front door. "Mr Salmon's the best horseman in the Fens. You were spoiled indeed. I was

so touched when he brought that splendid Suffolk
Punch with him to show you, that very first day — how
kind that was — and I remember neither of you batted
an eyelid."

I'm not listening to her. I'm surprised to hear from
some of the others marching down Fore Hill in a
crocodile towards the station that they've had letters,
sixpenny postal orders and even visits from *their* mums
and dads. It's cold now, and the leaves aren't
conker-coloured, they're gone altogether, just skeleton
trees. It's hard to hear what Peggy Burchwell is singing,
but I can make out the tune, and I know the words.

> *"Build a bonfire, build a bonfire,*
> *Put the teachers at the top.*
> *Put Miss Clarkson in the middle*
> *And we'll burn the blinkin' lot."*

When we get to Ely station we're allowed to mill
about a bit, like a bag of marbles that's been opened.
We can roll out and bump into each other. Archie
Markham is carrying a funny thing that's as big as him.
It looks like a vase made out of a basket, which Bobby
is jealous of because it's an eel hive and Archie can use
it back home to catch eels; the man he's been staying
with is an eel-catcher and he let Archie bait the hives
with dead cats and rats and horrible stuff like that,
which makes Bobby more and more jealous, until he
says, "If your eel-catcher likes you so much why is he
sending you back?" and then Archie bursts into tears

64

and they start a fight, which they have both missed a lot.

Archie tells Bobby he smells of beets and farts and they laugh and make up. Archie whoops then — he's spied some Beech-Nut on the floor. He shares it with us, biting the piece in three and then says that, anyway, this is only a "Phoney War", and hasn't been a war at all, no bombs falling, all our families are hunky-dory. We've only been away three months. We'll be back in time for Christmas.

That word, though. Bombs. I've managed not to think about them until now. Bobby and Archie love talking about them, running about with their arms out, like aeroplanes, making bombing noises. Is our house (Nan: I can't think of Nan) all blasted to the ground or bursting into flames? My fingers curl around the bar of soap in my pocket. I lift my hand to my nose to secretly sniff the silky smell and then hold it again, feeling its smoothness, turning it over and over. How happy Nan is going to be with me. She'll never want to leave, or go anywhere at all, after she's got the soap.

And then — horrible! — here's Elsie bustling on to the platform in her dreaded camel coat. We're on the train, we're just sitting down, the billeting lady is going to travel to London with us, and she stands up as she sees Elsie, and rushes to the window, lifting the curtain and pushing the window down: I think she's worried that it's something important, something forgotten. But I know what it is and my heart nearly stops. Elsie's found out. She's coming to get her blinkin' soap back! I clasp my hand tightly around it and begin singing, loudly as I can, so that no one will hear what Elsie is saying: *I'm going to hang out the washing on the Siegfried Line!*

The guard blows his whistle and the train slides away. When I look down the tracks are blurring into lines. Elsie is hurrying beside us on the platform, mouthing something and waving, but it's hard for her to keep up. She doesn't give up. She's breathless and redder than ever and at last I hear what she's saying, just as the train is picking up speed. "Bert! Uncle Bert sends you his love! He says goodbye." What? She ran all the way to tell us that?

Elsie's round face through the window is strange, worried. I remember that when I first met her I didn't think her expression unfriendly. She has big eyes, chocolate-drop colour, like her dog's. I see in them now something very puzzling, a thing I've not seen in anyone's eyes before. Mum has never looked at me like that, or Nan either. Although it's new to me, I suddenly know exactly what it is, and a feeling like a spanner turning over in my stomach locks it away. I think it's going to be useful to me. I'm going to store it up. Like the way I know who is hiding the ball behind their back, in the Queenie game. My way of reading people. Ah, I think. I want to smile. Elsie feels guilty. That's what *guilty* looks like. Even so. That Lux soap is in my pocket.

On the train home, I'm sick in a paper bag that the billeting lady holds out for me. She makes me stand near the open window in the corridor for the rest of the journey, eyes on me like a hawk. She thinks I'm "sickening for something", but I know better. It's just thinking that's doing it. Of Mum — where is Mum? Of the hospital, if we have to go there. Of the house with no furniture in it and no Dad there to shout, "Wotcher!" up to us and sweep me off my feet and tickle me with his scratchy beard and put his hand in his pocket and find a sixpence for me. The sick feeling from thinking about Vera again. Vera in a white bonnet, string tied under her chin, and a grey blanket, like a wet bandage, all soaking on her. Vera is a horrible, fearful thing, too ugly to look at or think about, and doing it makes my stomach turn over again, and hotness creep up from my belly and rush at me.

They must have had the funeral without us. Nan mentioned it before we left. Vera's with the angels now, learning to play a harp. There must be a miniature coffin somewhere with soap-coloured satin inside it and a boiled empty baby, like a penny guy. And Dad will never see her again, and maybe we'll never see *him* again. And if we don't watch out we'll all go exactly the same way. Boiled up in a big pot until our heads burst like steamed puddings in a cloth.

I know that's what happened, really. I don't think anyone's ever going to tell me, but I know it was Mum's fault. She didn't want any more blinkin' babies. Children made her go a bit doo-lally, Nan said. So she did something so wicked, or stupid, no one would believe it. Put Vera in a pot. Cooked her up. Or dropped a kettle of water on her. It's like when Nan used to cry, "Moll, what's got into you?" Has something got into

Mum? A devil, maybe. And now we're going to see her again, because the billeting lady says she's written to our mothers and they're going to be at the station to meet us.

I feel sick again.

But as the train chugs into that busy London station, under the high church roof with all the windows in it, like Ely Cathedral, and all the pigeons flitting about up there, and I'm grabbing my bag from the seat and pulling faces at Bobby, suddenly I see him. He's grinning through the window of the train and just holding a cigarette at his mouth in that way he has, his silver-blue eyes smiling, smiling. He has a smart black hat on and braces and a tie and a new-looking jacket, and he's chipper, that's what Nan would say — or is it dipper? Or maybe it's dapper. Anyway, he's one of those words, she really would say it, and he's dark and smart and sparkly. He's the loveliest, newest, shiniest thing I've ever seen.

"Daddy!"

He's wheeling me and wheeling me, and kissing my hair and kissing Bobby's head, as Bobby ducks away from him, and he takes a hand each and he's nearly crying as he hugs us. I can tell how much he's really missed us, the way he keeps his mouth buried in my hair for a long time, until the billeting lady comes up and says, all rude and stiff, that she has instructions to hand the children over to a Mrs Ida Dove and Dad says that's our nan and signs something, and he gives the billeting lady a wink, which sends her away all fluttery, like the pigeons. And clippy-cloppy on her shoes. When her back is turned, Dad makes this little movement, rubbing his hands behind her, as if her backside's hot. We're so happy that we're squealing, me and Bobby — we sound like the pigs when Bobby pulled their tails.

Dad says he knows a shop where you can get five doughnuts for fivepence, and let's go and buy them — and eat the lot! Or Sally Lunns, he says. You choose, kiddo.

"Can we go down Romford Market and see the eels in their buckets, getting the heads cut off of them?" Bobby asks. He's been obsessed with eels since Archie Markham got that eel hive.

Dad just laughs. "We'd better go see your nan. Tell her I've been and got you." He puts his face close to Bobby. "Tell her the old scallywag's out and about again!"

We both know better than to ask. Out from where? For how long? Any case, we're thinking about doughnuts and eels and Sally Lunns. I'm thinking of the soap in my pocket and Nan's face when she sees it. And Dad, with his sweet-smelling hair, glossy with the cream he slaps on it, the prickly feel of his face with all his stubble, like kissing a hedgehog. And a new toy — he says he's got something spanking new that we'll love. He promises to show us when we get home.

Where's Mum? I want to ask. Is Mum out, too? Which house are we going to? Is the house all bombed away or do we have another one? Why were you away so long? I fight these questions. Squish them down.

Dad loves me for my best skill: keeping mum, he says. Keeping my lips sealed. I can do that. He's so tall and so swingy, he can "show out" as he walks along, with all the ladies looking at him, and he has something new: a limp. As he limps by, the ladies cock their heads at him like little birds, their hands on their hips and smiling, so, so sweetly and kindly He's like something royal, like a prince or a soldier as he limps quickly through the station, touching his hat here and there to people. The dog's bollocks, Mum would say. Or a dream.

Keeping Mum

Christmas comes and goes with not much kerfuffle, just an orange for Bobby, which he can't open and tries throwing down the stairs, and a golliwog for me, and a Mr Jollyboy for Bobby that Dad found in a house after it had been abandoned. The Mr Jollyboy is the best thing in the world. That's the spanking new thing Dad was talking about. It's all wooden with a black cap of hair (just like Dad's) and a painted red shirt and black boots and jointed shoulders, knees and arms, and if you wiggle the stick in his back and put him on a flat surface, he can really dance. Dad does this for us and makes Bobby nearly wet himself laughing.

The Mr Jollyboy comes in a box with a picture of four laughing children on it, and a kind man with grey hair. The box says: *The most amusing toy of all times. Keeps everyone in fits of laughter.* I try not to feel cross that Bobby got the most amusing toy of all times when I'm Dad's favourite and I got a golliwog.

We're back now in the house on Lauriston Road, and we visit Mum in the London Hospital, and Dad says she's not all her ticket, which means she's not right in the head. She's waiting there for something. Some decision to be made — a court case, or something. I don't understand but I know she won't be there for long, that's what Dad says, and so of course I imagine that she might come home soon. Whenever I think of this my stomach turns over. I should be glad, I should want her to, but I feel sick and I'm ashamed of it. I keep picturing her in her hospital bed. She's in a pale blue nightie with forget-me-nots on it, all tied up at the neck, and she seems thin, suddenly, and old, and made of paper. She doesn't look at me when I step forward to kiss her — with Dad's hand pushing me in the back — and a thin worm of dribble glitters at the corner of her mouth. The hospital smells and the nurses aren't nice to us, and won't let us look at the little watches pinned to their pockets (although one of them gives Dad a cigarette and they all admire his limp) so we only go the once. Matron says Mum is just a dipso, which means nothing to me. I think I didn't hear her properly.

That nightie. *Forget me not.* I want to, though.

The months go by with me trying not to think about Mum, think about anything at all, but I listen to the grown-ups, and everyone is worried, all the time. Now it's late summer and nearly a new school term, and I'm seven and not six years old, and suddenly London is different. Yesterday, Sunday, there was a roar. Right on top of us. I looked up and saw a plane, like a silver fish, like a roaring shark, and I'm a little minnow in a pond. Three flash over. *Pop pop pop.*

Nan comes to the house and begs Dad to let us go away again because now there are air-raid sirens every single night and we have to spend so much time under the table. Weeping Willie, Nan calls the siren, and afterwards that's how I think of it: like Wee Willie Winkie, rushing through the town: are the children safe in bed?

After she's gone on about this, Dad says, Okey-dokey then, we should go back to Ely, to be billeted with the same family, and he'll talk to our teacher, Miss Clarkson, about it. I shout and put my fingers in my ears every time Dad mentions it to me, while Bobby looks at me in surprise and says, "Bang bang — all those rabbits! Didn't you like the plum pie we got?" In the end Dad says Bobby can go on his own and I can stay with him, as long as I'm a good girl and make him his breakfast every morning, and help him by filling a pram (Vera's old pram) full of coal whenever he tells me to and pushing it up to our house from wherever he finds it.

But a while goes by before it can be arranged. Nearly Christmas again and we've had a new bomb, one called Satan, which hit the Post Office Sorting in Mount Pleasant and now we won't get any Christmas cards from anyone.

When Dad takes Bobby to the station bits of London are roped off and wardens are not allowing cars to go up this road; there's a bomb in a square near the station that's unexploded. Dad just tuts and takes another direction. Bobby is excited: he's got his shilling knife in its leather case, and his rucksack with some barley sugars and his train ticket, which somehow the teacher got for him, and he asks from the back seat, "Dad, you know your bad leg — can I look at it?" and Dad nearly jerks the car off the road and looks at Bobby in the mirror, and taps his fingers on the steering-wheel and then says, "You cheeky monkey. You watch that!"

Poor Bobby looks startled. He didn't mean anything, he just wanted to look. Neither of us ever knows which things are going to make Dad cross.

Now we pass a road where a house has been burning and it's black and you can still see smoke coming off it and Bobby says, "Wow . . ." at the big pile of bricks, the scraps of cloth hanging on the bare walls at the side of the building and a man standing all bleary-eyed, just standing and staring at us, holding his cap and flapping at himself as we drive past. We pass piles of blue-green glass, watch men shaking frames from windows, sweeping the glass into little heaps. We fall quiet as we pass the open doors of a church, glimpse piles of sleeping bags, people with bundles of clothes, but Dad is staring straight ahead, whistling under his breath.

It's the first time Bobby and me are going to be separated. I'm sad, and I keep thinking that Nan said we should never be, that it's my job to take care of Bobby, but Bobby doesn't seem to be bothered — he's too little to care, I suppose, and the only bit he minds about is not ever meeting the Luftwaffe and managing to gather up any good shrapnel or, better still, any

73

bayonets. He can't wait to lie on his stomach on a boat, on the river Lark, holding a punt gun and waiting for the ducks to appear so he can shoot one. He says he'll make sure and bring us a chicken when he comes to visit and all the eggs we want. (I try to remind him of how mean Elsie was with our dinner, but Bobby has a short memory. When I carry on he says it's because I didn't help out enough with the beets and the Campaign; Bobby on the other hand is Not Afraid of Hard Work.)

"Save me some shrapnel, a whopping piece, if you find any!" Bobby says.

Best of all would be if I could find a gun, then I could hold off the whole of the Waffen-SS in the back garden.

His little face at the window of the train is more monkey-like than ever, with his hair recently shaved because of lice and his ears waggling as he mouths goodbye and waves to us.

Dad's new motor is not so nice as the old one, but it is a nice plummy red colour, and he has a lady friend called Annie, who's as skinny as a whippet. He leaves me with her during the days or nights when he's out and he says she's just a "brass" and will move out when Mum comes back.

Christmas goes by and Bobby doesn't come home, and I miss him. I try to care about the things Nan talks about — that posh people are coming from the West End after a night at a dinner to gawp at the poor bombed families, can you credit that? — but really I'm just wondering who is this Annie and what's a brass?

74

Also, what are these Motor Fuel Ration Books that Uncle Charlie gives to Dad? And does Dad post the letters I write to Bobby, in envelopes saying Salmon Farm near Ely, with all my sorriness for not finding any shrapnel? If Dad does, then why doesn't Bobby write back?

I try asking Annie about Bobby, as she's sitting on the sofa, buffing her nails with this little thing she holds in her hand, rubbing back and forth with the suede part and then showing me how pink and soft and polished her nails look. Annie just laughs and says, "Little boys never write letters!" and shows me her powder in a silver compact with a brush so fluffy it's like a rabbit's tail and her best gloves made out of cream leather, with tiny little holes in them in the pattern of a four-leaf clover. They're her lucky gloves, she says, putting them on a shelf above the mantelpiece. I'm not to play with them, mind.

She chats a lot, all the time, and she has hair like a bird's nest, and you feel as if even when she's not talking she'd like to be, which is tiring. No one mentions Vera, or Mum, or whether I'll have to go back to the country too if the air-raid siren keeps going off and the bombs don't stop.

Then one night, some time in the spring, Nan comes to stay with us because there's been a big fire at the docks, and everything, she says, is ablaze from end to end — warehouses, sugar, wood, food, spices. She says there's black smoke from one end of Poplar to the other, and you can't breathe for the choking feeling, and can't stir for an AFS man with a black face sleeping on his trailer, too tired to clean up before going back to the fire. She doesn't say anything about her own home but she sits in a corner crying into her sleeve. I make her a cup of tea but Dad doesn't say a word.

Dad lets her stay with us, and makes a bed up for her in what used to be Bobby and the baby's room, because she is his "muvver", after all, but you can tell he can't wait for her to go back home, because Annie and her friends — the Green Bottles — can't come over when Nan's there, and Nan listens to *Sincerely Yours* on the wireless and it makes her cry and Dad thinks Vera Lynn's rubbish. He calls it *Insincerely Yours*.

Uncle Charlie turns up one day with a new girlfriend called Shirley Edwards, and Dad says there'd be more room if Nan stopped round Shirley's just off the Vallance Road for a while, and after he's said this, I remember my question and ask Nan, "What's a brass?" and Nan turns around sharply to say, "Is that what he says about Annie, then?" and that's the end of it. She won't say another word, so I know a brass is something bad.

Not long after, we hear that a friend of Annie's has lost both her legs in a bombing, and a block of flats in Stoke Newington is burning and burning, and the shops near St Thomas's Square on Mare Street and a billiard hall have all been mashed to fire-sticks. The spire at St John of Jerusalem is all crumbled like a brandy snap.

We hear planes and they seem to me like wild duck fights in the air. They don't frighten me any more.

Instead they make me miss Bobby. If he were here he'd love to watch them, the silver shapes with the trails behind them. He'd love to watch until the little specks of shrapnel ping off the rooftops, or to cheer when one of them goes into a dive with a swishing noise and smoke pouring from it. Bobby would be able to tell me if I shouldn't cheer but groan: he can tell which planes are ours. I know he wants the shrapnel so he can swap pieces with his mates, but somehow I don't like rooting around in bomb sites — I think I'm the only child in our street who feels this way. I like new things and clean things, not dirty ones.

Nan goes to stop with Uncle Charlie and I know she's sad, and she'll never live in Canada Buildings again, but it's hard for me to be sad about that. I hear Dad saying she'll get a prefab now. All old people or people like Nan from Poplar are going to live in prefabs, they say, and I don't know why Nan isn't more pleased, because they will at least be new and have their own lavatories.

There is something new too about our house at Lauriston Road and that's the thing Dad doesn't want Nan to see. Dad has opened up the cellar and started doing his photography in there. It's supposed to be our shelter but we've been told we're not to go down there, and there's a key that only Annie has, and she keeps it up her stocking where she says Dad's not to be a naughty boy but has to "beg for it". Annie is usually one skinny coil of wide-awake energy, with these big dark eyes looking out from under her stack of hair, and wanting to say something to you, wanting to talk. One morning, though, I come downstairs in my pyjamas to find her flat out on our sofa, sleeping because she was out late in Bethnal Green and got caught in an air-raid and had to spend it down the tube, where she couldn't sleep at all. We'd been at home under the tables.

I spy the key next to her garters on the table beside the bed. I know it will only take me five minutes to see what Dad has down in the cellar and to put the key back so that no one will know.

The cellar door is hidden behind a wooden dresser. It doesn't move until I shove it quite hard, and then it budges a little bit, enough for me, being skinny, to slip behind the crack. I tiptoe, carefully as I can, and when the cellar door creaks as I open it, I'm scared for a second, thinking Annie'll hear me. There's no sound of her, though, so I step down the stairs carrying Dad's torch and bouncing a little circle of light everywhere as I go. It's freezing under my feet, and dusty, with a smoky black smell. I can't understand why we haven't got an Anderson shelter like other families and just have to go under the kitchen table and not down the cellar, but Dad says no one's to know the cellar's here, and he'll take his belt to me if I tell a soul.

Keep mum, she's not so dumb. It's a sign I read somewhere with a pretty lady on it, like one of Annie's Green Bottle friends.

It's not that exciting, though, down there. It's not what I thought. It's very small, not really a cellar at all, just a sort of space as big as a cupboard that you can stand up in. It smells nasty with lots of cigarette butts on the floor. I'm sure I can hear skittering, like mice.

All I can see in the trickle of light from the torch is a John Bull printing set, and a pile of photographs — they all seem to be of men, and one of them is Buster and another is Dad's brother, our uncle Charlie. Buster smokes these really posh cigarettes, Du Maurier, and that's what the smell is. Everywhere there are these cards. Grade Four cards. These stamps and black ink, which must be what Dad is hiding, probably just because Bobby and me would *love* to play with them. Bobby loves cards of all kinds. I have a little go with the stamp, putting the torch down to do it, pressing it on a scrap of paper in front of me, then picking up the torch again to shine the light over the words: *Wounded in action.*

Boring. What a boring thing to find, after all! I creep back towards the house and, using all my weight, shove the dresser back, properly, making a plate on it wobble. It's so disappointing, I don't even think I'll write and tell Bobby about it. He prefers cards with kings and queens of England on them, like the ones you get with Mazawattee Tea, and he always asks Nan to buy it, even though she says that's not her favourite kind, it's got a "musty" flavour. It's so that he can try and get the one with Queen Victoria on it. Victoria the Great, he calls her, like the film. (He's seen it loads of times. Dad says Bobby has "been and got himself a thing for Anna Neagle".)

Dad finds lots of things in bomb sites, and one day it was a baby grand piano, and he and the Du Maurier cigarettes man, Buster, pushed it into our living room and Dad played it. He'd had another row with Nan by

then, and asked her to leave. Still the planes twang the
sky and I try not to think of what Nan said, of burning
and smoking and what it must be like, crunching and
scrambling, the drumming sound, the smokiness,
gulping for air.

Dad is happy, though. Dad doesn't worry about
London burning. He doesn't worry about the
Frampton Park Road junction with Darnley Road
being all flat and dust and sticks with just a sort of cliff
of wall where houses used to be, most of it eaten out,
all crushed, red bricks dissolving into white powder. He
has parties with ladies over, Green Bottle friends of
Annie's. Another year goes by and London seems
quieter and it's not about fires but about waiting, and
parties, and *finally* having my ninth birthday and
getting a tiny red bottle of perfume with a silver top
shaped like a witch's hat, which I hide under my pillow.
It's from one of Annie's friends — a lady called Gloria.

Gloria is one of the Ten Green Bottles. The others
are Annie and Dolly and Beattie and Lily and Ettie and
Pearl and Josie and two more I don't know. They smell
of blue-bells and lilac — a sort of squeaky flowery smell
— and Gloria has a huge chest, like a shelf, you could
rest a cup of tea on. When she gives me the perfume I
pull the stopper out and it has a little black plug that
smells so strong that I think I might faint every time I
sniff it. Gloria has soft white fur on the collar of her
navy blue jacket and a hat like the lady in the Craven A
adverts.

Gloria says she'll take me out shopping with her one
day but I tell her that Nan says she'll tan the hide off

me if she catches me with one of the Green Bottles. This makes the ladies laugh and they all smoke their cigarettes and ruffle Dad's hair and ask him to play them something on the baby grand. He sings, "*Run, rabbit, run, rabbit, run, run, run,*" but that makes me cry thinking of Bunny, and Bobby shooting all those rabbits, so he plays some other ones, lovey-dovey ones, and Annie sits on his knee.

After she moved to Uncle Charlie's off Vallance Road, Dad sends Nan away whenever she comes to our house. I hear them one time shouting at each other in the hallway again, and then I don't see her for months on end. She even missed my ninth birthday and I'm glad about the Green Bottles who baked me a cake and gave me their sweet coupons, because otherwise, without Bobby, there wouldn't have been anyone. I keep going back to Lauriston School but there are signs up saying "Closed" because so many of the children are still evacuated that there are rows of empty seats and no teachers to teach them. I wander back home again. It's boring and lonely and no one seems to mind if I stay at home, so gradually I stop bothering to go in the mornings and instead go out with the pram to look for coal, like Dad told me.

Annie tells this story about a friend of hers who lived in a block of flats in Clapton where a bomb fell and a whole building got demolished. Annie's friend was lying in her bed, which fell through the ceiling to the flat below, and she ended up in a crater, in her pyjamas and not even injured!

They like these stories. Funny ones are best. Beattie says, "Get this. One night, Roger [Sly Roger] hangs his trousers on the bedpost, like he always does, and there's a blast in the house opposite, and his trousers get blown off of the bedpost and out the broken window, and he runs downstairs in his underpants to catch them!"

They giggle and smoke their cigarettes and tell some more stories about how funny it is to be bombed. Only Annie tells a bad story, about a friend of hers who put an asbestos blanket over her baby's cot to protect her, and the next day there was a bad raid and in the morning there was this huge piece of glass sticking into the blanket. "If that there blanket weren't there, it wouldn't half of done some damage," Annie says, and they go a bit quiet, and suddenly I think of Vera and want to cry. To cheer us all up they start chatting again, because after all it's quiet at the moment, no bombs for a while. They spring open their silver cigarette cases and snap off their mother-of-pearl earrings and let me try them; and Beattie shows me her eyeliner pencil, and how she draws a line on the back of her legs to make it look like she's wearing stockings, and lets me have a go.

One day, Nan comes to the door and starts knocking. It's a year later, early spring by then, the tree near the church dangles tiny catkins, like baby's fingers. It's closer to my tenth birthday than my ninth, and the war seems to have been going on my whole life. Nan keeps knocking, so loudly, banging the letter flap up and down and calling, that we all hear her and I have to let her in. She looks thin. She must have been ill, I realise, from looking at her, ill or sad or something. Why did no one tell me?

"But I'm better now, poppet," she says, as if she can read my mind, when I bury my head in her dress and cuddle her.

Nan takes one look at the goings-on in our front room and puffs up her chest and says we're in more danger here than from bombs and I'm to come with her, right away, back to Uncle Charlie's off Vallance Road. Dad says, "To that old slum, Ma? You think that's better for her than this?" and then she and my dad start arguing again, out in the hall, with Dad slamming the door and all the ladies trying to listen in, and we catch bits like ". . . your fault she's bin there that long," from Nan, and "I just about had it up to here . . . my grand-children . . . and a bleedin' load of whores . . ."

I don't want to go to the stinky house of Auntie Shirley and Uncle Charlie in Bethnal Green and I'm ashamed because, though I love Nan and I've missed her, I also love the things the Green Bottles give me. The tiny red bottle of perfume — will Nan make me give it back? They'd even given Bobby — home last Christmas on a visit to bring us eggs and chickens like he promised — a new bag of jacks, some Meccano and a whole box of Lotts Bricks. Won't he feel the same?

But when I hear the door close and see, out of the window, Nan looking up to our bedrooms, her collar up, I can't help it: I run outside after her, and fling my arms around her. She seems to have grown so much smaller, in these years.

"Fetch your coat, gel, and come with me down Vallance Road," Nan tells me, and I run inside to get it. Dad is back on the piano plink-plinking away and no one sees me leave.

"It's OK to be tight on the seafront in Brighton, but I say by Jove, watch out if it's Hove . . ."

"You done the right thing . . . Made a choice. Good gel," Nan says, taking my hand as we walk down Well Street, right to the bottom, past the barber that Dad goes to, pumping steam from the hot towel steriliser in the corner, then cross over and go on towards the Cambridge Heath Road. Nan plans to walk the whole way, I know. Long distances are nothing to Nan, and she's no money for the bus.

But we never get there. The evening's drawing in: it's black-dark very quickly with the windows boarded up and no streetlights on and the cars with black paint over their head-lights. Nan gets her white hankie out and ties it around my button so that it will flicker in the dark and show people where I am. We start to feel a bit stumbly, and I know that, really, Nan wants me for company, though she'll never admit it. I hold her hand and try to guide her safely to the kerb, but she's very slow. She has these strange puffed-up ankles as if she's got mushrooms stuffed under her stockings, and the darkness starts to move towards us, like a big black animal, licking up to our ears. We put our hands out, touch things and bump things: a person, a wall, just thin air. Now *our* ears are perked up, like dogs'. We can

84

hear other people's crêpe-soled shoes, all spongy on the wet pavements. Nan's scared she'll be knocked down, or attacked, in the dark — and she'd never let on to my dad, because he's a "useless great lump" and she's had to do "every bleedin' thing meself since my Alf went".

Cambridge Heath Road is full of puddles, and as we can't see them, we keep accidentally splashing one another's ankles. Nan's wool stockings are soon soaked. My legs are bare and the splashes are icy and startle me. But it makes Nan laugh. "My great-aunt Fanny!" she says, every time I do it, which makes us giggle.

"Pip pip!" Nan says sharply, when a shape is about to bump into us, and we hear someone say, "Sorry," and melt into the darkness. All you can see is black and grey patches where someone is wearing something light: a shirt collar or a handkerchief, like me.

Nan says just to stick to going straight, so we won't get lost. We've been walking for a while like this and we know we've passed York Hall to our left, because we smelt the steam from the baths there, and we know where we are now because of the smell of lavender in the museum gardens. Suddenly Weeping Willie starts up his lonely howl, making our insides turn over in fear. I hear the lavatory flush in the house we're passing, then another and another. People always do that before they go to their shelters. Two buses are pulling up and they stop at once; people pour out, heading towards the tube station.

"Dad says don't bother," I tell Nan. I know if he's caught in Bethnal Green he'd rather shelter under the Salmon and Ball railway arches, or round Vallance

Road, under the soot-stained viaducts, in a warren of small houses called Deserters' Corner and "do a little business" while everyone else is in the tube station, which smells so bad because everyone is frightened and there are no lavatories.

"It's mostly over now — there ain't no real danger," I say.

"My arse!" Nan says, reaching for my hand, crossing the road and pushing me towards the entrance to the tube. "I'm telling you, we hit Berlin two nights ago — they'll be wanting to get their own back!" She says this breathlessly, making me join up with the other people hurrying towards the entrance. Nan's face is shiny with sweat and then there's this strange sound, one we haven't heard before, really loud explosions, and Nan grabs me and screams and breaks into a kind of lumpy run, like a cow.

I don't understand what started her off, but other people are running, too, and there's panic. We're all hemmed into the steps, a feeling of being pushed, of slippery wet steps beneath you. It's so inky dark — we can't see them but we know the steps are like blocks of black ice, with just this one tiny bulb down the bottom, a finger of light pointing in a wobbly way towards us, and people tumbling over one another to get down there, jostling me and hurting my shoulders and stepping on my toes, and a lady crying, her hand on her huge stomach, all squeezed into a giant plum by her purple wool coat, shouting wildly to anyone who came near her, "Mind me baby! Mind out!"

And then a horrible sound, a frightening roar, and about sixty blasts, one after another, go off, somewhere down Vicky Park way, and people start screaming and pushing behind us. We're deep inside the steps — we must be quite near the bottom now — and Nan is still clutching my hand beside me but the person behind her is pushing her forward and she is being wrenched away from me, nearly twisting my fingers and I open them, and as the screams go up, I feel her hand snatch free — Nan! Nan! Her fingers clutch for mine but they're yanked away from me and suddenly we're all falling, a pack of cards, one on top of another — it's concrete and bones and soft chins all mashing up together, my nose slamming into something hard. I put my hand up and it feels wet — but I can't think: there's just an almighty feeling of being crushed, squashed, all the breath pumped out of me, and my knees buckling beneath me, and the pain of people toppling on to me and smashing me against the steps, and I can't see a thing but I know I'm going to die, and then someone is pulling my hair and I feel as if the top of my head is being opened up, like a boiled egg. I'm being lugged by the hair and told to *hold on, hold on*, and I'm pulled free somehow of the people on top of me, and a lady's voice says, "Gotcha!" and I shriek with the pain of having my hair yanked so hard. The lady isn't Nan. I can't see Nan anywhere in that mass of smelly wool and mothballs and rain and galoshes and wet black sticky stuff that might be blood or sick or I don't know what.

"They're kicking me!" another woman cries. I can't see her in the treacly dark. I don't think anyone else can hear her.

I'm so shocked I'm not even crying any more. I stop the hollering sound I made a second ago, and the same lady puts her hands under my armpits and drags me somewhere, and I have a feeling that maybe she's a police-lady or an air-raid warden or something, so I do as I'm told, but my heart feels sick because I know that what we're climbing over is bodies, is people — I can feel their elbows and their squashy soft bits and sometimes they breathe on me and I smell them and it's like the smell in the pig pen at Salmon Farm only worse because it's people. I hear them mutter things but it's all happening so quickly that I have to just do what the lady says, and get to the shadowy place where she tells me to wait, next to other people. We're all squished in a flat dark space, and I'm trembling so much that I feel as if the place itself is shaking. This must be what hell is like. A hell full of animals, sheep in a pen, stinking animal smells, and sounds of crying and wailing, and I don't even know if any of that sound is coming from me, but the lady says, "Be quiet, be quiet, wait here," and so I do, but I'm thinking, Nan! Nan! Where's Nan? And I look around and try to see her among the shapes, and I strain to hear her voice.

Somebody lights a match and, in the flare, I see the faces of grown-ups, mostly women: grey, big-eyed ghosts. There is a strange, moon-faced girl beside me, and for a moment I think she's Vera. But that's silly. She's much older than Vera — she's nine or ten, about the same age as me. She has a beret on, and she has shocked eyes, as mine must be, and a sparkly clip fixed on her beret.

Where is Nan? My scalp is stinging; I notice how much it hurts but I don't really care. My arms and legs feel black and blue with bruises; something black drip-drips on to the front of my coat. I think my nose must be bleeding.

"Stay there on the platform and say nothing!" the ARP lady hisses, as I try to get up and look for Nan. I sit down again. I close my eyes, and a little part of me thinks that if I just stayed here, closed my eyes and stopped thinking, no one would notice. They might leave me, everything would disappear. I could stay with Nan, wherever she is; give up.

I don't know if my nose really *is* bleeding. I might just be crying. I can taste salty blood and snot. A man lying beside me on the platform is making a horrible moaning sound. I feel the girl in the beret edge closer and perhaps she takes my hand, I'm not sure. I think I can see the clip on her hat twinkling; it looks a bit like a rabbit with two big ears. I blink and then wonder if that's really true; perhaps the shape was just a spark, something else. The girl has Shirley Temple curls sticking out of the bottom of her beret — they look grey in this light, but they must be blonde; her coat smells of wet wool. I can feel that she's there, without really seeing her, and this makes me feel better, like I should stay here, stay awake. I close my eyes for one tiny second, and a strange thing happens. I think it's not a girl at all but Nan who is sitting beside me, and I'm too tired to open my eyes and check. I'm sort of drifting somewhere, somewhere stinging and painful, but I feel Nan's fingers touch my cheek, and I'm glad, glad, glad, that she's still here after all, she's here with me, right beside me, and I'm not going to die, it's all going to be all right. Someone is singing a song I know well:

> "*Every Saturday morning, where do we all go?*
> *Stealing into mischief, oh dear, no!*
> *We go to the pictures where we sing this song.*
> *Every Saturday morning at the O-dee-on!*"

I look around, but the song is very quiet, it almost might be happening in my head. The whole place is quiet. I know the words, the tune, so well . . .

"Where's my nan?" I ask. "I never saw where she went."

Nobody answers me. I'm not even sure I said it or just thought it. The trembling carries on: we all seem to be trembling. It runs through my body and I feel as though the ground I'm sitting on is shaking. My knees are drawn up to my chin and knock against my chattering teeth. "*Tears won't wash with me, my gel.*" Was she here? Was she really right beside me? Pull yourself together, Queenie, and look for Nan.

Right: what colour coat did she have on? Her good navy one, buttoned up. But it's so dark, and difficult to move in here. Did I hear Nan scream, when we first toppled towards the steps? I picture her as she was leaving our house in Lauriston Road, craning up to look at the window for me, to see if I'd follow her, and her smile when I ran outside to join her. Then the moment where her hand was snatched apart from mine ... the tearing feeling, Nan clutching at me, trying to get some hold on my fingers.

I stretch them out now, and the girl I thought was beside me with the diamanté clip on her beret is gone. My hand touches wet concrete. Nan loves me: she must be here somewhere — she feels so close. I've never felt her closer, or stronger. I feel for Nan again. She *must* be here. Is that her, that dark coat? Did I see her just then, turning away from me?

Then in panic I wrench at the hankie tied to my coat and put it over my mouth as I realise, just too late, that I'm going to be sick, and a big sour wave of warm liquid spills over my hands, soaking the hankie and sploshing my coat.

Oh, Nan, don't turn away. Don't leave me, please. I forgot to tell you that I really love you too, with your silly sayings and your clacking teeth and your lumpy ankles. Nan, where are you? Nan! Come back.

My nan — Mrs Ida Dove — is among the 173 people, some say 178, who were crushed to death down that tube station that night.

After the all-clear, people help us out. I keep my eyes fixed on that girl, who I can't really see but only *feel* is leading me out of the darkness, the glitter on her clip the only flickering thing to follow. Somehow I'm taken home to Dad, I think by an ARP officer; there are quite a few children in the car, but I don't remember saying where I live, I just remember asking, "Where's my nan?"

I remember Dad's face at the door and his look; one I've never seen before. For a moment I think the wildest thing: that someone is sticking a knife in him from behind; he's about to topple forward on the doorstep. But he doesn't. The ARP ladies are shown in. Annie trots downstairs, looking sleepy, tying a silky violet dressing-gown around her. I hear mutterings in the hall and the phrase "two hundred dead" and that "the bodies are laid out in the church on Bethnal Green Road", can Mr Dove come and identify her . . .

The body. Bits of talking as Annie wraps me in a big blanket and goes to put the kettle on to make me an Oxo. Angry words between Dad and the ladies with their whistles and hats. The lady who brought me home saying something like "Of course it matters! For morale, for keeping up morale!" and then, even more tartly, "I won't ask why *you're* not in uniform, Mr Dove." Annie is crying.

"They're telling us we can't never talk about it," Annie says to me, as the front door slams, and Dad leaves. "So the Luftwaffe never find out. Or something." She's crying harder now, not seeming to notice her dressing-gown slipping open and her flat little bosoms peeking out.

"He loved his mother, you know." Annie sniffs. She strokes my hair, feeling in the pocket of her dressing-gown for her Player's. I remember the girl with the sparkly clip, and wonder if I'll ever see her again and whether she might give it to me.

I try not to think of Nan, of the hundreds of piled-up bodies, now dawn is breaking, all covered with trample marks, lying in the church. It's a horrible church, St John at Bethnal Green — ugly and plain, like a big box that no one cares about, with a nasty blue chipped door and a silly weathercock that always makes me think of a dart. I picture Nan as a bundle of knitted things, her legs sticking out, like the twig legs of a fat robin. Suddenly that horrible enormous heap of beets that Bobby had been loading, the colour of bones, of skeletons, comes into my head and sticks. I won't ever talk about it, so they needn't worry. *Tittle-tattle lost the battle.* But I'm still shaking, and I can't swallow. The smell of sick wafts all around me. My drink of Oxo stays in my mouth and then just dribbles out again, brown stains trickling down my dress. Hot tears mix with the salty taste.

I picture Nan, sitting next to the wireless, listening to her favourite programme, singing along. "We'll meet again . . ." Such a stupid song, because everybody knows that even the people singing it don't really believe it: they just *want* it so much to be true.

Then an important thought pops up: Thank God I nicked that Lux soap for Nan. The beauty soap of the film stars. All Nan's favourites used it: Vera Lynn, Deanna Durbin. All those posters about being careful with soap, using up every last measly ounce! Nan said Dad had fallen for the "squander bug", but I knew that the Lux had pleased her. She'd put it out in a little dish on her kitchen windowsill and she must have used it now and then, because it had a pattern on it of popped bubbles, which looked like lace.

I feel so strange then, thinking that. A terrible stretching feeling, as if my heart is yawning. But I'm certain, too. Nicking that soap is the finest thing I've ever done, and thank God I did, because Nan's life was hard, you can see that, and that soap was the only bit of *luxury* she'd ever known.

Bobby comes back for Nan's funeral. He's had scabies and he looks a fright, his skin all purple with the ointment they paste on you for it. He's grown bigger and talks all the time about punt guns and air rifles; he's got good at shooting.

The funeral is bewildering; there are so many coffins in the little church and so many different families hemmed in together, lots of people injured, with bandages on their heads and arms in slings, everyone whispering about what happened. It's nothing like the fancy funerals we sometimes see, with horses and black plumes. No one showing off, or properly allowed to say anything. "His face was that bruised, I couldn't identify him . . ."

They've done something fishy to the tube steps now, everyone says. Put rope ladders for hand-rails and painted the bottom of the steps white, to try and look as if they cared. As if they were helping people find their way in the dark, when everyone knew they weren't. Helping, that is. All concrete and bones and soft chins squishing up together. I keep expecting to see

Mum or Nan. I crane my neck for them and then remind myself: Nan's gone. Mum's . . .

Dad's wearing his best suit, pinstriped, with really wide trousers and a beautiful grey felt hat with a black ribbon on it. I stare at his face beside me in the line, but it's hard to read what Annie says he feels: any love for his old muvver. Instead he's darting glances left and right, shuffling his feet and smiling at people he recognises — is that the Southpaw Cannonball, old John Lee, the Jewish fighter, from the Salmon and Ball?

Bobby says something was going on in Victoria Park; the north-east corner had been fenced off that night. It was a "hot new gun site". They didn't look like guns to me when we passed by the park. Bobby whispers that they were anti-aircraft rockets manned by the Home Guard. On the evening *it happened* (that's how everyone talks about it, we all know what we mean), the rockets must have been fired over the heads of the people making their way to the station. The noise was frightening. It made people bolt, like horses.

Whenever anyone mentions it, I tremble again and a wave surges up. I'm not sure what it is, but it makes me rush to the lavatory because I keep feeling like I need to go. Every night since it happened I've woken and found myself standing in the middle of my room, opening a drawer, looking for something.

The ARP lady is at the funeral, smiling at me, but I never smile back. She has a dog with her, and I know the dog's name is RIP; it's a special dog for finding bodies, and it makes me feel sick. I don't want to pet it. My scalp still hurts from the place where my hair was pulled. Annie murmurs now that "Not a single bleedin' paper's mentioned it." She's looked and looked. "How can they ask us to never say nothing? People are in shock," she whispers, putting her face close to Dad's in the row. "Like it never happened."

"Two hundred East Enders don't mean nothing to them," Dad replies. He's not smiling.

After the service in church about Ida Dove, God Rest Her Soul, and all the other names, and the smell of the lilies, and the sound of quiet crying, like rain pattering on the roof, I feel as if I can't breathe, and I'm glad when we're back at ours. Bobby sits in a corner, flicking through his *Knockout* and trying to get somebody to give him a cigarette. But without Nan there to make it, there isn't even a funeral tea, just Dad on the piano and some of the Green Bottles singing. Annie lets me have a sip of her Mackeson's milk stout. It has a black taste, plain and warm like bath water, and my stomach rumbles.

Gloria, the one with the black hair in gleaming curls all around her head, the one who gave me the perfume and looks just like a doll with red lips and rosy cheeks, is wearing a dress in lovely peachy satin stuff, with black velvet trim around the pockets and collar, and buttons at the front that look like they'll pop when she waves her arms about, which she does a lot. She's laughing about something they call "the bomb lark". I'm outraged — is that what they call what happened to Nan?

Bobby nudges me in the ribs, telling me not to be silly. This is what they *do*, he says. Dad, he means, and

Charlie and Buster and the others. They make claims to the Assistance Board under different names, stating they lived in places they haven't lived in so that they can get they money for the bombed-out houses and the things that were in them.

"Do they?" I feel blinkin' silly. It's usually me who knows things, not Bobby. The Bomb Lark.

Dad is plonking away and Annie is singing that song about meeting again, don't know where, don't know when, and for once, for just a moment, for the first time, I look at Dad, and I see something in his face. Something about Nan. He must be thinking of how much she loved that wireless show, the one he teased her about, *Sincerely Yours*, he must be thinking about the words, *I know we'll meet again* . . . and he never will, will he? We'll none of us ever see her again as long as we live. But Dad puts his cigarette in his mouth and his head on one side and pounds away at the keys, and now it's a different song, the one about bluebirds, and the others are joining in, and whatever I saw in Dad's face isn't there any more, has moved away.

I'm glad to have Bobby back, but I don't think Dad is. Bobby is nine now and something about him annoys Dad — even I can see that. Bobby's cheeky, but he's small and he's not really brave like me. Dad calls him a milky — it means Bobby's like milky tea: weak. Bobby tries to cheek him, to stand up to Dad, the way I do, but then he'll lose his nerve or dart away to sit in a corner, reading about cars, about racing drivers like Woolf Barnato or Dick Seaman. Bobby wants to ask me about Nan, too, about what happened, but he daren't. I know that just from looking at him.

Bobby's happy that there's still no school and says he's never going back there if he can help it. Instead he's always begging Dad or Annie to be taken "down the dogs". He wants a job there or, better still, he wants to be a boxer, when he's older, maybe a featherweight because he's so small, but Dad puts his fists up and ducks and sweeps at him and then says, "Bleedin' hell, Bobby, you'll always be a milky — go and play with the traffic".

Bobby hangs about outside York Hall sometimes, watching the boxers, especially this one boy he loves, the Irish one with freckles and tufty blond hair and an impish face: Jimmy. He hangs around and tries to get Jimmy to sign his programme until someone shoos him away and then it's down the dogs with Uncle Charlie and watching the Kennel Boys. The dogs might work for Bobby as a job, because Bobby is "superstitious", Annie says. He has a system, involving colours, for making every simple decision, such as which sweet to choose.

Every day the Green Bottles are round our house. It turns out they knew our mum, knew her from when she first came to London from Dublin with her sister Brodie, and they tell me about her. Easily the prettiest of them all, Gloria says. "What happened to Brodie?" I ask.

They cough then. "Didn't she leave Moll behind, bugger off to America with a fella she met in the first month?" Annie says, and catches Gloria's eye and puts her hand over her mouth.

"Moll could sing beautifully," Gloria says, and "Weren't Moll the best Irish dancer?"

I whisper to Gloria that I have a horse named Betsy with a white mane and a pink ribbon and I keep her in the garage. Gloria ruffles my hair and tickles me under the ribs.

I can't get enough of hearing about Mum. Will you take me to see her? How long is she going to be in hospital for? They look at each other in a strange way when I beg that. I know they're hiding something from me, but for once I can't quite read their looks.

"Want to know why they call us the Green Bottles?" Gloria asks, trying to divert me, I know.

"No."

"Because of the bottle parties we used to have, up the West End. We wore these green dresses. Your mum was the baby. She weren't half pretty. She did it for six months. That's where she went and met your dad."

I clamp my teeth so I'm not tempted to reply. Annie looks up from patting at her chin with her powder puff and snaps the mirror shut. "We'll take you. Soon as your dad gives us the say-so, we'll take you to see her, OK? If you stop going on about her. Don't want to annoy your dad now, do we?"

Annie gives me a funny little smile when she says this, peeking at me with her big eyes from under her hair the way she always does, like she's afraid to look straight at you. I feel a stab of dislike for her. She's scared of him, I'm thinking. How pathetic. She's not like Mum . . . and I remember Mum, continuing to walk into the kitchen while he picked up his shoe, aiming the hard heel at her. Well, I'm not Annie. He doesn't scare me.

Not for the first time, I long for Nan to talk to. *She* would tell me, eventually, I think. (Somehow I've got the feeling that Mum isn't in the London Hospital any more. I don't know how I know this, or where I've got the idea from, but it feels like a certainty.) Nan wouldn't have meant to tell me, but however bad the news, I'd wiggle it out of her in the end. She couldn't resist me.

I picture Nan whenever I look at Bunny's tiny gas mask, made of black cloth and now hanging on its strap from the fender. I imagine Nan sitting up one evening to sew it. It produces a funny little pang to look at it, because two thoughts happen at the same time. How I'm not a child, and I can face facts; how silly that Nan would think I'd need such a babyish thing when I'm older than Bobby and not a baby. And at the same moment, another thought: how glad I am that Nan knew and no one else did — I am a child, quite a little girl, surely. I did need that babyish thing. Wasn't I only six or seven when she made it? I do need *something*, sometimes.

Bobby doesn't seem pleased to be back in London, even though now there are big balloons in the sky and Doodlebugs and he has taught me to listen to them, to listen to the moment when the engine stops — the important bit: that's the bit when it's going to happen, and you need to be sure that the plane has gone further than your house, that it's going to be streets away. Bobby lies under his bed shooting at planes in the sky with a pretend gun. He lines up his things in our room, on the windowsill, his cards about racing drivers, his bits of shrapnel that he's finally managed to get. There's something funny that I've never seen him do before: he has to touch everything twenty times before he can wear it. I mean his socks or his cap or his shorts: he does an odd little touching gesture, and counts — *one two three four* — as he does it.

"What do you think it's like getting squashed to death?" he asks, one night, when we're in our bedroom.

Of course I say nothing. Even so, the room swarms at me, like I'm in the middle of the worst nightmare and can't breathe. Shapes keep unfolding in front of me.

"What do you think it's like getting boiled to death in a big pot?" he asks, another night, in the same cold voice.

"Shut up! Blinkin' shut up, Bobby!"

He seems to wait until I'm just about to slide off into sleep to say these things. Of course then my eyes snap open and stay that way. It's bad enough that I wake up sleep-walking. Now he's making it hard for me to get to sleep at all. Bobby seems different, and sulky. I'm no longer sure if we're on the same side.

"I wrote you letters," I tell him one night, but he doesn't reply. Bedtime, alone in our room, is the only time this happens. Things we can't say in the day. In the darkness I can just make out his nose poking up into the stuffy bedroom air. The bed Nan used to sleep in.

101

One night, though, I hear him sniffling into his pillow, and when I whisper, "Bobby?" he sits up and thumps the pillow and wails, "Where is she, eh? What's he done to her?" And when I pretend I don't know who he means, he says he hates all of us and he wishes he could go back to the farm. That makes me cry, too, because Bobby has never been mean to me before, and I don't hate him, but I feel he's blaming me for something. I'm the eldest. I didn't save Nan, and I didn't save Vera. And I like the Green Bottles and to him that's one Great Big Betrayal.

Coming downstairs one day, swinging his monkey arms, he says rudely to Annie, "Why are *you* still here?" and he won't take it back, even when Dad comes into the hallway and unbuckles his belt.

"You bloody little bastard. You say sorry to her!" Dad shouts.

Say it, Bobby, *please*, I'm thinking. I clutch my fists inside the pocket of my pinafore dress and pray for Bobby to take it back, or Dad's mood to flit back to cheerful, lightning-fast, the way it does sometimes. Bobby starts to shake and he's looking like he wants to melt into the wallpaper but his mouth stays shut.

I try to wedge between him and Dad, but Dad shoves me to one side and says to Bobby, "You milky little —" and Bobby's big eyes are wider still. He manages to duck his head as Dad aims a blow at him, bolts upstairs and Dad thunders after him. I move to follow but Annie takes my arm and pushes me into the kitchen, where she closes the door and stands against it, biting her nails. She turns the wireless up. Still, Mrs

Mopp and Colonel Chinstrap can't cover up the noise. We hear him clearly, Dad with that frightening bark of a laugh, and then shouting. And nothing from Bobby. Just horrid thumping sounds through the floorboards that could mean anything.

"No fucking son of mine . . ." That's the only part I hear. I don't hear the end of the sentence.

Annie is humming, washing a mug in the sink, pretending. I'm digging my fists into my pockets so hard that I can feel the nails piercing my skin.

About ten minutes later Dad comes downstairs. I'm waiting for him. As the kitchen door opens I fling myself at him, fists tight, battering as hard as I can at wherever I can reach on him — his stomach mostly — with my fists. I expect him to belt me back, so I screw up my eyes and wait and wait for the roar, but instead I feel his big hands grasping at me, getting hold of my fists and holding them tight, so that I can't hit him any more.

"Little spitfire, ain't we?" Dad says mildly. And that's all.

He just sits at the table, whistling, and reaching for the Garibaldi biscuits to dunk in the tea that Annie is pushing his way, while I'm panting and staring at him, like a bull ready for its next charge. Annie is staring at him too and folding her teeth over her bottom lip as if she's trying to stop herself speaking. Dad pushes back his chair and picks up the *Racing Post*.

After a while, Dad flaps the paper down and grins at me over the top of it. He sighs loudly. "Shall I go and get that milky brother of yours a job as a kennel boy then?" he asks.

The kitchen is suddenly full of yellow light. Dad kisses the top of my head, and goes out to fetch his cigarettes from the pocket of his jacket in the hall.

Annie watches him, then puts the kettle on again, takes up her nail-buffer, and turns the wireless down low. "Still wanting to visit Moll?" she says. She's sorry for Bobby, too, I think, and guilty, like Elsie was that day, because she was a milky too: too scared to stick up for us. This introduction of Mum's name into the air feels wobbly, like the flame on a birthday candle. I daren't even answer, in case my breath blows it out.

My Education

It's a while before Annie mentions Mum again. The war is over. Mr Churchill says it on the wireless, and that day everyone goes up the West End at nine o'clock to shout and carry on, banging bin lids together. VE Day is the same day as my birthday so it feels as if everyone is celebrating with me, kissing Americans in their uniforms and climbing up lamp-posts, sending rockets streaking red into the sky. We sing "Bless 'Em All" and "Pack Up Your Troubles" and "Roll Out The Barrel", and no one mentions Nan or anything sad at all. It's the one day no sadness is allowed, Gloria says, no matter what you're feeling, because everybody in this world has lost *something*, it doesn't make you special. She holds my chin with her finger and thumb as she says this so she can look into my eyes, and she's smiling, but her look is hard to read.

Everyone wakes up the next day with bad heads and Annie says her mouth tastes like the inside of a budgie's cage; but here they are a few days later — they want to go out again, shout and joke and carry on some more.

"If you're off to see Moll, we'd better get you some decent clobber," Annie says to me. I wonder if she'd remembered it was my birthday. I'm twelve, and no one's given me a present, but now perhaps they will.

Annie takes me to a shop she knows, up the West End. Gloria comes too, and Beattie Rolls. Gloria looks the business. She has a fox fur on and diamonds on two of her fingers. And she looks fat. Fatter than usual. The fox fur round her neck has a pointy face and eyes and all, and lies there, gazing down at her bosom. I mean, I know from everyone else, from school now I'm back some of the time, or just from the wireless that, whether the war is over or not, these are hard times, that everything is in short supply — chocolate, stockings, eggs, meat, Pond's cold cream — but it makes no sense to me: they must be lying, because our house is always full of these things. Great piles of them, down in that cellar. I've never eaten so well in my life.

Beattie too, is wearing her good coat — dark brown velvet, with buttons in the shape of little brown butterflies, and court shoes in a glossy chestnut colour, a bronze-tipped toe, and a little brown bow, like a box of fancy chocolates. They have four shopping bags, exactly the same, and they give me two empty ones to carry.

"Now you just hold them bags and do everything we tell you," Annie says.

"And don't *say nothing*," Beattie says, drawing on her cigarette.

Saying nothing. My best talent.

So we go into the shop and Gloria keeps opening and closing her coat, and wrapping and rewrapping it around her, like she's hot and needs to fan herself. Beattie wanders round, picking up handkerchiefs and silk stockings, chatting to her, offering her cigarettes. And Annie picks up a chocolate brown pinafore dress, in soft wool, and holds it up against me. "Would that fit you?" she says. They're talking, talking all the time. They smell powerful flowery, a talcum-powder smell; it's choking me. My heart is pitter-pattering softly; I can see full well what they're doing.

Then we have to wait in line at the counter. The lady sitting behind it has her hair in a bun with a little net over it, and a cream lace collar on her blue dress, with the tiniest waist I've ever seen; the dress has a frill at the bottom and a sort of fake jacket attached to it. I can't help staring at it, until Annie, behind Beattie in her big saucer hat in the queue, nudges me. "Hold out the bag," Annie whispers. Then she steps forward to the counter and says, in a louder voice, a posh one I've never heard her use before, "My niece is admiring the peplum on your dress, dear."

The lady behind the counter smiles, says, "Thank you," and pats her bun. She has tiny hands too, as she reaches for the chain to pull the tin down that the money goes into. Annie hands over some notes and coupons from her book and I watch in delight as the tin is yanked up and disappears above us. Then it comes back down on its chain and some coins appear and the coupons have been stamped.

Annie has bought a pair of Dent's gauntlet kid gloves, cream-coloured, with tiny little holes in them in the pattern of a four-leaf clover, very like her other "lucky" pair.

"Oh, there's your brother!" Gloria says to me, nudging me, quite hard.

"Pop over and tell him we'll just be a minute," Annie adds.

Bobby isn't over the road, but I know better than to say anything, or even to look surprised. I understand at once what they mean. I'm holding two full shopping bags and I'm given a little push in the back by Beattie while the three women continue chatting coolly at the counter, admiring the gloves, complimenting the lady in the blue dress.

I keep walking. There is a man by the door who opens it for me. I wave my hand, as if I'm seeing Bobby over the road, but my heart is now worse than pitter-pattering; it's bounding around in my chest, like a puppy trying to leap out of its cage in the pet-shop window. Surely they'll hear it. Surely that man will notice how white I look, how tightly I'm clutching the bags, not hiding them or disguising them, brazening it out, how hard I'm concentrating on walking normally.

The man at the door coughs. He puts a hand out just as I pass by him and my blood turns to ice. I almost stop, give myself up. I wait, just for a second, and then realise he's giving me a friendly pat on the head. Like the sort a teacher gives their favourite pupil.

Outside the shop, I carry on walking. I don't turn my head or look back. I clutch the full bags and my hands are slippery with sweat. When I think I'm far enough my legs wobble beneath me — they've turned to string and will barely hold me up. I stand under a striped awning and wait. *Blinkin' hell*, I'm thinking.

And soon the Green Bottles are all around me, laughing and hugging me and smiling, and a car slides up beside us and we all pile in. Beattie lifts the bags from my hand, her hat tipping as she scrambles into the car, and all cool has gone: she's whooping. I recognise the driver — Sly Roger from the butcher's — and he winks at me, in his driver's mirror, and tips his cap to the others.

"Queenie! You're a fucking marvel!" Gloria says, stretching her arms out of her fur coat and shrugging it on to the seat behind her. "Bleedin' Nora, I'm hot!" she adds, while Annie tells me, "I never knew you had it in you — you're a natural!"

"She never batted an eyelid, did she, when you said Bobby was there? No need to spell nothing out for that one." Beattie laughs and lights up a cigarette, taking off her hat and putting it on the back window ledge of the car, patting at her neat hair with one hand. They rabbit on and on. They bubble away at me. How smart I am, how quick, how butter wouldn't melt, how pretty in the brown felt beret they've given me, hinting at the Brownies, at good girls and uniforms.

Annie hands me a bottle of ginger beer and Roger, hearing the top come off, says, "Hey, watch me bleedin' car!" but the Green Bottles all shout him down and tell him to cover his eyes, because Gloria's taking her big knickers off. The laughter that greets this remark is deafening, and it's true, too: Gloria is wiggling in her seat, and pulling down the pale blue nylon pants she's wearing, and she's immediately slimmer — her whole shape has changed. The pants are elasticated at the top and around the legs — they're home-made with terrible stitching and they look like giant baby knickers — and suddenly things are tumbling out of them: strings of pearls, stockings, lipsticks, compacts, even a tightly rolled child's dress, which I realise is the one I looked at, the chocolate brown wool pinafore dress —

"Should see your face!" Gloria says, and the others shriek some more, while Annie smothers me in a big hug. I see that Roger is looking at us all in his driver's mirror and grinning out of the side of his cigarette — he's not looking at the road at all. Gloria wants to stop at Harrods. Sly Roger practically knocks a horse down as he skids to a stop, lets us out.

A doorman opens the door to her and Gloria stalks in. A lady steps forward and puffs some perfume at her, and Gloria and I march right into the cloud of it. I'm nearly choking. "I need a lipstick," Gloria says.

There's a mood, somehow, like that perfume cloud, all around her. I can tell that Gloria isn't like the others. That she doesn't do it for the same reasons.

She stands at the counter, opening her purse. It's a gorgeous soft tan suede purse, shaped like a lovely fat

109

apple and with this satisfying clicky, swishy catch, gold metal with a cross-over snap, and I feel such a tick-tick-ticking feeling beside her as she opens it and, shoving aside her coupons, takes out a brand-new ten-shilling note. She's wearing the Dent gloves, Annie's gloves. The smell — the smell of leather and perfume and Gloria and *love* — wafts down to me, as I stand there, hopping from foot to foot, the note flying just above my head, like a flag.

"Now you look the business we can celebrate. I'll take you to see your mum, sugar, I promise," Annie says.

"But first we ought to go and see your brother. Ain't he a kennel boy these days?" Gloria adds.

My reward: the Green Bottles take me down the dogs. And after that to see Mum at long, long last.

I'd thought we'd go to "The Stow", with it's lovely white front like a big Christmas cake and the curved dog in his red jacket that I've gazed at so many times, arching over our heads like a crescent moon, but that's not the stadium Bobby works at: he's at Hackney Wick.

"There's afternoon races at Hackney Wick, and a proper crowd. War might be over but things ain't back to normal, thank God," Dad answers.

So we're now piling into the same car that slid up to me in the West End a week ago, and we're off to Waterden Road, only this time it's Dad who's driving, not Sly Roger, and "Look at you! All suited and booted," Gloria says to him admiringly, as she climbs in, but he's just staring stubbornly ahead, teeth clamped on his cigarette; he's not wise-cracking, not smiling.

It's a squash. Cigarettes and lily-of-the-valley mixed with the perfumed chocolates — rose and violet creams — being passed around from a padded lilac box. I crack one against my tongue and the sweet violet perfume floods out. The taste is a sad memory, strange. Like eating Nan.

Annie has her hair piled up in not quite such a bird's nest as usual. She's curled it into ginger sausages. Gloria has her fur on again and cherry-red lipstick, and Beattie is all blonde and sparkly with a big diamond necklace, and she's brought her sister Dolly — another of the Green Bottles — and they're both in black velvet and golden silk blouses, with ruffles frothing out of the buttons at the top and little gold satin flowers on their hats, all cock-eyed at a funny angle (but they say it's deliberate). I'm all dressed up, too, in my new dress, the brown pinafore. Gloria did my hair for me and patted powder from her compact on my cheeks and wetted a tiny brush on her tongue, dipped it in a square of black she has, and said, "Look up." As I did, she brushed it across my eyelashes. She hands me her compact to admire the effect: spidery lashes, like Vivien Leigh's. Whenever I blink I can see them: black spots, in front of my eyes.

Everyone is shrieking and laughing. The noise is deafening. It seems to go on and on, the celebrating, everyone happy and shouting for no reason. Our car is crawling along the Waterden Road. We're going to have to get out and walk — there's such a crush outside the stadium. Crowds make me nervous now, but there's no point in saying so. No one wants to talk about Nan, or be reminded of her, and even though Beattie and Dolly lost someone in the tube that day too, another sister, I think, they won't talk to me about it.

Bobby would say the Green Bottles are Raving Bonkers. Bobby seems in a bad mood all the time, these days, and the only thing I can think is that he's jealous. Jealous of the way the Green Bottles treat me, jealous that I stayed at home and he went to Ely, even though that's stupid, because it was him who wanted to go.

He's been working at the dogs on Saturdays and any other day he can bunk off from school. He's one of the youngest, but he takes it really seriously, being a kennel boy. He likes it, but I do hear him whining sometimes, arguing with Dad about it, and I realise that Dad and Uncle Charlie are asking Bobby to do things, and Bobby doesn't want to.

This morning he was in our bedroom, all important, eleven years old and getting ready to go to work, laying out his money on the bedspread, five one-pound notes. When I go to touch one, he put his hand over mine. "Hands off of my money! I earned that. You go and get your own."

Bobby's quirks are getting worse. Like he's convinced the colour yellow is unlucky, and if I wear a yellow dress he pulls a face and scowls at me and tells me to burn it and wear something else. The notes lay there, lazily, flatly, like they didn't care if I touched them or not.

"I only want to *look*," I told him crossly. "I don't need your blinkin' money. The Green Bottles will get me jellied eels or anything else I want."

He snorted, gathered up the notes.

"Got any tips?" I asked him.

He looked funny then. Like he couldn't make up his mind what to tell me. Suddenly he blurted: "British Girl. She's a grand bitch. A railer. But never put nothing on her. No matter what nobody says. Even Dad."

"I never listen to Dad," I said. Although, me being such a daddy's girl, of course that wasn't true. I'd always believe him the cleverest. Especially about dogs.

Bobby likes to use all these new dog terms to dazzle me, make me feel left out. Scrubbers, graders, railers, fliers, wide runners. He doesn't seem such a little boy any more. He likes throwing back his head to drop this Phosferine tonic into his mouth; he says it gives him "pep" and he's still trying to follow that Jimmy around, the freckle-faced boxer one. He nicks Dad's Brylcreem to stick down his hair, but he's still so small and I know it embarrasses him. He even smells different since he's been working at the kennels: the dusty fur smell, dog hairs and drool cling to his clothes. His ears stick out worse than ever. Gloria calls him Toby Jug and tugs at one whenever she passes him. Then he blushes a hot red and I feel sorry for him again.

"Head for the stand and I'll go and park the motor on Cassland Road," Dad calls to Annie as we pull up next to a long queue of people outside the stadium. The car door opens and we spill out on to the street to join the crowds.

"Why'd he bring the motor anyway, using up his ration?" Beattie asks, pressing down the ruffles at her throat and trying to stop them exploding up over her mouth.

Dolly laughs at her sister. "Why d'you think? Flash Harry — he's only sorry he can't park it in full view!" She flicks her sister with her gloves, then fixes her hat again, to make it even more cock-eyed, just like a flying saucer lying there. They tilt their heads together and giggle.

I follow the Green Bottles. We're drawing every eye in the crowd towards us. Old men are laughing, calling out things and sidling up to Annie and the others, young men in uniforms, opening their cigarette boxes like they're about to blow kisses from their palms, moving in close with flaring matches, close enough to gaze into the eyes of whichever Green Bottle they want to snap up.

"Queenie! Hold on to me, sugar," Gloria says, taking my hand as we go through the gates. Annie's sausage-head and twig figure in her green skirt-suit disappear in the crowd of caps and shoulders but Gloria doesn't click fast enough in her high courts to catch her. I wonder for a minute why it's Annie, not Gloria, who is Dad's girlfriend, when Gloria is so . . . sparkly and bubbly and sort of more *alive*. When Gloria is the one *I* like best. Maybe Dad doesn't like makeup and big bosoms, I decide. He likes girls to be plain and simple, like Annie. Or slim and pretty the way Mum is, not all lipsticked and saucy.

A powerful smell of vinegar floats up to me from someone's fish and chips and my stomach rumbles, but I'm shunted along and there's no moment to stop and beg for a bag of chips or some shrimps. Gloria is leading me to the tea bar in the standing area. A mass of old men in camel coats and hats are swarming like bees in a hive. She's lost the others but she doesn't seem to care: she wants to buy me a soupy thick mug of tea, brown as the river Lea, and find out what Bobby said when he left the house this morning.

"Come on, you can tell your best Green Bottle, your old friend Gloria, can't you? I know they know. I know Bobby would of told you. Is he working for London Joe's gang then or is it your dad?"

I take a big gulp of tea and yelp as it scalds my tongue. I'm thinking over what Bobby said, and why I was muddled.

"Where's your dad now, eh?" Gloria says. "He ain't looking out for us, is he? He's just thinking of hisself, doing his own little bit of business. Me and you, we should stick together."

I look around for Dad and see his hat in the distance, among a crowd of men's shoulders. A few moments ago he pressed a coin into my hand and said, "Be lucky, darlin'." I sip the thick tea and my nose is crowded with Gloria's perfume and the tobacco and salt and excitement in the air, and I wonder which of the Green Bottles is the best way to get to see Mum: Annie or Gloria?

"Well, Bobby . . . he did tell me something," I begin.

"I knew it!" Gloria squeaks. She twirls me around, trying to steer me away from the crowd at the tea bar and towards the bookie's pit.

"But, Gloria, if I tell you, will you promise —"

"Port and lemonade, girls?" butts in an American with a newly shaved chin, like a shiny side of boiled ham. He's smiling a toothy grin at Gloria. "Sherry, honey? What can I get you?"

Gloria shakes her head smartly without even glancing at him and crouches beside me again. She seems very surprised. "OK, what is it? You little — you're a right one, ain't you?"

"Can I visit Mum like Annie said?"

Gloria straightens up. She squeezes her fur coat a little tighter over her cleavage, and the silver locket she wears slithers between her huge bosoms. "Gawd — in that place? Are you sure? But you'd better be right then — and be quick too. Your dad ain't going to give me the nod, that's certain. Always has his favourites, does Lucky Boy."

So I tell her what Bobby said. That he started to hint British Girl was a good bet but then seemed to change his mind and told me not to bet at all.

"Bobby's lost his bottle," Gloria says mysteriously.

I do know that Bobby's been doping dogs for weeks. He loves to tell me his tricks: a straw in one of the dog's eyelids so that it blinks throughout the race. Tying up the dog's balls. Or chloretone wrapped up inside the sausage you feed them. Feeding them just before a race slows them down — that's the easiest way. Chloretone is usually for travel sickness in people, but it makes the dog's blood pressure rise when it first shoots out of the trap, Bobby says. The dog looks good at first, but soon fades.

"So. It's whether Bobby does what he's been told or not? That's a toughie. Must of told him to dope all the others . . ."

I don't know what she means. I wish I'd been concentrating when Bobby talked to me.

"No one can resist your dad — know that, Queenie? I don't know what it is about that fella. Luck of the devil."

I wait by the tea stand, wondering at this, while she flounces down to the bookie's pit, nearly tripping over herself to get a bet on before the traps come up. "You're sure?" she asks, coming back, staring at me. I'm not sure, so I shake my head but she accepts this, and turns to look at her race card.

I don't like trailing behind her to watch the race. As the lights dim and the buzz quietens to a sizzle, all eyes pinned on the traps lifting and the dogs exploding out of them, I'm still puzzling over Bobby and Dad and me, and how it got so complicated. I'm wondering if I did the wrong thing in telling Gloria, but I hope she'll keep her promise.

Five out of the six races have run. It's the sixth coming up and the dog in trap two, wearing blue, thank God, Bobby's lucky colour, is British Girl.

Gloria slipped away minutes ago to place another bet. Dad is staring at his race card and smoking one cigarette after another, trying to seem casual and playful and at the same time not really bothering to talk to anyone, or answer Annie's questions. We're milling close by the track, all of us (except Dad) eating shrimps with our little wooden forks and chatting, hemmed in on all sides. Gloria is busy plucking the heel of her shoe from the grass and doesn't look anybody in the eye. Dad keeps his nose in his race card but he looks up when Annie says, "The Flying Squad's here. NGRC. Did you reckon on that?"

She says it nastily, crossly, and Dad looks up, pretending to be unbothered. He puts a finger in one of her sausage curls, which has unravelled and is bouncing down around her ear.

"Relax." He glances down at me, then moves closer to Annie, to whisper something in her ear.

". . . it don't stay in the system . . . they can't test for it," I catch.

"That what Bobby says? Or do you *know*?"

I notice that Gloria is holding her little wooden fork in mid-air, closing her mouth thoughtfully around a shrimp and listening.

"He's a dead cert. Mad March Hare. He's like Mick the Miller — he'll be a Derby winner one day," Dad says loudly, lighting up one of his cigarettes. I glance at him. Surely he's not betting on Mad March Hare. It's British Girl, he's meant to bet on, isn't it? Then I wonder if he just says this to fool everyone, so the odds remain high, so no one bets on the real dead cert.

Dad's only pretending to read his race card. He lights another cigarette, shakes the match, grinds it under his foot. Sweat, a fine coating, shines along his forehead and his nose.

Suddenly I understand Gloria's comments perfectly. In some dim place I think I did all along. It's Dad who's been putting Bobby up to it. And the only really chancy thing is whether Bobby did what he was told today, or thought better of it. Let Dad down. I feel certain I know which.

"I didn't put my money on nothing! Can I, Dad? Just the Tote. *Please*, Dad . . ."

"No — ssh. Come on, the hare's running."

The crowd starts up the Derby roar. It's such a quick thing, a race. There's barely time to see the flash of ghostly dogs with their coloured jackets — I'm stuck between the furs and leather of the dog men and women anyway — but one thing I do see, as they shoot round the bend, is that the dog in the blue, the dog out of trap two, British Girl, she's flying, she's leaving the rest way behind', and Gloria can barely hide her excitement.

Mad March Hare, trap five, orange jacket, limps in fourth. Not quite last. He'd started off so well but there's no mistaking it. He definitely fades.

I glance at Gloria, who is staring at me and biting her lip until the lipstick comes off on her teeth. And I sneak a glance at Dad. He's beaming. His face is lit up, like the sun. He flutters his race card to the wind; all the fun, all the jollyboy let loose in him. He's off right away, towards the bookies, towards the paying-out booths. Then he's back, still grinning and trying not to grin, and giving my arm a squeeze and grabbing hold of

119

Annie. "Let's get out of here," he says, shoving through the crowds ahead of him.

He's so far ahead that I don't see it. Gloria has disappeared; I think nothing of it — she must have gone to the Ladies.

Then suddenly she's back, and instead of looking happy, she looks at me so sadly that I know at once something frightening has happened. She puts a hand on my shoulder and keeps pushing me through the crowd, towards the exit, and I only turn around to say once, "Where's Dad?" before I realise that, again, someone has been snatched from me.

"Don't fret, sugar, just keep walking towards the car," Gloria says.

Uncle Charlie drives us home in Dad's car, in a choked silence.

Gloria had been to collect her winnings and at that point, she says, she saw them. Dad and two undercover detectives ahead of us, suddenly bleedin' obvious, in their new camel coats, smoking their cigars, trying to blend in. A couple of kennel boys with them, including Bobby. Gloria had blocked me seeing them, hustling me towards the car with Annie and Uncle Charlie.

The car is full of hushed, half-sentences and strange conversation.

"You think Bobby's gone and grassed? How'd they connect it to Tommy?"

Bitter remarks burst from Annie, then Beattie, like traps opening: "The bastard, the stupid bastard!"

"I'd like to wring his jug-eared little neck."

120

They're sure it's Bobby's fault and that, somehow, it's no accident either. That Bobby got himself caught and along the way grassed up Dad and the trainer too.

I go over and over the conversation with Bobby, in my mind, trying to remember his instructions. I glance at Gloria, her profile beside me, the little brooch shaped like a sea-horse in diamanté on her collar. She's a proper little actress, like Mum said of me once. She's trying to act sorry about Dad, and sorry about Bobby, and maybe she is, but she's full of deceit too: her face tells me that.

What did Bobby mean for me to do? He definitely said not to listen to Dad. Not to put money on. But it seems like Gloria and Dad won, so Bobby must have changed his mind. Or maybe, as Gloria said, Bobby meant to disobey, but in the end, just couldn't resist Dad. Luck of the blinkin' devil. It's such a puzzle that my head spins, and I sit beside Gloria, relieved that at least she doesn't join in when Annie and Beattie say horrid things about Bobby.

Bobby wouldn't grass, would he? He's still family, even if he is in one almighty sulk. And he's not stupid either . . . so how could he get caught? And where are they now, Dad and Bobby? Gloria says it'll be Shoreditch Station. "Let's pray they ain't got nothing on them," she says. Gloria's winnings — I glance at her again and she is *glowing* — how much are they? How much did Gloria win?

Climbing out at the house Annie leans in at the driver's window and says to Uncle Charlie, "Tommy won't squeal. I can't speak for that young Toby Jug. But I know Tommy."

Annie clicks unsteadily towards the house, beckoning me to follow. Gloria stays in the car with the others. I give her a wave; a flutter. Gloria seems scared; she stares straight ahead.

That night I can't sleep at all. Our bedroom, overflowing already with Bobby's nightmares, is now swarming with fresh ones. I suddenly remember one of our teachers telling Bobby off, ages ago, at Lauriston School, for scrumping apples from a garden. "You'll end up in Borstal, my boy, that's where you'll end up." She said it not like a warning, but a fact. Sometimes I wonder why teachers and grown-ups do this all the time and how on earth they expect us to fight it. Fight the picture they have for us, like a tunnel, a route they're carving out in the earth for us to crawl along. We picture it too when they say it, of course. How else does the future happen? "You'll end up in Borstal. Mark my bloody words."

He did, too. Not then, but later. He got off with a warning, after the day at the dogs, but Dad got six months. And I got my promise: I got to see Mum.

Gloria arrives with no warning, and no explanation. The doorbell goes: Gloria is there. She's wearing a hat, I see it through the bubbled-glass window in the door, and as I open it, she's standing on our step, blotting her red lipstick on a folded piece of paper, pulled from a neat little pack. She looks over my shoulder. "Annie in?"

122

Yes, Annie is, but I tell Gloria that I'm all alone, and she seems relieved, tells me to get my coat, and hurry up: she has George the Greek waiting.

George, she explains, as we climb into the car, has kindly agreed to take us to the station. A great stink of cigar smoke nearly suffocates me as I open the door but from Gloria's mood — tense, quiet — I somehow know that I'm to say nothing and so I smother my coughs in the sleeve of my coat.

At the station she leans over to kiss George the Greek lightly and tell him with a wink that she'll pay up later. He turns his curly head to watch us both go and suddenly winds down the window to shout, in his powerful accent, "Yes, you will, baby — with knobs on!"

It's such an odd remark that Gloria and I suddenly put our heads together and giggle as we run for the platform. I've worked out what a brass is by now. I've figured out that the Ten Green Bottles do it when it suits them, although Gloria, being proud and vain, is the one who'd like me to believe otherwise.

On the train she's sober again, and drawing on her cigarette and checking that the corridor is empty before closing the door and sitting back down beside me.

"Now Queenie, you done good. You never told a soul, and that's the only reason I'm doing this for you."

Yes, a deal, I understand those.

"God knows, Annie wouldn't thank me, and your dad would skin me alive."

He would too. I know that.

She snaps open her crocodile-print handbag with a loud click to put her cigarette case away, and find the slim white holder she likes to use to smoke. I peep inside her bag to see if the lovely suede purse is in there, and Gloria softens. She offers me a comb and tells me to make myself look respectable.

"I'm doing this for Moll," she says. "Not that she deserves it. No, she fucking well don't. Excuse my French. But a deal's a deal. You've no idea how hard this was, Queenie. I had to write to the medical superintendent. I've had to cadge money off of George the Greek. You mind you're grateful to me, you hear?"

I do, I am. I nod hard, flipping the comb to the floor by accident and folding over to pick it up. But I'm scared now, too.

The train rolls on and the chimneys and bricks change into fields and, once, a shining fox flashes into a hedge and disappears. Suddenly Gloria says, "You didn't go to the trial, then?" and I say, "What trial?" and she shuts her mouth, fast, and when she opens it again there's a little smear of lipstick on her top teeth. I ponder this for a moment, wondering if she means Dad's recent trial (no one ever takes me to those) or something else.

The last thing she says as we get out is the thing that troubles me most. She understands at last, she says, that no one has told me anything; no one ever tells children anything. I suppose she is trying to prepare me.

"How old was she, then? Your baby sister — Vera?"

"I don't know."

"Was she older than a year? Thirteen months? Had she had her first birthday?"

"Yeah. I remember her birthday. Nan knitted her a hat. I made the pom-pom, you know, winding it round cardboard. It was pink with orange flecks —"

"Gawd. Over a year, was she? That's a shame. That's why. Under a year would of been better . . . It's a different law, then, see?"

I don't see, but I know better than to ask. We've now walked from the little country station all overgrown with brambles and with a lonely feel, horrible black birds pecking at empty fish-and-chip newspaper, and dog-ends, and have walked up a hill. I realise, staring up at the big fortress of a building in front of us, that if Gloria had warned me today, if she'd told me we were coming, I'd have said I'd changed my mind.

It looks like a whole town, not one building. It has high walls and two towers and sort of iron-railed balconies and walled gardens. Is it a hospital? It looks like a prison. The only big building I've ever seen is Ely Cathedral. This is bigger. And dark. And no one would ever want to make a model of it. I glance up at the windows, see the bars, and my eyes immediately spring with tears. I had never thought to ask why no one took me to visit Dad whenever he was away; but now, at this moment, I decide that they were quite right never to think of it, never to speak of it, never to ask me. I don't want to visit. I don't want to be here.

"Did you tell your brother you asked me to bring you?"

This surprises me. I didn't tell Bobby, no. And I don't know why.

"Don't you think he would of wanted to come, an' all?"

Yes. I do think that. It's just —

Gloria grips my hand in her leather gloves and snaps towards the gates. I somehow know from the way she does it that's she's thinking I've been mean, and I have, I know I have, but Bobby's sulky at the moment and, to tell the truth, I want something just for myself.

We fill out a visitor's book — or Gloria does. She gives Mum's maiden name. Is she pretending to be related? That must be it. Mum's sister, maybe. A lady comes, with a heap of heavy keys, a lady in a uniform who looks to me like a nurse. Like the nurse that other time, the one who called Mum a dipso. There is a tiny little Indian man shouting at the entry desk: he wants to see his wife. "Ssh, sir, please," the lady on the desk says, but he doesn't stop.

Gloria is asked to empty her pockets, and show inside her handbag, and when they spy matches, the nurses tut and say that matches aren't allowed in the visitors' room. "In case . . . you know," they say, looking pointedly at me.

"How's she supposed to light her fags, then?" Gloria sounds annoyed.

"We do it. We have matches. And there's a special brick for striking. Safer, you know . . ."

We're hurried away and another door is unlocked; we wait in the cramped space while this is done, and then we burst into the visitors' room. Every time a key is turned and a door opened, I expect her to be there. Mum. I expect her to look just as she did, or just as she *does* in my dreams of her. With her hair in auburn curls on top of her head, wearing stockings with straight seams. I'm working hard on this, on picturing this, on this lovely statue in Homerton I sometimes see that looks like her. Instead some weird smell keeps wafting up to me, a frightening petrol smell, or is it gas? A smell of that day, the day I failed to steal enough milk to keep us all together — and then suddenly there she is. And it is her, and she looks beautiful, but fatter and softer, and in a big tent-like dress made of dark brown material, and not like Mum at all.

Two nurses — both men, one with grey curling eyebrows like the barber at the barber on Well Street — are either side of her. As if propping up a giant doll. They bring her to our table, which is small and green, like a card table, and they put her on a chair. Her head sort of dives forward as if she really is a doll and they've dropped her. I think she's going to hit the floor, face first. But instead she grabs for me.

I hadn't expected that. I haven't said a word but now a little "Ow!" squeezes out of me and I almost pull away as she does it. I have to make myself sit still. She's sobbing. Her body shakes and her wet mouth is in my hair, her hot breath all over me.

I sit frozen and long for someone to peel her off.

Gloria's kind voice finally does it. I feel Gloria's fear, crackling beside me. She's murmuring, "Moll, how are you, gel? There now — calm down, gel, let her breathe now, Moll, there you go . . ."

Mum does at last release the lock on me and looks up. Behind her head are some drawings done by children and piles of games — Monopoly, Scrabble. Mum gives me a weird grin. "There she is. My big gel! Take a look at you. All grown-up. Where's your brother? Where's Bobby?"

I should have known she'd ask for him first. A little stab, under my ribs. Is that why I didn't tell him? Didn't want to share her.

"Where's the baby?" she carries on. "Was it your dad brought you? Or Ida?"

I glance, terrified, at Gloria. *Keep mum, she's not so dumb* pops into my head. What does Mum know about Nan? What should I say?

"Another day, Molly." Gloria rescues me. "You're only allowed two visitors at one time . . ."

"Huh?" Mum glances around as if expecting someone else, then slumps back into her seat. Her face is wet and Gloria offers her a handkerchief, which she takes and flaps against her face, the way you'd slap someone you wanted to wake up.

"Darlin'!" Mum says suddenly.

It's an odd sound, her voice. It comes out in a blurt, as if not from her mouth but somewhere else, like a voice from a film. Darlin'. That's not what I hear. I have such a clear, bright picture of her, from a time in our kitchen, standing with that leaflet in her hand, the one about evacuation and sending your kids away, and fanning her face with it, saying, "Shall I, then? Shall I send ya?"

128

I'm not your "darlin". You never loved me. You never even think about me.

I must be the wickedest girl who ever lived to think such a thing. I want to cry.

A couple of feet away a chair scrapes horribly as two nurses settle down beside us with notebooks.

Later, on the train home, Gloria says to me, "Never give you a minute's privacy, did you see that? Every word we fucking said."

"Got any fags?" Mum asks, now, abandoning the crumpled hankie and instead slapping the table, groping towards us. Her hand is fatter too. Her fingers are puffed up, and the skin grey.

"All right if we smoke, then?" Gloria asks the nurses. The one with the eyebrows, the barber one, gets up, strikes a match on a brick by the window and, cupping it with his hand, walks over to us and lights Mum's cigarette. Gloria seems thrilled that Mum's shown a bit of mischief — any of her old spark. I think Gloria is more shaken than she's letting on. I swallow tears and smile brightly at Mum, at anyone who might be looking my way.

The room fills with the smell of Player's. Almost, for a second, if I close my eyes, I can believe I'm there again, things are back how they were, with Mum sloshing her rum around in her coffee cup, Dad reading the *Greyhound Life*, baby Vera snoozing by the fire, *Children's Hour* rumbling away on the wireless in the corner and Nan knitting . . .

Instead of here, going back, on the train, remembering, Gloria sniffing beside me, patting my hand occasionally, saying, "It's the drugs, you know. She can't help it. They keep them drugged up to the eyeballs. She ain't half fat." And then suddenly, in a snort: "She was always such a beauty, your mum, such a fucking beauty!"

I stare out of the window, gently shaking Gloria's hand from mine. Nan used to read tea-leaves sometimes, for a laugh. Swilling the cup around, tipping it up, poking with her finger among the soft black sludge. "I see a ship," Nan would say. "That's you, Bobby, going on a long journey . . ." Or: "*There,* see? One day your ship will come in."

Always a blinkin' ship, it was. Why did she never see *this?*

The train slides through a tunnel and instead of green and trees it's my own face for a second in the black glass: my snub nose, my freckles. No, I can't remember anything more about Nan. She's fading, like a ball of wool unravelling until the last thread comes away and in the end there's nothing there. I close my eyes and sleep for a second or two but jerk awake. As I open my eyes I see myself suddenly. I think it's me: it's a girl my age — or is it another girl? — right in front of me, staring at me. A sick feeling creeps over me. Whoever she is, she's wearing my red flannel nightie with the drawstring ribbon at the neck and behind her is the chest of drawers in my bedroom, dragged open, as if she's been looking for something. I don't like the way this girl is peering at me, so I squeeze my eyes shut to get rid of her, and open them again, stare out of the window. The track smears into a wobbling line in front of me.

Then at last there's just Gloria again, and the green outside the window changes to the burned and splintered city with its brandy-snap pillars, its piles of charred bricks. I stare down at the railway track. It doesn't feel as if we're travelling along it. It feels like it's chasing us, just out of reach.

In the end I wished I'd never gone. I felt so guilty that I had to tell Bobby about it, a week or so later, and he just shouted at me. He said Mum was a dipso and an Alka Seltzer and he didn't care that no one took him; then he burst into tears. The visit spoiled my ability to picture Mum the way I wanted to. I wanted to imagine her like the statue of the Immaculate Heart of Mary on the church in Homerton on Kenworthy Road. That statue had eyes like Mum's: eyes that were glancing down, sarcastically, as if she wanted to laugh. Passing it always made me think of her.

That really was it. The end of our explanation about her. The end of the subject. She loomed large for us: she was a statue with sarcastic eyes and a stone heart carved on her chest that colonised our dreams but, honestly, she could never be mentioned.

I spent more and more time with the Green Bottles, and Bobby, being a boy, somehow couldn't, and that was when our lives seemed to divide, along strictly boy-girl lines. Bobby spent time with mates he'd made at the dogs, or trailing Jimmy the boxer, or just watching at the ring of the Repton Boys' Club and bunking off school.

Dad and Annie had some "news", they told us, one day, all smiles and secret looks: they were expecting a little baby brother or sister for us.

We thought of Vera, and said nothing.

I was supposed to be at big school by then, and Bobby too, but most of the time we both bunked off. I thought of Nan telling me to look after Bobby, and not get separated from him, and I tried, but the boys Bobby wanted to be with were a bit scary to me, and wouldn't let me hang around them. And he didn't like to be in school.

One day, Bobby was nicked for stealing an air rifle. He had to go to court and, of course, no one paid the fine for him, so that made matters worse. Dad was away, doing his time for his part in the dog-racing fixing, and money had dried up. I can't now remember the sequence of events — I remember a bright autumn day near Bonfire Night when Dad returned and took me to the brand-new Lesneys' factory in Hackney Wick to show me where the Matchbox toys were made, and said wistfully, "Think your brother's too old for a Matchbox car?" and I agreed that I thought he was. So Dad said he'd get one for the new baby when it came instead.

Then there was the day — a day when the weather perked up and daffodils appeared at Vicky Park — that Bobby pinched a bike and cycled past the Jewish Boys' Club on Fordham Street and got nicked by two coppers who recognised him. He abandoned the bike and tried to run but they chased him easily and caught him, and tumbled him to the ground, where one held him down while the other administered some good old British justice.

Oh, in those days you could do what you wanted to tear-aways. You could get them in the car with a kindly, "Come on, son, let's be having you," and once in you could pin their arms behind their backs and say to your mate, "Right, I've got him, let the little bastard have it!"

By the time he got to the police station Bobby had blood-stains all over him, but the arresting officers just shrugged, as if to say, "Well? How'd you expect us to bring him in?"

Bobby was in court the next morning, and fined a pound or two. This fine wasn't paid either — who had a pound to spare, when every penny was needed for the new baby? — and so his old teacher at Lauriston School finally got what she predicted: her picture for Bobby came true. Bobby was taken to an approved school in Hertfordshire. When — a year later — he absconded from there one night with his new friend Robby, he ended up at the police station again, and from there was taken to the allocation centre at Wormwood Scrubs, where Borstal boys awaited their fate.

Part Two

My Further Education

Me too. I ended up at a girls approved school eventually. I think Bobby went to his school around the spring of '46, and me a year later. I tried writing to Bobby, piecing together, from snippets Annie told me, that after he'd run away from the school he'd ended up in Hollesley Bay, a big farm Borstal in Suffolk, but Bobby's letter-writing never improved and I didn't hear back. I waited for that letter, and when it didn't come I threw myself into learning all I could from the Green Bottles about hoisting.

It was understood by all of them that I was the best. It helped to have me with them: I looked so innocent, in my pinafore, with the smattering of freckles across my nose. Sly Roger was always trying to put his hand up my skirt when I climbed out of the car and he liked me to sit in the front with him. (He'd bought another Chrysler off my dad at a knock-down price while Dad was inside again and that was what we drove around in.) The Green Bottles used to hoot with laughter to see me slap him off, not even slightly tempted by his offers (usually of something he was eating: a chip or a stick of liquorice).

We'd all get done up and go out for the day. It was a time when everything was short, everyone told not to be a squander bug. But that's not how I remember it at all. The Green Bottles were having none of that. Sometimes there were as many as eight of us.

In the West End there were shop walkers, and the Green Bottles taught me to look out for them. Something about their eyes, their expression, the way they fiddled with a jacket or a dress on the hanger but looking all around them, not interested in the clothes — I got this at once. My job was to let Gloria or Annie or Beattie or whoever know. The signal was my bending down to pull up my socks. This meant: "Shop walker in the area." If I pulled up the left sock the shop walker was to my left, if I pulled up one after the other, the shop walker was directly behind me. But if my socks were folded over at the tops, and equally matched, and I wasn't fiddling with them, the coast was perfectly clear.

I was mostly playing hookey from school. The first time a shop assistant asked me why I wasn't in school, I said, in such a posh voice, "I hev a music exam this ahfternoon and Miss hes given me the morning orf to prectise," that Gloria nearly wet herself trying not to laugh.

"Who learned you to talk like that?" she asked, later, as we were drinking hot chocolate in Debenham's off Wigmore Street.

"Margaret Lockwood," was my answer. I'd been watching old films at the Children's Cinema Club on Mare Street. My favourite was one about a posh lady who becomes a highwaywoman for the adventure. That was the voice I was mimicking.

So then Gloria took me to this friend of hers, to have elocution lessons. It was a house in Brancaster Mews with green walls and a big piano and a fireplace facing you as soon as you walked in, with flowers in a silver vase. Every time I went, the flowers in the vase were different, I noticed. The woman never let them go brown or droop. She was a tiny woman, hardly bigger than me, and wore glasses with little diamonds at the corners. She'd stare at me over the top of them and tap me sometimes, on my chin, or upper lip, with a pencil.

She'd make me recite things, poems, and tell me, in her funny deep voice, that I had to breathe from low in my belly, which she patted with her small, pink-nailed hand as she spoke. Gloria would watch her, waiting for me, sipping tea from a china cup that the teacher — I think she was called Mrs Sin-gin Sargent, or something that sounded like that — would make her whenever we arrived.

"The sense of danger must not disappear," I'd say. "The way is certainly both short and steep."

"Stee-p," Mrs Sin-gin Sargent repeated, pursing her mouth over the *p* to make it pop.

". . . short and stee*p*. However gradual it looks from here: look if you like, but you will have to leap."

And then it would be back to the beginning, to recite the whole poem, carefully, slowly forming each word, until the final verse, my favourite.

"A solitude ten thousand fathoms deep . . . sustains the bed on which we lie, my dear. Although I love you,

139

you will have to leap. Our dream of safety has to disappear."

"'Leap before you look', by Mr W. H. Auden," Mrs Sin-gin Sargent would say at the end, with satisfaction, and make me repeat it, popping the *p* and cracking the *k*.

"Much can be said for social savoir-faire, but to rejoice when no one else is there . . . is even harder than it is to weep . . ." I droned on, wondering what "savoir-faire" could be but liking the sound of it just the same. A great poem for a girl like me to learn. It was drilled into me, that poem, and in its way became my motto.

No one is watching, but you have to leap.

It's Gloria who's the boldest and the best, the one I want to be like.

This day, this one day, we're walking along Bond Street and she says, "How about some cucumber sandwiches and a spot of chocolate cake in the Dorchester? Just you and me."

After the trip to see Mum last summer I know she looks out for me, somehow. She says it's her job to teach me as I don't have another woman to do it. (Annie is big as a house and not coming out with us so much now the baby's nearly due.)

I haven't heard of the Dorchester but she takes my silence as a yes and hails us a cab. I watch closely how she does this. She doesn't wave her arm or shout like Annie or Beattie. She just steps a little closer to the kerb and tilts her chin. It's a nippy little movement. She

140

stares down the first cab driver who approaches and then it's just a flicker of her white glove, and the cab stops and we're climbing inside. She pats the seat beside her and sort of purrs at the driver, "Park Lane, please. The Dorchester."

We all like it best up the West End. We're sick of roped-off streets with signs about Unexploded Bombs, and pubs like the Nag's Head on Whitechapel Road. Saying, *Business as Usual*, but where the building is flapping open and hanging on by a thread. In the West End there are tiny purple flowers spilling out of window-boxes, and postboxes and telephone boxes gleaming with new paint. As the taxi slides past I squint a little, making the streets blur into soft putty colours with bright splashes of tomato red.

But as we get out and the doorman in his big hat sweeps us in, my mouth feels dry. The height of the ceiling threatens me, dangling the most dangerous-looking chandeliers over us. Gloria smoothes a hand over my hair and smiles at a fixed spot over my head, heading for the cloakroom.

She hands over her coat, a dark velvet, one she calls "tidy" but not her best, and as we wait there a fat, powdered lady arrives. Gloria steps back and says, "Oh, after you, my dear," and the lady hands her coat to the girl behind the desk, who gives her a button for it, with "26" on it in black numbers. It's a floor-sweeping silky sable fur and I see Gloria glance at it. I register her look. I wonder just how out of the blue this little trip was, really.

Bending a little, Gloria whispers, "Fat slug."

141

She then straightens up and allows one of the waiters to show us to a table.

We walk past the marble columns — the Promenade Bar, Gloria says — safest place in London, during the war, she tells me. Churchill had his own suite here. Everywhere is green and gold, full of fronds and gigantic sprays of flowers. Instead of fountains and streams there's bubbling chatter, and the sound of cutlery chinking, and crockery. It's just so big — high ceilings loom over us, and I almost stumble into a statue of a black boy holding some golden fruit next to a golden lamp.

As we sit down, Gloria notices that I'm trembling. The waiter is hovering, staring right through me. "Relax, Queenie," Gloria whispers. She picks up the menu and flaps herself with it. "My niece and I would like afternoon tea, please," she says.

He dips in a sort of bow, picks up our menus and leaves us.

Gloria leans in close towards me and mutters, "Just speak in your Margaret Lockwood voice." When I say nothing, she gets out her compact and uses the mirror to see who is sitting behind her. Then she takes the green velvet cushion I'm holding like a shield and puts it firmly on the seat beside me. "You know," she says, "I used to work here."

"Did you?" I can hardly believe it. Here, among the tinkling silver and the sparkling mirrors and the golden fruit and . . .

"Yeah. I was a chambermaid. Look, Queenie, we've earned this. When you've wiped round the bath of one of those fat slugs for the umpteenth time, you get to enjoy sipping from the best bone china, OK?"

The waiter reappears with a silver tray. He places a cup close to me, and a little silver tea-strainer in its own silver pot. Seeing my hand shake as I go to pick up the spoon, Gloria waits for him to leave and then whispers, "He's just a bleedin' waiter. A waiter! His mum works as a cleaner down the Troxy on Commercial Road . . ."

And yet to me, he seems like the poshest, scariest representative of another world I've ever come across. I look again at Gloria, grateful, and take a bite of the triangle of crustless cucumber sandwich she offers me.

"No vinegar?" I ask, which makes her laugh, for some reason.

I risk a glimpse around. The restaurant area is full of women, all of them drinking tea and talking. I'm struck by how much they use their hands when they talk, these posh women. That's all I can see. Hands: flapping, waving, wagging, clutching, grasping among the hot-house fronds. Their hands look like birds to me: dipping, now spreading, soaring . . . a restaurant full of birds, pecking over their crumbs, sipping at their tea.

And the chink of china sounding like coins in a pocket, jangling.

Gloria sees me looking and leans in to whisper, "Most of this lot were brasses. Dont half give themselves airs. They married their client, that's all. Me, I cut out the middle man and made money my husband, which, if you ask me, is *much* nicer . . ."

At the cloakroom Gloria is all charm and innocence as she seems to have lost the button with the number on it that allows her to collect her coat. I say nothing and the room swarms. I'm small and then big. My face on the outside of a kettle. A silver spoon.

"Oh dear, what was my number again, darlin'?" Gloria tinkles.

"Twenty-six," I reply, without missing a beat.

The fur is brought. The sable fur. The fat slug's coat: long, a gorgeous colour.

Gloria looks a knock-out in it. She slides her arms into the sleeves, strokes the collar up to her neck, as if she's petting a big, sleepy cat, and gives the girl behind the desk a cheeky smile. "Thank you so much, darlin'." She does a little twirl in the coat, almost giving the game away, she's so delighted.

And Gloria turns and stalks through the doors as if she's a big cat herself. I'm two paces away: I'm right behind her.

As we step outside I see the car. Sly Roger is waiting. Beattie is there in the back and we roll smoothly away, no great hurry, car magically appearing. This part of London is patterned with neat, distinct shadows. The pointy black spikes have disappeared — for scrap, Sly Roger says — and instead there are little wooden fences, almost like being in the country. Pointing up to a sky that looks like a clean blue handkerchief.

Beattie is admiring the sable, sniffing it, rubbing it against her cheek, stroking it. "Gawd, it's a beauty," she says. "Bleedin' hell. Must be worth about three thousand."

They carry on like this for a while and I learn that a really lovely mink coat would cost about three thousand pounds in Harrods but Gloria could only get about two fifty for this sable if she sells it to someone they know, who'll buy "crooked". She doesn't want to part with it and there's a bit of arguing for a while and then they start laughing about a friend of theirs who did a job in Bond Street towards the end of the war.

"So he's smashed the window of the shop and bad luck for him — bleedin' Special Police comes along. So this special says, 'What's going on here, sir?' And he's loading up the car, and quick as a flash he says, 'Unexploded bomb in the shop, sir, stand well back,' and blow me if the special don't help him load up!"

They giggle then. Put their heads together, snuffling like little pigs. "Best war we ever had . . ."

I know how shocked Nan would have been at that comment, but I push that thought aside. Gloria, Beattie, Annie: they're my family now.

I stare out of the window. Roger is taking us to a restaurant. The streets here are smaller and so pretty, with trees looming out of pavements, scattering pink blossom everywhere, and a frill of lilac pansies at the bottom of every window. I close my eyes for a moment, hearing only the purr of the black cabs and the *ting-ting* of bicycle bells through the opened car window. A lady's heels tap down the street like typewriter keys.

Even with my eyes closed, this could never be Hackney, or Poplar. Everything is being repaired. The lamp-posts are newly painted: black gloss. Each has a fat clump of yellow and blue flowers in a hanging basket. The scent of petrol mixing with new paint drifts

145

in through the car window, along with coffee beans from one of the cafés on the corner. This, I'm sure, must be how Paris or Rome or Venice or somewhere like that smells. The spring light is so sharp that the pavement is full of shadow puppets. I say to myself, remembering the taste of the cucumber sandwich, the crunch of green on white, that I'm probably a proper posh West End girl at heart. I'm going to have a flat one day with a window-box full of pansies and a tree with blossoms that litter the pavement with a thousand pale pink fingerprints.

And I'm going to look like Gloria. She's like Jane in the *Daily Mail* cartoon. All silky bosoms — my favourite bra of hers is a peachy satin number, swirled with stitching, and these great big pants with satin ruffles up the sides. I've seen her dress up when we're getting ready to go out, and she'll catch me looking and she'll pat her bum and say, "Will you take a look at that? No wonder I have them all slavering . . ." Then she'll curl my eyelashes for me with this little gadget she has and tell me again how special I am: "You're gifted, darlin', no mistake. If Queenie says the coast's clear, if Queenie's socks are pulled up — I know all's well with the world!" she says.

Up West it's not all rubble and houses gashed and luxury all nipped off. Rationing — well, there's rationing, I suppose, but you just don't feel it in the same way, not with the Green Bottles, of course. Nor the nasty cheap demob suits and children hobbling on wooden sticks and the old ladies with their faces stripped and stunned like they've burned and crumbled

146

themselves along with their houses. No. In the West End there are women wearing red hunting caps and silk scarves and check skirts and eating rich cakes. Not tortured poor women. Women like Nan.

Hoisting was the best possible way not to miss Bobby. There was so much excitement, and nervousness, there were just so many *feelings*, brilliant sweeping feelings, to fill you up, to push out any other thoughts. By the time I was thirteen I was the best. The Queen of Shoplifters — or the Best Green Bottle of All. They all said it. I would nick things for Bobby and keep them under the bed at home. A shirt in his favourite lucky blue. Brylcreem. A tortoiseshell comb. Taylor of Old Bond Street sandalwood shaving cream. (I didn't know if Bobby was shaving yet, but when he did, I wanted him to smell expensive.)

It was my daring the Green Bottles admired; my fearlessness. I never glanced back or hesitated or looked shifty. Shop walkers were trained to notice that kind of thing — a nervous look, a furtive movement. My heart might be going berserk, sweat streaming from my armpits down my ribs, soaking my vest and reaching the waistband of my skirt, but I was brilliant at hiding all of that, at ignoring it; at being, as Mum said all those years ago, "a proper little actress".

The Green Bottles would kiss me and feed me violet creams and praise me and dangle their warm pearls round my throat and squirt me with their Chanel No. 5 — so I just got better and better, more daring, more of a *bloody child genius*, as Gloria put it.

147

I remain grateful, whatever you might think, to the fabulous Green Bottles for all they taught me, despite what happened next. It was inevitable. The day came, naturally enough, when I was caught.

The morning starts with Dad yelling at Annie, trapping her in the door because she wants to go out, and a scrap between them, Annie screaming, that brings half the street out to see what's going on. Dad sticks his head over Annie's shoulder and booms at them, "Yeah! Stare all you like, you dozy bitches!" and they go back in again, to twitch at their curtains. The baby — Annie's baby, my half-sister, Gracie, who is about six months old — is sleeping through all of this, in the pram in the front garden where I've been sitting on a wall, swinging my legs and watching, so I decide to get her some shoes.

I can still hear them shouting as I turn down Well Street. My heartbeat is quick, the way it always is when Dad gets the dead needle. I never like to admit this to myself, how frightening he can be. Other memories will float at me, occasions with Mum, times when I'd bury my head under the pillow and whisper to Bunny, but I can't remember them properly, only the feelings around them. I push them away.

I try whistling as I'm bouncing the big wheels of the pram over every stone and crack in the pavement. The pram is a fancy navy and silver one. It has little silver handles to push to make the hood stretch up and a navy gabardine cover with little elastic hoops that slip round the silver buttons on the side. Trouble is, once

148

it's on you can't see Gracie's face. I peep in over this and check that her dummy is in her mouth and doesn't need a new dip in sugar. Saturday. I wonder what Bobby is doing, and when I might see him again. I'm fourteen, and floating through my head is some old storyline from a Nancy Spain detective story about a sleuth called Miriam Birdseye. *Poison for Teacher.* I like detective stories, especially ones set in schools like this one, with its "problem pupils", a phrase that makes me scoff. I'm also dimly aware that something doesn't feel right and that I have a faint stomach ache.

First I go in the ration shop run by old Mr Spinks. He was once a bare-knuckle boxer, and Bobby told me that one day, when Mr Spinks didn't like the fish and chips he was served, he threw the cat in the fish-shop fryer, so I'm scared of him. The place is too small anyway, so I just glance around and float my hand over some socks to mess up the neat piles and then leave. I consider nicking a pair for Bobby, but the stash under the bed for him is getting bigger and bigger, and today the thought doesn't comfort me.

Also the Green Bottles are in Margate for some reason, and I miss having them around to goad and praise me. I choose not to go towards Bethnal Green Road, like I normally would. I'm tired of the rubble — Stein's clothiers is just one pointed finger of bricks left standing. I hate seeing all the poor sad dogs nosing around, nobody to claim them any more. No, I'll go the other way. Not that Mare Street is different. I'm sick of everywhere being window splinters and dust, the buildings all broken open, showing their ugly insides, everything so exposed and jumbled up and frightening, the way you feel when you come home and find your drawers tipped out, after your house has had a spin by the police. Now it's like all the houses have had a spin. One big giant one, by God or the Luftwaffe.

Thinking this, I'm getting deeper and deeper into the doldrums, and I find myself outside James Brooke and Sons, and the only possible cheery thing I can think of is to get Gracie the new shoes. So I leave the pram outside. Red ones. Red leather with little cut-out clovers in the front and a red leather button on a fine strap. They're so sweet they make me drool. They're on a shelf next to some blue ones but the red look smaller — a better size for Gracie. I just pick them up and push the door and walk out into the drizzly rain with them. I'm thinking that if anyone stops me I'll say I was just trying them for size on Gracie's feet.

But no one stops me. No one is interested. I think about going back in for some socks but the rain is now falling harder, making a patting sound on the hood of the pram, and I don't have a coat, or hat. The baby will be fine with her waterproof pram cover. I slip the shoes inside it to keep them nice and dry and manoeuvre the pram around — the trick is to use all my weight at the back to make the front wheels lift so that I can turn it — and begin hurrying home down Mare Street. I feel flat. The red shoes are mouth-wateringly beautiful, but things look as ugly as ever. And I can't show them to Bobby and there's no point nicking a bun from Smulevitch's bakery for him, either . . . The dust and the rubble everywhere turns to slick grey sludge in the

150

rain. My stomach ache is really hurting. I need to go home and get some bicarbonate of soda. And when I have, I'm going to write to Bobby again. Annie mentioned there's a "Borstal hour" when they're allowed to write letters so maybe this time he'll reply.

Did I see a shop walker? There was someone looking at me and usually I would be so good at spying her. I go over and over this in my mind when I get home (in the end I took a meandering route, sloshing the pram wheels through puddles and forgetting my stomach ache, stopping at the sweet shop for some paregorics, then throwing them away because the smell brings back Nan so fiercely, kissing Gracie's nose and making her laugh) and Dad tells me grimly that the police have already been round asking for me. His mood has changed entirely since this morning. Anger always seems to leave him as suddenly as a match flame dies. He's dog-tired now and looks it, with a five o'clock shadow, his ice-blue eyes pale as water. He ruffles my hair with his huge hand and I grab it and hold it there, as he says, "Oh, sugar. What am I going to do if they take you off of me as well?"

I really think he means it. Gracie starts crying in her pram outside but no one goes to pick her up. Phew, I think, I've got away with it — the police have been and gone again. Yes, they know where I live, but it's hardly surprising: our family is pretty well known to them.

I show Dad the gorgeous dolly-sized shoes and he smiles, then sighs and frowns and says I'd better chuck them in the canal. When I pull a face he says gruffly that he'll do it for me. So that's where he is when the cozzers come back.

Annie lets them in. This time they have the welfare lady with them.

And that's how I ended up in the approved school in Kent. The very same day I became a "young lady", as Gloria had helpfully warned me in advance that I would. That is, I finally understood what the stomach ache was, as I sat squirming self-consciously on the nasty green seat next to the young policewoman in the police car. The first time I was nicked was the day I got my first period. The Curse.

But before I got to the approved school, I had my first glimpse of Holloway. Another day, another journey in a police car. They took me to the juvenile wing first, for assessment and to wait for my next showing in the juvenile court. I'll never forget it — the drive towards that awful gatehouse: the building just exactly like something Dracula would live in, I thought, glimpsed from the window of the police car. I craned my head to look up at the waving Union Jack, knowing this would be my last sight of anything gaily moving, anything *free* in a long, long time. Two stone griffins with keys clenched in their jaws glared down at me. There was a pause while the policewoman sitting next to me leaned forward to say something to the driver and a prison guard by the door. The car rolled towards the gate with horrible slowness, to allow me to fully take in every word carved above it. *Let this place be a terror to evil doers.*

I'm sure I cried then, but if I did, I wiped my nose and cheeks with my sleeve and made sure the policewoman didn't see it, licked at the salty taste and told myself that would be the last time. If I cried, it would be because I'd allowed myself the luxury of thinking about Mum, or that I couldn't stop thoughts of her. Remembering that one visit to her, that haunting, castle-like place. Holloway was bigger and scarier than the secure hospital had been, with no countryside around it, just gargoyles and griffins and ugly stone things. That would be me, now, my life, I thought. Stuck in stone. Mum would never know I was here, in the Borstal wing, with the Borstal brats, waiting for people to assess me and write about me and decide, as they had with her, what to do with me.

When approved school was first mentioned in court, I pictured it like I'd seen in *Picture Post* with sexy girls in pointy sweaters fighting and pulling each other's hair. But Holloway was nothing like that. I asked if I could go to the toilet and as I reached the cubicles in the remand wing, flanked by two officers, something skidded out across the floor from under the large gap at the bottom of the lavatory door. My new status as a "young lady" allowed me to understand what this paper item was, but did nothing to reduce the shock of seeing such a thing — soiled too — as it bounced off my ankle.

But approved school was better. A house in the country with locked doors, but no bars on the windows. Thirty girls, mostly tearaways and hoisters and "good-time girls" — it filled the papers, the problem of "good-time girls"; there was even a film with that title, about this real case, the "cleft-chin murder", done by a girl with her GI boyfriend, and the policewoman who came with me to prison was full of it, kept talking about it excitedly and wanting the prison guards to tell her more.

Approved school had five dormitories with six beds in each, and a big recreation room, where we were taught to make pineapple upside-down cake.

What I remember about that school now was the smell in it — a smell of old food, puddings and gravy, and of mothballs and damp, dirty coats hanging in the hall. We had to have daily walks in all weathers, but laundry and baths were only once a week. An unclean, unloved smell. Also I remember this: there were no mirrors. You brushed your teeth staring at wallpaper or bathroom tiles. You brushed your hair by asking the girl next to you if it looked all right. The nuns who ran the school must have thought that mirrors would make us vain, or tempt us to smash them, perhaps make weapons of them.

But fourteen-year-old girls need mirrors: it's the time in your life when you're most puzzled by what you look like, the time you are most anxious to see yourself reflected, to know who you are, whether you're pretty and desirable, or even that you exist. And so I think that the other girls, and particularly Stella, became my mirror. We spent so much time together, seeing only other girls like us; seeing ourselves. We somehow knew without asking things about each other's lives that others would never guess at. And we learned how others saw us too, our reflection in the world. That phrase of Elsie's, "East End slum kids", came back to me sometimes, when a certain nun looked at me, usually Sister Grey, who shrugged her shoulders with a great flourish and told me I was the wickedest girl she'd ever come across in her long, long life. "You're wicked through and through, Queenie Dove." (I'd found a field mouse, and put it in her desk. Which wasn't wicked: it was funny.)

It turned into a competition then. Between me and Stella, I mean. We both had pride and wanted to be the best, and we started to goad each other. Who could be the wickedest? Who could make the nuns despair the most?

Stella arrives the same day as me, along with another girl, who's skinny and buck-toothed with bad-smelling feet, called Valerie Tomlinson.

Stella is a tall girl with close-together eyes and straight hair that she swishes over her shoulder in a way Nan would have said was showing off. I look at this girl keenly, taking in her big bosoms and her shoulders-back posture, and the way she is making tiny chewing movements every so often with her mouth, moving something around in there, as though she's trying to chew gum, although there are signs everywhere saying it's forbidden.

"So many of them . . . that's three new ones this week!" says the wobbly old nun we're to call Sister Grey, sitting at the table and looking hopelessly at our

155

forms. "We shall have to build another wing if this carries on."

"I blame war fever," the other nun says. This nun has her back to us and is built like a gas cooker, straight up and down. She has a voice full of opinions. "These girls are boy mad. They go for anyone in a uniform and the *American Influence* didn't help, either."

This makes no sense to me since I'm in for hoisting and nothing whatsoever to do with boys or "war fever"; what's more, the war's been over now for two years so what on earth are they talking about? The tall girl next to me titters and shifts impatiently from foot to foot. She seems a lot older than me so I'm surprised to read (upside down on the notes on the table in front of me) that her birth date is only the year before mine. That makes her fifteen. Impressive, then, that she's already got Sister Grey snapping her ruler on her desk in irritation.

"You think that's funny, do you, Miss Stella S —?"

Better still, I recognise Stella's name as that of a big Jewish-Irish family in Bethnal Green and I beam recognition at her, so far from home in this country house in darkest Kent. She seems to take a minute to decide whether to beam back, running her dark green eyes over my crumpled pinafore dress and my straggling brown hair before finally moving the gum to one side of her mouth, and half smiling.

"And is that chewing gum, young lady? A disgusting habit — give it to me!" screams Sister Grey. This funny old nun is slightly shaky all the time: her head, her hands tremble, like she's a cup of milk on a train journey, ready to wobble over at any moment.

Sister Grey pushes the wooden ruler towards Stella's mouth and indicates with a shove that she's to put her gum on the end of it so that Sister Grey can walk with it to the wastepaper basket without having to touch it. Stella sticks out her tongue and, with finger and thumb, deposits the rolled up belly-button-sized piece of grey gum on the end of the ruler. Of course, it sticks a little, and Sister Grey gets to the bin but can't flick it off. She gets agitated then, obviously regretting that she asked Stella to do such a stupid thing — why didn't she just make Stella put it in the bin herself? — and the other nun turns around and stares at her, clearly thinking the same thing, and shaking her head, which makes me want to snigger, and almost feel sorry for Sister Grey. I can see at once how it is between those two nuns. A bit like me and Stella. Sister Grey, now really flustered, shakes and stammers and squeaks, and in the end throws the ruler into the bin, and wheels back towards us. Her upper lip is sweating.

"Disgusting! You're thoroughly r-repulsive, you girls. Now get to your rooms."

Stella grins and glances at me. The girl with the smelly feet looks worried and tries to hurry out of the door. First point to Stella, I think. Battle lines are drawn.

"What you in for?" I whisper to Stella, clutching the three belongings I've got with me in my dolly-bag: Annie's nail-buffer, Annie's lucky gloves and Annie's empty cigarette case. They were the only things I managed to grab that day — which feels like an age ago now — when I was first taken for a ride in a police car. Not exactly practical, but since I can't harm myself with them, I've been allowed to keep them in my room.

"Too much war fever with too many boys," Stella whispers back, and I giggle, excited by her willingness to spill the beans. Maybe approved school might teach me something useful, some of those things to do with men and boys that the Green Bottles were always hinting at and laughing over, but never quite spelling out.

It takes a long while to fall asleep, that first night. Stella is in the bed next to mine, and we've been whispering for hours after lights out, and finally I slip into a twitchy sleep, and start dreaming at once. I'm standing above a huge staircase. It's so long and steep that I can't see the bottom; it shelves suddenly like a cliff and you can drop off the end, I know that. Someone is beside me holding my hand, and I think at first it's Nan but then I see her about halfway down, waving at me and smiling, showing her pink denture-gums. So I try to turn my head to see who's beside me, thinking it must be Bobby, but my head won't turn, and I somehow know without being told or without seeing for myself that it's not Bobby, it's someone else. I want to see that person, and I start to panic a little, not knowing if it's someone or something I should be scared of. Is it a nice person or not? But my head won't budge and whoever it is is just out of range. And the panic goes and instead I'm sad because Nan's a ghost, and there's nobody else on the staircase and I feel awfully lonely. I glance over the edge, wondering whether to take a step. Stella's snoring breaks in then, startling me awake for a moment. When I sink back again, I can't find the dream, no matter how hard I look for it.

Dear Bobby,

I've made a friend here and her name is Stella. She's teaching me lots of things like how to smoke. We've found these butts the gardener leaves in the garden where we do work in the allotment and even though they are only Capstan and very squashed up and taste a bit soily we can stretch them out and light them with matches nicked from the kitchen and it's great. Hope you are finding some nice cigarettes in Borstul and have found a good friend like I have. I hope that they are letting you do your Important Touching of things Twenty Times before you put them on.

Love your Loving sister,
Queenie

I push the letter under my pillow, where it sits on top of a small pile of others, tied together with an elastic band. I've finally stopped trying to post them, or expecting a reply. I'm not sure that my other letters even reached Bobby — I always gave them to Annie or Dad to post, relying on them to buy me a stamp, and I realise now that they probably didn't bother.

Sister Catherine — the Big Cheese — sends a note to call me into the office and makes me sit there waiting

159

while she sharpens a load of pencils. I don't mind being there because most of the school day is so boring, just full of rules rules rules, like stand up to talk to the teacher and wait until you're spoken to before saying something, and don't ask questions unless you're asked to, and don't sit there in silence like a big lemon when I ask you something, young miss. Anyway, I've been sent to Sister Catherine's office partly because today I wouldn't stand up when Sister Grey asked me to and partly because there is going to be a visiting Ed Psych (educational psychologist) and I'm to be tested on things like my memory, which any nincompoop could tell you is *brilliant*, and then this other thing to do with my verbal reasoning or something and then this thing called the Stanford-Binet for my IQ — Intelligence Quotient.

Sister Catherine has a thick brow that sort of joins in the middle and shadows her eyes. She suddenly looks up from her sharpening of pencils, sighing really loudly, and says, "You've been here some time now, Queenie. Nine months, I think. And so little improvement. Don't you want to be a good girl?"

I say nothing.

"What would it take, I wonder, for you to be *obedient* for once?"

"Miss?"

"It's Sister Catherine, Queenie, as well you know. If we can change with the times and call our pupils by their first names, the least *you* can do —"

"Sister Catherine, people in Nazi Germany was *obedient.*"

"*Were* obedient, Queenie. People in Hitler's Germany *were* obedient."

"Yes, Sister Catherine. They did what they — were told and that's why they did all those terrible things to Jewish people. I don't want to be obedient, Miss. I want to be an old scallywag — like my dad."

She sighs even more loudly, and sips at a mug of tea on the table. "Indeed. Well you're obviously a clever girl — as well as a downright cheeky one. It's such a waste, that's all I'm saying. You could put your cleverness to a better use, Queenie. You're making life hard for yourself, with this resistance to rules, and your time here is ticking by and you've been sent here to *improve*, do you understand? To —"

She gets cut off then, as a tap on the door is followed by it opening a little and a curly-haired ginger man stands there, a great hulking man with a ginger beard and a stupid smile on his face. The ed psych. He shakes Sister Catherine's hand and they chat for a moment or two — the usual stuff about the shocking rise of juvenile delinquents since the war — as if I'm not in the room. Then he turns to me with a big phoney smile and says, "So, this is the troublesome young missy herself, is it? Well, let's get started, then, shall we?" and he leads me to the recreation room where the lingering smell of pineapple upside-down cake makes my stomach rumble. He has lots of papers, and a timer with a dial that he turns once and sets on the table.

Stella passes the window to the room on her way to gardening duty outside, and sticks her tongue out at me, annoyed, I know, because *she's* not being tested.

She then turns her back to the window and lifts up her skirt, pressing her bum in her navy blue knickers against the glass, hoping that the ed psych will turn round. I blurt out a laugh so loud that I'm sure he will, but the stupid giant just frowns and pushes a piece of paper towards me, and says I'm to "give it my best shot".

"Sister Catherine tells me you're quite a puzzle to them all, Queenie. Quite the most troublesome girl they've ever had . . . but then you're clearly such a clever one, too. She says you're good at maths but to Sister Grey it seems like a lucky guess most of the time, because she says when she asks you, you can never show your workings. You know, how you got the answer. So to them it seems like a fluke, or that you might be copying. Do you know what a fluke is, Queenie?"

A fluke. Like being lucky, you mean?

He pushes the paper towards me again, and the pen, and stands up, heading towards the window. The line of girls in their navy hats, which look like flying saucers on their heads, is aiming towards the allotments, carrying trowels. Stella's skirt is shorter than the rest, the waistband rolled over twice to achieve this, her bigger than average backside fanning out the pleats even further — I can always pick her out from the rest. Him too. Old Giant Ginger Beard is studying her.

So I begin writing on the paper he's pushed at me, and when he asks me questions I answer them, each one, just saying whatever comes into my head, and not trying to be cheeky. The room seems to be getting smaller and I watch him closely, noticing strange things about him. He's fiddling with his tie, tugging it from side to side and stretching out his neck, trying to loosen it. His eyes keep going to the window. His palm, when he puts it down on the wooden table, leaves a sweaty print. And his breath is coming out short, as if he's been running.

"Now I'm going to show you some pictures, Queenie, and some words, and I'd like you to say which picture most fits which word."

He shows me some dumb pictures, badly drawn, and some written words. *Incision*. I choose a knife, of course. *Inspiration*. I point to a picture of a woman diving into a pool.

"That one? You're sure? What about the man painting — don't you think that might be . . . inspiration?"

"You said I could say what I wanted. Now you're telling me. That picture's a man. And I'm a girl so I was thinking of myself. I think *diving*. When I dive into something, I feel inspired."

"So. What do you think *inspired* means, then, Queenie?"

"Um. Like you really want to do something. Like you just think of it one day. Like you're a genius because you dream something up that isn't real yet . . ." I pause, waiting for him to tear his attention back from the window and the girls in the garden outside. ". . . sir."

He turns back to face me, really slowly, and I struggle not to laugh. "Quite. OK, let's go on, then, shall we? I'm going to say a series of numbers and I want you to repeat them back to me in exactly the order I say them. Shall we start with five digits? Here goes . . ."

I get his attention eventually. I drag his attention back from watching outside. I repeat the numbers to him, and then he reverses the order and I repeat them again. This startles him. He coughs and sits up straighter in his chair. He adds ten more numbers to the list, making a great show of writing them down and covering them with his sweaty arm (his sleeves are rolled up now, like we're in a fight or something) and he reads them out to me carefully and I say them back to him and then he checks his own list.

"Hmm," he says, turning to face me at last.

He adds ten more numbers, writing them down on another bit of paper and then he reads them out kind of quickly, gabbling, like he doesn't want me to hear properly, and I repeat those ones to him as well. He stares at the paper in front of him as I do it, holding it close to his chest so I can't read what he's written.

"Queenie, do you have something like a mirror under the table? Are you reading the numbers?"

"We ain't allowed mirrors, sir."

"Can you see the numbers through the paper, is that it?"

"No, sir."

"Do you have an accomplice? Is there a girl outside somehow reading you the answers?"

He swivels round quickly to look into the garden, but it's green and still and full of trees. No skimpy navy skirts, or hats, or fat backsides and thighs in sight. He writes something on his notes in handwriting that, even

164

from here, I can see is ugly, the letters all cramped and forced.

"Hah!" He seems thoroughly annoyed and agitated, and pushes his chair back so hard that it tips up on the carpet as he stands up.

"Can I go now, sir?" I ask.

"Yes, yes, I suppose so. Go back to Sister Catherine. I've other girls to see."

He watches me as I leave the room. I know he does: I feel his eyes on the back of my head. My head, though, I'm thinking. My collar. My hair. Not my backside, my short skirt, not like Stella. I'm beginning to understand other ways to do it, the ways it might work for me. To do that thing Stella talks about. Wrap a man around your little finger.

A few weeks later I have a moment of *inspiration*. It comes on a day in early summer when the window-cleaner leaves his ladder up against the first-floor window — our bedroom — and I whisper it to Stella that night, and I can tell she's annoyed she didn't think of it first because she swears she's already escaped once from another approved school and she's an Old Hand at it and done it loads of times. I'm not sure I believe her. Anyway, I know what's really getting her goat is that it's me who thought of it first because she likes to know more than me on every subject. She loves teasing me because I haven't done it with a boy yet and I Know Nothing Whatsoever about men and I didn't even know that if you squeeze a boy's willy long enough this squirty stuff comes out, which sounds too

165

disgusting to be real and not something you'd think up yourself, unless someone puts the thought into your head. (Once it's in there it's hard to budge it.)

My plan is to climb out of the bedroom window, down to the gardens and then just leg it. All day I'm beside myself with nerves in case the window-cleaner remembers where he's left his ladder, or anyone else sees it and moves it. At tea-time I take one last peep from the dining-room window, and the feet of the ladder show it's still there. We've no belongings to take with us, no money, just a few saved-up cigarette ends, and we'll have to go in our school uniforms because the clothes we came in with were "filthy", according to the nuns, and full of lice or something and got destroyed.

That bedtime we wait in our dorm until wobbling Sister Grey has trembled through her last check on us, and we pretend to be asleep with our nighties on over our skirts and blouses. Valerie and Margaret are asleep, but two of the other girls are awake and stare at us as we strip the nightdresses off in the dim light and put our outdoor shoes on without socks. Then Stella wedges open the window and I gingerly stick one leg out.

"Quick — quick! Don't mess about, Queenie."

It's scary not being able to see too clearly; just a little light trickling from the moon as I grasp the grey wood of the ladder and step backwards down it, Stella's shoes almost on my hands as she hurries to follow me. It's a cool evening, but nice, not damp, not icy, just fresh.

Soon we're pelting through the garden to the allotments, the ground all soggy. We're stepping on the fresh rows of things, the lettuces, and collapsing the poles, but there's no one around and, unbelievably, no one has looked back from the house towards us, no light went on, and we're sure no one has seen us. Then Stella tries the door of a greenhouse, darts into it and, panting, pulls me in there with her. It smells lovely: warm glass and grass and tomatoes, fresh and green and alive. We huddle in the corner, panting, gasping and giggling. It was *that* easy!

Stella says we should eat some tomatoes to keep us going, so we do, feeling for the fruits in the dark, biting into the fat balls until the seeds spill out over our tongues and then, when we feel sure that no one saw us leave, that no one opened the door to the house, we creep out again and leg it through the allotments and scramble over the hedges towards the main road. They are high and we have to throw ourselves at them. I can feel my face getting scratched and my arms too, but Stella, giggling beside me, keeps me going.

And then we're over the other side and blinking, staring at the soft grey track in front of us. It seems to be a hedge-lined road. Stella says she knows exactly where we are, and how to get to London. I'll have to trust her, she says, and I wonder — but privately, I don't say it aloud — whether I do or should ever trust anyone except myself.

We walk for about a mile. Stella says it's a shame we're in uniform, but never mind, some men love that. Stella is full of mysterious comments like that. The things she tells me about men are so unlikely that they

167

make me goggle-eyed. I wonder whether she exaggerates her stories just to see how far she can go. "Your face!" she loves to say. The squirty story was bad enough, but on our long, dark walk together she tells me the dirtiest, most revolting thing. It was this man she used to see, who paid her good money not to let him do it to her but *just to go to the toilet on her chest*. And not even a number one, either: a number two!

"No! You're making that one up! That's like — well, it's just the sort of thing the nuns say, like men are sort of worse than animals. Anyhow, I don't even think an animal would do that."

"You think you're so bleedin' clever, Queenie Dove."

"I am clever, too! I just — you know, I don't think any fella would do that."

"They would too, and worse . . ." she says darkly.

We walk further, smoking the Capstan fag-ends we brought, one at a time, sharing one between us to eke them out, and then I need to relieve myself, and crouch down near a hedge at the edge of the road. Something moves, rushing out just at the moment when I hoick up my skirt and making me jump up and squeal. Stella screeches with laughter and says it was just a rabbit. Suddenly there's the rumble of an approaching engine and car lights. A lorry. A Bedford lorry, we make out, as it comes closer.

Before I can say anything, or run to hide, Stella sticks out her thumb and wiggles her bum right in the beam of the headlights and the lorry jerks, brakes screaming, and shudders to a lunatic stop.

Somebody leans out of an open window — we can barely see him in the moonlight, just the red lit end of his cigarette — and he opens the door and grunts something that sounds like get in.

It's high up in there and warm, and there's a little photograph of Rita Hayworth, dangling from the rear-view mirror, in this long black dress and wearing only one black glove. The lorry smells of fat men and beer breath.

"Too young for a wine-gum, are ya, girls?" the geezer says, offering Stella the packet. His voice is squeezed out, like he can barely breathe.

We both take one, and chew thoughtfully.

It's clear to us both what he's after, and after five minutes of driving Stella says she'll go with him if he takes us all the way to South London, because she's got family there and knows we'll be allowed to stay, no questions asked. He keeps looking for a lay-by, a place to pull over and stop, tapping on the steering-wheel with his hand and sweating.

I'm petrified by now. Stella's confidence is amazing to me. When he pulls over and she nips round the back of the lorry with him — it has a sort of flat bed in the back — I can hardly breathe, I'm so scared for her, sitting high up, staring into the dark, wondering if I dare nick one out of his packet of Player's and settling for another black wine-gum instead. When she comes back I stare and stare at her but she looks exactly the same. He starts singing after that. What if he picks on me next? How long before he expects me to do it, too?

Stella keeps him talking, but sure enough, as we get closer to South London, he starts sweating again and nodding towards me and saying, "What about her then, little Girl Guide, is she a virgin?" So Stella gets him on a promise and says I'll do it with him in the toilets at the first petrol station we reach. I nearly scream when she says this. I'm sitting nearest the door and I almost open it there and then, flop out on to the road and let the next lorry flatten me. Stella is sandwiched between me and him and she pinches me, the part of my leg she can reach, and shoves me in the ribs, and keeps talking. Not talking dirty, though, like he wants her to. She keeps changing the subject. Even in the state I'm in I can tell that Stella *is* clever at this, and that I could learn a lot from her. She seems to know that she mustn't crank him up any more than he already is, like not shaking a bottle of pop. He might just explode then and there and skid us off the road.

So we come to a petrol station and yellow lights flood over us and he pulls the lorry in. He gets out and opens the door on my side, grabs my arm and points me towards the toilet. He follows me and he mutters in my ear, "Right, Little Miss Chesty, get ya tits out . . ."

But Stella screams, "Leg it!" and kicks the back of his knee, which makes his leg buckle, and as it does, I manage it — snatch my wrist from his hand and yank away from him, shouting, "You filthy dirty pig! Your willy smells!" and he's startled by me shouting and probably by *what* I'm shouting — which doesn't sound much like a grown girl but like the sort of thing a child of six would say — and he doesn't want people to look

170

at us so he dumps my arm and I run hell for leather after Stella, just following her to wherever it is she's going, and a pale light is opening up, and it's so good to be back near houses and buildings and smoky fires and buses . . . When I catch her we laugh hysterically — we double up and our ribs ache. We have to crouch behind some bins. We're laughing so hard we make the bin lids shake as we lean against them; they rattle like cymbals at the end of a big show — and that's what it was, I'm thinking: a really Top Dollar performance.

We ended up staying with some Aunt Maggie of Stella's in South London for two weeks. Maggie had mostly raised Stella, it turned out, after Stella had, time after time, run away from home, from a step-father who was always "after" her and who farmed her out to his friends for a price. Maggie was a hoister too and was on nodding terms with Gloria, and other Green Bottles who, I began to realise, were pretty famous all over London; definitely the best at what they did. So I took pride in telling this Maggie that my dad had taken up with one. Probably the first time I ever spoke with any pride about Annie.

My mistake was to go back to Lauriston Road. Of course I'd hoped to see Bobby, though that was stupid because Bobby was far away. I told myself he might have escaped too and no one would have told me. And I wanted to see Dad, and Gloria, and my baby sister, although Gracie was more of a toddler by then, not a baby, and a half-sister if you want to be pernickety.

171

The police got wind of it right away and that was how I was caught. I ended up back in a police cell, screaming and yelling, while they got a welfare officer to come and fetch me. It was a month after my fifteenth birthday. I must have looked a sight — hair unwashed, strange clothes that Stella's aunt Maggie hoisted for me that didn't fit — a pair of dark slacks and a ribbed turtleneck sweater that really drowned me. I saw what they were filling out on the form about me. This screw wrote down that I had "mental health problems".

That did it. Those words. That was the first time I had one of my rages. The power of it, how it roared in me, this anger, scared me, too, if the truth be told, as I sat in that cell, nursing it, feeling it grow and grow like a dark monster inside me. He left me in this police cell on my own, all night, just occasionally lifting up the hatch to peek at me, and I felt this monster swell until it took up the entire cell with me. When the officer came back in the morning with my cup of tea I flew at him. Chucked the slop bucket at him. He ducked. Then I picked up my tea and threw that, too. Right in his face. I'll show you! *Mental health problems*. I'm not Moll, I thought, just sitting here and taking it.

Of course, all it did was to make everything harder. Another visit to the juvenile court. "Beyond parental control," was the verdict, for both me and Stella. And I got a proper sentence then, not a country-house approved school but a place for young offenders. Two long years. No cigarettes. Toilet-cleaning duties. Lights out at half past eight. Keeping your cell spotless and fighting with your cell-mate, who was the most slovenly cow you'd ever come across. No proper knives and forks, just a spoon. Sitting on your stool, staring at the wall so that you could save up your library book because you only got one a week and, if you let yourself, you'd gobble it up in a day. Watched all the time through the little spy-hole. Cleaning out your chamber pot and nearly chucking up when you swilled it into the slops bucket. Stella got sent to Aylesbury and I didn't see her for those two years, not until I was released.

Sometimes now I wonder if those terrible rages were part of some hormonal thing for me, you know, just a normal part of growing up, the way migraines or stomach cramps are for some girls. They used to shock me, really, and I could never predict when one might sweep over me. "You're your own worst enemy," one screw said to me, after another occasion when chucking my stool around in my cell had earned me a spell in solitary and a week on Diet 1 (bread and water). These days the probation officer would have some trendy term for it — you know, something like Self Sabotage.

I wondered sometimes, too, about all those tests I'd done, and what they might mean. Back at approved school, a week after Ginger Beard had left, and before we had cooked up the plan to escape, I'd asked Sister Catherine if I could look at my results.

"You know perfectly well what it says here," she replied, flapping the pieces of paper he'd given her.

I blinked innocently at her.

"You no doubt got hold of your file and changed the figure," she continued. "This handwriting is pathetic . . ."

When I remained silent, she was forced to say, "Should have put something more realistic, shouldn't you? 180! Recite some Shakespeare, can you? Explain Pythagoras's Theorem? Thought not . . ."

I was biting my nails, I remember, a new habit I had developed to help squash the desire to bite her. My mouth was too full to answer.

"You're a deceitful minx. But no one has an IQ of 180 and certainly not a wicked little heathen like you, Queenie Dove."

And that was that.

My Apprenticeship

That, then, was my education. I was about seventeen by the time I got out, and had learned plenty. The girls in the young offenders' place found it hilarious that I was still a virgin and had loads of suggestions for how to put that right. The way they talked (like Stella), I realised that it was *unheard of* for a girl like me not to have been interfered with by somebody. Gloria and Beattie and the other Green Bottles must have been protecting me. I mean, Sly Roger. And others besides.

I couldn't wait to meet up with Stella again and, best of all, Bobby. He'd been let out a few months earlier. The year was 1950 and boys were looking different: a sort of American style. You know, cut-back collar with large-knotted tie, Boston Slash Back haircut and a housecoat jacket in light fawn, normally with brown flannels to match. And there were dance halls everywhere, with jiving, and no one over twenty-five, a few American stragglers left over from the war, and coloured men. There was still rationing — that was a shock, I'd thought it would have been over by then — but things *had* changed, and so had I: despite all the terrible bread, cubes of cheese, sweet tea, and stew with big lumps of pork fat in it, I'd got myself quite a figure. (I've never been one of those women who looks at herself in the mirror and takes everything apart — critical, you know. What a waste of time that attitude is! Young girls today make me sorry for them, always dissecting their own bodies, like they're one of those maps of a cow in a butcher's shop. Me, I take my lead from Gloria. I look in the mirror, slap my lovely fat behind and say to myself, Yep, Queenie, *looking good!*)

I had a tiny waist, just like Scarlett O'Hara. (If I pulled the tape hard it read eighteen inches.) I suddenly had hips, which made the fabric of my dress stretch in these sexy creases across the thighs. As for that lorry-driving geezer back then calling me "Chesty" — what can I say? I mean, I didn't ask for them. But they don't half draw the eye, and if I left one button on my little cardigan (always bought a size too small) undone and wore the bras that Gloria showed me, those conical numbers that pointed them like missiles, well, it made me laugh to see men's eyes pop. They just couldn't help themselves, even the nice ones.

Bobby could hardly believe it was me, that time, when I came back home and we went up to our favourite café on Bethnal Green Road to celebrate. I saw at once that he'd changed too. I didn't know what

175

to say about it. Maybe it wasn't a change exactly, but a certainty, a solidifying of something that had been there all along. Or more likely it was just that I understood more, you know, that I'd learned after my time inside that such things existed.

"Queenie. Would you look at you? All grown-up!"

He gives me an awkward hug, and that's as much acknowledgement as we make about the years we've spent apart. But he's beaming at me, smiling and smiling, and he has a soft dark shadow across his top lip: his first trace of a moustache.

"I've got a load of stuff for you at Lauriston Road. Did Annie show you? A blue shirt . . . but I suppose it would be too small for you now. And maybe they chucked them out . . ." I start telling him.

"Don't worry. I've got this mate — he can get me anything like that."

I try not to feel hurt. I watch him carefully. Mario brings him a mug of tea, a slice of fried bread and a huge plate of bacon and mushrooms ("No eggs!" Bobby insists, with panic in his voice). Mario ruffles his hair and says, "So nice to see your sister back, eh, son? She's a beauty, huh? Some nice boy fall for her now, eh?" and beams at me, and nods towards the new waiter, standing at the counter. "Like my nephew, my Tony!" shouts Mario, while the bloke he's pointing to stands behind the stacked plates with his black silky quiff, shoulders stiff with his attempt to ignore his uncle Mario's words.

176

Bobby looks Tony up and down, then slowly straightens his hair, using a comb from his back pocket and the mirrors above the wood-panelled walls, to make sure it's just so.

I notice Bobby carefully touching everything, whispering the numbers to himself and counting. I notice him looking at the Formica table top, which is almost a shade of yellow, though it might pass for cream. I want to ask him, "How was it, then, in Borstal?" We heard so many stories about the beatings. Stella knew a boy in Borstal too, and he'd told her about another boy who once messed his pants on a long training exercise, a long walk, and the screw made him take them off, there and then, and rubbed his face in it, so that he was covered, stinking, and you could barely see his eyes for the brown shit all over his face.

I try not to think of this as it's making me want to be sick. And it's not just Bobby's quirky superstitions I'm worrying about: it's the other thing that frightens me more. Surely they beat him for that, if not the screws then the other boys. Or did they encourage it? Was that where he learned it? Was it forced on him? This bit doesn't ring true, though. I know my brother and I remember now, sipping at my tea, watching him carefully, the way he was already doting on that older boy, Jimmy, that Irish boxer boy, and liked to mope around after him, and Robby, too, the boy he absconded with, there was something about him . . .

"I'm boxing you know, down at Repton Boys' Club," Bobby says, as if he's reading my mind. His mouth is

177

stuffed with the bread he's chasing round his plate, mopping up brown sauce.

"Great," I say.

"And I've got me some work, too." Bobby glances around the café. The place is heaving, every seat filled. The customers are mostly known to us, and definitely known to the owner, who shouts things every five minutes, like "Geoff! Need a top-up? Maria, was that three sugars now, darling, or four?" The door is open to the street to try to ease the smoky atmosphere but it's still one big swirl of cigarette smoke and hot gusts of frying fat. From a lorry parked outside, a man traipses in and out of the café carrying boxes raised on his shoulder, tomatoes, oranges, which he stacks behind the aluminium counter, where it's Tony's job to slam the keys of the till and pay him. I notice Tony looking my way, glancing from under very black eyebrows and then glancing back, not wanting me to see that he's clocking me. I sip my tea and allow myself a teeny smile.

"Who ordered a weak lemon tea? Was it you, Billy boy?" shouts Mario to someone else. He seems to battle through the fug of sizzling fat to land the mug of tea on the table.

"Yeah . . . there's a Firm I'm fixing up some cars for . . ." Bobby says.

"Cars? But you can't even drive!"

He looks miffed then, and pushes his chair back, replacing his knife and fork really, *really* carefully. Like he's going to be inspected on it: the exact placing of knives and forks on plates. "Paddy's teaching me. He's

178

a grease monkey. He works in a garage down Hackney Wick owned by the Firm. You remember Paddy?"

I don't, but I pretend to, for the sake of easing the conversation again, making things smooth between us. I want to say that it's OK, it's all OK with me, whoever you are and whatever you do, but instead I beam at him, and grin and grin, and try to show him with my eyes how much I've missed him and how glad I am to be back.

"Hear anything? About Mum, I mean?" Bobby asks.

A plate crashes noisily behind the counter. There's a second's silence and then the hubbub starts up again. I look down at my mug and count to five. I don't know about you, Bobby, but I get by *not* thinking about Mum, and not wanting to hear anything about her.

"Annie said she'd been and gone and had an accident in there. Set fire to her skirt with a fag or something," Bobby continues, watching my face carefully.

"How does Annie know anything about Mum?"

"Gloria. Gloria visited Mum. She said . . . Mum was in a bad way . . ."

"No," I reply, after a long pause, spilling sugar on to the table from the spout on the container as I check it's working, then casually stirring my tea. Round and round. "I haven't heard anything at all about Mum. I know she's still there. That's all."

"Well, we've had ourselves a taste of it now, ain't we? Nuthouse, hospital, Borstal, prison, all the same . . ."

A tremor runs through me, now he's mentioned her name. I push my mug away. Mario is on to me at once, asking if I want a refill, but I quickly shake my head.

179

"What do you think of Gracie?" I ask Bobby, changing the subject. "Proper little madam, don't you think?"

And the mood is shifted by the sudden shouts from Mario: "Old Bill's outside, everyone — everybody parked nicely? Everybody all righty?"

Bobby and I take it as our cue to get up and leave.

What eased the feelings, the prickle that Bobby talking about Mum started, was one thing: a trip up the West End to practise my art. It took a while before I dared. Months went by, and I itched to go. I waited until after Christmas, until a day when I thought I might explode if I didn't. Money was tight, of course. I'd been making do on what Bobby gave me, and living at Lauriston Road with Dad and Annie and that whiny spoiled princess Grace, sharing my old bedroom with her. I had coupons but I decided to leave those at home. I had another way to get the things I needed. Makeup, clothes, that sort of thing.

On the bus there, I could hear that screw's voice in my head, telling me I was my own worst enemy, but I shook it off, thinking, Only if I'm caught. Which I won't be.

Pancake makeup. Satin blouses with pussy-bow neckties. Department stores where my old gift for spotting the shop walkers had not deserted me, and my talent for subtly rolling the clothes really, really neatly and walking confidently to the door with them in my bag was as strong as ever. Eyelash curlers. Eyebrow pencils. Nylons. I wore a coat with big wide sleeves, and

180

piled corsets and stockings up them until I could get to a loo and put them in the bag. These were the days before cameras and electronic tags. These were days when department stores were the most glamorous places you could hope to be.

After I was back in the habit, it was easy to stockpile the stuff I needed, to make the change into life on the outside. One time I got involved in a long natter with a girl on the makeup counter in Harrods about cold cream — stocks were low, I think she was trying to keep us entertained — and when she was distracted for a moment by another customer I managed to slip a little tub of Elizabeth Arden face cream into my bag.

It would have been nice to go with Gloria or Beattie or some of the other Green Bottles, but those days were over. They had gone their separate ways, or perhaps got themselves boyfriends, or in more than one case (Josie and Dolly) were inside, doing time of their own.

What comes back to me now about those trips on my own is standing in the Ladies Powder Room in Harrods afterwards, leaning against that cold tiled wall, my hands trembling. I remember dipping a finger into that fondant pink cream, and thinking: it smells like freedom. Or perhaps, to be more accurate, I just thought, never again. This is the life for me. Another time I dabbed myself with the most expensive perfume in the world, or so it was always said, from a lovely shiny black bottle with a red cherry top: Joy. I'd wait until the shaking in my body calmed down, or until I heard the cubicle door next to mine swing and knew someone else had come into the Powder Room. Then

I'd walk out with a spring in my step, smelling of money and Joy, in a way that would have made Gloria proud.

"Shame your brother's a rooty-toot. A fruit. He's gorgeous . . ."

Stella, of course, doesn't mince her words. I think about denying it, but decide not to bother. It's not as if Bobby can hear her. We're in a noisy underground dance hall at the Angel, Islington. Bobby is here with his coloured friend from the boxing club, Landy. We like the way that new places have sprung up since we've been away, mostly coffee shops, but Stella has yearnings to go up the West End, where the men she says are "more dangerous" and where it's *really* happening. This place belongs to another era.

"Too many local boys and old-time spivs here," Stella decides, drawing on her cigarette, and lounging against a pillar so she can watch the dancers. Behind them, on a raised platform, is an eight-piece band. Stella's annoyed because we've been here ten minutes and no one has yet asked us to dance. She only wants to dance with a coloured fella anyway and there's just a handful here, because she's heard they're the best, definitely the best, dancers.

"Not him," I say, pointing to a tall one in an air-force uniform, trying to jive. "Look at him — he's got two left feet."

"Everyone says it about the blacks, Queenie. It ain't just me. They're naturals . . ."

"Just because everyone says it don't make it true."

182

At this point, a man steps our way. He's been walking round the circle of girls at the edge of the room, sizing us up. Stella pushes herself forward and sticks her tits out, nudging me and making it as clear as she possibly can that she fancies him. I recognise him at once from the café in Bethnal Green: Mario's nephew, Tony. Our eyes lock as we acknowledge, with a sort of embarrassment, that we know one another, and his look seems to say that, yes, after all, maybe his uncle was right and I might well be a beauty. Tony takes his hand out of his pocket and grinds his cigarette on the floor. Then he just leans forward and taps me on the shoulder: my signal to dance.

We slouch together on to the dance-floor, and I'm aware of Stella's angry flouncy gesture as she swishes her hair over her shoulder and narrows her green eyes, watching our hopeless efforts to dance with each other. A bit of shuffling; Tony puts his hand in the small of my back once; we stare again into each other's eyes and give up.

His eyes are a pale colour, impossible to work out in this light, but he has thick, silky black lashes and black eyebrows so that they are all you notice, sort of hypnotic they are, and he looks a bit like Montgomery Clift. He assesses me with equal openness and seems to like what he sees: I'm wearing a black dirndl skirt with bands of coloured ribbon round the hem and a nylon petticoat to stiffen it out. I've cinched it in further with a thin black belt and I have on a low-cut black lace top, black shiny courts and Tahitian black pearl earrings.

183

(I've nicked all this: a South Sea Island girl look, based on a pin-up calendar.)

"Let's go up West," Stella says, breaking in and tapping me on the shoulder pointedly. She has to shout over the music and I feel a blast of warm breath on my cheek as she does. "This place is dead as a doorknob — I mean, *a swing band?* Come on, Queenie . . ."

Tony stops dancing and pulls out a cigarette. He flashes the pack towards me and — after a second's thought — towards Stella. We both take one, and stand once more at the edge of the dancers, smoking. I like the way Tony smokes, holding his cigarette very lightly, inhaling gently like he doesn't really need to, lifting his chin and tilting his head ever so slightly to blow smoke out of the side of his mouth, not in my face. He continues to stare at me.

"The strong silent type, are we?" Stella says, shouting again.

"Can't hear myself fucking think over this racket," he replies mildly.

"Well, we're off," Stella mouths, signalling over his head at Bobby, who has lost his mate Landy to a blonde in a red dress. "Up West. Ciao, *Tony*. See you." She says "Tony" with a pointed Italian accent. He doesn't rise to the bait.

Tony turns slightly to see who Stella's waving to. He nods to Bobby, and is it my imagination or does Tony seem pleased that it's only my brother, the pansy, I'm heading up West with?

Outside on Upper Street, Tony and Bobby have a five-minute chat about the fact that Bobby's nearly old enough and surely just about to get call-up papers. Tony's done his national service, he says (he's older than I thought, then), but he knows a fella who has an enlarged heart and who'll impersonate you — you know, give your name, anyway, they don't know what you fucking look like — and fail the medical. He's done it about seven times now, for seven different medical boards.

"How much?" asks Bobby, and I know this strikes him as a good solution.

"Hundred quid," Tony says, walking away from us. "Talk to my uncle."

"Fucking hell," says Bobby, more to us than Tony. "I think I'll get me dad to do me a medical certificate, off of this doctor in Stepney."

Tony gives me a sort of wave, but the way he walks off, decidedly, hands in pockets, tells me that's my lot for this evening. He gave me the tap on the shoulder. He's not going to beg, for God's sake. I stare after him, making sure not to show Stella or Bobby with the smallest gesture or expression that I'm in any way disappointed.

Bobby prefers a pub called the Bag o' Nails — near the Wellington Barracks at the back of Buckingham Palace — to coming to Soho with us. Stella rolls her eyes, and whispers, "Guards officers." So we go on our own. We end up having a hot salt-beef sandwich in the Nosh Bar near the Windmill, and we're starving, biting into the thick white bread and the juicy slices of meat so that the fat dribbles down our chins, making our lipstick slide off our mouths. We dab at our lips with Quickies, clean ourselves up in Stella's pocket mirror.

Then to a spieler in Ham Yard, and because we're young and new, all these men keep coming up to us. Stella plays along — she's fearless — but they get on my wick, and the truth is, like that time in the lorry running away from approved school, I'm a bit frightened. The place is full of the Maltese pimps I've heard about — Epsom Salts (Malts), Stella calls them — and they don't look friendly. Although it was a few years ago, I do remember hearing in school about Black Rita, found shot in her bed in Rupert Street.

I sip my port and Guinness standing up, trying to spot the next man about to make a pass at me and head him off. It's a crush, and so noisy with shouting, music from over the street, and the men squeezed in the fug of smoke at tables, now and then smacking down cards with a yelp. Stella weaves between them, her hand at my elbow, guiding me to the dingy basement lavatory. She wants to know about the Firm Bobby's working for. Haven't I noticed that London's changed now we're out and it's not The Whites running things any more? Billy Hill and Jack Spot teamed up, she says, to get rid of them and she'd be interested to know who Bobby's been working for since he left Borstal — because you want to be sure, she says, staring at herself in the cracked square of mirror as she redoes her lipstick, that your brother's backed the right horse.

As I'm coming back up the stairs from the lavatory, one of the men, this short Yank with a sweaty head, gets up and makes a kind of lunge for me. He's sort of half out of his seat, and I can't help myself: my hand just comes out and swipes him, really hard, across the face. My temper again — I'm instantly embarrassed and sorry for him. A couple of his card-playing friends look up — one big heavy is obviously from Scotland Yard, you can spot them a mile off — and laugh at him as he rubs his cheek.

He's standing up, dazed, and Stella has wedged herself beside him, at his ear, apologising. "She's a virgin," she whispers. "Ten quid."

The man freezes. He was about to step behind a screened-off table where his friends are, but instead he moves closer to me, elbowing Stella out of the way, and looks me up and down the way Dad studies a greyhound. My palm stings where I slapped him, and I rub it down the side of my skirt.

As she sees his hand go towards his jacket pocket, Stella moves in again and says, "We need another ten quid key money. Key money, you know. For the room." She jerks her head towards the door and towards Archer Street and beyond, to some imagined hotel far away.

The Yank is grinning now. We're squashed up against one another and he is pressing against my chest. He puts an arm around my waist and squeezes up closer. "You really not popped your cherry, honey?" His breath is hot in my ear and smells of whisky and cheese. "Or you just kiddin' me? Cos, you know, I don't really care — I'm *loaded* . . ." and he brings out a whole wad of one pound notes, that he doesn't bother to count.

Stella gives me a Look. The notes are hot, down my bra, tucked in.

"OK, it's just over there. Soho Square. We'll show you the way," Stella says. She's pointing confidently but we're not near Soho Square and I know she has no idea where the nearest hotel is. Now my palm is really stinging, and sweating too. I know what she's about. What if he gets nasty?

We pick our way across the sticky beer-slopped floor and through the crowd to get to the door. Not easy in a stiff full-circle skirt that swishes around threatening to knock glasses to the floor. I lean against the door and it gives. We tumble out.

"Leg it!" Stella screams, and we're off, tottering, careering, running — squealing, actually, we can't help it. We race up Archer Street, past a couple of coloured blokes already queuing with their instruments outside the Musicians' Union. They watch us and whistle while Stella pauses for a second to consider climbing up a fire-escape ladder near the stage entrance to the Apollo but thinks better of it, seeing the height we'd have to climb and hearing the Yank come out of the spieler behind us. She tugs my hand and we stumble against the stage door where a brass is fixing her stockings and tells us to shove off so we run on, past the tramps sleeping on Rupert Street. A six-foot tart, wearing nothing but thigh-high boots and a red bra laughs at us as we pass a half-open doorway, and Stella squeals again. She drags me in the direction of Brewer Street market, where they're already starting to put up the stalls, and there's a clank of metal in the distance.

Finally, panting, ribs aching, we stop in the bad-fruit-smelling alley under Maurice House, knowing we lost the Yank long ago. My ankle turned over once in my heels and pain shot up my leg so now I take my shoe off to rub it and Stella leans against me, laughing and breathing heavily.

Stella's doing this quiet, soft sort of cowgirl hoot. I don't think she planned it, but it was the speed that threw the Yank off. He shouted once, made this hopeless gesture with his arm. He must have been drunker than he seemed in the spieler because he gave up the chase so quickly. I hardly dared glance back, but over my shoulder I had a sense of him, just outside the closed club door, stumbling along a little way, then caving in heavily against the doorway of the Artisans' Dwellings on Archer Street. A sorry pang twangs through me. Then I remember his whisky breath, and him squeezing up close to me, shoving something hard against the side of my leg. I might be a virgin, but I'm not an idiot.

I feel like hugging Stella, with the relief and the triumph. Rolling. A well-known trick. Getting the key money for the room and then not putting out. Thirty pounds in total! Silly sod thought he'd given us twenty. That's fifteen quid each and a bloody great gold-mine we've just discovered.

So, that was how we started, Stella and me. Or, how I remember it, our first business venture. Chance, the first time, and after that, more deliberate. We never got quite as much money as on that first occasion: we usually asked for twenty and settled for ten. We did it for a few weeks on our own, finding we could make nearly two hundred pounds a week: a phenomenal sum at a time when working in a Lyons Corner House would have paid us three pounds a week plus tips. We used some of it to pay the rent in advance on a lovely flat, one on the new council estate in Well Street that I'd had my name down for since getting out of the young-offenders place: the Frampton Park Estate.

It was a top-floor flat with a balcony and a washing-line and a little hatch from the kitchen to the front room. The rent was three pounds ten shillings a week, but we didn't bother saving any money after we'd paid the deposit: we used it to buy all the things we could think of — a brand-new gas cooker, blue and red patterned curtains, soft pile carpets, new beds and cabinets, a whistling kettle and sixty bottles of Babycham to keep in a crate in the kitchen. Sipping one from a dainty glass, I would look out and watch birds and clouds and see the poor damaged spire of the church over at Lauriston Road. There was talk of rebuilding it. A new one made of copper, which time would turn a pretty shade of green. But still, that flattened me a bit. I thought I should have aimed for somewhere further away.

Yanks in Soho were generous. Gamblers were easy because they were already distracted. We had to avoid the Epsom Salts and any girls they ran, who'd tear our hair out if they caught on that we were stealing their business. Stella didn't stick to rolling: she was soon back to her old tricks. She genuinely did need money for the key, and she'd disappear for ten minutes — the ten-minute rule: one of the Malts had started that to make the most of business — while I waited nervously downstairs, just inside the door, smoking cigarettes one after another, waiting for the next likely punter to send up to her. Then one night this greasy old fella pulled Stella into the doorway of Barney Lubelle's sax shop and started laying into her with his fists. I was screaming blue murder. I took off my stiletto and went for his eyes and we managed to get away, but it shook us. In the end, what we needed, though we hated to admit it, was a heavy, some muscle. A man to be in the background if anyone, you know, took it to heart.

That was where Tony came in. The third time I bumped into him he was driving a car down Well Street back in Hackney. A nice car: a Rover saloon, glossy burgundy with black paintwork. New-looking. Much too flash for someone who worked part-time in his uncle's café. That told me he did other things. Hadn't he boasted to Bobby that he could get an impersonator to fail the national-service medical for him for a price? He didn't seem to work for a Firm but he definitely had money. He was strongly built. The window of the car was wound down and he rested his arm on it, shirt-sleeves rolled up above the elbow, the skin tanned and softly furred with hair. It was the top of his arm that really impressed. Even through his shirt-sleeves you could tell it was about the size of my thigh.

He had film-star looks. Like I said, Montgomery Clift. Or maybe even Tony Curtis. Something intense that you couldn't fail to notice, that drew all the girls in

191

a room to him. Black hair, short at the sides but folded at the top of his head in a not-quite-stiffened quiff, a full mouth, those unusual eyes. That day he smiled and opened the car door, smiled again briefly as I said, "Nice," to the burgundy leather seats, and took me for a spin, and though he didn't say much, his actions said it all. Like he nodded towards a bracelet I was wearing and caught hold of my wrist to look more closely at it and a little shiver ran along my arm. I was thinking, he's smooth all right, he's confident, because he held my wrist a little too long and then looked straight into my eyes until I blushed just a tiny bit. Then he seemed satisfied, and dragged his eyes back to the road.

It was Stella who asked him directly, eventually, when he dropped me off, back at the flat on the Frampton Park Estate. I knew she was jealous, steaming, that it was me who seemed to have hooked him, but she put that aside and her practical nature took over. She made him come in for a cup of coffee (he wanted Italian coffee, of course, dark and bitter, but we only had Nescafé). "We need a driver," was how she put it. She showed him the bruises on her arms from the man in the doorway of the sax shop and asked him if he knew what rolling was. "Queenie's a virgin, can you believe?" she added, for good measure. We both peered at him when she said that, to watch how his pupils expanded. The irises, once I saw them in daylight in our kitchen, were the palest of blues. I felt dimly that his eyes, or maybe his colouring, made him familiar to me, that he resembled someone I already knew, but it was years later that I realised who it was. Dad, of course. How corny was that, and shouldn't it have been a warning to me? That my first love was, in some way only vaguely noted, like my father.

And there's another thing that didn't occur to me then, in those early days of meeting Tony, days when it felt like everything he did was charmed, every gesture or glance: the way he rested his hands on the tan leather of the steering-wheel as if he was about to start playing the piano when he was waiting at traffic lights; the way he sometimes narrowed his eyes, staring at me, like I was some kind of blinding sunlight; the way, if I stood close to him, he was always so clean-shaven, never even a suggestion of stubble, as if he shaved and bathed three times a day; the way he strode into a room and paused first, possessed it, snagged all eyes before he would move or talk. I loved the way his hands smelt of coffee grounds from the café, or faintly of oil from his car, and how this combination was good, masculine and sexy, when it came from Tony. But the thing that only occurred to me later was this: Stella. She wanted him first and went for him, and Tony chose me. Well, I'm sure you've figured out by now that I'm vain, or that I'm proud: I like to compete and win. That might be why I fell for him, after all, or why I stuck with him for too long. Simply that he singled me out and made me feel chosen, the best. I was young and silly and, God, above all else, I wanted to feel that.

So this first night Tony drives us up to Soho, and we agree a cut: three pounds for him and three pounds ten shillings each for me and Stella, per client. He shakes his head slightly when Stella suggests this, as if it's not the money that matters to him.

"You're tough as old boots, aren't you? You can look after yourself . . . I'm just coming along for the ride," he says.

I'm sitting up front with him, acknowledgement of my almost-girlfriend status. I catch Stella's eyes in the rear-view mirror, see the irritation. She has a new hairstyle though, and it looks great. Short but sort of piled high. Me, I've gone for another pin-up calendar. Flat ballet pumps, Capri-length slacks, shirt tied just under the bust. I sleep in rollers to make my fringe really puff up over my black-linered eyes. It's a warm evening, with a holiday feel to it. The streets are full of girls smoking on doorsteps and boys flattening their hair with combs. Nice wholesome teenagers from milk bars.

Stella slips out and disappears the minute we arrive. She says she'll see us later, around eleven, when things start to change and the clientele is more to her liking. Tony parks on an old bomb site. First we head for a café he knows, past the smells of Russian tobacco, of French pastries from the bakeries, of Italian sausages and Algerian coffee, past the slim girls in their headscarves and slacks milling on the streets, past the sandwich-board man advertising a concert by the Trinidadian Steel Band, past a huddle of West Indians laying out some cards on the pavement and towards the Italian cafés on Brewer Street. This doesn't feel like going to work, I'm thinking, trotting like a little dog beside Tony's huge strides, it feels like a date.

Tony chucks his hat on to the crowded hat-stand by the door and squeezes us into a booth. The tiny woman in black behind the counter has already spied him and comes racing over, flapping menus at us and shrieking, "Tony — Tony, where you been? And who's this, eh, who's this lovely?"

Tony gives her a short smile, friendly and comfortable, and orders us coffees while we decide. The Gaggia machine at the counter swishes noisily. In truth, I know he's going to decide for me. Red wine in tooth-mugs and a huge bowl of something hot and tomatoey, with fragrant green leaves on it, and cheese to shake over it from a glass sugar-pot. At least, Tony says it's cheese, but to me it looks like yellow semolina, and it stinks to high heaven. I do my best not to let on I haven't eaten this kind of food before, and to answer Tony's questions without speaking with my mouth full.

I like the things he asks me. The more he wants to know about me, the more glamorous I feel, the more conscious I am of my bracelet tinkling, and my hair curling softly at the sides of my cheeks in the new style, my soft expensive perfume floating up from my wrist. Yes, I think I'm the most beautiful girl in Soho when Tony asks me questions about myself. How many people have ever asked me simple things like how do I know Stella and how come he ain't seen me around in Bethnal Green before?

My "adventures": that's how Tony describes them, and I'm glad, because that's how I think of them too. But what seems to be hovering over the meal, what has squeezed into that crowded café with us, is Stella's

195

remark in our kitchen on the Frampton Park Estate. I feel sure he's remembering it too. He eats with hungry, serious attention but every so often he looks up at me and then I see it in his expression. I recognise it at once; the word for it pops into my head just as easily as I named that look of guilt in Elsie's eyes all those years ago. And I'm deciding, while telling him about Dad and Annie and that day at the dogs, I'm deciding, in a quiet way, somewhere in another part of me, that, yes, I'd like to. Give up my virginity to Tony.

"So you escaped the school in Kent. What d'you get up to next? Your next adventure," he says, offering me a cigarette from his pack and standing up, the signal that it's time to get to work. I realise I've hardly found out anything about him. I've noticed he has money in his wallet, but as for what he says . . . a few basics and that's all. Tony was born here, to an Irish mother and an Italian father. His father was interned, one of those "enemy aliens" that got sent on a ship to Canada at the start of the war, and died when the ship was sunk by a U-boat. The way he tells me this I know that it isn't unimportant. In fact, I'd say, from his dazzling eyes, fringed with blackness, scarily intense, that this is probably the one essential fact, that it burns underneath everything else about him. He says that the thing to remember is that it is not so very long ago that places like this had their shop-fronts smashed, did I know that? And most of their owners sent to the Isle of Man, you know that, Queenie? I shake my head but try to look concerned, to look like the sort of girl who would never make fun of an Italian accent. Not like

Stella. Somehow I know that now he's told me about his father he's never going to mention it again.

He pays, and fetches his hat from the hat-stand, leaning over the counter to give the tiny old waitress in her enormous white apron a kiss. She shrieks and shouts and moans about the shortage of this and the lack of that — how's she supposed to make a living when you can't find almonds for love or money? I know she's just trying to keep him a little longer. It feels to me like the whole place wants to bask in Tony's attention, that every woman in there is wishing she was me.

It's an eventful night. I catch up with Stella, and we drink some vodka from a flask she's brought. She's cross because one of the Messinas' girls insisted she move on from the room she was using on Glasshouse Street so she's come to join me. She'll give rolling a go, she says, because she's aching, you know, down there, and she needs the laugh. We make a few feeble attempts with the young crowd passing us, and after a bit of banter, one possibility emerges, an older fella, not nice-looking but clean at least, well-to-do, and only about five foot eight, with this silly braying manner. Stella whispers to me that his sort, public schoolboys, usually lick the stamps on the other side, and where's Bobby when you need him? But I nudge her fiercely and tell her to ssh, because he's leaving his friends behind, he's crossing the road with us, he seems to mean it.

197

Stella gets the money first — ten pounds, each note carefully counted out — and then tells him she'll go on ahead to sort the room. Me and this bloke are to follow after five minutes. We stand awkwardly while the silly short geezer smokes his pipe and refills it and keeps looking me up and down, then suddenly tries to kiss me, with his stinking, pipe-smelling mouth. I try not to be too rough as I tug away from him, saying, "Later, darling — come on, my friend must have sorted the room by now . . ." and lead him in the direction we've planned, and where I know Tony will be loitering.

The vodka and the red wine have kicked in a little and I find myself woolly in the head, falling ever so slightly against him as we start walking. We pass the French pub on Dean Street, where Stella will be waiting, counting to a hundred, like a game of hide and seek; the plan is for me to start running then, where drinkers are still standing outside, and where we will be in full view, and the punter will feel too daft to follow. In my flat ballet pumps I can usually run quickly — outrun anyone — but somehow, I think it must be the alcohol, my jerking away from him doesn't quite work this time, and he's much swifter than I'd imagined, and he chases and catches me and pulls me towards a parked car, which he says is his. Now that I've made an attempt to run, I'm not sure what to do. I can hardly go back to pretending that all is as it should be, so as he opens the car door and jostles me to get inside, I start screaming.

Tony appears like a black cat, skulking in the shadows. I look around in surprise, wondering where he could have been watching us from to materialise so quickly. And in an instant I feel the mood crackling around Tony, and my heart quickens and I'm breathless from the tussle, and panting.

"It's fine, this — gentleman's just getting in his car — nothing —" I say, re-knotting my blouse under the bust, patting my hair and groping for one of my earrings, which seems to have dropped off. I know Tony carries a razor; everyone does. The sort that slides open; a Kropp razor. I want to rest a calm hand on Tony's arm, but feel strongly that I shouldn't, that it would be a mistake.

"I paid ten fucking quid! I did!" says the man, in his posh accent, taking it all in: Tony as my minder, or perhaps my pimp. Poor sap still thinks he should get his money's worth.

"Queenie — walk back towards the French pub," Tony says, in a cold, low voice that I haven't heard before.

"Queenie? Fucking 'Dorothy', you said —" squeaks the fella, then makes a snuffled, startled sound and I turn away from him, from his short, suited figure, not wanting to see any more.

I begin walking. A dark thick fog is closing in, the coal-smoke filling the air, along with the garlic and cigars. I can hear music from a jukebox, but that's streets away, along with the holiday mood of earlier, the coffee bars and girls in their full skirts, smoking their Craven A's. Here it's so foggy suddenly that I can't see my own steps on the pavement, only hear them, the soft leather soles of my pumps. At last I can make out Stella

199

at the end of the street, a slim shape in a fuzz of grey, waving madly, calling, "Come, come on, I can hear the Old Bill . . ." So I run towards her without looking back.

My absorbing all this, my understanding of Tony's mood, my anxiety, locks at once into a certainty, an inevitability. It's deeply familiar, as familiar as mash and liquor. It's not a reason to give him up. The certainty of its regular appearance makes you afraid, but you also long for it to happen, so that then it can be over. Prison taught me that. The nose, the instinct for it. Prison, and a childhood with someone like Dad. It's just this: your body can always predict when something violent is about to kick off.

It was later that night or, I should say, early the next morning that Tony came to claim his payment; the gift he was promised in our kitchen by Stella. He came round to the flat as a pink sky was breaking over Well Street, knocking softly on the door, having run, he said, smiling broadly, the five flights of stairs in one minute flat. I quickly snatched out my rollers, and opened the door wearing a new nightdress, a black and pink nylon négligée, hoisted, I have to admit, a few days earlier, with Tony in mind.

He made us drinks, in highball glasses he'd brought with him, and he poured a lot more gin in mine. "For the pain," he said plainly. I remember how I felt beforehand. I felt wobbly, almost dizzy, with fear, with anticipation. I wanted to — I'd heard so much about it. I wanted to know what everyone was talking about, what was going on in Soho and behind net curtains everywhere, if the *People* was to be believed. And I wanted to secure Tony as mine.

When he kissed me, lifted my hair from my neck, I was surprised that a man so strong-looking could be so gentle, so affectionate. He took my hand and led me into my bedroom, which felt old-fashioned — the hand-holding — I mean, and then climbed on to the bed with me, carefully folding down the blanket first, peeling back the top sheet and smiling, grinning, as if to disguise his seriousness.

He was studied, in his behaviour, and deliberate, as he always was, and there was a mood about him, as unmistakable as the violent one had been. It should perhaps have been disturbing, but was, as I remember it, only thrilling. Tony, I realised, did not like to be thwarted. Maybe I should have known better but I was a girl, and longing for someone to want me, so back then, the force of his personality, how *much* he wanted me, was new to me, was the trick and the power; it was dazzling.

I came to dread it, of course, Tony's wanting me. The violence of his feelings, the strength of them. But not that night. That night it was all new, and changed everything. He took care; he was practical; he knew what he was doing. But then he grew crazy, and I loved that he couldn't be deliberate any longer; he wasn't in control of himself. I felt like I stepped out of myself, watching, astonished, while someone went mad in a china shop. We woke Stella up; she was hammering on the wall, he made such a racket. And though I was embarrassed, he was undeterred. He had to have me three times, every which way he could think of, until I relaxed a little and his repeated worried questions and pauses to gather strength and pour me more gin did the trick at last, and it stopped hurting.

He leaped up then, and put on the bedside lamp. The room was full of a strange new smell, powerful. It soaked into the sheets and floated up from my skin. This time he wanted to watch my face, he said, sitting on the edge of the bed and slipping his hand under the covers; he wanted me to feel it, too.

I propped my head up on my elbow, turned on my side towards him, smiling.

Yes, in those early days, I was crazy about Tony too; Tony was a marvel, he could do no wrong.

Rolling isn't much fun when it gets to October and the nights start drawing in, and the gas-lighter is coming by as early as six o'clock to light the lamps in the deepest streets of Soho where this weird old man with a beard goes from post to post, flicking open the casements of the lamps with his wand. It's too unpredictable for us to continue rolling for long, good though the money is, and there are too many brushes with the Messina brothers, especially the frightening one, Gino, the one not shy of using electric flex on his girls if they disobey him.

"You saved much for the rent on Frampton Park Estate?" I ask. Stella looks like I just asked her if the atomic bomb went off. To change the subject, she wonders where Tony is — didn't he say he'd look out for us? She's had to fend for herself these last two nights.

"He's on a job," I tell her, which is as much as he told me, although now that we're officially going together, he has at least admitted what it is: he does indeed work for a Firm. He provides and fixes up the cars for blagging — robberies; and he's often the get-away driver. His boss, I somehow picked up, was behind the huge recent raid of gold bullion, valued at forty-five thousand, just outside the Dutch Airlines offices, off Theobald's Road, which the papers were full of. Only sign of it for me was that Tony was flush suddenly, peeling off crisp white five-pound notes in an inexplicably familiar way. The way Dad used to be.

"Tony don't want me going out rolling, anyhow," I tell Stella, proudly.

"What — bossing you round already, is he?" Stella says, her eyes on the window, watching the pavement outside on Frith Street, cars pulling up, couples arm in arm, five Chinese girls in blue aprons sitting on the steps outside their workplace, smoking and laughing; the place shedding its daytime colours and characters for the darker, smokier ones of night.

"No . . . just taking care of me. I like it, actually."

"Well, I hope he's keeping his socks on in bed, then. If he's taking such bloody good care of you."

I look a bit wide-eyed, pretending I don't know what she means. I wouldn't dream of asking Tony to use a French letter. In any case, I know he'd refuse.

"He's like . . . he's told me about the other way," I say, wanting to defend him. I don't like Stella's

203

suggestion that he's bossing me around; I don't like her thinking that anyone could boss me around. "You know, the Catholics' way. Safe times. And then, when it's not safe, he can, you know, pull out . . ."

"*Pull out!*" She nearly chokes on her tea. Leaning forward, she whispers, "I've heard him, Queenie. I wouldn't want to vouch for his self-control . . ."

I blush, and stare down into my omelette and chips. Then we both crack up laughing.

"God — who's that?" Stella blurts.

A silver Rolls-Royce has just pulled up on the kerb of Frith Street, outside the window of the café we're in: the Caterers' Club. All the while we've been talking Stella's been only half listening, craning her neck to see the comings and goings outside. We like it here because, although it used to be a place for waiters and chefs coming off their shifts, it's now well known as the hang-out of some famous show-business faces from the theatres nearby and some of Arthur Rank's starlets.

I have my back to the window so I can't easily turn to stare. I have an impression of the swanky car sliding by and parking, the commotion it's causing, a black-haired woman in a fur and a curly-haired little girl.

"Is it Lady Docker?" I ask. The woman steps into the café, holding the little girl's hand, while the car keeps its engine purring and the man stays inside, fugging it up with his cigar.

"Queenie!" A blast of Chanel No. 5, a froth of fur coat: I realise at once that it's not Lady Docker, it's Gloria.

"How lovely to see you, darling!" she says, beaming, and nodding to Stella. The little girl bats big eyes at us both. Gloria opens her bag and gives the child a shilling, then swiftly flips open her compact mirror to admire herself. Still the glossy black hair, piled on her head in curls, cherry-red lips, and impressive shelf of bust. I'm calculating how long it is since I've seen her. Not since approved school. She looks . . . older, with a more angular face than I remember. But then, staring at the creases fanning out from her eyes, as she puffs at her nose with powder, I think I just didn't realise how old she was. Older than Mum. Twenty years older than me. So she must be nearly forty now.

Gloria turns to the child and says, "Go ask at the bar for a big glass of chocolate milk, there's a good girl . . ." and the girl turns on her heel while Gloria squeezes herself onto the banquette beside Stella. Her voice, surprisingly posh, reverts to Cockney when she tells Stella to "shove up, gel".

"That your daughter?" Stella asks, watching the child skip to the counter in her velvet-collared red coat and shiny black shoes.

"Oh, if only . . . We like to think so, don't we, sugar?" Gloria says loudly, so that the child can hear. "No — it's my Ronald's little girl. Lost her mum, poor love. Ronald's a widower. His loss was my gain." Gloria gives a little wave, through the window, to the old gent in the car outside. He gives a shy wave back and looks hurriedly forward, as if afraid to catch our eyes.

"He thinks you're working girls." Gloria laughs. Stella gives her a sharp look. "Dear Ronald," Gloria continues, beaming. "Wouldn't touch a brass with a barge-pole. Not these days, I mean. He'd be terrified I'd leave him. What a treasure! Everyone should have a Ronald." Gloria sighs happily.

"What does he do?" asks Stella.

"This is my friend Stella," I say.

"How d'you do, dear?" Gloria, quite a bit heavier than she used to be, squirms a little in her seat to extend her hand to Stella, to show that she's not offended by the direct question about Ronald, then pops her compact away in the pink fur lining of her crocodile clutch-bag. I find myself hoping that she might have a handbag I recognise, or a compact or cigarette case, but everything looks new. Four years. Nearly five. I'm being silly, I tell myself, to imagine that she would have the same things.

The curly-haired child returns and stands radiating sullenness towards us. She bangs her glass of chocolate milk on the table so hard that a little puddle spills. Gloria dabs at the splash with a napkin. "Betty . . ." Gloria murmurs ". . . careful, sugar. My Ronald . . . cars. He owns a big company." She whispers which one, as if the information would cause a riot, then looks around the café, and back to Betty, dabbing gently at the child's chocolate-milk moustache. "He started life as a used-car salesman, did Ronald . . . just like me dear old dad!" She cracks a huge laugh, her gold earrings jingling as she moves her head.

I find myself thinking, How funny that it never occurred to me you had a dad, back then. Or to wonder about your family at all.

Now Betty slurps loudly at her drink through a straw, standing up so that she can blow bubbles in the tall glass and make the maximum noise and fuss. Gloria smiles indulgently at her, patting her arm, then turns her attention to me. "So — great to see you! How *are* you, Queenie?"

"I'm fine . . ."

"I heard from Annie you were . . . back."

"Stella, get us a milk and a dash, will you?" I suggest.

"Huh? Why me?"

"I'll give you the money . . ."

Instead of getting up, Stella just signals to the waitress, making it clear she's staying put. The waitress, standing idly at the counter, puts her pencil behind her ear and hurries towards us, beaming all her attention on Gloria, obviously under the impression she's famous.

Gloria is staring at me, and opens her mouth as if she's going to speak. I think my eyes must show panic, or something, a silent plea for her not to mention anything, not to mention the subject I'm afraid she's going to mention, because whatever she was going to say, she closes her mouth again; seems to think better of it.

"Well," Gloria says, after a few moments filled only with the sounds of Betty slurping up the dregs of the chocolate milk, "I only popped in here to get Betty a treat. Ronald hates this part of town. We live in Mayfair now . . . and we've got another place down in the country. You'll have to come to the house, Queenie."

207

Standing up to leave, Gloria says formally to Stella, "Lovely to meet you, dear. Look after your friend Queenie for me, won't you? I'm very fond of her. And, Queenie — you think about what I said. Everyone needs a Ronald . . ."

When she leaves, she carefully puts some notes under my plate and tells me that dinner's on her. I wait until she's in the car outside before glancing down. Fifty pounds, in brand-new notes.

Stella and I can't stop talking about her after she's gone. "Did you see that handbag?" Stella says. She *is* like Lady Docker, Norah Collins; we're always reading about her — didn't she marry that director from Fortnum & Mason first, and then he died, leaving her a quarter of a million pounds richer? And that was before the fella she has now, the Daimler one. Yes, the excess of it all appeals to us: gold-painted Daimlers, mink bikinis, three husbands. "Shame that the Shirley Temple brat comes with it, in Gloria's case," Stella says, but I disagree. It's clear to me — and, again, gives me a sudden new view of Gloria, the Gloria from my childhood, that Gloria loves kids. Probably wanted some of her own.

"Forty's ancient, so it's too late now. Gloria's — you know — she ain't half a motherly person. I bet Betty's a real bonus," I say confidently.

We've been wasting our time with this rolling lark, we decide, after our glimpse of the gold-and-fur-lined life of Gloria. Much too dangerous and, at the moment, it's too nippy as well. Yes, Soho is lively, and it's definitely a step up from getting ten shillings for giving some old geezer a plate in Cable Street, with the saddest, shabbiest tarts of all, but there are richer pickings elsewhere, we suddenly realise. Stella says she was talking to this girl called Ruth, who was one of the Rank girls, in a film with Diana Dors. She knows her and another girl called Vickie, who works in a higher-class place, a club, with members, where not just any old rag-and-bone man can come in, and you can meet all sorts: racing drivers, actors, dukes, business-men.

"My granddad was a rag-and-bone man." I pout, pretending to be offended.

Stella laughs her brilliant throaty laugh. And that's how we move on to our next job, working a little bit further west. Stella's in hearty agreement with Gloria. Everyone needs a Ronald.

It takes a while but we track her down. We go and visit this girl Ruth. She's working at the Little Club on the Brompton Road in Knightsbridge. It's winter by then. Soho is still strung with bedraggled left-over bunting in red, white and blue but this area of town looks to me like it didn't give a toss about having a new queen: bunting is common.

It's early evening in winter, before the night takes off. I'd talked to Tony, told him that Stella and I had been thinking of getting a proper job, receptionist or something, in a smart West End club, and he said he knew a fella who owned that kind of place, and would ask around for me.

Ruth lives in the flat above the club on the Brompton Road, where she's employed as the manageress. We can smell the wealth as soon as we get to the door, and the sense of exclusivity is what appeals most; that's what we want. People have to sign in this little black leather book when they arrive. Members only, which keeps out the riff-raff.

Stella and I sit with Ruth, smoking and sipping our coffees from these lovely white porcelain cups. Music is tinkling up to us from the club downstairs as the pianist warms up. All Ruth's underwear is drying on the little electric fire — every colour of the rainbow, bras, lace panties, giving off this warm fresh laundry smell, mingling with her perfume: Christian Dior. Classy.

Yes, she's sophisticated, and smart, I'm thinking, and very pretty in a delicate, fine-boned kind of way. She's been in this film *Lady Godiva Rides Again*, with Diana Dors and Joan Collins, and she shows us the photo of them all, lined up in their bikinis. We can hardly recognise Ruth: her hair is black and she's plumper than the fine-featured, jittery blonde in front of us.

"I'm pregnant there," Ruth says, without explaining further.

Diana Dors is easily recognisable: in the middle, of course, hogging the limelight. Joan Collins is the prettiest, with sort of high-falutin' eyebrows that make her look the cleverest too, and a Tahitian flower in her hair. I know Stella is disappointed that her own audition for Rank did not go well: she was told she was boss-eyed. (Her eyes *are* ever so slightly close together, come to think of it, but bloody hell, says Stella, so are

210

the eyes of that new child actress everyone's going on about: Susan Bleedin' Hampshire.)

Ruth has a black silk scarf tied around her neck and dangling earrings in Whitby jet. We're laughing like school-girls over her "little black book" and the kinds of people in it. I notice that she has one hand that's sort of crippled and, seeing me glance at it, she tucks it under her and sits on it. I feel guilty and look away.

As we talk, the couple in the bedroom on the very top floor, above us, are going at it a bit too theatrically, so Ruth gets her broom and bangs it on the ceiling, her eyebrows nearly slipping back into her hairline as she stretches up to do it; then we both snigger again. So. High class though this club is, it's familiar enough.

Ruth is fidgety, never seems to sit still, obviously why she's so slender.

"How did you get yourself this job?" Stella asks.

"Oh, I met a bloke ..." Ruth replies vaguely, jumping up to put the photograph away in a drawer. She sits back down, looking as if she's made her mind up to trust us. "Do you know my friend Vickie Martin?" she asks. Stella nods.

"I met this fella through Vickie. Stephen. I think he's some sort of doctor, a back specialist or something. He's helpful ... you know, elocution lessons, how to tell if a wine is corked, which knife and fork to use. That sort of thing. Helps you fit in. Talk to the toffs."

"Queenie's had elocution lessons," Stella says, giving my arm a little punch. "Can't you tell?"

Ruth gets the Pernod out then, pouring it into these tiny little cranberry-tinted sherry glasses and we sip it. The door to her bedroom is open and I glimpse white tassels, white-painted walls and furniture, white bobbles dangling from the white curtains. She's certainly trying to convince somebody of something.

She gets up to put a record on. "Here In My Heart". Al Martino.

"Didn't I see you in Harrods the other day?" Stella says to Ruth. "What'd you get?"

"Oh — let me show you, it's a dress, with these pleats that open up. Look!" And she rushes next door to the bedroom to get the dress. While she's there I hear the lavatory door open and, thinking she'll be a minute or two, I seize the leather book Ruth left on the floor between us.

"God, Stella, listen to this! King Hussein of Jordan. King Farouk of Egypt. The actor Victor Mature. Lord Montagu of Beaulieu. Billy Butlin. Peter Rachman. Stanley Baxter. Stephen Ward. The Maharaja of Cooch Behar . . . and get this, Stella, Sir Bernard and Lady Docker!"

We fall about laughing. This is the golden ticket for sure. An exclusive club. That's the kind of job we want, and that's where the Ronalds of this world will definitely be found, we're certain. But, better still, it's a world where you can be furlined and dripping jewels: where you can be *self-made*. You know, like people always say about businessmen. He's a Self-made Man. That's me. Queenie Dove, twenty years old. I've made myself up.

My New Job

That's how I got my second job, my first proper job, you could say. Tony was as good as his word and spoke to his boss who, among many other businesses, owned a private club in Curzon Street. I was thrilled: Mayfair, not Soho . . . definitely the part of town I was aiming for, and being a receptionist meant it was indoors at last, in all weathers. My job was to sit at a little desk as members of the club came trooping up the stairs, offering them our big leather book to sign in, smiling, sounding well brought-up, and looking pretty. Also to be discreet and not say anything dumb if — say — the Marquess of Milford Haven came in or the Maharaja of Cooch Behar, probably with Stella's friend Vickie Martin. Not to acknowledge Vickie as someone I knew, just a polite "Good evening, sir, good evening, madam." Not to bat an eyelid if a girl I knew from the East End as Stella Capes signed herself in as Mariella Notvony, or Anita Wimble as Pat someone or other. For this I got ten pounds a week and the use of the tiny flat upstairs.

I left the Frampton Park Estate flat to Stella, who was always hopeless with money, and supposed to be covering the weekly rent. I soon discovered it had never been paid, and there were eviction notices and a big metal bar and council signs all over the door. One night we arrived late with Tony and left the motor running on his Rover. He broke the door in with a crow-bar and we managed to rescue boxes and boxes of our stuff, and squeeze them into the boot to drive them over to the flat in Mayfair. It wasn't meant for two, but Stella and me shared the double bed and she moved into a fold-up in the kitchenette whenever Tony stayed over. All I remember now about that flat was the smell of Nescafé, which we were always making, and that it had a huge white-painted window to the street below and — at last! — geraniums spilling from the window-box, lovingly watered by me.

Stella got work at the club, too, as a regular hostess, serving drinks to customers in the lounge-room where there was a piano and a bar.

The women members of the club fascinated me as much as the men. I spent hours at my desk, studying every detail as they came chattering up the stairs in a cloud of perfume, let their gentlemen friends take their furs, tripped on their heels into the lounge, casually ordering their gin-and-Its. I don't mean the Vickies or Stellas: I mean the Duchess of Argylls and Lady So-and-Sos, or the young debs. The ones born to it. I wanted to see how deep it went, or if it really *was* something I could do myself, work at. Not just clothes and the jewellery, although that was part of it. Not just the way they walked, although that too — chin lifted, shoulders back. No swaying of the hips; too vulgar. I studied their nails, their hair, their teeth, the smell of them, the handbags they carried and how they carried them, their skin, the straightness of their noses. I felt frustrated: there was something I was missing. When I really examined a *lady* (we never said "woman", in those days), I doomily concluded that her difference

214

from me was indeed deep, and hard to fake. Bones and flesh grown from good food, not just in one lifetime but over generations. The jaw, the size of the ears. And most of all the profound certainty of where the next meal, the next hot bath, was coming from.

Well, I couldn't do anything about the basics. Skin that had been pampered by expensive creams rather than cooped up in an airless tenement or inside, except for the exercise hour, does have a peachy quality, of course it does — you only have to glance to see that. Younger poor girls might pass more easily than older ones: Stella had good bone structure, a nice jaw-line, but her teeth let her down. I suddenly thought of Annie — I'd popped in to see her and Dad the other week. Though she was only about forty then, because of her skinniness, a lifetime of under-nourishment, Annie had a face with no padding at all; it caved in on itself. She looked what she was: hardened.

I loved that job and soon discovered two things: there were two clubs, the legit one and another one, just as there were two leather books, one under the counter and one visible on top, and one of them offered quite a peculiar menu. Also this: posh men, educated men, ministers and dukes and barristers, were no different from the types we'd been meeting in Soho: their brains, as Stella put it, were still in their balls.

I decided then that I wanted to look the part, so I went to Diana Dors's favourite hairdresser, and Mr Teasy Weasy turned me into a platinum blonde. I put my hair up in a sophisticated French pleat to make me look a little older. Then I sat on my cream leather stool

215

at Reception, winding my legs around the base; admiring my cream ankle-strapped wedges, hoisted, in lieu of my first week's wage, from Anello & Davide on Oxford Street.

I would, at some subtle signal or playful remark from the gentleman signing in, open my eyes wide and produce the Other Book, then sit back down on my stool and pretend to be busying myself with some paperwork while he flicked through it — with apparent casualness but you could always feel the atmosphere changing, pick up on that strange, flickering charge that meant he would soon point, with a quivering finger, at someone's name (usually French) or description ("London's First Dusky Maiden") and push the book back towards me. Without saying anything, I'd make a softly spoken phone call, and chalk up my "extra" fee, my commission, in a red notebook. The chosen lady appeared in record time (they were all housed in flats nearby) and accompanied him to a hotel where the Soho Don — Tony's boss — had a deal with the proprietor.

In those days, the fastest money for me would surely have come from joining those girls in their profession, and I've often wondered why, apart from the brief bit of rolling, I never did. It's not as if I was prudish about sex. Once I'd done it with Tony, I knew sex was the easiest barrier in the world to cross, if I wanted to, and it showed me that whatever people *said*, sex was happening everywhere. He showed me something much more important, though. Perhaps not many women get this with a first lover: he showed me what *I* could feel, the scope of strange pleasures *my* body was capable of. It wasn't all about him. I was most interested in this.

Once, at the approved school, I remember Sister Grey saying to Sister Catherine, after looking at the files for a new admission and sighing theatrically, "How come *all* these street girls claim to have been abused by their fathers or uncles? I ask you — how likely is that?" Based on my experience of running the club, based on the approved school, based on Ruth and Stella and everyone I knew at that time, I'd say: very. And so I've come to the conclusion that this seems to have been the other reason I didn't join the oldest profession. I wasn't interfered with as a child or young girl; I hadn't already had my boundaries invaded, or been brutalised into feeling that this was my only worth, my only ticket to success — my sexiness. I knew I had brains too, and more than that: flair and brass neck. Determination. More than once, when an older man, or one I didn't fancy at all, rested his hand on my backside, that powerful craving to slap him surfaced. Scared of losing my job, I'd squash this down and sugar it with some polite "Oh, no, *I'm* not on the menu, I'm afraid . . ."

I suppose I just didn't have the proper lack of care for my own feelings; the ability to ignore the anger I felt if someone pug-ugly happened to touch me. This got in the way, of course, of any possibility of pursuing a "Ronald"; a sugar-daddy. I'd leave that to Stella, I decided. I'd read enough magazines going on about how you can tell when he is The One. None of them mentioned the fizz in the stomach just above the pubic bone that I felt whenever I looked at Tony. But they did mention how a room lit up whenever The One was in it. I wouldn't say the room lit up: to me it was more that all the light was sucked from it, concentrated on this one dazzling spot — the spot where Tony stood chatting, or smoking, or laughing, running a comb through his hair.

Later there was a Diana Dors song called "The Point Of No Return". I saw her sing it once in the Bal Tabarin, you know — or was it the Revue Bar? Anyway, one of Paul Raymond's places. I didn't think much of Diana's voice, actually. Little girly, ordinary, sort of falsely perky, not true like my favourites, Sarah Vaughan or Billie Holiday, but somehow the lyrics of this silly Diana number were the ones that stuck with me. *Why not give in? Let yourself go*. On the back seat of Tony's new racing green Rover 3.5 coupé, I let myself go with knobs on.

Still, it was also an eye-opener, working at the club. I won't pretend I wasn't astonished at first and delighted by how fast I was learning. French polishing wasn't what I had thought it was at all. Whipping, tying, Golden Rain — Stella had been right all those years ago when she'd told me the sorts of things men wanted to do to and on women's bodies. And the *kind* of people who wanted to do it! Judges, government ministers, senior policemen, members of the aristocracy, actors, photographers, film stars, company directors, names that I'd seen elsewhere in the papers, usually making statements of outrage at the state of British society, and I had to keep a straight face when they politely enquired whether a certain young lady possessed a bat — you know, a cricket bat — and went into great detail about what kind it should be.

When we were rolling, working girls were picked up all the time by the police, fined thirty shillings, and were back on the streets the next morning. The fine was part of the job, you know, a kind of tax. Business booming on the streets of Soho was tolerated, up to a point. Stella told me about one brass, "Fifi" (they were always called Fifi), who, when a bloke wouldn't pay, left him tied to a bed and went to get a policeman to make him cough up! But I think by then, around the mid-fifties, attitudes were starting to change. The various exposés in the *People* about the Messina brothers meant that the police had to be seen to be cracking down. They did eventually arrest Gino Messina, and things went a little further underground with private clubs like ours, backed by heavies, sweeping the business off the streets.

In the summer of 1955 there was something much more frightening and shocking than that to preoccupy us, though. That was the summer the woman we'd met in her little flat, Ruth, the manageress of the club in Brompton Street, was on trial for her life, for the murder of her lover, David Blakely. Tony got us tickets — God knows how, they were changing hands for about thirty pounds each — to sit in the Number One court of the Old Bailey.

Stella tried hard to catch Ruth's eye from the public gallery, tried to offer her comfort, or a smile, or just recognition — anything — but throughout the proceedings, Ruth simply stared out, dressed in her two-piece suit with the astrakhan collar, her white blouse newly pressed, her hair freshly dyed. She pretended not to see us, not to hear when someone in the gallery yelled, "Blonde tart." In the end we wished we'd never gone. We didn't feel like friends or supporters: we felt like part of the baying crowd.

Ruth looked dejected, hard and cold, nothing like the delicate person we'd last seen giggling and pouring us dainty glasses of Pernod, springing up to show us her pleated new dress. Her voice fell in the hush of the courtroom, where everyone seemed to be holding their breath, as the judge donned his black cap and condemned her to death. I've never forgotten it. "Thanks," Ruth said, without a trace of irony.

"Can you imagine killing anyone?" Stella asks, very suddenly and not at all quietly, staring out of the bus window on the top deck, later that day, on the way home.

I weigh my answer.

"That bit when she said . . ." Stella goes on ". . . *I had an idea that I wanted to kill him* — that didn't half startle the judge. Did you see his face? Can you imagine saying that?"

The evening is warm, muggy, the bus stuffed with cigarette smoke, making our eyes water. We're due at the club in two minutes' time and at this rate we won't be there for another twenty. I wipe at the window with my sleeve.

Stella turns her green eyes to me, aware that I haven't said a word. I'm picturing it, all of it, Ruth so

220

alone, so "upset": her word, a word you use for a child's feelings, surely. What was it she was feeling, really? So desperate, so enraged, so desolate . . . none of those words seems to do it. I know what rage feels like, I'm thinking, so I try and remember that. Times when I've lost it, didn't care what damage I caused to myself or anyone else. That prison officer I tipped the slop bucket over. The freedom. I close my eyes. I imagine how it might have been if I'd had a gun. The white-out feeling. Was she drunk? No one said she'd been drinking. Hooking my finger around the trigger. Can I imagine it? Almost. I try again.

Pulling the trigger. Ending everything, giving it up. The man you love, the children you'll never see. Is it possible to imagine nothing, not-existing, blankness? Yes, almost. Something else looms up at me: a round face. A baby. It's nothing to do with Ruth and it squeezes little hands around my lungs.

"I need some air," I say sharply, thumping down the stairs to the lower deck of the bus, breathing deeply.

"Blimey, what's the rush?" Stella says, clumping after me. She nearly falls against me as the bus lurches. She ties her headscarf under her chin and winks at the conductor.

"Let's call in the Star, see your brother and his crowd of fruits," she murmurs, beside me in an instant, and just as swiftly returning to playful mood.

"We're due at work at seven o'clock," I snap. The bus rumbles along. A lanky West Indian man tips his pork-pie hat and stands up to give an old lady his seat. She shakes her head furiously at him, flapping her hands and resolutely standing, as if the seat's contaminated. Stella chews her gum, still pondering Ruth. Me too. Imagining her in that dress she showed us. The heels of too-small shoes pinching her ankles, her shifting her weight from foot to foot. Sweat trickling down her ribs, inside her dress. A low stomach pain, lying like a hammock: remnant of her recent miscarriage. A gust of Christian Dior puffing from her handbag as she takes out the gun. Lifting that .38 Smith & Wesson in her slightly crippled hand, the hand I saw her slip in embarrassment under her skirt that day in her white, white flat. Now she holds it steady, as she waits for that bastard David Blakely to appear.

That night it's Tony, though, not me, who is jolted awake by a nightmare. The bed is clammy, the sheets twisting round him, his body shiny with sweat. He pierces my sleep with a strange whimpering moan, the sound a cat might make, and then a shout and a thump — he thumps the pillow — startling us both awake. I wrap myself around him and try to soothe him, and he says thickly something about birds, all the birds flying away, he says, leaving the island — where are they? And barbed wire everywhere. "Collar the lot!" Tony mumbles, into his pillow. He always says this when he's having a nightmare.

I get up to make him Nescafé and bring it back to bed and snuggle beside him. Stella is out with one of her new finds: a man called James who works in the international gem trade, and is her ticket, she assures me, to a life furrier and sparklier than Lady Docker's.

She's in his London pad — he has a house in the country too, of course — so Tony and I have the flat to ourselves for once.

I put my cheek on Tony's naked chest, let the soft fur tickle my nose, breathe in the smell of his skin, the coffee and bay-rum hair oil, listen to the steady thump of his heart, like the throb of a big engine in a factory. He shifts me off to sit up a little and sip at the coffee. He hasn't properly opened his eyes and, after a couple of sips, he puts the cup down, next to his hat and his Kropp razor on the bedside table, and lies on his back again, black hair all sticking up like a paint-brush. Soon his chest is rising and falling again in a deep sleep. I hesitate to go back to sleep, to turn off the bedside lamp: I want to listen to his heart for longer. This time, closing my eyes, my cheek pressed to his chest, I think of it ticking, like a gold watch, dropped into a dark cave. He's so solid, and strong, male and real and vivid and hot and beating and . . . Words keep coming, keep piling at me. They pile up and shore up and scream at me that never, *never* in my wildest dreams, no matter how wicked I might be, could I do what Ruth did, what Mum did: kill a living thing, put an end to something — make something, someone, dead.

Most nights at the club Tony is there. He comes upstairs, signs in, smiles and chats to me, then goes through another door into the bar, but he usually sends a glass of champagne out for me, which I hide under the counter to sip between club members arriving.

Sometimes he comes back to chat for longer, and feel me up when no one else is there.

One night this white-haired gent is talking to me, in his Basil Rathbone kind of voice, silly bow-tie and a hunted look, leaning over the counter, obviously hopeful about the Other Book. He's actually talking about the dullest of things, the London pavements being hard on your feet, and I glance over my desk top to see that this old chap is wearing sandals, and his feet are bare with painted toenails, which he's obviously wanting me to admire. As I lean over to do this, I become aware of Tony, glowering, just a few yards from us. The gent clocks him, too, and, murmuring something, seems to think better of asking me anything more and goes on up the stairs to another room in the club. Tony comes over to talk.

"I'm the jealous type," he says. He hands me the champagne glass he's brought me, eyeing the books under the counter meaningfully. He leans over and kisses me. "Take the evening off. Ask Stella to cover for you."

"Oh, yes? What're you offering? A night at The Ritz?"

"No."

Tony stares at the counter again, as if fixated on something. I take a sip from my champagne glass, glance around me. Two girls, student-types, no doubt from St Martin's School of Art, wearing bright scarves, reeking of Carnation perfume, clatter up the stairs on the arms of a man so tall and spindly he looks like a ghoul. I offer them the book and a pen, smile in my best professional way.

224

"Marshall Street baths," Tony says, when the girls have signed in and gone through to the bar. "Hot bath. First class. Bring your own sixpence and a clean pair of knickers."

"You don't half know how to spoil a girl." But I'm trembling: I feel my nipples tighten, even as I pop next door to ask Stella if she'll cover the last half-hour of my shift.

We take a taxi to Marshall Street, and Tony smokes all the way. He sits close, but doesn't touch me. I can feel the muscles in his leg through the fabric of his trousers. I'm thinking, I love the way Tony holds his cigarette, cupping his hand like that, and I love the way he draws on it so deeply — the same way he does everything, seizing the most pleasure possible from it.

"You're very beautiful," he says. I'd been looking out of the window. I turn around in surprise.

"Blinkin' corny!" is all I can think of to say, but Tony doesn't smile. His eyes hold mine. I can't look away. Instead I surprise myself, after a moment or two, by nodding, and then, after a second or two longer, smiling and saying, "Thanks." I somehow know that Marshall Street baths is somewhere Tony takes girls, has taken girls before. I don't know how I know this. I know it with a strange kind of jealousy that mixes with the hot, deep, fizzing feeling in my stomach of something else.

I see I'm right by the way Tony enters the building; the way he pays the attendant, who lets us in by a side door, and by the silent way that money is given, towels

225

offered, and the man looks me up and down. We step through into a long chlorine-scented corridor, past banging doors and down a rabbit warren of corridors ponging of talcum powder and sweat, into a room that Tony has the key to and unlocks. I've only ever been here on a Friday afternoon when the cubicles are singing with children and people shouting, "More hot water in number three, please!" I almost expect someone to turn the brass clock on the door, and tell us how long we've got. Tonight it's eerily quiet, and this is obviously some kind of private arrangement. The room smells strange: of baking wood and mushrooms. The enamel tub in the centre is steaming with water, and someone has added bubble bath: a lavender froth sits on top of the water. Tony puts his towel down on the brown-tiled floor, takes off his socks and shoes and begins unbuttoning his trousers.

His seriousness suddenly cracks into a big grin as he tells me to get undressed. "Come on, Queenie Dove — too posh are we to get in the bath with your old fella?"

"Are you my old fella, then?"

Tony's naked skin in the electric light is the colour of a new penny. I glance down and then quickly up again, giggle a little. Even after all the times we've been together, I feel like I've never stood in front of him as bare as this, like he's asking me to now. He stands very still, then nods briefly in reply. It strikes me, in a funny way, as some sort of declaration. I somehow know that this is as close as he will come to telling me he loves me.

226

My face bursts into a broad smile, and I kiss him. He breaks away, turning his back to me as he climbs into the tub, gasping a little at the heat. I lean towards him in the water as I undo my blouse. Steam makes my cheeks hot and pulls at my curls. My skirt brushes against the side of the tub and is soaked through. The air is liquid and the whole place a big hot cloud; I can only make out a blurred Tony in the heat. I can't help laughing and throwing a flannel towards him, leaning forward to whisper something filthy in his ear, and kissing him again. I'm thinking, as a button flies off my blouse, and my stockings fall to the floor in a wet heap, that another thing I love about Tony is how unashamed he is. I put out my hand and the tip of his penis feels like velvet. I hold it tight, watching his face. He's all mine, I'm thinking.

He's telling the truth about the jealousy, though. I can't understand this: he never minded me rolling. "Because you're mine now," he says.

"You know I'm a flirt, Tony. I never mean nothing by it . . ."

One night, after work he comes to pick me up and take me to a club back in Soho where he still has some business to do with his boss. It's just a clip joint — a one-room job hidden behind a Chinese laundry, with a telephone and a radiogram, full of smoke and musicians and girls smoking American cigarettes. We're handed whisky as we get in the door and Tony strides ahead of me. I recognise a girl — a brass — from Bethnal Green who I'm doing my best to ignore. I'm over-dressed for this place. I don't even like to sit on one of the chairs, not that anybody could sit down in here. It's packed, and it's not a crowd I fancy either, just touts and bookies, whizzers, that kind of thing. I look around for Tony. There he is, leaning against the fruit machine, talking to a tall man with a huge back, flat as a blackboard, whose face I can't see. I watch Tony slick his comb through his hair, the familiar gesture, the way he runs after it with his hand, smoothing; I imagine, without smelling it, the bay rum. It's four in the morning, my legs are aching and I want to go home. Back to my lovely little Mayfair flat. Why did I even come up here?

So I trip over to Tony, my heels sticking on the beery floor, and tap him on the shoulder. He ignores me. I do it again, a bit harder, and I'm just about to say something when he wheels around with mad force, grabs my wrist and, with his other hand, slaps me so hard across the face that I think he just bashed one of my teeth out. I stagger towards the bar. The man Tony is talking to turns lazily to stare at me. The noise in the bar seems to stop for a minute — girl clouted by her boyfriend — and then carries on. I can't see him — it hurts so much. My hand flies up to my cheek, and I feel sure something is crumbling in there, like a macaroon.

"You bastard!"

I grab the nearest thing to hand, an open bottle of beer on the counter top and try to hit him with it. Of course, all that happens is the beer sloshes out, and Tony puts his hand up, grabs it and stops me, but then he starts pushing me outside, upstairs, towards the door. I can feel by the way he does this, his hand on my arm tight enough to twist the skin, then behind me, shoving, how angry he is, and my heart is beating so fast that I feel like I might be about to have a fit, or burst into flames, or something, and I'm ashamed, being shunted outside like this, and at the same time struggling and trying to get away from him.

When we get outside, on to the street in front of the laundry, I start screaming at him — *How dare you slap me who do you think you fucking are* — so he slaps me right back again, and under the lamp I can see that his face is really blazing, and he keeps backing away, saying, *Don't make me, Queenie, don't make me, you hear* . . . His pupils are so wide that his eyes are black, and I know what that look means. I saw it that foggy night when the punter got rough with me, and Tony told me to walk away, tried not to let me witness it. But haven't I wondered all along what simmers at the bottom of Tony's dark heart? I've wondered just what Tony is capable of, how far he might match me for temper and rage, and now I'm about to find out.

Look, it wasn't so bad. He left me bruised and shaken, I had a cut lip, but Tony walked off — he tried to walk away from me. I could see that this was his way to limit the damage he might do, that he knew himself, and was ashamed, too, and frightened. The worst of it was having to hail a cab, blood dripping from my mouth into my handkerchief, my hair mussed, skirt filthy, and feeling like some tramp as I gave out my address and the cabby said, "Huh?" and asked me to repeat it, like he didn't believe me.

It was later, creeping into the flat, not switching on the light, but fumbling along the wall, trying not to wake Stella, that I started to shake. I stopped where I was and felt myself trembling, like a train was rolling through my body. Familiar; horrible. My skin felt cold, as if I'd just taken all my clothes off and stood in an icy wind. I put my face against the wallpaper. I let my knees give a little. I smelt the paint. My throat closed up. Tony, my lovely Tony — I tried to shake the picture of him: the way he'd looked at me, the way my head jerked on my neck as he hit me. Not once, not twice, but — what was it? — *three* times. First with the flat of his hand and, when I didn't fall to the floor, when I kept shouting at him and coming at him, he hit me in the jaw with his fist, nearly splintering it. I tasted blood from my cut lip, and ran a hand along my jaw-line up to my ear. I thought of Moll, then, bouncing back, saying to Dad, after he'd thrown his shoe at her, "You think that fucking hurt?" I still couldn't believe it. No one's ever going to throw a shoe at me! Isn't that what I'd said to myself? And here I am, and it's Tony of all people. Tony, who I thought had saved me, who loved me at last, better than anyone.

Tony is sorry. He's made me a gift, a tiny wooden heart, smooth, ebony. He carved it himself. He's hung it on a silver chain. He stands just inside the door to the flat, on our Welcome mat, not knowing if I'll let him put it on me. I step towards him, into the circle of his hands, and he clasps it around my neck.

I try not to feel disappointed that it's not something costly, something in a red box with tissue paper.

Tony watches me carefully. Next he produces flowers — a big bunch of roses, red ribbon. Better, I think.

"You all right? You all right, Queenie?"

I nod, not trusting myself to say anything, and he puts out his hand and touches my cheek, and when he sees that I'm not going to shake it off, his whole face changes: the light comes back into his eyes. He ruffles my hair, kisses me.

"I tried to tell you, didn't I? I tried to stop you . . . I'm a shit sometimes, you know that . . ."

Yes, I think. I know that now. I can't pretend I don't.

So we jog along as before, and the only change is, we're both wary. As if — the phrase pops into my head — the gloves are off, and we both know what's what, and we don't want to fight again. Tony only takes me to fancy places on my evenings off — no sleazy clip joints any more to do business. He takes me to the Gargoyle on Dean Street, with its lovely painted ballet dancers on the walls and a four-piece band downstairs, and to the oldest dance club in London, Murray's, on Beak Street, which feels more like a grand hotel than a club, where everyone is dressed to the nines and a great long American bar stretches along one wall, making the whole place glitter. Tony knows everyone and it seems like he can get in anywhere, so Stella, impressed, starts to join us, her new boyfriend (James the gem dealer) in tow, to laugh at the way the showgirls' naked bosoms bounce when they dance, and to try to spot a star — is that Cyril Ritchard over there? Isn't that Lewis Casson?

Night after night, Tony appears beside me at my reception seat at the club, handing me a glass of champagne, always waving tickets under my nose. One night it's the nativity play at the Interval Theatre Club — he knows someone backstage — and I wonder if I won't lose my job, taking so much time off like this. Is that perhaps part of Tony's plan?

I'm ill that Christmas, a heavy cold, and I spend two days in bed with Tony. Stella is away at James's place so we have the flat to ourselves again. We take a flask of tea to bed, and whisky, and despite my red nose and snuffling, Tony spends most of his time hot and naked under the covers, running his hands over me, never tiring of telling me how lovely I am, how much he wants me. Even when I'm thick with cold and my head aches, he can always do it, make strange waves rise in me, make me change my mind.

Nearly a year passes like this. A truce. And then it's my birthday and he calls in the morning early to announce that he'll take me tonight to Wheeler's Oyster Bar, best Whitstable oysters in London. I'll be twenty-three. He leaves, telling me to put my best frock on, and says he'll be back for me at seven. He's excited about something, a secret. I think I know what's coming.

Stella and I make a special trip to Liberty's to mooch around in the lingerie department. It's strangely quiet, like being in church.

"Not exactly *husband* material, though, is he, Tony?" Stella says, as if reading my mind.

I'd never told Stella about our fight. I'd crept in that night and the next day when she saw the state of me I said I'd been drunk and fallen, and I've wondered all along if she believed me. Now I look sharply at her. "What d'you mean? He's gorgeous." I snort, in a sort of whispered sneer.

"Well . . . he's from Bethnal Green. His uncle runs a caff."

"Shut up! That's just it. He's like us. He knows what's what —"

"Well . . . thought you had your sights set on a country pile somewhere. A double-D-shaped pool like Diana Dors, a chauffeur-driven Jaguar . . ."

"When did I say that?"

"All right, then, maybe not the double-D-shaped pool but, you know, a fella who can choose a nice bottle in a restaurant and buy you a diamond necklace."

"Tony's reading a book about wine. And, blimey, you're not seriously saying he couldn't get me some tom?"

"OK, OK, he could get the tom, but . . . well, for how long? I mean, before he's nicked or the Soho Don decides to make him eat a red-hot poker or something. I thought you wanted those things for *keeps*."

"Keeps! Nothing's for keeps, is it? Especially not a fella."

We're angry, but whispering out of the sides of our mouths, wandering around, unfolding bras from their tissue-papered boxes and getting the snooty sales girl to

233

pull out drawer after drawer of silk French knickers. I know I'm annoyed, not just with Stella but generally. Something about the whole subject of marriage — not just to Tony, but to anyone — makes me mad. An angry, *bored* mood swells over me, the feeling I had that first night in Holloway, every day the same, the same four walls, over and over . . .

Remembering Holloway always makes me long to nick something. The sales girl has her back to us, opening yet another drawer; I slip a satin Berlei bra up the sleeve of my coat, stuffing it like a handkerchief, without even glancing around to see if anyone is behind me or watching.

Outside, I'm thrilled to discover that the peach-coloured bra is even my size. I dangle it haughtily in front of Stella, who has come out empty-handed. These days, I mostly do it to keep my hand in, the hoisting. I hide it under the bed, never even wear it. Half the time I throw the stuff away.

"Anyhow," I say, in a softer tone, soothed now that I've nicked the bra, like a baby who got her bottle back. I carefully fold the soft fabric and squeeze it into the inside compartment of my handbag. "Why is it always about hooking a man or getting spliced? How — you know — blinkin' old-fashioned is that? Is that the only way to do it? I want to make my own money — don't you fancy that?"

Funnily enough, as it turns out, that's exactly what's on offer. Stella's wrong about the wedding proposal. Tony has a proposal all right, but it's more original than that. The Soho Don is putting up the money for a jewellery heist. And he needs two girls to play the role of fiancées, to choose the rings. There's two thousand in it for each of us. And another thousand if Stella can introduce him to James, her boyfriend, because tom always needs to be fenced, passed on. The Soho Don has heard that James is an international gem dealer, and in his book, such people always have their price.

I said yes to Tony's proposal. I didn't hesitate — it was the best offer he could ever have made, I was thrilled and flattered, and started planning right away: the wigs, the outfits, the timing. But that night we got drunk and had another fight, a bad one. Tony said I'd been ungrateful about the oysters (I said they were like snot), and had behaved like a bloody tart in Wheeler's, spending all my time hoping to spot an American film star — in short, according to Tony, I'd been an all-round spoilt middle-class bitch.

I remember that bit, the exact words, because I had a sense of wild surprise as he said them — I almost wanted to laugh. I didn't, though. Laugh, I mean. I took one look at his pale eyes, now black again — *spoilt middle-class bitch* — then Tony roared, like a bull, a sound so peculiar that the hairs on the back of my neck pricked up. He rushed at me and gave me a hard shove in my stomach. The door to the downstairs floor was open, and I tumbled. Before I knew it, I'd bounced down three stairs. Not the whole way to the bottom. I lay there on my back, winded, and Tony glared at me for a second. He looked shocked. I thought he was going to help me up. The bedroom door opened, and a sleepy Stella appeared and then stood there, as if she didn't know what to do. Tony thundered down the stairs and *stepped over me* on his way out. Stella ran to me and I lay there, gazing at a crack in the ceiling, feeling not so much in pain as ashamed. My lower back hurt, but I didn't think anything was broken, so I let her help me up, saying, "Don't fuss, don't fuss, I'm fine, just a bit winded," while Stella said, "The bastard, I can't believe he did that to you — what if you'd fallen to the bottom? You could of broken your neck."

The worst part was that Stella had seen. I couldn't quite push it out of my mind; Stella wouldn't let me.

Never mind all of that. A sum of money I'd never dreamed of earning had just been offered to me. Stella gave me whisky and I spent the rest of the evening telling her about the heist, and talking about how it might be done — what would we have to do, should we go and look at the jeweller's first, make sure we knew exactly the layout of the back room, the room we needed to be shown into so that we could pick our engagement rings? Stella caught my mood. She forgot about Tony in talking up all the possibilities: would the drawers be locked? How would we get the owner to leave the cabinets open? What security did they have? she asked. Just an alarm button, Tony had said, usually under the counter, we'd have to check it, make sure we never let the bloke get near it. We'd wear wigs and sunglasses: would people think sunglasses looked a bit weird inside a shop? No, they might think we were famous or something. And white cotton gloves, of course, for the fingerprints . . . "But how will we try on

236

the rings?" Stella asked. "Oh, we won't let it get to that . . .

As we were climbing into bed, and after we'd switched out the lights, Stella said, "My step-dad used to knock Mum around. Another reason I was always legging it. It weren't just what he did to me. I got sick of the sight of them fighting. She'd give as good as she got but, you know, Queenie, you're half Tony's size. He carries a razor. That's all I'm bleedin' saying."

That Kropp razor. Sheffield ground, Made in England, with a blade, yes, that Tony loves sliding silkily from its cover. That's not the half of it. For the robbery, Tony had already told me, he'd bought a German Luger, an automatic. He'd shown me it earlier in the evening, and the two magazines it came with, one with six cartridges, one with seven. Twenty pounds, it cost him. Easy enough to find one since the war — there are tons of them knocking around if you know where to look, Tony said.

I heard what Stella said, but the lights were out so she couldn't see my face; I said nothing. The next morning I had a bruise on my bottom that looked like a black ink stain. But apart from that, nothing was damaged. I had reason to worry particularly about *damage* because I suspected, though I hadn't dared to think about it properly, I might be expecting.

Despite what I'd said ages back to Stella, I knew Tony's method of family planning wasn't foolproof. Some of the girls I knew swore by the diaphragm, but of course you had to persuade some doctor, pretend you were married, go through the palaver of having one fitted, and then remember to put it in all the time, and smear it with that disgusting jelly . . . and if Stella was right, men hated it, and could feel it. The blinkin' thing sprang out of your hand and shot across the floor just as you were squatting in some bathroom somewhere trying to get it in . . .

Abortions, though they weren't called that — I'd heard them talked about often enough by girls in our rolling days, or girls at the club, too. Everyone had had one, or knew someone who had. There were knitting needles, or a seriously dangerous, but quicker, way involved having amyl nitrite wafted under your nose and a sort of womb scrape. You could be back at work the same evening, as long as you could stand up. Or there was a doctor in Streatham who would do you safely for fifteen quid. Worst of these stories and the one that stuck in my mind was about a girl called Cynthia. She went to a really sleazy place, and a syringeful of — can you imagine? — *Daz* was squirted up her. She laughed when she said this, and we were expected to as well. Washing powder. "You could of bleedin' done it yourself and saved your money," Stella said, and the others, listening, passing round a cigarette, laughed again.

But there was more. Cynthia said she had pulled her knickers up and struggled home on the bus. And she started coming away — that was how she put it. The others nodded — they all understood: they knew what was coming next, but I didn't. I had no idea. When she talked about the pain, the blinding pain, and the thought that she was going to give birth there and then, on that bus seat, either that or die, I felt hot; I was going to be sick. They were sitting on the fire escape outside one of the theatres, the back of the Apollo on Archer Street, in the early hours of the morning, smoking, legs dangling down on the black-painted ladder to the street. Cigarette smoke, the smell of fat from an open kitchen door somewhere, and the perfume that was always around then: Evening in Paris. My stomach turned over, and I leaped down from the metal perch — it was quite a long drop to the bottom of the ladder. I marched off somewhere. I didn't know where I was going, but I kept walking, practically running. It was a boy, I'd heard Cynthia say. She'd been crying by then. A tiny boy: he could fit in her palm, but she saw his thingy, and everything. She saw him clearly, the shape of him, red and bloody, and she wrapped him in newspaper and buried him.

Oh, God. Not me, then. I couldn't do that.

The day of the heist, Stella and me are silent as we get dressed, checking ourselves in the mirror in the hall, then grinning at one another, sort of shimmering with excitement. I feel just like I did that day we escaped from approved school, how we had to get through all the hours of the day before we could really go for it, with our mouths watering the whole time, our salivary glands prickling, like we were just about to tuck into the best meal of our lives.

We've got our instructions. We've been through it, over and over, with Tony, Joe, and the driver, Jimmy. We've got everything we need in the car: wigs, fur coats, sunglasses. It's been decided that I'm the only one who should open my mouth: I'm the only one who can *pass*. There are two cars, two drivers. The Soho Don has paid for these: two ringers (switched number-plates). The idea is that we'll jump in the first car, then ditch it near Waterloo Bridge where another will be waiting. That's the genius. They won't be looking for the second car.

All I have to do, I'm thinking, as Stella's white-gloved hand rings the bell of the Bond Street shop, and as Tony straightens his jacket and glides up beside me, is use my talent. Do my best. For myself, for the baby, for the future. I feel like I'm stepping on to a stage to pick up a prize. I'm sailing over the threshold, arm in arm with Tony. These are my best skills — all the things the Green Bottles taught me and more. Balls of steel, Gloria used to say. And eyes in the back of my head. And something else — something really special and mysterious. I can feel it kicking in now, as I'm smiling, *smiling*, at the man in the gold-rimmed specs, who adjusts his tie and smiles back.

"Oh, darling," I say, lifting my sunglasses, but only the faintest bit — just enough to point out a diamond the size of a gob-stopper to Tony. "That one's exquisite . . ." And then I turn to smile in my queenly way again at Gold Specs. "Is there a private room, perhaps, at the back?" And I lead him, this man, like a poodle, away from the panic button in the front of the shop and into the back room. There he will unlock drawer after drawer, and cabinet after cabinet, never daring to offend us by locking them up again, and

Stella will be cooing softly all the time, like a pigeon, and then Tony will quietly, gently, close the door to the back room behind us. Joe will be standing in front of it, and it will be too late, as the prickle of something registers with Gold Specs, sweat springing instantly to his forehead, at the very same moment that Tony pulls a gun from inside his coat and points it.

We move fast then. Me and Stella open our bags, no finesse, then throw in whole cases, trays, boxes. These are big bags, deep, huge in fact. The size of a man's brief-case. Funny how no one noticed that when we came in.

"Don't move," Tony says, and Joe stands the other side of this bloke, listening at the door: there is another man, lighting his pipe — old-school security — and a shop girl, pretty in her pale blue dirndl, at the front of the store, but they're paying no attention to what's going on in the back room. Still, we have to walk past those two before we can leave. My heart is clamouring, scrabbling, it feels like, as if there's a whole bunch of desperate kittens in my chest trying to get out. The same old feeling, the jabbering, glorious, *alive* feeling I always have: my head is dizzy with smells — the leather smell inside Stella's new bag, the Windolene of the glass in the shop, the stink of a spray of lilies, old cigar smoke. The powerful smell of sweat coming off the man with the gold-rimmed specs. And the acid smell of diamonds — that most of all. Their smell and the feel of them. Even through my cotton gloves I can feel them, shivering, like living things, long strands rattling and shrieking into my bag.

And then these long seconds have passed. Tony stays behind to cover Gold Specs with the gun, as the rest of us trip politely out of the shop; past the blue skirt at the counter, who has her back to us, doesn't notice our faces behind our sunglasses, the size of our leather handbags and the way we clutch at them; past the bloke with his pipe, who is chatting her up, doesn't notice the clipped way we're walking, practically running, doesn't see Joe's hand folded meaningfully inside the top pocket of his coat.

It's only in the street, climbing into the car — Jimmy's got the engine running — that I hear shots, two shots, and a shout that sounds kind of stunned and unbelieving: oh, God, Tony. None of us had bargained on blinkin' Tony. He's taut as elastic and he just went ping.

I think there's screaming, somewhere. It might even be me. We keep the car door open and we're bouncing along the pavement with it like that as we pull away and Tony comes running out and flings himself in on top of us, a heavy heap, and Stella screams at him, "What did you do, you stupid git?" and are there people looking, I don't know, are there any witnesses?

I'm calm now, flat as a slice of cold ham at the butcher's. "Just drive," I say, leaning forward, talking to Jimmy. "No one's following us. Just drive to where we said . . . and put the wireless on." Jimmy keeps his eyes fixed on the road, and slides easily through the lunchtime traffic. I run hands over myself under my fur coat as if I'm checking that I'm all here, as if it was me who was shot at. I'm pouring with sweat inside my dress, dripping down both sides of my body, like someone just ran a garden hose over me.

"I'm pregnant," I say to Tony, in a whisper — but, crammed in the back with us, Stella hears me and gives a strange, jerky sort of yelp.

"Huh?" Tony shakes his head, staring at me.

"I've clicked. I'm expecting a baby," I say calmly, as the car weaves skilfully, Jimmy's eyes always on the rear-view mirror, and we approach our drop-off point.

"Oh, doll, oh, baby, Queenie — Queenie!" Tony reaches for me, and throws his arms around me, burying his face in my neck, hugging me so hard he knocks half the breath out of me.

I'm suddenly aware of Stella — who has been quiet, so quiet, through all of this — that she's squirming in the seat beside us, crazily tapping at the window, then reaching for the handle. "Jimmy! Pull over. I'm going to be sick!" she shouts, and we pull over, but only for a second, so she can splash sick into the gutter, before speeding off again towards Waterloo Bridge, all praying that the Soho Don has done his bit and the promised car is waiting.

That's the easy bit, the robbery. The waiting, the getting away with it, that's something else. The thrill ebbs away and your limbs feel heavy and dead and the cigarette in your mouth tastes of nothing but ash and the food on your plate is colours and smears and you just push it around, put your knife and fork down and shove it away from you. All you can do is wait, and it gives you a headache, the worry, the fear, that something will go wrong. We listen to the wireless, and pick up the papers, and wonder. What's going to happen now? I jump out of my skin if there's a knock at the door. Stella nearly flies through the ceiling one time when she hears a siren pass outside in the street. It's such a big jump that afterwards we look at one another and burst out laughing.

I picture Tony's gun, now that I've seen it. "It's at the bottom of the Thames — I chucked it," Tony says, and I wonder if I believe him. Falling asleep that night, my eyes flip open as I remember it, the Luger, and smell the sweat again of the skinny bloke with the gold-rimmed specs. All this in yellow light, a kind of heat, like a flash-bulb just went off. Then I close my eyes again and it's fine: there's no gun anywhere. I tell myself, Tony said he got rid of it.

Finally, about a week later, the heist is mentioned in the paper. Stella brings it upstairs and we pore over the account, feeling like film stars: they found the abandoned car, as we'd meant them to, by the river at Waterloo. Tony says the Old Bill probably guessed who was financing it, but they couldn't prove it and there were too many at Scotland Yard who were already in the pocket of the Soho Don — he's sure we're safe. The papers go on about these two dark-haired, well-spoken women, who "might have been hostages forced into taking part in the robbery" — and Stella squeals with joy. "Can't no well-spoken girl ever do a heist, then?" she says. "Bleedin' stupid, these journalists, aren't they?" It doesn't occur to the reporter that we might have been wearing wigs; that we might not be "dark-haired" at all, nor innocent, nor threatened at gun-point. It's only Tony who is given a proper description; he's the only one anyone got a good look at. The witness, still recovering from shock, is a Mr Alfred Richardson, senior sales assistant, who, "despite being short-sighted, is certain the man was in his late twenties, dark-haired, around six foot three in height, and well built". Mr Richardson was "terrified when with no provocation whatsoever the gangster fired two shots at the ceiling".

No provocation whatsoever. Tony fired at the ceiling. It's only when I read this, feeling relief, that I realise I'd been imagining something far worse. I'd thought, I'd not wanted to think, but I'd heard the shots, and Tony had been panting and running, and I'd wondered . . .

I shake this from my head. I feel certain that I know Tony. I know he's got a temper, that he gets mad sometimes. Gets the dead needle, as Nan used to say about Dad. I don't like it, but it's part of the deal. You can't just love bits of someone. *All of me, why not take all of me* — isn't that what the song says? I know exactly how bad Tony can be and, well, if he can love me like he does, despite *my* faults, well . . . I can do the same for him.

That night our money comes through, our payment, and that's all that matters. Tony brings it, and Stella and me are really quiet, like schoolgirls, as we open the envelope, sitting on the cream carpet in my flat, stubbing our cigarettes in this glass ashtray Stella loves, with the big red letters, "CINZANO", on the side, and a bottle of champagne beside us, then whooping as we see the notes and, suddenly, Stella leaps up, showering me with money. She sticks a roll of fivers in her hair like a curler. She pretends to eat it. She sticks some down her bra and glances up at Tony, pushing out her tits.

"Smell it, Queenie — go on, gel! Tell us, what does money smell like?" she says, tumbling backwards on to the rug, laughing.

I pick up a few notes where they've landed and sniff them. What does money smell like? Paper, I suppose. I sniff again, try harder. "It smells inky and sweaty," I say. "Or maybe just new." I don't know. God, it smells like disbelief.

After all that. To be nicked a month later by a young shop walker and a policeman for such a silly small-scale thing. A teddy bear. Some bootees. Baby stuff, literally. A pair of the loveliest white cashmere bootees. And I tried to find a soft white rabbit, like the one Dad gave me when I was born, but had to settle for a teddy, a very small one, serious-looking, with chocolate brown eyes. I was in some sort of dream, sliding around like I was on castors. Maybe it was the hormones because for once my talent — or should I say my *luck*? — deserted me: a shop walker spotted me right away.

Well, there was another reason, perhaps. I mean besides hormones. Tony and I had another big fight. It started because the tension was so high, the waiting, and one night I said something about that Luger, about Tony losing his temper, and maybe — I can't remember — I think I might have said something to him like "You're a fucking liability"; I was shouting I think, and before I knew it, Tony had kicked me, really hard, kicked me under my ribs, and I was doubling up and I couldn't breathe. I was trying to say, but I couldn't catch my breath, the words wouldn't come out properly, "The baby, the baby — what about the baby?" And Tony smacked me in the face, slammed the door and left.

So it's later, it's after that, after I've calmed down, and smoked every one of my cigarettes, and bitten my nails down to the quick, and worried about the baby and run my hand over my stomach and wondered and wondered: is everything all right? It's to make everything OK. That's the reason I did it. I could have paid for them a thousand times over, the cashmere bootees, the teddy, but that wasn't it: that wouldn't work the magic. I had to chance my arm. The baby is fine, I told myself. And just to prove it, I'll go and get it some things, some baby things, and then it — *she* — will be real. I felt sure that I was having a girl. I could see her: a baby, with black hair and blue eyes like Tony's, and fully formed arms and legs, and a little heart that beat.

So now, here I am, and I'm cold again, with that icy feeling in my skin. I'm marched to an office at the back of the department store, and that teddy is plonked on the table between us, where he sits, staring severely at me.

I'm thinking, as they're talking to me, thank Christ there's nothing to link me to the jewellery robbery. Nothing at all. After the fight with Tony I went to see Gloria. I gave her a big envelope with my money in and asked her to keep it safe for me. She looked at me: she was worried about me, she said, but there were no bruises on me, so she didn't ask any questions. "You're the only person I know with money of your own," I told her. I didn't add, so you won't be tempted to dip into it.

Someone brings me a cup of tea. Staring at the bootees, I tell them about the baby, but it cuts no ice. If anything, the policeman they've called in taps his pen even more sharply on the table. The shop walker glances at the store manager and they all look back at me. They tell me I can call my brief but I'll be denied bail. It's a night in the police cells and then remand at Holloway, given my track record in "absconding". They mean from approved school.

"Not exactly a first-time offender, are you, miss? We've got officers at your place right now," the bloke says nastily. "What do you think we'll find there?"

Full skirts and net petticoats and scarves and bikinis and ballet pumps from Gamba, in every colour under the sun. A whole hoard of things nicked over the last few months. I'm picturing them as the airless grey room I'm in gets smaller and smaller, and I stare into my cup of tea. I want to close my eyes. I say nothing, but I'm shaking my head. I know I've done something too stupid to believe. I can barely believe it myself. But at least the cozzers won't find the tiniest speck of a sparkler. Not one note of the money. That's what I keep thinking, as I sit there, swallowing my grey tea, and my heart sinking, sinking, sinking. Whoever said it had been right. I *am* my own worst enemy. Didn't we almost get away with it? I'm the only one who had to test things to the limit, who had to push her luck just that tiny bit further, the only one who had to *do this*.

That night I sleep in the police cell at Shoreditch. A police doctor has examined me to see if I'm telling the truth about the baby. He does it dangling a fag from his mouth, ash crumbling from the end and dripping on to my chest. I know for sure I've clicked: I don't need the bastard of a doctor to confirm it. I feel so sleepy, sort of drowsy and thickened, slower. I dream all night long of jewels, dancing in front of me. I'm stretching out my white-gloved hand towards them and then my hand feels strange to me, like it's not mine at all. I stare at it and follow the arm, the velvet sleeve, and see that I'm right: the hand belongs to someone else, someone who looks like Princess Margaret — a dark-haired woman who is sitting on a table, like a stuffed toy, staring severely at me. Then she bursts into her twinkly royal laugh and I wake up.

Holloway, remand wing. Noisy and hellish. Always women shouting or crying or screaming at one another. No one thinks they should be in here. Bellyaching about their innocence or the unfairness of it all, worrying about their kids or their old man, that's all they do night and day. It's all coming and going, visits from dock briefs; there's always a screw panicking and other screws arriving like a swarm of ants to press some poor screaming wretch back into her cell. People being let out for court appearances, family visiting, new prisoners arriving, it's disturbing. The ceilings outside the cells are so high that walking into lunch along the narrow corridor the sound bounces and the place is alive with ranting and echoes.

I remember it well from that brief visit years ago. The central atrium, the four radiating wings and right in the middle a great show-off staircase, as if the whole blinkin' place is some kind of fancy film-set. The choking feeling of the artificial lights, how everyone's skin soon looks grey and strange, as if we're all under water. The metal pimples along the walls — emergency buttons: how tempting it is to push one yourself, just to get into some trouble, just to bring on an event. It's so frenetic on remand that you almost long to be a lifer, to be on the top floor where things are quiet and regular. We live for the arrival of the Jolly Trolley, six o'clock, with whatever sweeties we've been allowed by On-site Pharmaceuticals. In my case it's just sleeping tablets, but it's still the highlight of the day.

So, Dad and Annie come to visit me, bringing Gracie. I have a second court date soon, and they're here to "keep my spirits up", Dad says. He's grey, these days — he's nearly fifty. His eyebrows have stayed black and bushy, and with a more solid build, and all that pent-up strength, he looks like he should be twirling up the lather in the Russian baths — but he still has his old sparkle, and manages to make me laugh, picking on one of the women screws who he says looks like Uncle Charlie in drag. Dad laughs — glances shiftily up and down the room — then coughs and heaves. Annie pats him worriedly on the back. "Your dad's got to take it easy," she tells me. "The doctor says."

He's had a health scare, I gather: his ticker. And —
he doesn't tell me this himself but Annie does, proudly
— he's got a stall on the Roman Road. Flowers.

"Blinkin' hell, Dad — don't tell me . . . You ain't
planning to go straight?"

He looks embarrassed, shifts in his seat, says
"Nah —" and then, catching a sharp look from Annie,
shrugs. Gracie sits there, quiet in her yellow hair-ribbon
and yellow cardigan, always watchful. Gracie is ten
now, and clever, Annie says, "Like you, Queenie." You
know Grace is *listening* and you know that Annie and
Dad haven't quite got her measure. She could stay at
school, even pass her eleven-plus, the way she's going,
according to Annie. Dad swells up a bit, looks proud,
when she says this. I feel a stab of something fierce, but
I say nothing.

"I don't understand how you're back in here," Annie
chats on, not noticing. "Why didn't she sentence you
then and there?"

"Oh, it's because they asked for other offences to be
taken into account. Or something. They found out
about — well, a couple of other occasions."

Twenty-two other occasions of hoisting, to be exact.
They're so determined to hang those on me, they never
even looked around the club. Never sniffed out
anything at all. They were so obsessed with catching
this one girl, this hoister, that they missed a whole
industry.

"So, that woman — the magistrate, she said
something about not being able to give me a sentence
as long as I deserved. Can you believe that? And they're

waiting for further reports or something. I don't know. I think it might be to do with, you know . . ."

"Oh, yeah. How you keeping in yourself?" Annie says, which is her way of asking about the baby. She was there in court. She heard the prison doctor's report read out. Dad glances at his watch. I know I don't show yet but my hand drifts towards my stomach and since I can't think what to say I just leave it there. A bun in the oven. For some reason I think of Nan.

"Stella's been to see me," I mutter.

Annie replies, too quickly, "That's nice."

"And Bobby."

"Glad to hear it."

"No Tony, though."

"Oh."

"We had a fight . . ."

"Well, Queenie, I think our time's up," Dad says, standing up, looking nervously behind him, as if expecting someone to put their hand on his shoulder. I knew he wasn't listening, but does he have to make it so obvious that he wants to go?

"Isn't this where, you know, that woman was hanged?" Gracie asks suddenly.

"What?"

"Your dad's right — we oughta be going," Annie sweeps in.

"Take care of yourself." Dad gives Gracie a shove towards the door.

"See you in court on Thursday," Annie says. "We'll be rooting for you."

"Ta," I say. It comes out small so I clear my throat and try again, more heartily. "Ta. See you Thursday."

Hard not to wonder how much Annie's rooting is worth. Just as well that, as usual, I've made my own plans.

What that magistrate said about terrible childhoods has hit home a little, but not in the way she meant. It has made me think about the baby. Never mind *my* childhood, too late to alter that, but there's no way I'm going to have a baby born in prison. Women do, of course, all the time. I once read a horrible statistic that babies born behind bars — to convicted mothers — had a fifty per cent chance of ending up inside themselves, before the age of eighteen. Well, *prison* is not the neighbourhood I'd want any child of mine to be raised in.

And then I thought again about Dad going straight, and Annie's shy glance at him when I accused him of it, and what I caught in that look. Hopefulness. Optimism. And Gracie in her yellow hair-ribbon that Bobby would have run a mile from. The whole scene makes me angry, and sick. Dad can do this now, can he, do it for Annie and Gracie but not for me or Bobby, not for Mum? The truth is, he's getting old and fat, lost his nerve, and he's using Annie's nagging as an excuse to give up. It troubles me. It makes me want to get him on his own and shout at him. It makes me want to get hold of Gracie too, and shake her hard.

So it's a long walk back down the winding stone steps to my cell, past the walls with the scratch marks from other desperate prisoners. Gracie's comment about Ruth flares up in my mind — last summer, we were standing by the wireless at nine p.m. exactly, listening to the pips, and knowing that was the time, the exact minute . . . I crush that thought. If I give birth in here, I know I'll never see my baby again. She'll be adopted in a jiffy: that's what they always do. I'd serve the rest of my sentence without her. My dock brief gave me the possibilities and, even with a short sentence, that's what I'm looking at. Giving birth in prison.

My cell-mate, an old brass called Rita, is waiting for me, wanting to share her squares of chocolate and tell me about her little grandson Thomas, how well he's doing, and all sorts of other codswallop I'm not interested in. I don't want to think about Gracie with her piano lessons and eleven-plus and Mummy and Daddy at home, just like in the storybooks. All I know is, no daughter of mine — I don't know why I'm so certain it's a daughter, but I am — is going to start life here. I thrash about on my thin cot, scrunching the blanket up to my ears and listening to the murmur of voices. Of clicky steps and keys jangling outside the door and the racket as the Jolly Trolley passes by. Then, at last, a bit of a hush for the evening. The loneliest sounds in the world: the flap lifting and shutting on the spy-holes as screws walk the corridors, checking up on us.

I drift off a little but my dreams since I've been pregnant have been so powerful that I'm not sure if I'm sleeping or hallucinating. I'm back in that high-castle place, where I visited Mum that day with Gloria. And there she is, as she's been all this time, in her nightie.

254

Newspaper and fag-ends floating round her feet. Her face one minute vacant and depressed, hopeless; the next alive with spite and rage, as it could be, sometimes. *Shall I, then? Shall I send ya?* I'm saying to her, and laughing. Then she's suddenly a girl herself, and giggling, and she has a white horse, and flowers in her hair, and she's in Ireland, a place I've never been, and we're girls together now, skipping. We have new names, both of us, little-girl names — I think we must be sisters, and I'm saying to her, *Come with me, don't be left behind, come on to a better place, the one I'm going to with my new life and my new things, lovely things, and not the bleak grey fog of your life, not the docks, not the gutter — no, this place is full of books, everything is rose-pink and white here, full of cherry-blossom. Come with me, why don't you?*

But you really want to leave me behind, she says, and in the dream, I know at last. She's dead. The spy-hatch opens. I think perhaps I screamed, or shouted. The cell is black again and I can't see Moll's face — she's just a dark, shrivelled child, a little girl with nothing — and I'm crying now. I know it was my fault. I'm an evil daughter, a bad girl. I took a new name, I took new things, grabbed at things — I *wanted* things. I rejected her, whatever she tried to give me that day I visited. I left her there holed-up to rot. She didn't leave me, give me up, as I'd always felt. I abandoned her.

Thursday comes and I'm dressed in my normal clothes to go to court, as remand prisoners always are. I'm flanked by two women guards, and they park on a side street outside the court. As we go into the building, I ask one of the warders if I can go to the lavatory. I'm lucky as it's the Mother Hen one, who knows I'm pregnant. She glances at my belly — quite flat, actually, but I know she knows and she nods at me, sort of embarrassed, and says she'll wait outside. So far so good.

I'm inside the lavatory, and I listen quietly by the door. I start counting, I can't help myself. Come on, Stella, come on. One Mississippi, two Mississippi . . .

Then I hear heels clicking down the corridor outside and Stella's familiar cough, loud enough to let me know she's there. I know she'll be wearing a wig but there's a moment when I think, Oh, my God, maybe someone's recognised her. Could they connect us somehow? I step inside a cubicle, lock the door and stand on the closed toilet lid. The flush chain dangles from the cistern and gently taps against me, as I lean forward, trying to wedge open the window. It's green with the ivy growing on it outside, and has a stiff little catch at the bottom, encrusted with grease and rust. I prise at it, desperation rising in my stomach.

Keep talking, Stella.

This is my chance, this is it, the only one. I have to grab it now. I push and push at the catch, wedging my thumb under it to try to lever it up. It's not locked, just stuck with years of locked-down filth. And then, finally, it gives, with a spring, and one nail wobbles loose and drops to the floor with a clatter so loud I think my head will explode. I hold my breath, and heave myself towards the window. An envelope of window. It's slim, but then, even four months pregnant, so am I. I push the glass out and upwards, like a door flap. I've taken my shoes off and left them on the lavatory floor, toes pointing outwards so that if Mother Hen peers underneath it might look for a moment as if I'm sitting there. That may give me valuable seconds.

It looks a long way down. There's a couple of bins I can head for to break my fall, which will have to be face first. I've wiggled out far enough to the waist to free my arms and shoulders and find myself where I hoped I would be, in an area that stinks of bad drains — the rear entrance to the court, just like Stella described it — so there's nothing for it but to push myself forward and try to steady myself as I crash on to the nearest bin. I wipe my stinging, greasy hands on my skirt and take a couple of heaving breaths, bending double. I try to pull myself together, look around.

Where's the wall Stella thought I could climb over? Surely she didn't mean that one. I have to run and throw myself at it — I realise, with a sickening dread, that Stella must have forgotten how short I am, and that I'm pregnant too, and not as nimble as usual. I hurl myself at it again and manage to snatch at the top with the tips of my fingers, bricks scraping under my nails as I haul myself with all my strength — with a strength that surprises me — and sort of fling myself violently over the other side, tearing my blouse and scraping my arm and cheek, but only dimly conscious of any pain, bouncing back on to my feet and half running, half walking down the main road.

Now the next problem: where's the blinkin' motor? Where's Tony? I smooth down my blouse to try to look respectable, praying that no passer-by will glance down at my stockinged feet and wonder about me. I think I can hear voices, blokes' voices, and at any moment I expect to see the silver badge of a police helmet glinting in the sun.

My stomach rushes at me, and I have to turn towards one of the spiked fences to throw up in someone's garden: my usual reaction to nerves, made worse by the pregnancy. Surely they will have noticed by now in the court that I'm gone and raised the alarm. How long can Stella keep the screw talking? Tony, where the fuck are you?

Then, at last, it's there: the loveliest sight in the world, a car with its engine running and the window open, and inside it is Bobby, my lovely darling brother, in a mohair suit and a spanking new trilby: monkey-faced Bobby, grinning from one blinkin' ear to the other.

The car is spanking new, too. A red Austin-Healey 100, like something from the London Motor Show, one of those sports cars with a cream side panel, just shrieking to be noticed, parked on Queen Victoria Street with the engine running.

I rush to it, and fling the door open. "Blimey, Bobby, you flash git — what a motor to pick!"

His foot is on the accelerator before I've even slammed the door shut and his grinning doesn't stop, his mouth is stretched wide. "Is that all the fucking

258

thanks I get? Thought I'd greet you in style — you know, in the manner . . ."

I lean over and squeeze him, making his hands in their leather gloves wobble on the wheel a bit. He nods towards a bag and I reach over and pick out what he's brought me: a hilarious Diana Dors wig and a pair of cat's-eye sunglasses — and we're off, squealing up Liverpool Street, our hearts soaring towards the true blue sky, heading towards Hackney, laughing and shouting: hysterical. I've never loved my brother more.

He takes me to a new flat, in Bethnal Green, wanting to show it off. He's got a new boyfriend. No cozzer would connect Bobby and the new boyfriend with this place: no one will look for me here. He doesn't tell me this, but it's clear the Austin-Healey 100 was a gift, and someone else is paying the rent on his new swish home. It's hilarious, the décor. Cockney Moroccan: rugs, leather, tassels, silk hangings, little tea-glasses on a brass tray. I look around in wonder, then sit down heavily. I dab at my cheek with one finger, feeling a long scratch, like the little raised teeth of a zip.

"You OK?"

"Yeah. Could I have a drink of water?"

He brings me it in one of the Moroccan tea-glasses, and offers me a cigarette too, from some silly scented tray. My hand is shaking but I sip slowly, trying to calm myself. "Where's all this swanky stuff from?" I ask Bobby. I remember a conversation with Stella, in the lavatory of the spieler at Ham Yard all those years ago, when she said she hoped Bobby was working for the right Firm. Everyone knows that these days it's the Krays, not Spot and Hill, who are running things. The Soho Don set them going, like a big gold watch.

"Later," Bobby says. "Stella says you're — she told me . . ."

My brother, the hard man. Can't bring himself to say the word "expecting".

"Yeah, I am. That's OK. I feel OK. Just because I've clicked I can still work, you know. I'm not an invalid."

"We got to hide you. You can't go up West, or any of your old places. Look, see here, what I built . . ." And he shows me how, in one of the wardrobes, behind his rows of stiff new shirts (all from the same shop on Jermyn Street and mostly blues and whites — of course, yellow is nowhere to be seen), there's a false wooden panel. If you peel it away there's quite a big space, enough for me to stand in, even when I'm fat as a whale.

His new place smells like disinfectant, for all the Moroccan leather wafting around. Bobby seems to have grown even more strange in his habits, and compulsively fastidious; maybe it's his reaction to those years when Mum let him stink the place out like a little animal. Again I wonder if this is a boyfriend or a boss. Probably safer not to ask. In any case, probably both.

Bobby seems agitated, can't sit still, smoking and prowling. "D'you mind if I go out? I could pick up the papers at King's Cross when they come out. See if they mention any breakouts by remand prisoners."

"Good idea."

He wanders into the kitchen and I follow him. That, too, is all spanking, like something right out of one of the London shows. All mod cons. Not a banana or a lemon allowed to spoil the colour-scheme: pale blue and tomato red. He leans his back against the refrigerator and he's staring at me. "You heard, then? Did Gloria tell you?" he asks.

"Heard what?" But I know. I do know what he's going to say, and why it's him somehow, who picked me up, not Tony.

"Is it Mum?" I ask.

"Yeah."

I stand there smoking and staring, and there's a funny little movement inside me, like bubbles popping. Quickening. The baby. "I had the weirdest dream about her, when I was inside," I tell Bobby. I'm dry-eyed. Neither of us is crying, but our voices are very quiet and the kitchen feels full, shimmering, so that's there's hardly space to take a breath.

"I know you visited her that one time," Bobby says. "I always meant to . . ."

"We should of gone again. We should of both gone. What happened?"

"You know she burned herself? She was ill for a good long while after that. Heavier drugs. Then . . . she never recovered."

I'd known. I'd known that night. That I would never see her again, and I'd made no effort to see her or find out.

"Will there be a funeral?" I try to make my voice sound neutral.

"We missed it. Like everything else."

Bobby's face. His eyes glitter, but no tears fall. I watch him carefully and he looks away, puts his hand up, as if to hide his expression from me.

"I'm hard to find," he says, "moving about, you know. Dad didn't know about this place. Annie tried sniffing around . . . I had to wait till Gloria found me."

I think of Dad and Annie visiting me in prison, and wonder. Dad's cowardice meant he always avoided talking to us about Moll, acted like she didn't exist, after Annie moved in. What little I knew, I'd found out from Gloria and from guesswork. I'd figured out what Mum's sentence must have been: indefinite. Probably Mum had hoped that pleading criminal insanity would mean a lighter sentence than prison, that going to a hospital would be easier. She hadn't reckoned on secure hospitals, and drugs, and her own hopelessness, or the "indefinite sentence" idea, the fact that for you to get out, someone has to be interested: someone high up has to care, has to plead your case before the medical superintendent.

So Dad hadn't bothered to tell me. I remember now how quick he was to get up, during the visit with Annie and Grace, how shifty. How he wasn't really listening to me; in a hurry to get away. I thought at the time it was because he was embarrassed at Annie blabbing on about him going straight, or about his ticker. But now I see. It was more than that. The bastard knew; he'd decided not to tell me. And — this is something I cling to, this is the only thing that makes it bearable — I think he was ashamed. For once in his life he was

262

ashamed of his own ducking and diving, knew himself to be a coward. Maybe my dream that night about Moll just confirmed what was hovering around us, unsaid.

"Do they think she — done it deliberately?" I wish I hadn't said this. I don't want to know the answer.

Bobby sighs then. If I put out a hand to touch his skin it would rustle, like sandpaper. He looks so old and tired. His fingers are tap-tapping on the counter. He stubs his cigarette in a saucer he then carefully washes and turns away from me. "Who knows?" he says quietly, and I wonder if he does, if he's keeping it from me.

He turns back and we stare at one another. Then, expressionless, he nods, and opens the refrigerator. It's cavernous, all gleaming white shelves: empty except for one pint of milk. He pours me a glass and hands it to me. I stare at him. He's only about five seven. Jockey-sized. On tiptoe I can almost reach him. He's not that little monkey-boy I stole my first bottle of milk for, but we're motherless again, I think, unable to stop such a funny old-fashioned expression popping up. Fending for ourselves.

"You have to eat," he says, a little sheepishly. "For the . . . you know. I'll send Stella over to visit, and whenever you hear this knock . . ." he raps a little tune on the door frame ". . . you'll know it's me or a mate."

I nod, sip the milk.

"OK? You OK? You don't mind me going now?"

I do mind. "I'll be all right," I say. "You go off. I know you've got stuff to do." Then, "Bobby?"

He looks at me as if he's been expecting this question. "What do you think?" I say. "D'you think he ever loved her?"

"I don't know. Yeah. Maybe. In his way."

"And d'you think she was, you know, what they said? Not her ticket? Was it the way Dad treated her? Or was it, you know, the baby? What if — what if it happens to me?"

"God, Queenie. I went away. I was — what? — five years old. I don't remember nothing. Why the fuck are you asking me?"

I nod, and he tries to smile, to soften what he just said. "And . . . you know, if you make yourself a tea or something, use a coaster."

I almost laugh, but instead I nod and make a big fuss of washing out the glass in the bowl in the sink.

After Bobby has gone I shed a few tears. Only a few. Then I wander round the flat, picking up red velvet cushions, and sliding paintings to look behind them. I play a game to see if I can spot anything yellow at all, one tiny spot of it, but I can't. Then I sit on the lavatory (even in this room it's red-tasselled curtains and a velvet rug) and feel half my body peel away. I'm surprised to find how much I'm shaking. I hold my hand to the mirror, watch it trembling. My teeth even seem to be chattering.

Queenie, Queenie, who's got the ball?

I stand in Bobby's bathroom for minutes and minutes, noticing myself shaking, and waiting for my teeth to stop clattering, looking at the long red scratch down my cheek, feeling the salt snake into it. Watching my reflection calms me. It's hard to be in a state when you watch a person in the mirror doing it: it seems daft.

I pour a second glass of milk and carry it into the bedroom Bobby said was for me, and — popping the glass on to a red leather coaster — I slip between the sheets. They're new, straight out of the shop; still ironed. The thought of my brother tenderly making up this bed for me, planning to bring me here, makes me cry again.

I wish I could feel Tony's arms around me, bury my face in his chest. Or feel his hot, heavy leg suddenly kick out and be flung over me. He'd do that sometimes, in his sleep. I loved it, being locked under him, knowing he was trying to keep me there, to claim me.

Maybe — a tiny, rebellious thought this. How lovely it would be to give up, to be — what was it that Sister Catherine wanted? To be obedient. Easier to do than this: it takes all of your strength. And then it's never enough. You can't just do it the once: you have to keep doing it, over and over again.

The next morning I'm woken by that little knock at the door that Bobby told me about and I open it gingerly, expecting Stella. There's Tony: taller than I remember him, shinier, darker, more beautiful, glittering. I can see from his expression that he doesn't know if I'll let him in. He's swallowing hard, and not smiling.

He's brought me roll-mops and the *Express* and, yes, I'm in the papers, as the "First Woman Ever to Escape from Holloway". The fact that I wasn't actually in prison but was on my way to court and hadn't yet been charged doesn't stop them having a field-day detailing the "pint-sized good-time girl who goes by the name of Queenie Dove", her history of stealing and absconding and her "shocking disregard for the law". My hair colour, it's noted, might be blonde, auburn or black: I've been known to wear a wig. The piece goes on to say that I'm four months pregnant and unmarried, believed to be "caught up in a gangster's underworld". I grin, unable to stop a little blaze of pride.

Tony watches me read, leaning against Bobby's counter, drinking the coffee I've made him, and helping himself to more sugar, cube after cube, until the coffee is almost too stiff to twirl the spoon in. "I've brought you something else. My mum knitted it," he says. He rummages in the pocket of his coat, glances at what he finds there as if he's surprised, or embarrassed, but hands it over. A knitted baby hat springs open in his palm. White with a bobble, and tiny, like the bonnet for an imp, or a fairy.

"You told your mum?" I take the little hat, and lift it to my face. It smells faintly of cheese and fat from a chip fryer.

"And this," he says, producing a little box, black. Inside is a gold christening bracelet, the size of the circle my finger and thumb can make. He watches me turn the bracelet over, testing the spring, and lifting it to the light, looking for the hallmark. This is automatic behaviour. I'm not thinking at all about christening bracelets, or white knitted hats, just remembering a fresh new bunny, white, with a pink ribbon bow.

Tony nods as if I had spoken; he gulps the crystallised coffee in one swig. "Doll — I'm sorry. Never again, I swear, I'll never lay a finger . . ." He pulls me forward in a kiss and the familiar hot fizzing feeling flickers up from my groin to my mouth in one long flare; a match being struck. I wonder if Tony was genuinely afraid, or if he understood. There was never a question of whether I'd take him back. It was only a question of when.

Those months in hiding went by in a blur of boredom and loneliness, alternating with fascination at my pregnant state. I flicked through magazines to learn about the "nest-building" I'd be sure to experience, the happy anticipation and the desire on my husband's part to busy himself with home improvements in preparation for the Big Day. (It was true that Tony was carving the baby a cradle.) It was boring if Stella or Bobby or Tony or Gloria or Dad and Annie couldn't visit, but pregnancy made me endlessly sleepy and over-warm, so it was possible to spend hours, sometimes days, just like a caterpillar snuggled in Bobby's red and tasselly bedroom, only emerging for feeds and fattening up. I couldn't go out too much in case I was recognised. The only stab of envy I felt was when Stella told me a tale of high-rolling in L'Escargot Bienvenu and the Savoyard, with her new gourmet boyfriend who knew all about snail seasons and which restaurant Prince Antoine Bibesco had courted his princess in.

Sometimes I wondered if, despite her amazement at my "bravery", Stella wasn't a bit envious of my pregnancy. She liked to horrify me with tales of the men she knew who wanted to do it with "preggies" — "Like those little birds, you know, who follow fat hippos, trying to peck them . . ."

It was unthinkable in those days to raise a child on your own: if you'd been foolish enough not to take the opportunity of an abortion when you had it, you had to go into a mothers' home and give the child up for adoption. But I was a criminal on the run: being an unmarried mother couldn't be any worse. Not that Tony was against us getting spliced, but it was impossible, in the present secretive and complicated arrangement, for us to think of how on earth to achieve such a thing.

I was thankful for Stella's visits, for the blast of cold, coal-smoked air from the outside world she brought with her. And Gloria too. With Gloria I made plans that I didn't discuss with a soul, and week by week, she released to me a little of my stashed robbery money so that I could buy food and help Bobby out here and there. Two thousand pounds was an enormous sum, in those days, and would last a long time, properly eked out. (Stella splashed out on fancy cars and high rolling, so we never discussed how much she had left, or whether she'd made plans for the future.) The weeks dragged. On a good day I felt snug as a bug in a rug and thought nothing could go wrong. On a lonely one, I'd long to hoist, because only hoisting could lift my spirits and take away the gravelly feeling that some big wheel was rolling over me, flattening me into the ground.

268

★   ★   ★

One day in late December, Stella brings over a black wig and a heavy fur coat big enough to cover me, and playfully insists we go and get some things for the baby. "You've not been in the papers for a while. Surely they've got better things to think about than one little gunman's moll from Bethnal Green." Only Harrods will do.

Tony brings a car and puts on a chauffeur's cap to look the part. It's a freezing day with the whole of Knightsbridge like something glittering on a Christmas card. Our heels make that lovely fresh crunch in the frost and our noses are tipped with pink and nothing, *nothing*, could be nicer than to be out and about that day, carrying a baby under my fur coat, in the sharp fresh air.

Tony waits for us as we load up and I haven't lost the gift: I manage a dozen nappies, safety pins, plastic pants, a gorgeous pale pink nightdress with silky ribbon at the neck, a tiny pillow, sheets, scratch mittens, blankets with silky trimmed corners, a fancy carry-cot, a posh grey pram ... Actually, we don't hoist the bigger things. We put them on a tab. It's the account of a very well-off gentleman of some importance who used to come in the club. He'd bought me perfume and stockings once and I'd come to Harrods with him and memorised the number of his account by looking over his shoulder. I'm amazed to find that, like lots of numbers, it's still in my head. The shop girl lets me sign for it and smiles and says, "How lovely — might be a New Year baby!" as I sign with a flourish. Poor sod —

he'll probably see the list of stuff one day and have a heart attack, thinking some mistress is in the pudding club and about to blackmail him.

Stella thinks this is a hoot, but one glance at Tony's face tells me he thinks otherwise. "How come you remember that geezer's account number so well?" he asks me later, when we're on our own in the Dog and Duck on Dean Street.

"I don't know. I just have a good memory for numbers or something . . ."

"What — after one fucking glance?"

His look is threatening, and I can tell by the set of his jaw how angry he is, how much he's trying to hold back. For the baby, I think. Now I'm so big, it's impossible not to see how vulnerable I am, like Humpty Dumpty, or a big egg that might easily smash.

Then, later that month, Tony thinks it might be OK for me to go to the New Year's Eve party at Winston's Club on Clifford Street, as long as I'm in disguise (and partly perhaps because being pregnant does make me genuinely unrecognisable — my face is puffy and my bosoms are up to my chin). He'll tell everyone we're married and I can cover up with the fur. I'm thrilled because Winston's is a new club and looks awful ritzy: I've seen the poster everywhere — Barbara Windsor, in her sparkly bikini, and Amanda Barrie with their "augmented cabaret" . . . I'm longing for a touch of the old glamour, to see the New Year in. Winston's isn't quite the old crowd — so not too many chances of someone recognising me, and I've heard that stars like

Gina Lollobrigida and Gary Crosby (son of Bing) go there.

We never end up there. Stella wants to call in first at this new place in Soho, a bombed-out church that's been converted into a club. It's mostly West Indian guitarists and coloured dancers and Stella's got it into her head that it's much the most fashionable place to be. We can hardly move in the crush. Tony brings us two enormous warm rum punches, with slices of lemon floating in the melted butter, from a bar decked with bamboo and fishing net. Stella and I jiggle on the floor in a version of dancing, barely able to see one another through the smoke, buffeted around too much to really move, but smiling at each other, tapping our toes and nodding, like crazy pecking birds.

The band pauses for a break between numbers, sipping their beer, and I suddenly need to rush to the lavatory, battering my way through the elbows and hot bodies to get there. As I flush the loo behind me I glimpse a little red tadpole swimming away. What on earth is this? Something to do with the baby? I'm just about to whisper to Stella, waiting outside the cubicle for me, when a great juddering pain swarms all over my belly — Stella takes one look at me as the door opens and, without bothering to tell Tony, lost somewhere in that cavernous place, rushes us outside to hail a black cab.

That forty-minute journey back to the East End is the longest of my life. Stella is dabbing at my face with Quickies to wipe away the sweat, squeezing my hand, and watching the meter — we're going to have to do a

271

runner, she hasn't any money. She gives me a clean hankie to bite on because she doesn't want the driver to know what's happening, and I'm like a cat in a box, scrabbling to claw my way out every time a new pain strikes. She's already asked the girls in Soho a few weeks back and found out about a home in Lower Clapton that will take me in, no questions asked, if I can hold on until then and not have the fucking baby in the cab! Tony has paid the woman up front; it's all sorted.

That night I have two surprises. The first is that the woman who opens the door to me and Stella in the net-curtained terrace in Lockhurst Street is none other than Beattie Rolls, a little fatter and less glamorous in her apron and slippers, but easily recognisable as one of Annie's Green Bottle friends. She smiles and ushers us in. This is what she does for a living now. This and abortions.

The second surprise — after hours of grunting and struggling, up on all fours like an animal, in a back room on a bunch of blood-sodden sheets, with a baby who seems like someone trying to get out of a sweater when they've not quite lined their head up with the neck-hole — comes later. Like other times in my life, I note the pain, and choose not to comment, only ducking my head like a horse and biting down on the various whisky-soaked rags Beattie brings me. Stella chews her nails and flaps uselessly, but she did have to stay behind to "pay" the taxi driver for our journey — me being too big to leg it — so although there isn't time to say so, I'm grateful to her.

There is a moment when I think I'm standing at the edge of a cliff, staring down at a black and boiling sea swirling beneath me. "I don't want to have a baby," I say to Beattie. "Can we stop now? I've changed my mind." Beattie is calm, she keeps mopping my brow and patting the small of my back, and she doesn't answer. I look down at the churning sea, from the great height, and wonder if I should jump. There's Mum at the bottom, in the water, and Nan, too, and all the other women who've had babies, eddying around and panicking, but beckoning frantically to me. Surely Mum is holding up a little wrapped thing, and it's terrible, it's going to sear me with pain worse than I can ever imagine, than anyone could ever imagine, and I won't get through it. There aren't even words for it. How will I be able to do it and survive?

Then Beattie is gently bringing me back down to the grassy side of the cliff edge and the sea is calming, stops madly churning and rearing up at me, and another contraction passes over.

"That's it, my gel," Beattie says. "Nice and slow. Easy . . . holding yourself back . . . that's right . . ."

My baby arrives at last, just as the sky erupts into red, flushing through the net curtains, on the dawn of the first day of 1957. Beattie swears and sits back on her heels, wiping her hands on her apron; Stella bursts into tears.

I fall on my back on the mattress and the bundle is handed to me, warm and strange, and slipped on to my chest. A little heart beats against mine. And that's the second surprise. The name I had for her, for the little

273

girl I always knew I was carrying, just won't stick. Ida, I'd planned to call her, after Nan. The little warm thing, light as an empty paper bag, hastily wiped clean and wrapped in a white muslin cloth, stares up at me. *Ida*, I try again. But she seems to be studying me, each almond-shaped eye open and quizzical, a very stubborn gaze. I want my own name, she seems to be saying. Don't give me something that belongs to somebody else. I glance away from the baby's face, overwhelmed by the clamouring feeling inside me every time I look at her.

Beattie kneels beside us, bringing me a cup of tea.

Maria. The name floats in from somewhere. I feel a shiver run through me, as Beattie suddenly says, "Is it me, or is it chilly in here?" and closes the window to the bedroom. Too late: the name has flown in and settled, like a moth. Maria.

Becoming a Mother

That first week with Maria was like falling in love. Nothing in my life before or since has felt stranger than that unreal week. The baby was magical: the faint vanilla smell of her; her dark eyes, which as the week went by altered in colour from inky blue to the blue of a mussel shell to a lighter, more astonishing colour, vivid as a thread of blue ice in snow. I stared at her tiny fingers, lifted up her hand, marvelling at the lightness of it, like a rose petal. I felt that she was studying me too. Perhaps not *marvelling* quite as much. I almost wanted

274

to apologise in advance. Thinking of that magistrate's comments. The terrible-childhood idea. I'm so sorry it was *my* life you landed in. This is it. This is who you got. I'll do my best . . .

At least Maria wasn't born into squalor and starvation. I found myself doing little calculations like that, trying to weigh up the ways in which my life and hers would be different. The tasselled Moroccan flat was filled with sweet-smelling freesias and roses, and fruit — someone even found bananas from somewhere, though I had to hide them when Bobby was around. There were constant visitors that first week: Stella and Tony and Gloria and Beattie and Bobby, and each of them lifting the baby and gazing at her as if she was the most breathtaking, astonishing, miraculous thing — which she was, of course. She slept soundly, snuggled in cashmere, her wrist encircled by a gold christening bracelet. She didn't enter the world with her mother in shackles either, in D Wing of Holloway Prison. But I did go back there, sooner than I'd hoped — my spell of cashmere and gold, freesias and fruit, was brief.

Here's what happened: about a week after the birth, Gloria was visiting. I was suddenly in staggering, burning agony, wondering if something wasn't very wrong. I went to the bathroom to try to examine myself with a mirror, but somehow I couldn't even crouch down to do it: my body, from my vagina upwards, was ablaze, and the next thing I knew, I blacked out. I had no memory of falling, or of anything else after that. If Gloria hadn't been there, who knows what might have happened, how long it might have been until someone came.

I woke in a hospital bed. Metal bar behind the pillow at my head. Handcuffs on my wrists.

After I'd given birth, Beattie had stitched me, rubbing me first with an ice-cube to numb the pain and doing it as fast as she could, giving me a huge slug of whisky to get me through it. It was brutal, but that pain was nothing to what I felt on waking up in Homerton Mothers' Hospital, to the sight of police and doctors and that clinking sound between my wrists and the knowledge that I was defeated.

I knew Gloria would be sorry that she did what she did. She told me later she was scared, more scared than she'd ever been, and she'd thought I was going to die. She was right: I would have died if she hadn't made the decision to get me to hospital, driven me there herself and left me in Reception — not wanting to be caught aiding and abetting a prisoner on the run. But that wasn't much comfort then. I *wanted* to die. Turned out I had septicaemia from the stitches and, without antibiotics, the feverish spasms that were shaking my body from my bowels to my head would have cost me my life. That was nothing to me. All I could think of was how stupid Nature is, as my dumb cow-like body continued to produce milk from my aching breasts, flooding my hospital gown, not understanding that it had all been for nothing and there was no use for that milk now. It would never reach the baby. How could I know when I'd see Maria again?

Part Three

That's the story, then, of Maria's birth, and how I managed to have her *born free*, as the song goes, although I was facing a longer sentence than ever for absconding. The septicaemia, the doctors told me, meant that my Fallopian tubes were buggered (I'm not sure that's the word they used) and I'd never have any more children.

Gloria was right to take me to hospital, though it took me a while to see it that way. What made me forgive her was this: she kept Maria. She persuaded her old man Ronald and, by some greater miracle, she persuaded Welfare and the rest of them to let her take care of Maria, unofficially foster her while I was inside, and that there was no need to give her up for adoption. She did all of this without dropping anyone else in it — Stella or Tony — or offending Dad or Annie, who also wanted to take care of Maria. She even managed to win her step-daughter Betty round by persuading her the new baby was a novelty, a little dolly to play with rather than a threat. And as soon as I was allowed visitors and out of the prison hospital, Gloria got done up to the nines and brought Maria to Holloway in a bonnet fit for a princess. Gloria was a marvel. The resourcefulness that I'd seen back in my early hoisting days, that gift for deceit and beguiling others, hadn't left her. She was a force to be reckoned with.

Then Tony came, and he brought Maria too. I sobbed to see him holding the tiny baby so tenderly on his lap, and when he left with her, assuring me that Gloria was outside in the Rolls, that "Maria won't want for nothing, doll, you can be sure of that," he had included in my parcel some tobacco and papers (he knew they went further than cigarettes in prison and tobacco was valuable currency), some soap, socks and the small square of white muslin that Beattie had wrapped Maria in when she arrived, hoping, I suppose, to comfort me because it smelt of her. I sniffed it once, alone that first night, and the shock of longing swept over me like a wave, almost knocking me off my feet. I had to fold the muslin and stuff it into the back of my cupboard. I never reached for it again.

Holloway hadn't improved any in my five-month absence. I had a new cell-mate: a coloured girl called Tracey, with huge eyes and scars all the way up both arms. She had the habit of farting like a man whenever she felt like it, then cheekily saying, "Pardon," as if she had forgotten herself, and yet she was the one always putting in complaints about me: apparently I disturbed her at night by sleep-walking, and going through her pathetic belongings, helping myself to things. She went on and on about this photograph of hers she said I'd nicked, of her little boy back home in Jamaica, called Matthew. I did see it once, I remember it, stuck on the wall above her bed with toothpaste. It couldn't have been her son because he looked ten or eleven and she was about twenty-two at most. He was standing barefoot outside a shack: a skinny Negro boy with a very stern gaze. Yes, I remembered the photo well enough and, yes, it was now not in her cupboard and — yes, OK, after some rummaging — it was discovered in mine. That didn't prove anything. She could have put it there herself.

I don't know about the sleep-walking. I rarely slept, or remembered sleeping. My sleep was scraped and scratched all night long by the sound of a baby crying. A newborn baby's cry. Like the mewing of a cat.

"Why doesn't somebody pick up that baby?" I'd say to Tracey. If she was awake she'd shake her head and tell me to fuck off: there was no way I could hear a fucking baby from our cell. Lock-up was at eight forty-five p.m. and it was the most terrible moment of the whole long day: the time when I knew I had to face it again, hours and hours of that baby crying and not being comforted.

I grew to understand eventually that it wasn't outside the cell at all and that no one else could hear it; I learned not to mention it again to the prison doctor, the screws or Tracey, and finally to accept the extra medication I could have to help me sleep. The Jolly Trolley was everyone's friend in prison, but remembering Moll, I was wary, and if I could, I wanted to get through nights without help from "Pills on Wheels" or the "sweet shop". I saved them up, the pills, determined only to use them for the very worst of nights.

Gloria was devoted, and every visitors' day, she brought Maria in to see me. She kept a diary and wrote down what Maria had done, and showed it to me: every feed, every hour of waking, every nappy change and gurgle was in there. Gloria assured me she'd bought Dr Spock's book and was following his advice to "respond to the baby's needs", and not doing strict four-hourly feeds, or refusing to pick Maria up when she screamed blue murder. Her Ronald was a bit tight with money and Gloria didn't have her own, so we'd decided to use some of my whack from the jewellery robbery to pay for extras. That decision made me feel better at once, as if I was more in charge.

"You don't let her cry for long, then?" I repeated, holding the sleeping Maria, stroking her dark tufty head. Minutes later, my fingers were registering the little packet of tobacco Gloria had successfully sneaked in, hidden in Maria's towelling nappy.

I managed to smile for Gloria; I knew she was trying, but it was so hard to cuddle Maria, feel her to be the only living thing in the grey stone of Holloway, and not to be sick with worry: surely the place would defile her in some way.

Those nights after Gloria's visits were always the worst: they were why I saved up my sleeping tablets. Tracey's advice, in fact the advice all inmates give, was not to imagine it — life on the outside, they mean. You get by just living day to day, focusing on the present. Your routines: breakfast, gardening duty, lunch, work in the kitchen, tea-time, exercise yard, if you're lucky, dinner, lock-up. Or the same routine hour by hour, but with your smokes, your bits of smokes, eking them out. Forget what's going on outside and your "bird", your time, will fly by, swallowed up in the long grey corridor that forms prison life: that's the popular view.

Well, I'm Queenie Dove, and I like to do things my own way. Yes, those were the worst, darkest years, and I don't want to dwell on them for longer than I have to here. But I didn't deal with it by cutting off or shutting down, or fogging myself over with drugs.

Sometimes when I woke to the sound of a baby crying, I'd lie still, soothing myself with the knowledge that it would quieten down eventually. This time it's Vera, I'd think, remembering how we used to call her "Baby Grumpy" and how grizzled and old she seemed, compared to my light, vanilla-scented Maria. Remembering too the gin we used to put on our fingers, me and Bobby, to calm her, and how heavy she was for a little girl of six to pick up, which was how old I was, I realised with a jolt. The struggle to walk with Vera; half dead with sleepiness myself; the effort to quieten her cries; Vera's head banging relentlessly against my shoulder. What a lot to ask of me.

I'll be a better mother than you, Moll. I'll get out of here in one piece, and I won't give up, or forget my daughter, or turn to drink. I won't go *fucking doo-lally* either.

Towards the end of my second year, Dad visits on his own. No Annie or Gracie. This is unusual, and puts me on edge at once. He's forgotten to bring me anything, no smokes, nothing. It's near Christmas and there are pathetic decorations in the visitors' room — you know, paper chains, that kind of thing, stuck to the windows with Sellotape, sagging over the chairs. Dad talks about his flower stall, and then about Bobby: have I noticed how much weirder he is, these days, how he even counts the beans in his plate of baked beans? I ask about Maria. Yeah, Gloria brought her to visit last week and he took her to Santa's grotto down the People's Palace, in Mile End; she got a box of coloured pencils. And other bits of chit-chat, and then long silences. I find myself staring at the clock, trying to make out the hands behind a little loop of coloured paper. What's Dad doing here? He shifts uncomfortably in his chair, crosses his leg, picks a fleck off his sock . . .

Then time's up. He scrapes back his chair and coughs, and coughs again, and says he's heard something. So that's it. Something he wants to tell me, about Tony.

It can only be one thing. It can't possibly be anything good. I stare across at the door, then down at my hands. I'm standing up now, gripping the back of my chair. Then down at my toes, in their prison-issue sandals . . . I'm not listening. I want to put my fingers in my ears, and inside I'm silently humming, blocking Dad out. *La, la, la* . . .

"Yeah . . . This was before he met you, an old girlfriend of his, but just the same . . . This fella says he beat this bird black and blue, knocked two teeth out. She was in hospital. The London. Broken jaw, two broken ribs. It was after Tony's dad got sent on that boat, that one what got hit by a U-boat on the way to

Canada . . . You remember how all the Eyeties was sent to Canada in the war? Either Canada or the Isle of Man? You know, 'collar the lot', Churchill said . . . Anyhow, Tony beat this bird to a pulp, this fella says, not just, you know, a little slap . . . It weren't a pretty sight at all . . . I'm telling you . . ."

Why? What on earth do you think I'm going to do with that piece of information? I'm staring at him so hard that he starts to look nervous. He's pulling on his jacket.

"Yeah, well, I just thought you should know. Tony's bad news. Put her in *hospital*, he did, Queenie . . ."

And in the end, that unleashes me.

"You're such a fucking hypocrite, you know that!" My voice stops others in their tracks. The place crackles: they love a fight.

"What — wha —"

"Put her in *hospital*, did he, like you did to Mum?"

"What —"

"Yeah, except not for the rest of her life, eh, just a bit of a bashing, rather than getting her put in *hospital* for the rest of her fucking life . . ."

"What? Your mum was sick, Queenie, she weren't her ticket, nothing to do with me, I never . . . I don't know what you're on about . . ."

"No, but someone had to sign the papers, didn't they? Someone had to commit her there and then leave her there —"

"No, you're wrong, gel. It was the courts, the courts what decided."

I'm on my feet suddenly, and the room itself seems to be pounding, like a big drum. "Oh, what the fuck! What do I care? Get the fuck out of here! Don't come here telling me about Tony! I don't want your advice! I don't want nothing from you!" And I'm screaming by now, and the room is erupting, the screws moving towards me as I'm picking up a chair, with a terrible sense of achievement. I see the look in Dad's cocky blue eyes as I watch him duck. A look so *ashamed*, it's gratifying. At last, for a moment, I made my dad *know* something.

Look, I wasn't stupid. In fact, after I'd calmed down, and thought it over, in a tiny part of me I even felt touched by Dad's efforts, touched by the one and only attempt he'd ever made to be, well, *fatherly* towards me. To try to protect me. I knew I'd forgive him by the next visit; make it up with him. It's just that it was too late. And easier said than done. I've learned that people are surprisingly judgemental and angry with women who get hit by a man. Everyone's advice is the same: leave. It used to make me feel like saying, "Yeah, OK, why don't you leave the man you love, the father of your children? Why don't you leave tomorrow if you think it's so blinkin' easy?"

"But my fella's not beating me up," they say. "*He* doesn't have a temper." Those people are so bloody sure that if they accidentally did fall in love with a person who had an unpleasant personality trait, they'd leave at once. Well, I'm no angel myself. Tony puts up with my temper, doesn't he? I can handle him. That's always my reply, to myself, to Dad, to Stella, to anyone else who tries it. I'm the strongest person I know. I don't need your advice. I can handle *anything*.

We drive to pick up Maria from Gloria's on a spring day in 1960. Tony is outside in a car I don't recognise, waiting. I come blinking into the light. Everything is bright, and loud, and bigger — I can hardly believe it. Tony leaps up and throws his arms around me with such force I think he's going to topple me. I can't stop rubbing my eyes. He looks different, older, of course, even though I've seen him on visits. His eyes are as striking as ever, but he has these deep grooves alongside his mouth even when he's not smiling, and he's bulkier. When he hugs me he doesn't feel the same: there's a thickness to him that wasn't there before. He hasn't shaved and the stubble coming through is grey, giving his face a fuzzy outline. Or is that just me? Does everything look fuzzy because I'm blinking so much?

I'm carrying my little bundle of belongings, which Tony throws in the boot. And I feel ashamed because what I'm wearing, slacks and blouse, feel wrong, out of date. "Don't be daft — you look like a little honey," Tony says.

Tony grins and grins, telling me about all the things that are new, all the things he says I'll be surprised by. But I've been reading the papers. We get *News of the World* and the *People* in prison. Tracey was always going on and on about the riots in Notting Hill and that coloured fella who got killed last year. Tony talks about what he calls "technological changes" — I'm stunned to be outside, I can't really concentrate — and how he and a mate, Jimmy, tried to get hold of these new argon guns, high-powered electric torches that can blast through metal so that they can break into safes. Tony did a little bird of his own for nicking six argon guns: eight months in Durham. And it's absolutely clear that any money he made has gone.

The main difference, according to Tony, is the club scene. Was that new café open when I went in? Next to the delicatessen on Old Compton Street? Yes, I say, it was — it had just opened.

"Fucking hell, that all went mad," Tony says. He tells me about kids coming from far away, the suburbs, just for one night. Pavement's always full of them. He does this funny little hand-jive movement with his hands on the wheel to show me.

"I hate that Lonnie Donegan record, though, don't you?" I say. Tracey'd had a wireless and for a half-ounce of tobacco she'd let me listen to it for an hour.

Tony starts singing it, in old-fashioned music-hall style: "'Oh . . . my old man's a dustman, he wears a dustman's hat . . .'" until I laugh and whack him and tell him to shut up. He has a good voice, though: a rich, lilting voice. I'd forgotten that.

"Is it all kids, then, teenagers?" I ask, trying to keep the anxious note out of my voice. The sense of being old now, of having missed something, being locked away while it was all going on.

Tony glances at me and his look is reassuring. Like he just flicked a hot brush over me. He assures me it's not just teenagers. And we both agree we like Adam

Faith, and he sings one of his too, for a while: "'What do you want if you don't want money?'" There are swanky places too, Tony says. Churchill's and the Beehive, and Winston's — the new club we were heading for that New Year's Eve: it's become the top spot; yeah, that's the number-one venue in the West End. Also this place called Murray's, posh place, do I remember it? Stella works there now as a dancer. She has to get all these fellas to buy her drinks and then they charge them the earth, and Stella gets paid in what she calls scalps, how many losers buy her a drink. He'll take me. But Hackney, though. Back home. I won't recognise it. So many blacks — they're everywhere. There's cafés in Clapton where you don't see a white face, just all these pork-pie hats and a Blue Spot radiogram and pinball machines . . .

"Where we going to be living, then?"

"I'm renting a place. Not far from where you and Stella was — Frampton Park Road."

He'd told me once, when visiting me inside, that he'd left the Soho Don. I knew from before I went in that the control of London was changing and what Stella said was true: it would always be best to be working for the right Firm. The impression I got, and I didn't like to delve, was that now Tony was working for himself, piecemeal, casual things as they came up, if they were tempting, but generally, since Durham, trying to stay out of trouble. Mostly he was back working in his uncle's café. I'm relieved, because this means the likelihood of him being banged up for something is smaller. It also means we won't exactly be rolling in money.

"Back there? Near Dad and Annie . . ." I try not to sound disappointed. My mood is crackly, brittle. I can't quite believe that I'm actually on the outside. That someone won't come along and click handcuffs on me, haul me back inside. Also, Tony keeps mentioning that we can get spliced now, we can get our little baby girl back and have a big do at St James's Church in Bethnal Green, or the Italian Church in Clerkenwell — wouldn't that be *fine*, doll? I say nothing in reply to this. An elastic band tightens round my lungs; I feel like I can't breathe. "Can we open a window in here?"

It doesn't take long for Tony to get fresh. This is what he's convinced I've been missing most in my three years' bird. That I'm about to explode, right? I'm smoking one cigarette after another, dragging deeply, blowing smoke towards the open window, as we leave London for Kent, where Gloria's house is, and he's leaning over, squeezing my knee, smoothing his hand over the cotton of my slacks and up to my crotch, smiling at me, trying to unbutton my blouse with one hand. "Leg-over and chips is what you need, doll," he says.

We decide to pull over in a lay-by and push back the seats; Tony takes off his jacket and shoes and produces a bottle of whisky. We're on a country road. I look up from my position pinned under him, legs painfully braced, feet on the dash, and see it all over his shoulder: birds, sky, a tree covered with pale pink blossom, like a giant lollipop — the world again.

Rumble of the odd lorry passing us, and mad twittering sounds from the birds. The tang of diesel and orange peel and plastic and whisky and Tony's skin. It's too much, it's nearly choking me.

Tony is hot, frantic; scuffling. Like we're having a pub fight. He gets my knickers off and quickly unbuttons himself and gets inside me — he hasn't lost any of his urgency and he hasn't learned to pace himself either. Just as I start to get interested, it's over for him and he's kissing my neck and sighing happily. I almost push him off me, but I stop myself, count to ten, ask for a hankie, and hold him for a while. I try to disguise the drumming of my fingers, pretend I'm just stroking his back.

It's fine: I'm in a hurry too. I want to get to Maria. I wriggle about awkwardly to pull my knickers and slacks back on; Tony combs his hair in the rear-view mirror, whistling and grinning at me. We open both windows and hit the road again. I'm drinking it all in: fields, signs, petrol stations. As long as I live a petrol station will never look as good to me as it does right now.

The long driveway from the road to Gloria's house is intimidating; we both fall silent. There's a little cottage to our right that I think at first is the house, but Tony — who's been before to visit Maria — tells me it's the gardener's cottage, one of several dotted about the property. Perhaps because it's in Kent I keep being reminded of the approved school. I almost expect Sister Grey to come running out and sweep me inside. Ronald is away, Gloria has told me that. She's indicated that he's often away, and she's glad of it. He's quite a drinker, and mean, as it turns out, and "daft old Gloria" has "been and gone and fallen for him, after all", she's said.

It rears up at last, this grand house, grey stone, closed-looking, huge trees, an enormous lawn, tennis courts and a swimming-pool. A scale I hadn't imagined. I mean, I'd seen Gloria, the Rolls, the furs, the pearls, but those things seem like small-fry next to this. A house is something else. I'm surprised to find that I'm not just overawed, I actually feel afraid, and I can't understand why. I wasn't ready, *I hadn't yet imagined this*, is the strange thought that pops into my head. No sign of Ronald's silver Rolls. There's a white Jag, though; Tony parks next to it and leaps out to admire it.

To my surprise it's Gloria herself, not a maid or butler, who answers the door. And she's reassuringly Gloria — glass of champagne in one hand, cigarette elegantly poised in the other, yellow silky dress stretched across her vast bust so that she looks like a ripe canary, all warmth and delight at seeing me spilling over as she ushers us into the kitchen and plonks glasses of bubbly in our hands.

Maria is out towards the back of the property with Betty and the nanny, she says. The nanny? Gloria had assured me she'd been raising both girls herself, with no help at all. I don't ask her about this, just note it, silently. I suddenly need to go to the lavatory; I think I'm going to be sick. Gloria shows me where it is, and I *am* sick, just a little — the champagne, no doubt, or the whisky, or just the shock of it all, after three years of sweet tea and stewed greens. I sit for a second or two in front of the clean white toilet bowl, closing my eyes and trying to draw the strength to get up and go back.

Then we're standing in the kitchen, gazing out to the garden, which backs on to fields — part of the property, apparently — and where I can see a young woman in a navy uniform and two girls. I mean to run outside, but find I can't move. Gloria prods me gently, and I step closer to the window. One of the girls is very small, barely more than a toddler. Black-haired, a scrap of a child, in a white cotton dress, being lifted in the arms of the nanny. I can't see her face. I should know her face, every eyelash, but a picture of her always fades, much as I stared hungrily at her on visits. She kept changing week by week, growing, changing — her eyebrows lifting and darkening, her chin firming up, her eyes widening and sprouting longer lashes, silky-black like Tony's. This is just what children's faces do, of course. Generally you see them every day and you don't notice. The gaps between visits made it impossible not to. As if I was seeing, in front of me, time passing. All the moments of my daughter's life I was missing.

So, for longer than I mean to, I just stand and stare at the window, savouring or putting off the moment, I'm not sure which. After a second or two, tears spill down my cheeks. I can see clearly what the three figures towards the field are looking at: a white pony. Gloria has bought Maria a pony, all of her own.

It's dark by the time we're ready to leave. We've had teacakes and hot chocolate and I've prattled away to

Maria while she has given me her usual hard stare, only occasionally replying with one-word answers that seem to come from nowhere.

I try to squish the anxiety that I'll never be able to give Maria the things that Gloria did. How will she accept life with Tony and me in Frampton Park Road after this? Maria eats daintily, and looks to the nanny for prompting: is she allowed another piece of teacake, should she now put the napkin on her lap? I can see that the person she's most relaxed with is Tony, who tickles her and suddenly scoops her up with rough kisses, calling her his "honey bunny" and making her squeal. Surprise assaults of affection: I remember them well. Dad used to do that.

Later, Tony packs Maria's stuff into the boot and carries her to the back seat, telling her sweetly to lie down, while he tucks a blanket over her. She keeps lifting her head up like a tortoise. She looks bewildered as Gloria leans in to land kiss after kiss on her and Betty leans in too to say a weak goodbye, offering a formal handshake.

The nanny takes Betty inside. Tony slams the car door, saying pointedly to me. "Thought you ladies had a bit of business to sort out?" I know he's trying to get Gloria out of the way. It's also clear that Maria has no idea she's coming with us, and certainly not for good. Tony says firmly, "That's enough now. Don't get Maria upset." He gives Gloria a kiss and a pat, then shoos us inside the house so he can sit in the car outside on the expensive gravel with the engine running, while Gloria and I pop upstairs.

In the master bedroom, Gloria digs about in her wardrobe for an envelope. The rest of my whack, which she's been keeping for me since the jewellery robbery. I've calculated there should be about £1,400 left, after the money I'd been giving to Bobby for sheltering me, and other bits and bobs I'd told Gloria she could use it for while I was inside. Gloria hands me an envelope, which feels light, but I don't open it, not in front of her. That would be rude.

In any case, Gloria is sobbing suddenly. Sinking in her yellow dress like a lemon soufflé, mascara blackening her cheeks, the strands of pearls round her neck clattering painfully as her chest lifts and falls; sitting on her purple satin bed, all ruffles and flounces, clutching at me, saying, "Don't take Maria — sheesh all I've got . . ."

Alarmed, I lift the glass from Gloria's hand and put it on the bedside table. Now I'm so close I see that she must have been drinking steadily all day: she's sodden and glazed, her eyes barely focusing. A toot from the car horn outside makes me jump. Tony will be tapping his fingers on the wheel.

"Don't be silly, you've got Betty —"

"Betty hates me!" She collapses backwards on to the bed.

The one person I don't expect to see like this: Gloria. Pouting, playful, bubbly, kind-hearted Gloria. I don't know what to do. How to thank her, how to *repay* her. I sit down on the bed beside her, take her hand. "Gloria — you can see Maria every weekend or as often as you like, honestly."

She gazes up at me, and struggles to sit up, brushing at her face with her hands and giving a watery smile a go.

"Maria will want to visit, won't she, to see her lovely pony?" I say.

And, strangely, at that Gloria collapses again. "I've got *nothing*," she wails. She sweeps an arm around the room, vaguely indicating the purple velvet curtains, the white dressing-table, the half-open door to the dressing room stuffed with mink.

Taking my own child feels like stealing, is my grim thought, as I close the door to Gloria's bedroom, sneaking across the landing to the staircase. Does nothing really belong to me? What do I have? What can I wrap up and tie in a bow and pass to Maria? Not a pony, or a white bunny rabbit. Is it nothing, like Gloria? Is that what I have to pass on, one big fat *nothing*? Gloria's despair washes over me, as I creep away down the staircase of her grand house. Fine fingers of glass from a crystal chandelier point accusingly every step of the way.

So is *that* why? I wonder. Why I was tempted out of going straight, retirement you might call it, tempted to risk everything, risk Holloway, all over again. Because I thought I was useless, nothing anyway, under all my bravado? Like that Marilyn Monroe quote — what was it? About only wanting to be somebody so badly if you fear you're nobody, really.

No, that doesn't strike me as true, actually. It strikes me as corny, the wanting-to-be-special idea, or if it was true for me, it was just a tiny, weeny bit true. There were other reasons. Other pressing reasons. We'll come to those. Give me a chance: I'm trying to be honest here.

I wanted to give Maria a life as different from mine as possible, but it wasn't easy. Seeing Maria with the white pony didn't make me feel happy for her. Instead I had this horrible grudging feeling that I didn't even have a name for then, but knew well enough. I'm sure *that* was what was in the package wrapped up in ribbon; that was what Moll passed to me. A shameful feeling, a taboo one that you shouldn't feel towards your own daughter, but you do. It makes me wonder if anyone can ever give their child something they don't have themselves. Don't we pass on exactly what we don't mean to, despite our best intentions? After all, what had Maria had so far? A locked-away mother, and an only-there-some-of-the-time father.

I didn't realise that then. There was a way to go before I saw that. No, at that point it was all about Tony and picking up where I'd left off, and having a laugh with Stella, doing all the things I'd been denied. I was only twenty-seven years old, and I had a lot of catching up to do. Oh and it seems it was me who had paid for Maria's pony in any case. Gloria had dipped into my money over the three years: no wonder the envelope felt light. Old habits . . .

Living with Tony, with a man, was not what I expected. We rubbed each other up the wrong way; we were both independent and loved our own routines. I couldn't cook, producing burned toast and eggs so floppy they wriggled off the plate; he wasn't a bad cook but if he'd worked in the café all day he wasn't about to do it again in the evening and, anyway, cooking is a woman's job.

He slept longer hours than me; he liked to lie in of a morning, and if Maria woke him, he'd be in one of his tempers, charging like a bull at things, frightening us both. He kept on and on about getting hitched, and I kept fobbing him off. I didn't know why I didn't want to. I just used to tell him that I'd never imagined myself married, and Tony would reply, "Surely every bird does," or if he was in a bad mood, "Fucking hell, Queenie, you ain't no spring chicken." If he was in a *very* bad mood he'd call me a bitch and say I should be glad that anyone wanted an ungrateful old cow like me, but he was always sorry for those outbursts, and I'd scream equally ugly names back at him, and then feel sorry for *him*. I didn't have a good reason not to get married and it was in the days when "living over the brush" was something quite shocking, frowned upon, though everyone knew someone who did. I felt I was being unfair. I didn't understand myself.

We scraped along like this for a couple of years. Money was tight — we were living off my few remaining savings and Tony's wages from the café — and in the end, Tony accepted that as the reason not to get married. But it drained us, the fighting.

And once again, it got nasty. One time Maria stood between us — she actually plonked herself right between us — and I saw that she was red in the face and shaking from head to toe. Tony came tearing at me

298

and pushed her out of the way, and she was screaming, *screaming*, and I was trying to duck as Tony's fist came flying, and trying to sweep Maria out of the way all at the same time, and I did think, I suddenly thought, this is how it was for me, too — and, *be honest for once, Queenie, it wasn't all right, was it? It was terrifying* — and as I tried to allow this thought to form I was also fending off Tony with the nearest thing to hand — a pan, a heavy pan, and I smashed one of the light-bulbs as I swung it and it popped and Maria screamed again . . . and I told her, *Run, run upstairs, don't come down!*

That night I cried into my pillow, remembering Maria's little red face, her bravery, standing between us, and yet the sight of her, how scared she looked. I've never seen anyone shake that hard. And then suddenly my sobbing was about Moll, and myself, and remembering. Taking Bunny to bed with me, hiding under my pillow, holding Bobby's little sweating hand and how I dealt with it by thinking, *I'm not like her, why does she let him do that to her?* and hating her, and furious with her, blaming her, for *allowing it*. At this thought, I sat up in bed and crept out from beside the snoring Tony and went to stand at the kitchen window, looking out towards Well Street. What Stella had said before I went inside came back to me. *You're half Tony's size.* Wasn't Moll half Dad's size? Why on earth had I been mad at her for so long? Wasn't it unfair to expect her to have been able to stand up to him, defend herself against him?

299

I went next door to check on Maria, sleeping with her nightie rucked up and her face hot against her pillow. I tugged the cotton material down over her bottom and covered her with the sheet. And then I lay on the narrow single bed beside her, my face close to hers. She breathed out, and the smell of cherry-flavoured toothpaste wafted towards me. And I kept remembering her placing herself between us, trying to be strong, trying to prevent a twelve-stone man hitting me, with her tiny-girl bulk. How long before she realises she can't save me and can't stop the horrible scary things from happening all around her, and switches to hating me?

Maria was such a funny little thing. Flitting, flickering. It was as if she faded in and out of existence, like electricity being switched on and off. I'd be doing something — vacuuming, lighting a cigarette, chatting on the telephone to Stella, about to pick up a book — and I'd look down, suddenly conscious of her, like something was on fire right beside me. There she'd be, shimmering. A dark, glittering child. Angry, like Tony. Other times she'd be running. On the way to Vicky Park, off to visit Granddad and Annie, or her big cousin Gracie, she'd be bowling by, fast as a blown leaf, giggling, in her own little world, and I'd try to catch her and swing her up or kiss her or even get her to smile at me. Nothing. It was as if she couldn't see me at all. I didn't exist. She'd keep on running, whirling, chasing birds. I worried about her. I talked to Stella, who I didn't see that often now — I think it must have been the summer of 1962 — and her reply surprised me:

"Well, you didn't think you'd get off scot-free, did you?"

That stung. Stella meant the years I'd been inside, of course. I hadn't expected her of all people to rub my nose in it. Stella often asked me, looking round the little flat in Hackney, didn't I miss the rush, the glamour of my hoisting days? She'd learned to drive, and her boyfriend, this huge fat man she'd met at Murray's, who had two other mistresses in London and only liked sex once a week without looking at her — he liked it really cold and official, she said, from behind — had bought her a cherry-red Mini that she was driving around in. Hard not to feel a twinge of envy, seeing her in that car, and yes, I did miss hoisting. I felt a kind of twitchiness when my life was so dull that made me want to do something to stir it up. A fight usually did it. A huge fight with Tony. The pattern was the same: the drama and the adrenalin and the rage, and then the fog, the strange foggy sweetness that always enveloped me with such reassuring predictability along with the bruises afterwards.

So, this one night Tony comes home for his dinner and immediately I sense a mood. A warning mood. He's excited. Hopping from foot to foot, hiding something. He did a little job, he says. Nothing big. He rolls his eyes, meaning, I can't say more in front of Maria.

I'm in the kitchen in my apron — yes, really! — heating some peas in a pan on the stove; Maria is looking at a book of numbers on the table. She's started school by now and she loves it, as long as she's

301

allowed to sit in the home corner and read all day. She's lost in this book, only once glancing up from it to ask, "How many sweets are there in a quarter of pear drops?"

"I don't know. Fifteen?" I answer.

"Good. Because I ate four earlier so I've got eleven left."

That's what she likes to do, Maria. Little calculations, figuring stuff out. Tony kisses the top of her head and puts his hands round my waist at the stove. "Got something for you, doll," he says. He's twittery and agitated; he produces a box. A little black box that pops open and sparkles. "There you go. What d'you say to that?"

There's nothing I can say. Not now, not in front of Maria. I pretend to be pleased, and kiss him, and slip the diamond ring on and admire it, extending my fingers as if I'm a film star, as if I'm Marilyn, only not poor Marilyn, no, news of *her* is everywhere . . . All the while my heart is ticking like a time bomb and I'm thinking, God, no. Not if you were the last man on earth.

So we sip Babycham and eat the tinned peas and gammon steaks I've made us, and I run Maria her bath and read her stories and tuck her in, and Tony flicks through the paper with his feet up and his slippers on, half watching *Z-Cars* on the telly and all the while the feeling is brewing in me, swelling and filling every inch of me. I've been waiting for this somehow. Waiting for the moment to make things *unmendable*.

But the moment doesn't come, and we watch more telly and I make us a cup of Nescafé and the evening drags on, and soon Tony's yawning and saying, "Let's go up to bed." Of course he thinks his luck's in tonight, because of the ring, and I won't have a headache like I've had every night lately. And even then I get a reprieve. It seems as though he's going to accept mildly my murmured rejections; we're going to be able to just fall asleep with a grudging kiss, and his leg flung over me, and if I'm not careful I'll wake up and it will be tomorrow and I'll find myself engaged to be married to Tony and the key will turn for ever on a life I'm already locked into, but ludicrously feel I could still escape at any time. There's no logic to it. The only thing I know is that it's got to be done. Now.

"Tony. I can't do this. I don't want to . . . marry you."

His face in the half-light in our bedroom seems to melt. He's lying beside me; his side is to the wall, mine to the door. I'm already primed for feminine duties: to be the one ready to get out of bed to bring cups of tea, comfort a sleep-walking child. I don't know what I expected from Tony: roaring, gnashing of teeth, thumping the pillow — or me, perhaps. Instead there's a sadness so forceful that I think I must be mistaken, I must take it back. I surely can't be saying this, can't be deciding three people's future all alone like this. Tony lies still for a while, then reaches a hand for mine. From the way the bed is shaking, I know he is crying.

★ ★ ★

Later, in the middle of the night, I'm almost relieved to find myself shaken awake, to find the sadness gone and replaced: Tony shaking me, his strong hands tight around my throat, his coffee-smelling breath hot on my face, hissing at me, "You ain't never going to take Maria, you know that? I'll fucking kill you first. Or kill her."

Not for one instant do I think he could do it, strangle me. Kill me. He's frightening, yes, but I'm made of rubber, I'm sure of it: I'll bounce right back.

I'm up on all fours in a flash, grappling with him. I reach for a mug, at the side of the bed, and smash at his head with it. He lets go of my throat, and rolls away from me, only seeming to be half awake, now groaning in pain. I've cracked him a huge whack on his temple.

"See?" I'm shouting, careful to yell from the hallway, at some distance from where he's holding his arms round his head, staunching the blood with a sock. "I can't marry you, you stupid bastard. That's why! See? See what I mean?"

One Last Job

So. That's another reason I had to do it. Come out of retirement. That last big job, I mean. To get some money, some independence, to support Maria by myself but, more importantly, to escape from Tony. You don't reject a man like that and expect it to end there.

If you want to know why women stay with a violent man, it's simple. Because instinctively we always know that he will become dangerous at the point we leave him. As long as you stay, you're convinced you can manage him, appease him, control him, match him, keep him sweet. Leave, or try to, and his threats become real. To kill you, kill the children, kill himself. He might well do it now because he's desperate; the full force of him is unleashed. If you're leaving him, he's got nothing to lose.

The sadness returns, soon enough. New Year — 1963 — comes and goes, and with it Maria's sixth birthday. I feel dimly that I'd rather Tony was angry than sad, because only when he's angry can I feel certain I'm doing the right thing. I pack some stuff in two cases and leave Tony slumped over a coffee in the kitchen, Maria's defeated birthday cake on the table, candles and icing all mashed up, wrinkled balloons bobbing round the floor, tired old faces. She runs to say goodbye to Daddy, thinking it's a short-term thing I'm sure, flinging her arms around him and then, when he clutches her, saying squeakily, "Daddy! You're holding me too tight!"

We go to Annie and Dad's in Lauriston Road. I tell them we've had a row, but nothing more. In any case, I know that Tony won't be able to stay away. Four days later, he turns up, battering the door. Dad is out, Gracie too, but Annie and Maria and I jump out of our skins, recognising at once the quality of the knocking.

"Take Maria upstairs to the bedroom," I tell Annie.

305

I open the door to Tony. He's drunk, unshaven, black-eyed and sizzling with anger, like a lit firework on the doorstep. "I want to see my daughter." Everything about his face, his words, reveals his mood. As if he can't actually see me, he's so thick with malevolence.

"D'you think that's a good idea? In the state you're in —"

"I want to see my fucking daughter!" he roars.

I hear a couple of locks turning somewhere. A dog barking. A window opening. Just like another time. That day I was first caught hoisting, when Annie and Dad were fighting, here, on this very doorstep.

"OK, I'll get Maria. Stay outside. We can go to Vicky Park. But, Tony, tuck your shirt in. Try and sort yourself out. She'll be upset, seeing you like that."

I'm determined to talk to him as if everything is normal. As if I'm not wondering about that Kropp razor, which he sometimes tapes open, and whether he has it in his pocket. As if my whole body isn't braced, like a dog's, to attack, or defend, or whatever is needed.

Tony allows me to close the door and go back inside. I stand in the hallway for a moment, rest my cheek against the raised shapes on Annie's wallpaper. Annie's worried face appears at the top of the stairs and then Maria darts out, a flickering black and white shape, running towards us. "Daddy! Is it Daddy?" She races towards the front door and, without hesitating, flings it open, throws herself into Tony's arms.

And I'm thinking, again, Can I really do this? Break them up? She loves him. She loves him more than she does me. What right have I to make this decision, to deny her the only father she'll ever have?

I watch them for a moment or two. He's down on one knee, on the pathway, burying his face in Maria's hair. He's holding her very tight, and once again she squeals: "Daddy, you're squeezing me!"

Then he looks over her head at me, and I see it, but too late. There's no love there for Maria. This is all about punishing me. In an instant he sweeps her up and he's off, running. He strides away, down Lauriston Road, before I can follow. I dart out after him, not bothering to fetch my shoes, iciness under my bare feet, screaming and shouting, and watching helplessly as I see him bundle her into a car, a car he'd parked out of sight but that tears off in a moment, as if he left the keys in, the engine running. Like a get-away. His talent, of course. How could I hope to follow him?

An old man comes over to me, to where I've sunk to the ground. I think I might be crying.

"Is that your husband?" the old fella asks. When I say nothing, he points to the telephone box near us with his walking stick. "Shall I call the Old Bill for you?"

Call the police. Should I? That would be a first. Annie has come running out on to the street after me, and she's brought my shoes. She puts an arm around me and nods to the old man, dismissing his help, and huddles me up on to my feet, ushers me back towards the house. I'm sobbing, but I'm also stunned. I can't think straight. I can't believe my own stupidity, that I would let Tony get this close to us and not realise he was going to do something. As if he would take a rejection lying down.

"When Gracie comes in, I'll get her to fetch your dad," Annie says. "He'll know what to do. Your dad's got friends, you know, someone who could sort Tony out . . ."

I can't bring myself to answer her. To voice my worst fears. That it would be too late. That before anyone could get to him Tony would do something to Maria. And that it wouldn't be enough to sort Tony out once. He'd never stay away. I'm not numb any more: my mind is racing. Am I really made of rubber? Perhaps it's wood, like that wooden heart Tony once made me. Whatever I'm made of, I'm an idiot. Where has he gone? Should I phone the police and get them to chase him?

There's a commotion outside, and Annie leaps up, thinking no doubt that Dad's returning. But someone is pounding with a fist on the front door. Annie opens it, and a tumbled Maria, violently crying, is heaped over the threshold, then dumped on the Welcome mat.

"You fucking bitch!" Tony roars. I slam the door in his face, rushing towards Maria, hugging her and holding her. What was that all about? Was it just meant to be a threat? Or did he regret it, think better of it? That explanation somehow rings true. Tony's moods are unpredictable, and I know he despises his own temper, tries to get a hold of it.

Once again, I feel how terrified Maria is: her body trembling, her teeth chattering, her arms clamped around my neck.

"*Save me, Mummy,*" she keeps crying, which makes no sense. She's home now. But I understand what she means. I have to get us away. Somewhere Tony won't find us. Not Gloria's — that would be the first place he'd think of. Bobby's in a place on Vallance Road; Tony knows that, too. Maybe I can go to Stella's for a while. I don't think Tony knows where her new flat is, the one belonging to the fat boyfriend who likes the clinical sex, although it won't take him long to find out.

That's when I realised that money was the key. Enough money to move somewhere Tony can't find us, somewhere he'll never think of. Enough to start a new life, and save us both.

OK, enough excuses. Yes, it was a huge risk to take part in a robbery of that scale, just when I'd got my life on track, when I was out of prison, had got my daughter back, and was trying to go straight, to give Maria a different life from mine. Yes, yes, I've tried looking at my life, and how I got here, and I think I've covered quite a lot. Genetics, parents, family background, social environment, the wider society I found myself in, blah, blah, blah, peers, education, values of those around me: yes, yes, you must admit, I've covered all of that. What have I left out? What else makes you who you are? Have you ever asked yourself that? Do you believe in destiny, Fate? God's guiding hand? I don't, I have to say. No, I'm pretty sure there's no such thing.

I'm staying at Stella's flat in Mayfair with Maria. It's a squash for three people, and it means Maria can't go to school. Also, as we're all sleeping in the same bed, Maria and I have to make ourselves scarce for one hour every week when the huge fat man comes around. At least Tony hasn't yet figured out where we are, and we've been here six months, scrounging off Stella and using up the last few quid of my saved money.

To my horror, I miss Tony sometimes. I feel sickened by the way that a song, a particular song, like that Roy Orbison one, "Falling", can catch me off guard. I feel quick to bruise, like a peach. Just a snatch on the wireless, that aching plea to be forgiven. Tony had a good line in aching to be forgiven. Stella jumps up whenever she hears it and switches it off.

So we edge along to the summer of 1963. The summer of the Profumo Scandal. Everywhere you go you hear Randy Mice-Davies jokes and record shops are selling a daft album full of silly songs about the case; there are Profumo cartoons in all the newspapers. Stella is particularly obsessed with following it all, because she met both Mandy Rice-Davies and Christine Keeler a couple of times; both of them worked at Murray's as dancers or showgirls, on and off, like Stella. Stella remembers Christine as being striking. She had haunting eyes, like an Egyptian goddess's, Stella says; an extraordinary face. What surprises Stella is how the girls are always presented like best friends in the newspapers. Stella remembers them fighting. She remembers a time when Mandy chucked a whole load of Leichner theatrical powder over Christine in the dressing room. Well, threw it into the air. It whirled around in the fan and landed on

Christine's hair as she was sitting there in her Red Indian costume, doing her makeup ready to go on. And another funny thing: Stella remembers Christine as a blonde back then and Mandy as having dark hair, almost black, with a fringe and kiss curls on each cheek. In the papers it's always the other way around: Christine with her snaky black hair and her mate Mandy a daft blonde in a petal-strewn hat, swaggering out of court.

Anyhow, we follow all this gleefully, poring over the photographs, heartily approving of the fact that Christine and Mandy are, according to the press, still going to Vidal Sassoon in Bond Street throughout the trial to have their hair done; or that Mandy comes out of the Old Bailey in that lovely wrap dress, giving everyone a whirl.

Stella remembers suddenly, reading about the trial, that the name Stephen Ward means something to her. Wasn't Stephen Ward a name in the little black book belonging to Ruth Ellis, all those years ago, when we went to visit her at the Little Club? What a strange coincidence, but Stella's sure she's remembered right, that Ward knew Ruth's friend Vickie, who was killed in a car accident in 1956. And there's another name from the Profumo Scandal that prompts a memory in Stella. The landlord Peter Rachman, ripping off all those coloured tenants — a one-time lover of both Christine and Mandy. But she can't remember why or how she came across his name before. I remember immediately: he was in Ruth's book too. Small world, Stella says.

★ ★ ★

Just about to get smaller. Because the robbery was introduced to me through two separate routes. What a criminologist would no doubt call my "Social Milieu". The main players were all people Bobby knew. That's Bruce Reynolds, Charlie Wilson, Buster Edwards and Roy James. Three of them were boys he knew from Borstal; another was a racing-car driver he'd known from his kennel-boy days at Hackney Wick. One of them had been at primary school with us; another at primary school with Stella. They're all about our age (thirtyish). Too old to be the Beatles but still wanting their five minutes of fame. Not that I remembered meeting any of them before, but they were deeply familiar, just the same.

Only one of them, as far as I knew, had links to either of the gangs that might mean Tony would know the plan — the Krays or the Richardsons — and that was a bloke called Tommy Wisbey. It soon became reassuringly clear that Tony wasn't invited. His heavy drinking and wildness would have been known and would have ruled him out. Also, surprisingly for the time, the Krays weren't behind this plan. The money was being put up by someone else, though no one ever seemed to know who.

The second connection was through Stella. Her fat man bought his properties with the help of a solicitor, John Wheater. She mentioned him casually to me; she was thinking of trying to buy a flat of her own, and had been talking to this John Wheater about it. He had an Irish friend, handsome, who was always with him; this fella had a couple of rich girlfriends who intimidated Stella. She was always trying to get the two men alone. She did finally, plying them with whisky when her boyfriend was away, visiting one of his other mistresses. These two men started talking to Stella — daft lugs — about a robbery, the biggest ever, they were involved in. She had no doubt, years later, that the Irishman was the one referred to by the robbers as the mysterious "Ulsterman", who tipped them off about the train leaving Glasgow. The train they were about to rob. The solicitor John Wheater was later arrested and sentenced to three years in connection with that same robbery. I'm sure you know which one.

It's Bobby who suggests it first. Says he needs my help, and there's a really good whack in it for me if I do. We're round at this terrible place he's now living in, on Vallance Road, a real slum. "Yours must be the only remaining one," I tease him. "I thought they were all demolished." I have Maria with me, and I'm nervous. It can only be a short visit: Tony might find us here.

Bobby's in some sort of trouble. He's left the Firm, or his boyfriend — he doesn't say which and I don't ask — and he owes someone a lot of money. An enormous sum, something like twenty-five thousand pounds, and there's no way on earth to get that kind of money without a really huge job. Why does he owe it? Because he was gambling with it, and it wasn't his to flush away, but he believed his luck was in (he always believes his luck's in), and he kept piling more and more bets on, that seam of optimism in him, like a strip of mercury, poisoning everything.

He can never hang on to money. I've wondered about that before now. How money that's "won", that lands in your lap or is stolen, perhaps never feels quite real or solid. If he tries to translate it into real things, bricks and mortar, it just puffs away.

He's making us a cup of soapy-looking tea in the kitchenette attached to his living room, and pacing around, talking about this fella Bruce, the leader, and how I'd better say yes quickly because it's all set for about a fortnight's time. Every so often he pauses, clutches at his ribs, winces.

I noticed a toffee-apple seller on Vallance Road on the way up here. I send Maria outside with sixpence to get one, so I can look at Bobby's ribs.

Under his jacket, his lovely Prince of Wales checked suit jacket that I know is his pride and joy, under his pale blue shirt, I find sodden bandages. He lets me discover them, but pulls away from me when I put my hand out to touch. "Leave off. I'm fine."

I take my tea and sit on the sofa, hearing Maria's returning footsteps outside his front door. He'll never tell me, I know that but, all the same, the words leak out: "Who was it?"

He's trembling, I notice. His skin is a watery grey colour and his eyes are bloodshot. He gives an almost imperceptible shake of the head, meaning, "That's as much as I'm going to say."

"Have you got a television set?" I ask Bobby, opening the front door to Maria's light knock. He says no. I turn back to him then, aghast at the thought that just occurred. "It wasn't Tony? It wasn't because you wouldn't tell him where we are?" A cold slick of sweat forms on my back as I wait for his answer. Slowly I become aware of a little dark form in front of me, and the sound of splintering toffee. Maria.

"Maria — here, pet, go into Uncle Bobby's bedroom and put the wireless on. See if you can find that song you like about the devil in disguise." Maria eyes me suspiciously over the top of her toffee-apple but does as she's told. I close the bedroom door behind her.

Bobby sits down heavily on the sofa and makes it clear that the subject of how his ribs got broken is closed.

"Right. Give me a cigarette and tell me about this job, then," I say.

Bobby opens his packet of Player's and offers me one. "Not any old job. It's only the biggest job you ever heard of." He explains. The biggest train robbery in history. A Glasgow-to-London mail train. A travelling post office, in effect. A train due to arrive in Euston at four a.m. on Thursday, 8 August, but with a dash of luck and quite a bit of planning, most of it now in place, will never get there with its £2.6 million pounds in mailbags, all neatly in packages and helpfully marked with the amount of cash contained within. Bobby will be one of those on the track, hauling the mailbags. His whack with mine combined is likely to sort us both out. We'll split it. He can get the man he owes money to off his back — that's all he's prepared to say about it — and bugger off to Spain, where he's happy to live for the rest of his life. I can leave London, live anywhere I like. Anywhere that Tony can't find me. Give Maria the life she deserves.

"Give *me* the life I deserve," I say. I'm not going to make my daughter the scapegoat. I'm not going to be one of those mothers moaning, *After everything I've done for you* . . .

I'm thinking of that day with Stella, after the jewellery robbery. Those banknotes: prancing in our high heels like show ponies, tossing our hair. Two and a half million pounds. What does two and a half million pounds *look* like?

"We need you to stock the hideaway, kit out the place," Bobby says. "We'll do the main bit. You won't be on the track, but we need a bird for the shopping, for stocking this farmhouse we're going to hole up in afterwards, because — well, blokes look suspicious, don't they? Blokes don't buy food."

You have to laugh.

He tells me a bit more what the set-up is. As much as he thinks I need to know. His job is to find the ringers — the cars with plates — but also to be on the track. They'll be using Land Rovers and an ex-army lorry. Everyone will be in army uniforms and balaclavas. There's a meeting in South London, and he wants me to go.

"Bruce says girls are unlucky. Crime's a man's business."

"Who is this Bruce?"

"I want him to meet you, see that you're as good as any bloke . . ."

"Better."

He grins at me. "So you're in, are you, Queenie?"

As if one of us has signalled that the discussion is over, we both suddenly stand up. Comical, somehow; formal. We stand smiling at each other, trying to pretend just for a while longer that there's a possibility I might say no. Finally, Bobby laughs, and then winces, and I go to hug him, then remember.

"That day at Hackney Wick," Bobby says, as I go towards his bedroom to fetch Maria. "The dogs . . ."

No need for me to ask him which day, or why he's bringing *that* up again, after nearly twenty years . . . I pause, my hand on the door handle, nod, say, "I know. You made a decision. Not necessarily the wrong one. You were more scared of Dad than the thought of going to Borstal."

"So, are you more scared of Tony? You should be."

"Bobby. How much will my whack be? That's all I need to know."

I open the door to the bedroom and an unusually docile Maria gazes up at me. She's lost in her toffee-apple, sitting on the bed, gnawing at it, her face red and sticky, much of the bedspread smeared with it. Bobby won't like that. On the wireless it's not Elvis but Tony Bennett crooning away. I stand and listen for a moment, and for the first time in months and months, I'm not scared: my heart is rising and rising, like a balloon.

"Oh the good life . . . to be free and explore the unknown . . ."

★ ★ ★

Even all these years later, so much is written about it, about them, that's rubbish. The line that always makes me laugh is the one about the "criminal mastermind" behind it. It's like no one could actually imagine a bunch of working-class criminals, most of them knowing each other from poor bits of London or their time inside, actually planning it together, carrying off something *that* cheeky — the crime of the century they called it — without a posh bloke to boss them around.

I remember the *Sunday Telegraph* going on about this shadowy evil genius, a miser living alone in one room in Brighton. An "uncrowned intellectual king of the underworld". One thing they did get right is that, yes, most big crimes have connections to each other: most cons come from the same families, going back a few years, and we know each other. We meet at school. We go to the same pubs. We go out together, get married, have kids together. You've seen that.

Funnily enough Ronnie Biggs, the one who ended up being the most famous of all, was just a bit player. A petty thief, part-time handyman friend of Bruce's who'd spent more time in prison than out of it. He'd started off in 1946, nicking pencils.

One thing that's agreed in all accounts of the robbery was that there were people involved who were never named, or caught. One book, by this Piers Paul Read, called one of them "Bill Jennings". I don't remember any Bill Jennings. Bruce, in his own colourful account, called one of them Frank Monroe. I don't remember any Frank Monroe. There was a retired train driver, giving specialised advice, whose name changed every five minutes: was it Stan, Peter or Frank?

The other thing that's agreed is that only about a seventh of the original £2.6-million haul was ever recovered. One writer on the robbery, the best in my view, said, with obvious frustration, "Where the rest went, only the surviving robbers know. And, as usual, those who are still alive are not saying."

I see him once that summer. Tony. I'm on the bus with Maria; he's in the street. He looks . . . handsome. He runs a hand through his hair, and I see a flash of his wrist under the cuff of his shirt. Even now, it's possible to see that wrist like a signal, like a flag rising, a message. *See how you still love me, doll*. He's walking fast, though, along Bethnal Green Road, with his usual deliberation. He walks as though he's chasing something.

"Look, there's Daddy!" Maria squeals, and waves. I grab her hand.

Am I wrong, I wonder, to be afraid of him, to keep his daughter from him? How will I ever know? All I know is that I don't want to be one of those women you read about. The ones discovering their husband jumped from a balcony, or gassed himself in a car, and took the kids with him. The wives who say, "Yes, he threatened it, but I *could never imagine* he would do it, do a thing like that to his own child."

I've seen that gun, the Luger. I never believed he chucked it, not really. And when Dad told me about that girl — the girlfriend before me, the one Tony put in hospital, was I surprised, really? My problem is just as it's always been: I have a good imagination. I *can* imagine it.

The meeting, then. Bobby is silent all the way there. Just as we get out of the car, he puts his hand on my shoulder and squeezes it. Then he steps up to the door, knocks sharply. A bloke opens it, who says he's Bruce. There's a woman hovering in the background as we step in. She moves upstairs without a word, a whiff of baking powder and disapproval as she bangs a bedroom door on the landing above, where she's obviously been told to make herself scarce. A child's voice calls to her. I think about Bruce's comment that crime is a man's business, suppressing a smile. Oh, yes. We're just the wives and girlfriends: mopping up.

Bruce takes us into the front room, where the television screen has been covered with a white sheet, pegged to the curtains. He's sort of brainy-looking, dark hair, starting to recede, soft moustache, beginning of a double-chin, black-framed glasses. What I notice straight away is his posture, poker-straight, army bearing. Or like a teacher, somehow. The glasses perhaps.

There's a couple of bottles of Scotch on the coffee-table and two ashtrays already full of fag-ends. About seven men sitting around. Introductions done quickly — Bobby's sister, I think you know her? That kind of thing. They're so close to the Big Day that tension smoulders in the smoky room like a heat haze.

I find myself wondering if one of them is a new boyfriend of Bobby's. Which one would it be? The tall one with close-together blue eyes is handsome, but there's no sign that any of them is a queer. I decide I must be wrong and it's not about that for Bobby. It really must be about escaping, and the money.

There's one introduced as Jack and he's really swanking in a mohair suit that looks hand-tailored. I notice a pricy-looking watch on one wrist but he's not flash, no other jewellery. He's the only one not smoking. He also has manners. He stands up when we're introduced, nods, smiles, runs a hand through his blond hair, sits down again, carefully tugging his trousers so as not to spoil the creases with his knees. I suddenly feel a tremor of excitement that I've barely yet allowed myself. Perhaps this job might have the odd little bonus for me, beyond the money.

This is just last-minute stuff. The Up Special has been thoroughly checked out. The HVP coach (High Value Package) is the one they want. This is the core group, but there are others, about the same number again, and the railway worker, needed to beat the railway signalling system and teach the others how to uncouple the carriages. This is trickier than you might think if you don't know what you're doing.

"Draw the curtains, Frenchie," Bruce suddenly says, and a slim man jumps up and the room is hastily darkened, while Frenchie fiddles with a film projector. The one Bobby called Footpad helps himself to a slug of Scotch, topping up his glass without offering it to anyone else. I sit down next to Jack, as close as I dare to those long, folded legs. He budges up a little for me. I'm conscious that I can feel his thigh and I try to move away but there's no room on the squashed sofa. His thigh muscle radiates heat towards mine through the fabric.

We're shown a brief wobbly film of the train, then this place called Sears Crossing, all projected on to the sheet pegged to the curtains. At one point the woman from upstairs bursts in with a tray of tea and the light makes us all blink. Her husband — I think this must be Charlie's house — says to her by way of explanation, "It's Frenchie's — war stories, love. Just leave that on the table, ta, we'll put the milk in."

She glares at me. A bunch of men watching Frenchie's war films? In that case, what's *she* doing there? As the door closes, leaving only a frame of light, Jack places a hand on my knee. No one else sees it. The room is dark. I stay absolutely still, but I don't shake it off. It rests there, unmoving, like a leaf that just fell innocently from a tree. We both stare straight ahead at the screen.

I gather that the train has been studied over and over, and these seven men are familiar enough with that side of the operation. They just like going over it. The way they all looked up so shiftily when Charlie's wife came in with the tea was so like naughty boys caught in school that I wanted to laugh. Now we're sitting in a dark pit with dust motes dancing in the strip of light from the projector between us, and it's like being bats in a cave. The room has that feeling: the high whine of something that passes back and forth between us, over and above what is being said. *I've missed you.*

A bit more discussion and a few grumblings about having me on the team. Just like Bobby said, they wonder if it's unlucky, having a bird on board; it's like having a girl on a ship.

"I love being called a girl," I say. I'm thirty years old.

Bobby begins sticking up for me. The lights come back on. Jack's hand has miraculously disappeared from my knee. Bruce, silent throughout this discussion, grins, pushing his glasses up his nose, and tells everyone to shut up. It's going to be all right. He's the boss. Class dismissed.

We'll reassemble down at Leatherslade Farm. Bobby will drive me. My job is to stock the farm, Bobby's to fake the number-plates and provide (nick) the remaining necessary equipment: the army uniforms. There's an army base nearby, Bobby says, so it will look more natural to have an army convoy. How else would you explain that number of men near Bridego Bridge?

We say brief goodbyes and Charlie's wife hovers again in the background as we leave. Jack taps his forehead at me in mock salute. He beams me a mischievous smile, too, over the head of the smaller bloke, Frenchie, and adds an appreciative glance at my cleavage for good measure. The *tension* in that cave of a front room I've just spent four hours in is almost too much for a body to bear. I'm taut as a guitar string.

★   ★   ★

These are the things I buy to stock Leatherslade Farm: eighteen tins of luncheon meat, nine tins of corned beef, forty tins of baked beans, eighteen pounds of butter, twenty tins of peas, thirty-eight tins of soup, fifteen tins of condensed milk, thirty-four tins of fruit salad, thirty-two pounds of sugar, seven loaves, nineteen cans of Pipkin beer.

I do it over three days in early August. Bobby helps me, posing as my husband. We go to different grocers so as not to arouse suspicion, Maria dancing around the boxes as I lift them into the car, looking like the perfect little family, away on a holiday. I have to do all the hefting. Bobby is fit enough to drive, but his ribs are tender and they need to knit together, so I won't let him stretch or bend too much.

Jack sends a big sack of potatoes, a barrel of apples, via Bobby. Seems he has a fruit stall, a legit one. He adds a note: "Tell your sister there's plenty more where that came from. And I notice you don't get many of *those* to the pound, if you don't mind me saying." I remember him clocking my cleavage earlier. Cheeky sod. Shouldn't make me laugh, but it does.

Then we go to a different grocer on the Chatsworth Road for the cheese, the Bovril, the Saxa, the biscuits. Next we get coffee and tea and Jammie Dodgers and ketchup. I add Brillo pads and rubber gloves. There'll be plenty of cleaning to do.

Seventeen rolls of toilet paper. Eleven inflatable rubber mattresses. Pillows. Sleeping bags. Blankets. A dozen Pyrex plates. We fill three car loads and take three separate trips to Leatherslade Farm. Journeys full of the smell of orange peel and Bobby's walnut dashboard. The village of Brill suddenly appearing at the top of a hill, the picture-postcard windmill, and those vast, swanking views of Oxfordshire. We laugh about everything. A house called "Commoners" and a sign for "Boarstall" which sounds alarmingly close to a place we all know well. Even, bumbling along the caterpillar of a road, a sign for HM Prison Bullingdon makes us laugh, rather than shudder, and we wave madly, in case any of our mates are inside.

Leatherslade Farm takes a bit of finding, the first time, and we can hardly ask a local. We've been told by Bruce it's up a longish track set back from the road, in the Oxfordshire countryside, between the villages of Brill and Oakley.

It takes us two attempts to find the track, it's so well hidden. There's a milking unit next to it, and the sound of a cow clanking against something metal makes us jump as we sit in the car, windows down, smoking, uncertain if this is really the place. To our left it's all tangled brambles and early blackberries, red and hard, but I need to relieve myself, so I squat down beside the car on the damp grass. Then Maria wants to go, so I help her with her knickers and hold her skirt up for her, laughing when the sheep in the field beside us, who have been watching us anxiously with their ears sticking out, suddenly bolt in alarm. A huge buzzard is circling overhead. The track leads upwards to the farm, well hidden by a low wall covered with ivy. Bobby waits impatiently.

Maria's never seen me this excited. I catch her staring at me, staring and staring, and flashing me one of her lovely dark smiles. I'm in my element.

The "farm" is actually a farm cottage and a load of outbuildings on about five acres of land, on a little rise, almost directly below Brill. It's surrounded by garages, outhouses, sheds; big enough to hide a five-ton lorry and a Land Rover. Ivy, a dense hedge and loads of thick green mean that you can't see it from the track below. But from the house, from the top rooms, with binoculars, you can get a view of the road below. A big pile of tyres, machinery scrambled with green growth . . . It's clear no one's used the place much in a while.

I'm there already the night before it kicks off. Bobby has left, one last trip back to London with Maria to drop her off at Stella's, then return to Leatherslade Farm. (We've both agreed Stella a part of the whack, for helping to hide me these last seven or eight months.) Bobby's planning to be back again by midnight. We all have walkie-talkies, and radios in case they don't work, so we can contact one another. Phone lines are going to be cut, so the walkie-talkies are essential. I'm left behind, making the beds and unloading provisions into the larder, smoking with the men who are already here. There's a basement, with a trapdoor, perfect for storage. I leave some candles and matches at the top of the step in case the torches fail, and close it again.

Jack strides into the kitchen.

326

The curtains are pulled down everywhere, even over the door. The place is ablaze with yellow and orange flower patterns and it's a warm August evening but someone has lit a couple of gas lamps and put some cocoa on the camping stove, which is taking a long time to boil because the flame is so low. They obviously got fed up and left. It's like being inside an Easter egg.

"We could hole up here for a fucking month," Jack says, opening the larder door and grinning. He helps himself to a glass of ale from the Pipkin can he finds there.

"Gloves," I remind him. He isn't wearing his. I wipe the place where he handled the larder door; I'm wearing pink rubber gloves.

He turns me round and kisses me. He pushes my head back against the closed larder door. He runs his hands all over me, murmuring into my neck. I peel off the gloves and the smell of rubber wafts up to me. When men pawed me like this in the past I always hated it; it's strange how differently I feel now. Perhaps I've been waiting for this. Jack's the only man I know who doesn't smoke and he smells fresh, like a new shirt from a packet. It's hot in the kitchen. My eyes are closed. I'm thinking if I do this it will seal things; it will be over with Tony and me. And I'm surprised at the little stab that this thought gives me, even now . . .

Jack takes hold of my hand and I glance down at his fingers. He has a small scar across one of his knuckles. He nods towards the nearest bedroom where I've recently made up the bed — mattress, pillow, sleeping bag. But as I turn I see a hair — one of mine, bleached

327

blonde, attached to the handle of the larder door. I pick it up.

The walkie-talkie on the kitchen table rumbles into life as a car rolls up, and I hear someone arriving at the front door, just as Jack is laying me on the opened sleeping bag and rolling down my stockings. "The Ulsterman!" someone shouts. Bloody hell. The job has been postponed for twenty-four hours. I gather it must be the arrival of Footpad, from the voices and the sounds of ice and whisky being poured in the kitchen. Someone moans loudly, achingly, and there's the sound of chairs being scraped back. One topples over and another voice says, "Shit! The cocoa!" as the smell of burning chocolate curls into our bedroom.

Jack pushes the door closed with his foot. I stifle a giggle at the sight of him, blond hair all over the place, trousers propped up at the front. He slicks down his hair with both hands, kneeling over me. He's vain but that's all right with me. So am I. Slowly, teasingly, he starts unbuckling his belt.

Look, I know it wasn't all larks. They didn't plan on hitting the driver, but the bloke they'd brought with them couldn't drive the train from Sears Crossing to Bridego Bridge, and something had to be done to persuade the driver to move it that last half a mile to where the rest of us were waiting. It wasn't like any of them had guns — you have to give them that — just a couple of coshes. In court one of the rail workers said he heard a shout: "Get the guns!" But Bruce remembers it differently. "Get the cunts", that's what was said.

If you ask me, the problem boiled down to one person and that person has never to this day been named or caught. Not Buster Edwards. Buster said he hit the driver, but there are lots of different stories and there was a book deal in the offing and they wouldn't have got it if someone hadn't owned up so Buster did. Oh, yes, I know he's the one you love the most, the cheeky chappie, the diamond geezer. You've got your version of him. That's not how I remember him. He was a boxer — Bobby knew him from Repton Boys' Club. He was part of the Firm run by Freddie Foreman, and Buster's favourite weapon, according to Bobby, was an iron bar. Even so, there's so much dispute over who hit the train driver. I'm not sure even those of us who were there know, unless we were at that end of the train. Unless we were *really* there.

On that and other things, can you really believe what a bunch of crooks tell you? Especially when they keep contradicting themselves. Were there fourteen or fifteen men involved? Or eighteen? Have you ever wondered who the ones the convicted keep mentioning are, the ones who were never brought to trial? Who was that small figure, pocket-sized, like a jockey, army fatigues, dark in a balaclava, stocking mask squishing the face, slender enough to trot along the moonlit track, under that hunter's moon, swift and low, virtually invisible? Who was it that covered the green signal with a glove to stop the train while the two others took care of the driver and his mate?

329

★ ★ ★

We're nervous, at Leatherslade Farm, waiting for the message. Buster's chasing chips, pink with ketchup, round his plate with a fork, the others are playing Monopoly, rattling the dice and buying up hotels. Jack is dressed, now, the memory of him tight in my belly, already in his army uniform, staring down at his cup of tea.

"Christ, we look like Popski's private army!" Bruce says, but no one answers. Walkie-talkies crackle into life, and when they do, a surge runs through us like we're all wired together. *Check. Check. Check.* People standing up, pulling on their balaclavas.

It's in the lavatory — the outhouse — that Bobby catches hold of me. Hustles himself in there with me. Locks the door. I stand against it, staring at him in shock. He's crying; he's shaking. I've never seen him like this. He can't do it, he says. His ribs. He can't lift mailbags. Sweat is pouring from his face, mixing with the tears, and there's a suffocating feeling in this tiny room, which already reeks of nervous male piss. He sits on the toilet seat, the equipment — stockings, balaclava, army fatigues — across his knee. *Put them on for me. Cover your face. No one will know. If you keep your mouth shut . . . I don't know — can't you strap your tits down?* And then he's sobbing, truly sobbing, like I haven't seen him do since he was a little boy, since long before those Borstal years, when he was small and lost, when no coin had yet been flipped, when it was still in his hand, shiny and new, ready to toss towards the future. Now he's clutching at his ribs

330

and I'm terrified they'll rupture, he'll spill out, that it will all have been for nothing. He needs that whack, he sobs.

And more than that. "Look," he says, and he's practically screaming, "they only went and painted the inside of the lorry!" A shiver runs up and down my back, his voice sounds so frightened. I follow his eyes. A tin of paint, that's all. A squashed tin of yellow paint. *Please*, Queenie.

And so. That train, lighting up the night-sky as it arrives. A sound rushing in my ears, of blood, of money, of something else. I remember. That's all I'm saying. Whether I was there or not, believe what you like — all the men say I wasn't, could never have been. They'll concede that Bruce stayed with his pal Mary near the Thames, after the job. They'll admit that one of them had a German wife who collected him in the morning; that Footpad used a girl he picked up as an attempt at an alibi to say he was in Ireland at the time. But a bird on the track, or down on the embankment, lifting mailbags? No bleedin' way. Even Bobby would tell you that I was never there. Jack knew. I'm somehow sure that Jack could tell it was me. Maybe I'm wrong because it was dark and no one was looking at each other. We were simply working, efficiently, quickly, putting our talents to use.

That clanking sound as the train is uncoupled. The tang of hot grass, metal and cat piss. The taste of nylon stocking in my mouth; the feeling of my eyelashes being stuck. I can't even blink. And someone or something, like a lover, you know, that long-delayed, always-expected something we live for, which never quite arrives, calling to me through the night air.

What I remember now is a fox streaking across the grass. I don't know if anyone else saw it — saw her. A vixen; cubs in front. I was on the track, and she was whisking along the embankment — grey, ghostly in the moonlight, her low tail stroking the ground, ears back, nosing the cubs in front of her. She disappeared and appeared again as I glanced up, like a scarf weaving through a magician's fingers. I blinked, tried to concentrate. The mailbags were heavy. There were a hundred and twenty. My task was to stand there, say nothing and heave the bag passed to me on to the man standing at my right, who would heave it on to the waiting lorry. Give nothing away about how heavy I found them, not make any kind of feminine grunt or sound.

The vixen had been keeping her body low, swift but unhurried. Pretending to be casual instead of what she really was: *intent*. Every inch of her twitching with it, and in that strange light she seemed ablaze. I can't now remember the drive back to the farm, or how I lifted and threw those heavy bags, stood my ground. I just remember that vixen, the only thing glowing in that soft grey night. She was beautiful, I remember thinking.

For most of us, myself included, the habit goes as deep as *Brighton* in a stick of rock of boasting. Exaggerating. Lying, if you like. Or, best of all, saying nothing.

Perhaps I'm making it up, you know, putting myself at the centre, everywhere that mattered. That's me. Right at the heart of the criminal world since I landed there in 1933.

The papers said at first that a million was stolen. When I read that a shoot of anger went through me because it was such a lie. They knew it was more than that. They were playing with us. Just like that day years ago in Bethnal Green when I lost Nan. The bastards think they know what it's good for the British Public to hear. Two and a half million was worth a hell of a lot back then.

Three days later me and Bobby are back in London. We've missed one of our drops — a bag in a telephone box near the farm that got abruptly left because the Old Bill is now crawling all over Leatherslade. But the whack is so good that we're not complaining. We follow it all on the television and on the wireless through the night until the early hours, when we get back to Stella's, hugging ourselves, drinking hot sweet tea, keeping the curtains drawn at her flat and trying hard not to whoop and holler too much, in case the neighbours hear. Sweating, flushing, hot, cold, whenever we hear things. *The police believe the robbers are holed up within a thirty-mile radius of Sears Crossing. The train driver, Jack Mills, is still in hospital. He suffered lacerated injuries to the back of his skull . . .*

Bobby's suitcase is here at Stella's; he's already packed. He's still not fit, and winces as he leans over. I

333

gently take the suitcase from him and lift it myself.
Maria and I go with him in the taxi to Gatwick to wave
him off; our own plan is to leave later today. Maria
keeps saying, "Will you have to put your arms out, you
know, like wings, like a bird, to fly there?" Stella is
going to drive Maria and me to the Fens, later today, to
the same village I was evacuated to as a child, so I can
find a place to rent. "Maybe someone will recognise
you," Stella says. What — that little East End slum girl?
I don't think so. In any case, there's nothing at all to
link me to the robbery.

My plan is to rent a cottage — perhaps in a village
outside Ely — get Maria into a nice quiet country
school, lie low for, say, two years, and then when I'm
settled, buy a house in the city of Ely, a cottage at the
bottom of Fore Hill, maybe the cottage by the river I
saw that day when Bobby and I first arrived, as
children, and had the strange feeling about. I remember
the sense that there was someone inside it, someone I
knew. Funny that.

"Come and visit, won't you?" Bobby says.

"Look after yourself," I tell him. This handful of
words will have to do. We hug silently, hoping our
bodies can say our goodbyes. We break apart.

"Stay out of trouble," he replies. We can't say more in
front of the taxi driver. We still don't know if we've got
away with it.

Paying the driver when I return from the airport is
the first time I've drawn on the money. They're all used
notes, hard to trace, mostly in the form of one-pound
and ten-shilling notes; green and brown with the lovely

severe face of our queen on them. I hand the notes over, waiting while he gives me my change. My hand is sweating — the notes shimmer in front of me, threatening to dissolve. Then I recover, give the cabbie a big grin. Lean in at the window with some of my old brass neck, waving another pound note at him. *Keep the change*.

A week later, a postcard arrives at Stella's. San Pedro, Costa del Sol. Whitewashed houses bristling with red geraniums and a wide strip of blue sea, like a runway. She drives to Ely to bring it to me. We wander round the marketplace, and then down by the river, arm in arm, and she slips the postcard into my pocket. No message, sensibly, but I recognise Bobby's handwriting on Stella's address — big, capitals, curly loops. I smile, and when I get home to my slightly wonky, ivy-covered cottage in a village nearby, I prop it up by the fridge.

A month after that he sends Stella a photograph. She brings that the following Sunday. I stare at it for a long time before tearing it up. It's Bobby lying by a swimming-pool, wearing sunglasses. Bobby, who always hated water, flattening himself out alongside the blue square, dipping one hand in, a big fat cigar poking out of his mouth. The pool is surrounded by shrubs, and orange trees.

A memory floats back then. Something about Bobby as a child on the Salmons' farm, when he came back on his own here without me. How he loved the horse, the outdoors, the *good* dirt, as he always called it, and how it was before Bobby's superstitions, his insistence on

335

lining up coasters, mats and towels kicked in. I remember that Christmas, too, when he first saw an orange and didn't know what to do with it, threw it down the stairs in frustration to try to open it. Now he's lying beside his pool surrounded by orange trees, more oranges than anyone could eat in a lifetime.

By 1964, most of the train robbers had been brought in. I followed the stories, reading the paper, watching the television, always waiting, expecting. But I knew I needn't be worried. No one was looking for a woman. No one grassed. No one expected those long sentences, but still: no one shopped anyone else. And because Bobby had sat out the whole thing, hiding in another of the outbuildings, his prints weren't on the mailbags or any part of the train and no one was looking for him, either. Stupid Roger Cordey was the first to be arrested: he answered an ad for a garage to rent that had been placed by a policeman's widow. When he paid up, three months' cash in advance, from a thick wad, she raised the alarm. Leatherslade had quickly been identified as the hideout. Fingerprints were found on the ketchup and the Monopoly box and on the drum of Saxa salt. (I remember seeing Buster shaking it everywhere like he couldn't get any out, even when it was pouring.) Ronnie Biggs's dabs on the Monopoly cards. The public loved that. "Can you believe that? They played Monopoly with real money!" I heard this woman say, in the butcher's on Market Street in Ely. I longed to tap her on the shoulder, say casually, "It was

Ronnie Biggs's birthday. They didn't just play with it, they rolled it up and smoked it, like cigars."

Jack Mills, the train driver, gave his testimony in court, and was described in the papers as "nerve-shattered" and "a broken man". I don't know how the others felt about this — I can never ask them — but I always had a horrible dive in my stomach whenever his name came up. Bobby's argument was that it wasn't just the bastards who hit him but the British Railway Board who shafted him, since he was off sick for a long time afterwards, and stopped work for good only later, and never got any kind of compensation from his bosses. The Railway Board defended themselves, saying that the driver's sick leave in the year following the attack wasn't as a result of the train robbery but because he had leukaemia. They claimed one of his medical boards had proved this, but the doctors had chosen not to tell the driver, and they didn't want to be the ones to break the bad news. I'll let you draw your own conclusions about that.

Jack, my Jack, was one of those never brought in. We didn't see each other again after that night, though. I knew we wouldn't. Jack was proof — to myself — that I could get over Tony, and a distraction, but he was never going to be a contender. There were dramas and escapes — Biggs, of course, most famously, and Charlie, too, later. There were newspaper deals and books and films, and eventually first-hand accounts by people like Bruce, claiming to tell the truth, the whole truth and nothing but the . . .

Stella and I put our heads together and laughed, every time another story came along. There's so much that's disputed that it's barely worth trying to get a version together. Some claim it was Charlie who gently wiped the driver's face with a blood-soaked rag. Neither Bruce nor Buster will tell who it was who helped the driver, sat with him, held his hand, offered him a cigarette, while they waited for the train to be shunted forward to Bridego Bridge. Who exactly was there and who did what is never agreed. "What happened to the huge stash of money? And maybe there were others on the track that fateful night . . ."

There was one detail that interested us. Poor Footpad. He was caught by some traces of paint on his suede shoes, the same paint found in the cabin of the lorry, and matched to the paint in the outhouse at Leatherslade Farm. Yellow paint. So maybe Bobby was right to be frightened of yellow, after all.

Luck again. Can I believe my luck? I don't know. Isn't even luck something you make yourself? Stella doesn't agree, and later — I mean, the following week, the next time she visits us — we argue about it. "Even in hopeless situations, there's usually something you can do yourself," I say. "You can make things better or worse."

So Stella says, "Well, all right. What, say, if you was drowning? No lifeguard around, no rope to hold on to, nothing. And the current's strong and you ain't got no strength left and can't fight it? That's just plain *unlucky*."

"Unlucky might be how you got there, OK, how you start out. But once you're in the water, you can still do things. Thrash around. Carry on struggling. Or close your eyes, give up. Or . . . *think* about it. Use words, try to make sense of it, even while it's happening — tell yourself a story about it . . ."

"A story," she says. "Trust you to come up with that!"

She snorts then, lights another cigarette, crosses her long legs and leans back against a postbox on Lisle Lane. She's seen a bloke she recognises, her visits here are so regular, and is giving him a hard, appraising smile. A country postie on a bicycle. He pauses, adjusts the satchel over his shoulder, before smiling back.

I do miss Tony sometimes. It happens most often when I go to pick up Maria from her school — in a thatched building, can you believe? — and she skips to the car in her gingham skirt and red cardigan, and I think of all the things Tony'll never see: Maria in the nativity play as a sheep with woolly ears tied on her head; Maria winning at hockey with a ferociously determined centre-forward position; Maria standing proudly in front of the whole school to receive her badge as house captain. This morning on waking she says to me, "Mum, did you know that there's a kind of squid with two hundred and fifty-six thousand teeth?" I didn't know a squid had teeth. She's imaginative, and clever — so clever that sometimes I catch myself having that exact same thought Nan voiced about me: "Where did you come from?" Or maybe: how did I ever deserve such a lovely bright spark as you?

But then I discover that whatever decision I took, however guilty I feel about leaving him, Tony wouldn't be seeing any of these things anyway. Tears are wasted on him. Stella told me recently that he's inside, Durham again, doing a good long stretch. Armed robbery — and this time his trigger finger found its target, as I knew some day it would. Maria is growing up in the cookies-and-milk life I can provide her with, and I'll leave it up to her whether she wants to see him when she's older. She knows where to find him.

I miss Nan too, sometimes, remembering all she gave me, what a loving person she was. I think of all those people who died that night in Bethnal Green and I wonder — not for the first time — why I didn't. Why somebody, or something, saved me. Was *that* luck, then? Or something else? Somebody helped me, the woman who pulled me by my hair, but more than that, I remember the strong feeling of a person sitting beside me in those worst moments, feeling for my hand. Maybe Nan, maybe someone else. Wasn't there a little girl wearing a beret with a sparkly rabbit clip?

Am I ashamed of how I got here, that it wasn't honest, that it wasn't legal or — what? — regular or orthodox . . . *Conventional?* Is that the word? I told you at the start I wasn't and you won't catch me repenting. People love to believe they're so much better than they are. People who have never been tested, they're so quick to judge. What do they really know about themselves? All I'm saying is this: unless you've been there, found yourself with nothing but your own talent . . . that bright spark, my naughtiness. *Look if you like, but you will have to leap.*

One day, driving Maria to school, in a mad rush as usual, turning right on the Stuntney Road, I glance up and see Ely Cathedral on the horizon, sitting there, as always, above everything else, dominating. The Ship of the Fens. And I remember Nan and the tea-leaf sludge she moved around with her finger in an empty cup, not so much reading the future as indulging a family trait she passed down to me: relentless hopefulness. Optimism. I see her soft skin, her blue eyes, the same blue eyes Dad has, and now Maria. "I see a ship," Nan would say. "One day your ship will come in."

Acknowledgements

Queenie is a fictional character. However, events at Bethnal Green tube station did happen, as described, and a group called Stairway to Heaven, led by survivor Alf Morris, has been campaigning for a permanent memorial. You can donate to the fund: www.stairwaytoheavenmemorial.org

My warmest thanks to Professor Lorraine Gamman for her insight, expertise, helpfulness and generosity. Thank you also to Jake Arnott for his enthusiasm and help, and to Iris Cannon, Frank and Margaret Bowles and Josie Bowles for sharing their war-time reminiscences. Thank you Suzanne Howlett for her perceptiveness and clarity. To good friends Sally Cline, Geraldine Harmsworth, Kathryn Heyman and Louise Doughty, for keeping me going. To my agent Caroline Dawnay, for her clear-headed professionalism and kindness; to my editor Carole Welch and her assistant Ruth Tross, for invaluable input into the first draft of this novel.

I'd like to acknowledge the following:

Paul Bailey, *An English Madam, The Life and Work of Cynthia Payne*, Jonathan Cape, 1982
Brendan Behan, *Borstal Boy*, Hutchinson, 1958

Diana Dors, *Behind Closed Doors*, W. H. Allen, 1979

Lorraine Gamman, *Gone Shopping: The Story of Shirley Pitts, Queen of Thieves*, Signet, 1996

Pip Granger, *Up West: Voices from the Streets of Post-War London*, Transworld, 2009

Peter Guttridge, *Crime Archive, The Great Train Robbery*, National Archives, Kew, 2008

Muriel Jakubait, with Monica Weller, *Ruth Ellis, My Sister's Secret Life*, Constable & Robinson, 2005

Bruce Reynolds, *The Autobiography of a Thief*, Virgin Books, 2005

Mandy Rice-Davies, with Shirley Flack, *Mandy*, Michael Joseph, 1980

Donald Thomas, *An Underworld at War*, John Murray, 2003

Barbara Windsor and Robin McGibbon, *All of Me: My Extraordinary Life*, Headline, 2000

Damon Wise, *Come By Sunday, The Fabulous Ruined Life of Diana Dors*, Sidgwick & Jackson, 1998

Jennifer Worth, *Call the Midwife*, Merton Books, 2002

Keep Smilin' Through: Memories of the Home Front 1939–1945, Doghole Publishers, 2005

For about ten years I've been involved with the Royal Literary Fund and received a great deal of support from them. I will be forever grateful for that support at such a crucial time, and I'd like to state that once again, and thank Steve Cook in particular.

ONE WEEK LOAN

OWL